Kim Kelly lives in the Central West of New South Wales. *The Blue Mile* is her third novel.

Also by Kim Kelly

Black Diamonds
This Red Earth

The Blue Mile

KIM KELLY

Pan Macmillan Australia

First published 2014 in Macmillan by Pan Macmillan Australia Pty Ltd
1 Market Street, Sydney, New South Wales, Australia, 2000.

Copyright © Kim Kelly 2014

The moral right of the author has been asserted.

All rights reserved. No part of this book may be reproduced or transmitted by any person or entity (including Google, Amazon or similar organisations), in any form or by any means, electronic or mechanical, including photocopying, recording, scanning or by any information storage and retrieval system, without prior permission in writing from the publisher.

Cataloguing-in-Publication entry is available
from the National Library of Australia
http://catalogue.nla.gov.au

Typeset in 12.5/16 pt Adobe Garamond by Post Pre-press Australia
Printed by McPherson's Printing Group

This is a work of fiction. Characters, institutions and organisations mentioned in this novel are either the product of the author's imagination or, if real, are used fictitiously without any intent to describe actual conduct.

Papers used by Pan Macmillan Australia Pty Ltd are natural, recyclable products made from wood grown in sustainable forests. The manufacturing processes conform to the environmental regulations of the country of origin.

For Nin & Nana

They lie, the men who tell us, for reasons of their own,
That want is here a stranger, and that misery's unknown;
For where the nearest suburb and the city proper meet
My windowsill is level with the faces in the street.

Henry Lawson, 'Faces in the Street', 1888

At present I am afraid there is nothing very hopeful
to be said for Australia.

Otto Niemeyer, Bank of England, 1930

How many cares one loses when one decides not to be something
but to be someone.

Gabrielle 'Coco' Chanel, ageless

One

Yo

There aren't any trees in Chippendale. I see this now, this evening, as if I'm seeing it for the first time, as if I'm not stepping out the door of the Native Rose for the hundredth time to find this street treeless. Cleveland Street. There are telegraph poles here, a mile of them all along it, but there are no trees. Only telegraph poles, which used to be trees.

I look the other way, behind me, where there are trees. I can see the tops of the figs of Victoria Park, but they're in Darlington, and beyond them the trees at the university, fenced off from us. Precious trees, they must be. I look down at my boots: here, on the footpath, in Chippo.

Keep looking down at these boots, until they stop swimming about beneath me. I'm a bit shickered, I see, and very possibly for the last time, for a while at least. I've been drinking here at the Rose since three, drinking my last pay too. None of which discredits the fact of there being no trees in Chippendale. There is not a struggling blade of grass to piss on in Chippo. Only telegraph poles.

'Move it along, Yo.' Jack's fists smash down onto the back of my shoulders as he jumps off the step of the pub behind me, more shickered than me, on the rum for the last few.

'Move it along, the pair of you.' Cully closes the door after us, pretending he's not happy with our efforts to empty our pockets into his till. We're the last out. I'm almost always the last out. Round the corner into Shepherd Street, O'Gorman's dragging his heels ahead of us, Finnerty and Nash ahead of him, two dozen or so heading home. Any ordinary Thursday evening, it could be, each of us having dutifully played our parts in the daily transference of cash from factory to publican.

'Giz a smoke then.' Jack takes the tin from my pocket and helps himself, leaning into me too hard, so that I fall over my feet and into the gutter – with the last of my tobacco flying over the road and mostly into a pile of horseshit.

'Too clever, Jack,' I thank him for it.

'Oi sorry, Yo.' He's looking at the horseshit, reckoning the for and against.

I shove him along: 'You spoon-headed idiot.'

But I soon pull him back as we near the corner of Pine Lane. The factory. Our factory. Foulds Boots, from which we got well and truly booted today. The low sun is coming off the windows on the building, making them golden, and Mr Foulds is standing beneath them, locking up, saying goodnight to Mrs Whitby who oversees the girls. Three hours ago he was saying he was sorry to us. Jack takes in a breath beside me, but before he lets it out again, I say: 'Leave it.'

It's not going to help us much to be in trouble as well as unemployed, and Foulds is not a bad sort of fella. At least he bothered with an explanation. It's the fault of this 'trade depression business biting in', he said; and that the girls will take a third as much as us now that we're men, he didn't say. I turned twenty-one on the nineteenth of June, exactly six months ago today, should be grateful I was kept on that long, bad planning on my part that I didn't see it coming. Didn't look. Jack'll be twenty-one come

February, not that you'd know it, the veteran way he drinks, but that's meant Foulds'd have to put his pay up too, or risk the fine from the inspector. He's not a bad sort of fella, Mr Foulds, no. He wouldn't underpay a man, wouldn't risk a fine – he's avoiding that by not employing any men at all.

It's the week before Christmas; I was going to buy Aggie a new dress.

My own fist curls into a ball, a hot ball of anger. Useless anger.

Foulds sees us over his shoulder and he's quick to be off, going round the corner a block out of his way to the train. Home to his family. Somewhere in Petersham, he lives. There'd be plenty of trees there. I'll bet he's got a garden, with his own tree in it, kids hanging off it everywhere. I'll bet he sleeps well in his bed, without much of a thought for us, if he has a thought at all.

'It's all sorry O'Paddy to some!' Jack shouts after him, and I pull him back, pulling myself back too.

'Leave it, Jack. It's all O'Paddy to the cops too, you know.'

He stops still on the footpath. Staring at nothing, the uselessness coming over him too. Staring at the future, at tomorrow, no work to get to. Nothing.

Nothing but a worn out joke between us: 'You know O'Paddy's easier for them to spell,' I say.

So he says: 'I can't spell your name either, Yo.'

And I say, 'Can't argue with that,' as we start moving along again, because there isn't any argument in it. Jack's not a spoon, not really, he's not ignorant, but he can't spell, has trouble enough with his own name, Callaghan, despite Sister Joe's efforts with the ruler, too long ago now. I can still feel it, though, smashing across the back of my own hand: *Get to the Devil then, Eoghan O'Keenan. Get out!* Couldn't win an argument then, either.

Jesus, where am I going to now? Where am I going to find another job? And you know I'm not blaspheming with this wonder, Lord; I'm praying for the answer. It's going to be the same story all over Chippo. I will knock and ask at every door, at every *No*

Situations Vacant sign, at the knitting mills on Wellington Street, the shirtmakers on Abercrombie, the sweets factory at the corner of Mooregate and Daniels. I will take any work. But they'll all be wanting girls, if they'll be wanting anyone, paying them on air and lint and crumbs of peppermint. Not men. And not ones called Eoghan O'Keenan. Are men with names such as mine even considered to be men? Eoghan – *How do you say that again?* Yo-un, it's not that hard – Owen will do if you're not too keen on your whys, or you're not my mother, pity her. *Come again?* Ah, forget it. Forget we have names at all. Or a need for living wages. What are we then? Dead men?

No, get away with that. I'm living, all right. Only pissed, more than usual, and for the last time, O'Keenan. It's always the last time, isn't it? It is, this time, unless I can get another wage of some kind. I tell Jack: 'We should go up to Redfern in the morning, try at the Lebbo places.' The Syrian factories; I've heard they've got a new one, bed linens and that, and their shirt makers have always got work on of one sort or another.

But Jack says: 'The Lebbos?' Turning his lip up as if I've just said let's go and see about work picking the filth off the legs of cockroaches, never mind the ten minute walk to Redfern to save the tram fare.

A job's a job, though, isn't it? I need the money. I don't care if it's not the proper wage they'll be offering, or what bargain makes the inspector never take a look in them Lebbo shops. We turn into Myrtle Street, our street, past Gibsons on the corner, the furniture factory, where I worked before Foulds, sweeping first, as a boy, and then lugging dressers and wardrobes and that, and no one's working there now. It closed down a fortnight ago, laying everyone off: seventeen men and boys; the Finnertys have not got a man in work in their house now. Jesus. Remember when I got the job stitching at Foulds, though? I'd thought I was something special, with the machine work. I thought I was getting some skill at it. I was there nearly three years – three *years,* that's a long time to be working anywhere in this world. But I know I do a good job when I'm at any sort of work: I have to. Why else would Foulds have kept me on so long on a man's wage? Remember: I've never been sacked before this day. Not even from my first job stacking the bottles at Quirks cordials – the boss there put me on to Gibsons when he was closing up to move out west. Because I'm worth a job. I have to get another job. I will get another job, trade depression horseshit or no. And I'm getting another one – tomorrow.

'Reckon I'll go up and say hello to Hammo tonight – you coming?' Jack says, picking up his pace with the idea.

'No,' I say; I won't be going up to say hello to Mick Hammond tonight, or any night. But I hear what Jack's suggesting: Hammo's done better for himself than anyone else we know, going in with Tex Coogan, looking after his girls for him at the knocker at Strawberry Hills. Why not be the dirty O'Paddys we were born to be? And end up dead quickly too: Tex Coogan is after a share of the coke trade up at the Cross, is the word. I tell Jack: 'You should leave that alone too.'

He doesn't answer me; he says, 'See you later on, then,' and he ducks under the verandah of his house, gate banging behind him, with the number seven swinging upside down on it beside the eight of number eighty-seven, hanging on by a nail.

I want to shout after him, tell him again, he should leave that alone, but I don't. It's his business what he does, and we've got different concerns. I cross the road, following the eternal fart of boiled cabbage and bacon bones home: if that's what you might call the place, when you're not calling it the gateway to Satan's arsehole. One hundred and twenty-two Myrtle Street, but there's no number on this gate.

And I can't believe my luck today as I find the Lord of Darkness himself is here in visitation: the front door's wide open and I can see right through to the kitchen, the shape of his boots stretched out there by the table.

My father is home, and far too early for it. It can't be six-fifteen yet. He won't have lost his job today, too, I can be certain of that: he's a carter for Tooths and rusted on with them. Only two minutes at a stagger up on George Street West, but he's never home before nine o'clock at least, staying on at Ryan's, the tap next door, as long after closing as is necessary to be certain my mother will be thoroughly, and I might say mercifully, unconscious with the Royal Reserve on his return, if he comes home at all.

Jesus. No blasphemy in this one either. I am a dead man now. He's heard I've been sacked, hasn't he. It's my wages pay the rent and put food on that table.

I'm not for a bashing. Fuck this. No. Not now, I'm not having this now, too. I turn around, going to the Callaghans', I've decided – I'll go and say hello to Hammo tonight after all. But I don't even get across the road. A motor car speeds past through a puddle that splashes right up over the pickets of the verandah and onto my boots. I see the shape of a woman's hat, in the backseat, as the motor heads round into Abercrombie at the Oak, a red hat in a white motor, taking a fast shortcut through nowhere. I could hurl myself after it, hurl myself across the roof of that motor to get away, get anywhere, but that Aggie chooses now to hurl herself at me: 'Yo-Yo!'

My little sister, wrapping herself around my knees, preventing any sort of escape, settling my fate.

'Evening, Ag.' I pick her up, little slip of nothing that she is. Seven, and small for it, smaller still under her head full of wild black curls, and telling me through her lost front teeth, 'You smell like beer.'

'I'm sure I do,' I tell her. Aggie: her blue eyes bright and fearful and wanting. Very possibly hungry. I stop still in her eyes for this second, her skinny arms around my neck as if they might afford me some protection. I say: 'We'll go out and get some chips in a bit, yeah?'

'Eoghan!' he shouts. Our father.

Aggie nods and I put her back down on the doorstep. She slips into the front room, where she'll hide under our mother's bed till he's finished.

'Eoghan, you scruttery fuck, get in here!' No scrape of the kitchen chair. He's not going to bother to get up and find me; he's so sure I'll come, to save our mother the bashing instead, or delay it, while anyone who hears or cares decides it's Kath O'Keenan, our mother, the one who has trouble with the drink. Jesus, but you know I could run and leave them both to it, run as both my brothers have before me.

But that Ag is waiting, and she's waiting for me, because I'm all that she has, bag of horseshit that I might be.

I'll take what's coming.

'*Screan ort!*' He smashes his fist down onto the table.

Yes, our father, telling me I'm damned. At least I might still be pissed enough not to feel it too much. Then me and Ag'll go out for some chips. We'll have to go to Kennedy's, though, up on Regent Street by the tracks: they're open late.

Olivia

'That's gorgeous, Ollie – *gorgeous*. I love those bebe roses.' Mother touches the brim of the vagabond I'm trimming, her lips brushing my cheek before she's out the door in a heady whirl of Chanel and jade chiffon. 'Toodles.'

'Will you be late?' I turn to see the tassels of her handbag disappear past the *COSTUMIÈRE* on the window. I stick my needle back in the pincushion and frown at the backwards lettering, fresh gold lettering that is Mother's response to international financial catastrophe: *The middlings will let us down now, you'll see,* she said of the ladies of modest means and the majority of our clientele, *so we must go upwards, Ollie. Up. Up. Up.* So that our window and our card now glitter:

EMILY COSTUMIÈRE
– Exclusif Couture et Chappellerie Féminine –
PARIS ♦ LONDON ♦ NEW YORK ♦ SYDNEY

And we've just this morning taken delivery of new 'mahogany' display cabinets and one velveteen chaise. In ivory. With gold brocade trim. So ostentatious, so obvious, I can hardly look at the thing.

Don't give me that face, Ollie, Mother said when the men brought the furniture in, *you'll get frown lines. If you'd be happier with 'MISS GREENE'S HATS & FROCKS' you're welcome to it.* She waved at the door: *Out in – in – in Homebush or somewhere. You can dress chickens as a sideline.*

That made me laugh, and appreciate her efforts, as I always do, if not always the sense of them. She's doing all this for me, to give me a chance, signing the lease here the week I missed my debut with a head cold I didn't have, which in April will be two years ago. It's not as though other offers of society or dancing with smelly old Barker College boys have run thick and fast since, and it's not as though I'd want them to, not now anyway. I love this shop. Our little salon, on the second floor of the Strand, up in the gods, snug between the optometrist's and Monty's Photography. It's me, my heart is here, and when I'm here, dreaming and scheming up my designs, I can forget that I'm five feet and eleven inches tall and that all I possess of the Greenes' wealth and position is the prominent placing of an aquiline nose. *If we were in Paris, you'd be muse to a thousand, Ollie,* Mother says, *you're gorgeous.* She's blind. Love is, isn't it? I'm eighteen, and three-quarters, and no one's ever looked at me as if I might be something worth looking at; certainly not the way Mother does. Don't look at that chaise either. Good God. Atrocity.

Back to my bebe roses then, my work, my salvation from all things atrocious, and our only means of paying for them. What I can't do with the twist of a ribbon isn't worth doing, and Miss Min Bromley is most certainly going to look gorgeous in this hat. We're designing her whole trousseau, and this is one of two afternoon casuals I'm creating for her. She's a very sweet blonde, and this shell pink is going to double her sweets so her girlfriends writhe in envy and must have one too – and won't ever get it because I only do one-offs. Minerva Bromley is also the daughter of one of the directors of the Commonwealth Bank. If she's pleased with her trousseau, we might indeed be travelling upwards. I stab my needle through the base of my next bebe with her other, less appealing connection: Minerva Bromley is also the cousin of Cassie Fortescue, with whom I went to school at Pymble Ladies, and the taunts still seem as nasty as they ever were: *Sticky, sticky, stick insect. Is she a bug or is she a boy?*

I transform into a Parisienne muse now as I stitch. I'll show Cassie and her ilk. One day, I'm going to be a costumière of international renown. I'm going to be as famous and fabulous as Coco Chanel.

'Ollie?' the shop bell dings with my name.

It's Glor, my friend, my newest and in some odd way my first real friend. Gloria Jabour, from downstairs. I turn and smile: 'Hello, lovely one.'

'Ollie, it's six-thirty,' her smoky amber eyes rouse on me. God but she's relentlessly lovely: I don't see her all day and it catches me up as if I'm seeing her anew. 'Dad says it's a mad mob of riffraff down at the Quay – he doesn't want you waiting for the ferry after dark, and neither do I. Come on, knock-off time.'

'All right.' I smile at that too: Mr Jabour takes his fatherly responsibilities so seriously he extends them to every child he knows. He's also our favourite and exclusive purveyor of all things silk. Jabour's Oriental Emporium – he's got a stock of gold-shot flouncery in at the moment that looks like it wafted in from Persia via magic carpet. I ask Glor: 'Anything come in that I must have?'

'Mmm, maybe a couple of samples,' she says with a teasing grin. 'Some fantastic Fujis, tough as leather, soft as cloud – in candy stripes. But you'll have to wait until tomorrow. Dad's locking up now.'

That he is: I hear the grille screech and thump over their shopfront, echoing up from the ground floor. A newly installed contraption, unfortunately necessary: there've been three robberies, in this arcade alone, this month. I'm compelled myself now to check our new cabinets are locked, the three of them we spent most of today fussing about with, arranging and rearranging our perfumery, our jewellery, our hosiery and glovery, and as I half-gag on an acrid whiff of the gleaming new polish I take some comfort at the thought that thieves would have a hard time heaving these things out into the street: well made, at least, even if the 'mahogany' is painted-on pine.

'Oh Ollie, the chaise – doesn't it look grand?' Glor spots the atrocity, as if it might be possible to miss it, and she bends to run her hand over the ivory velveteen, that firm, graceful sweep over fabric that says she could true-up the edges of the air if she had need to measure it.

But I look away, and I say, 'Grand, yes.' Distractedly, pretending my locking of the stockroom door now requires my full concentration, as I fight off a rush of resentment: well, you would think it grand, wouldn't you, Gloria. Chi-chi showiness designed to attract those who like glittery things. And money: all Arabs worship money, don't they. Equal rush of remorse for these thoughts as I think them, too; as if the Jabours don't work hard for their money. As if I'm any better. Above money. Still, a nasty little voice says I am. Grand. I'm the only child of Viscount Mosely, Lord Shelby Lawrence Ashton Greene. Shouldn't have a shop at all; shouldn't be worried about the debt this stupid furniture has put us in.

I keep a grip on the stockroom door handle, to keep this all locked in. Glor knows nothing of it, of course, no one here does – it's our private atrocity. As far as the wider world's concerned, poor old Daddy was lost in the war, and I would be happy to believe that if it weren't for the birthday cards, the payment of my school fees, and these days a contemptibly pitiful allowance that barely buys my thread – £15 per month. How old does he think I am? Ten? He's in Kenya at present, on a hunting expedition, and I hope a lion eats him. Forgive me. Mother might've picked herself up from the divorce and carried on, sent home from whence she came, but I didn't; haven't. I was only seven when he put us out to sea –

'Oh! And these fresh flowers, too?' Glor is now gushing over the white roses, the ones that are sitting on the magazine table by the chaise; the bold extravagance of two dozen white roses, which arrived this afternoon at about five past three.

'Oh yes,' I laugh, not looking at them either, and my laugh is so brittle Glor guesses that these are *not* part of Mother's refurbishment.

'Oh.' A say-no-more-about-it sort of oh.

The Jabours will have seen Mother flying by their window, jade chiffon whirling out to the waiting cab. His cab. This barrister chap: Bartholomew Harley. A criminal barrister, chasing Mother. And Mother chasing in return. *Darling Em,* the card says, *see you at 6.15 – try not to be* too *late. Bart x*. She only kept him waiting ten, if that. He's something heroic around town, name in the papers for putting some terrible razor-gang crook behind bars, and he's taking Mother to the Merrick Club, for the third time now. Which is where they met: in the Jazz Room. Which *is* part of the refurbishment: Mother parading our creations on the dancefloor of the latest and most popular place in town on Thursday, Friday and Saturday nights. Not a bad idea at all: her beauty alone is enough to draw attention. No one would ever guess, to look at her, that she herself is the seamstress, and no one could be more admiring of her glamour than me. But really. She didn't get in until almost two o'clock on Sunday morning. She's not known him a fortnight. This in itself isn't entirely unusual, but the *Darling Em* and the spectacular nature of these roses are. I don't like it. I haven't met him – I never meet them – but I don't like him either.

'Ollie?' Glor's concern is the sound of loveliness itself, but I turn away from her again, packing my bits and pieces into the drawers of my work table, brushing up my squiggles of thread ends. 'Why don't you come to ours for dinner? You could stay the night – Mum would love to have you over.'

Yes, I know she would, and genuinely: if Mrs Jabour could have the whole world over to her house in Randwick for dinner she would never be happier. But I can't accept the invitation, not tonight. I'd be there ten minutes, squeezed in amongst their big boisterous happy family, half of Beirut round the table, Mrs Jabour telling me I'm too thin, while her sister, Aunty Karma, pinches my arm to demonstrate it, and I'd be wanting to run. I tell Glor: 'Thanks, lovely one, but I've got so much to do with this trousseau, I'm going to plough on with it – at home, don't worry.' I'm already reaching for a hatbox.

'If you're sure . . .'

'I'm sure. Toodle-oo. Off you scoot. I won't be far behind you.'

'Promise.' She rolls those delicious Arabian eyes, because I will linger a little longer here. I always do. 'Lunch tomorrow,' she insists. 'Just you and me. Pearson's, yes? Before the silly season gets too silly and we don't have time to scratch ourselves.'

'Yes, that sounds fab.' I wave her out, and I will have lunch with her at Pearson's tomorrow. Plate of sweet, fat summer prawns: yummy. I'll look at those candy stripe Fujis in the morning, too, get to them before anyone else does – could be just the thing for a kimono I've half-conceived for Min Bromley's loungery.

But for now I go back to my ribbons, back to half-finished afternoon casual bebes, and I'm about to toss a card of the pink satin into the box when I decide, no, I'm not going to work on the trousseau at all tonight, not taking this vagabond home with me. I'm going to have some fun of my own. Design something especially for Glor. Something snazz, for Christmas. I do love her so. But what shall I make her? It takes a while to come to a decision, staring into the limbs of our hat tree, our style samples that ramble over the steel display frame that covers almost the whole of the back wall, but finally I see it: a little taupe sisal mid-brim I'd almost forgotten we had. I pluck it and pack it into the box with some silver and bronze ribbons – colours that will look more than gorgeous against those amber eyes and that creamy, flawless skin.

I pat the lid down on the box with that swish of good feeling I get whenever I'm about to begin something new. Not knowing what it will be until it is, letting inspiration take me. With a little help from *Vogue*: I lay the October and November issues in my portfolio and clip it closed, swing it over my arm, hatbox following, and as I lock the door of the shop behind me, I look up through the glass roof of the arcade to see the sky is the most divine shade: gold-shot teal. Magic-carpet sky.

And it is getting on for late: *bonggg . . . bonggg . . . bonggg . . .* the Town Hall clock strikes seven as I scoot down the stairs around the lift well, through this dim cavern of shut-up shops, only the Aristocrat Cafe across from Electrolux still open, at the George Street end, and it'll close in a minute as well. Out on Pitt, Ned the barrow man is shutting up too, tossing his leftover bits and pieces of fruit into a crate and tipping his hat to me, 'Night, miss.'

'Goodnight to you too, Ned,' I reply under my brim, already scooting past him.

Mindful of Mr Jabour's warning of mad mobs, I quicken my steps, keep my eyes on my mary-janes and my mind on their rhythm, soon joined by the oompah-pah of a Salvo band playing 'Good King Wenceslas' in front of the Commonwealth Bank on the corner of Martin Place. I don't stop to hunt about for change to pop in their box, though; I've barely got tuppence for a tram myself and whatever I do have I shall be spending on Pearson's prawns. I don't look up.

There is quite a mob out tonight, mad or not, a lot of shoes. I keep my eyes on my mary-janes; I really must give these a fresh coat of paint: starting to look like crumbling stucco. Certainly can't afford a new pair. Glance up as I near the corner of Hunter Street, where Bartholomew Harley's chambers are, and where Mother met him for lunch at the Tulip on Tuesday. *Bart.* I really don't want to think about him, them, about what this might mean for us, if . . . No, that won't happen. I just hope she's safe with him. I'm sure she is; of course she is. She knows what she's doing, even if it might not be immediately apparent to anyone but herself; even if the neckline on that jade chiffon plunges just a little too . . . dramatically.

Take a deep breath. Take in the salty smells of the harbour drifting up on the warm breeze and I'm here, at the Quay. Glance up again as I cross the broad boulevard of tramlines and there's no one about. No mad mob anyway, only the normal quantity of late-ferry stragglers, and a few tramps, the usual poor souls; the blind man with his cup and his sign under the awning of the kiosk: SPARE A BOB FOR A DIGGER. Not from me tonight, I'm afraid – my ferry is here, I see, and I just about scoot through the old beggar for it as the deckhand reaches for the board rails of the gangway.

'Please, wait!' I call out across the wharf, hatbox clattering against portfolio.

He doesn't look up.

'Wait!' I shout, and I make a leap for it.

'All right, miss, where's the fire?' He shakes his head as I thump aboard, bumping his shoulder. He says some other disparaging thing but I don't hear it as the whistle blows.

Blowing me and my embarrassment round to a lonely seat up near the bow. Where the water looks strung with fairy lights, there are so many vessels dotted about – it's a dream. I close my eyes for a second and see a beaded evening cloche: teal, gold, pearl. Mmmm.

Open them again as the ferry chugs under the great claw of the Bridge, as it is so far, this Dawes Point end. Look out across the harbour at its matching pair in the north, at Milsons Point. Two monstrous, grasping claws, they seem. Black against the teal dream sky.

I don't know about this Bridge creature. It's a necessary evil: that awful ferry crash with the schoolchildren last month, and half-a-dozen near misses every year, the harbour is just too crowded at peak times. This Bridge will also be something heroic, some kind of wonder of the world, if it succeeds in holding itself up, so they say. But no matter how wondrous it is, it's going to ruin the view. Our view over Lavender Bay. What will that do to the value of our house? It's only a tiny thing, a tiny, leaky-roofed cottage, but it's all we own, apart from hats and frocks. No one thinks about that sort of thing, do they, when they go off and build a bridge. Oh dear, your home is worthless now. Tough luck. Be grateful they didn't demolish our house with a wrecking ball, I suppose.

I shiver with the cooler breeze coming straight off the water. I shiver with the wonder of how precarious everything seems, and not just for Mother and me. For everyone, everything. Whole stock exchanges tumbling into the drink . . .

Look up into the great North Claw, reaching out into nothing. Imagine working up there, catching fifty tons of girder or what have you, dangling off a crane perched high on the edge of nowhere. I'd rather not. Listen to the clang, crunch, grrr of the workshops below, grinding on all day and night, and be grateful we don't live at Milsons Point. Good God, that must be appalling to live on top of. But I look up at the claw again now as the ferry pulls away towards McMahons Point and it's a different view altogether. I see the zigzag that will run along the whole arch, soaring from point to point, a glimpse of the majesty of it. The genius of its design.

And I'm swished right the way through with inspiration at it. When the ferry pulls in to the wharf, I'm the first to thump off, 'Excuse me!', bashing a man in the leg with my hatbox on my way. I don't stop to say sorry: I fly up the steps to the ridge top and home. To make a start on my creation for Glor. I've seen it now. I know exactly – *exactly* – what I want it to be.

Yo

'Shut your mouth, woman,' our father spits into our mother's crying. His face is grey with hatred and his mouth is an old scar ripped through it as he blames her: 'It's you who killed him.'

That makes the cop flinch. Constable Smith, I think he said, and no older than me, if he's a day. Never seen this one before, but he's getting his lesson in O'Paddy tonight. He's just now brought our brother Michael in through the back and laid him across the kitchen table. Michael's dead, and the grazes across his neck tell how. He's hanged himself, at the boarding house up on Goold Street, where he was living. Dying. I haven't seen him for more than a month before this, since he left the tin-pressers at Ultimo, where he was working; not laid off: sacked for drinking on the job. Drinking himself to death, here's the evidence. Lost two stone off him, at least; it's a wonder the weight of him could do the job. But it has. Found this afternoon when the landlady came for the rent.

But regardless of these facts, our father now turns his menace to the other cop, McKinley, who on any other day is a bastard to match him, and he tells him: 'You will find out who did this, who murdered this boy.'

I'm sure I look at him just as McKinley does: disbelieving. Doesn't want it known that Michael has murdered himself. Jesus, at what low place in the shitheap of hypocrisy does this sit?

McKinley shakes his head: 'We'll leave that to you, O'Keenan.' The cops have done us enough of a courtesy as it is, bringing Michael home, instead of tossing him in the morgue for the pauper that he is.

And now they're leaving, the constable saying, 'Evening, missus, er, sorry . . .' to our mother, who won't stop crying, if ever she has.

I look at Michael again. He's grey as our father, only he is in fact dead. My brother is dead; not me. I'm having trouble with this fact: half-relieved I'm not getting a fist in my face for coming in sacked. Jesus. Michael is dead? Yes, and he is not at peace about it. His jaw is crooked, as if he'd taken one there. Maybe he did. I wouldn't know. I didn't know him well at all. There's another fact to trouble me: twenty years under the same roof and three streets away after, and I didn't know him well. I can't remember a time he wasn't drinking. Always fucked or looking to be; he was never going to run very far. Twenty-three years old, he is; was. Never had a life. Never knew him. Nor Brendan, our other brother. He's seventeen and I've not seen him for more than a year. No one has. He could be dead too for all anyone knows.

Our mother is holding Michael's hand in hers, his dead hand, and crying, 'Michael, my Michael,' over and over again, until it's like a siren far away, from me, although she's right here, a kitchen table's breadth away.

'I said shut your mouth, woman,' our father says again, but softer, telling her something in Gaelainn, the language I don't know, calling her Kathleen and pouring her a glass of the Royal Reserve. Pouring blood into a filthy glass.

She takes it from him. She's let go Michael's hand and stops her crying long enough to drink it down, all of it. She'll drink that whole bottle now. She's had one already: I see the empty by the fire, the fire I lit this morning, which she's let go out and not lit again all day.

It is her fault that Michael's dead, and she'll never see it. I do, though. I see it all too well, this moment, in the claret stain of her face. A thief at the least, she is, for taking herself from us, for putting more of the Child Endowment down her fat red neck in grog than food in her daughter's mouth. Aggie. Jesus, she can't see Michael like this; I'm hoping she's stayed hiding.

'Eoghan, get Madigan,' our father says to me, telling me now it's my fault; telling me I'm to go and get Father Madigan at St Benedict's. 'Tell him your brother's been murdered, that he fell in with Coogan, got himself lynched.'

I stare at him again: the Devil has lost his senses. Madigan's no doubt already heard the truth of it; if McKinley told our father of it near five o'clock at the brewery stables, then it's bound to have been a dozen times across the road to St Ben's by now. Madigan is not going to bury Michael, and we've no money for it anyway. No one will chip in for a funeral, not even the Callaghans, not even any of them at Tooths – especially not them. No one will want to be near this. And I'm not saying anything with the breath of the name Coogan in it to anyone, or I'll be the one getting lynched.

'Pat, leave it,' our mother begs: 'Please. Pat –'

That brings his fist smashing down on the table again, making Michael's boots jump as if he might be brought to life, making our mother scream and beg again, 'Please, Pat!'

Why does she beg him? I ask you, Lord. She's always begging him, and that's what sets him off, the same as showing a cur your fear.

'Don't just stand there, useless fuck,' he spits his hatred into me. 'I said get Madigan.'

I nod at him, but before I go I look at our mother once more, taking Michael's boots off, taking them from the table as if that might keep the Devil from this house, her hands shaking from fear and grog, and now I turn my back on them, on the pair of them, and I walk out, up the hall to the front room, and there I reach under our mother's bed for Ag and drag her out by the ankle with one word: 'Shush.'

I'm holding Aggie's curly little head to my chest as the gate bangs closed behind us, holding her tight to me as I start to run, and I don't care if that man bashes that woman to death without me there tonight. I hope he does, so that he will be hanged himself, so that they are both gone and with them all the shame I've ever felt for being born to them.

I've taken the corner at Abercrombie and run halfway to St Ben's before I tell Ag, promise her: 'We're not going back.'

She says, not letting go of my neck: 'Are we going up to Kennedy's for chips?'

'No,' I tell her. 'We're not going to Kennedy's now.'

We're getting out of Chippendale, out of this scruttery shitheap, and we're never coming back.

Coming up to St Ben's on the corner, Ag asks me: 'Where are we going, Yo-Yo?'

'I don't know,' I tell her, the spire of the church to our left and the chimney of Tooths to our right. I am running through my life, thick with the stench of hops, the entire extent of my life set between George Street West ahead and Cleveland Street behind us. You can live and work and die here without ever going outside their bounds. Not me. Not Aggie and me. There's music coming from St Ben's, from the hall, a banjo and a fiddle winding round a tin whistle. The Christmas concert; I see Ellen Callaghan, one of Jack's little sisters, she's with Lil Casey, and they're walking down between the back of the convent and the church, in their emerald dancing skirts, flowers wound through their hair. I tighten my hold on Aggie: she can never be one of them girls, not if we stay here, and I will never kiss Lil Casey, because she'd never go with me, never look at me.

Where are we going, though? Where can we go? At the side of the brewery, at the stables, I see one of the other carters, Frank O'Toole, just inside the gates; he's cooling off his draught mare with a few buckets, late in from his run. He's an all right sort of fella, that one, not one of them our father would consider a mate, not one he drinks with, but I step up my pace to get past him, past all of it. The band at St Ben's is pounding out 'God Save Ireland' now and my head is pounding with my boots from the skinful I had myself this evening. The last ale I will ever have, I promise myself, again, but a promise to the death this time. If alcohol should pass these lips ever again, then the Devil can have me too.

I tell Ag, for want of another idea: 'We'll catch a tram, yeah? Into town.'

'Can we?' Aggie tightens her hold on me as we turn into George Street West, where I keep running, dodging this way and that through the traffic across the road and right past the tram stop because we can't stop here, not right in front of Ryan's Hotel. I keep on up to Railway Square, where the clock on the tower of Clark's strikes the half-hour. I look up at the clock: seven-thirty. I look at Clark's: I was going to get Ag's Christmas dress there, though I've never been inside before, or in any department store. And I can't remember the last time I caught a tram.

I keep running, right through the crowd around Central Station. I keep running right past the fish-and-chips on the bend into the Haymarket, though I know Ag is starving for her tea. I keep running even though I need a smoke; Jesus but I need a smoke now.

'Are we going to get a tram, Yo?' Ag asks me. She never complains, my sister. Ever. She asks, but she never complains.

'In a bit, Ag,' I tell her. I won't let you down. Ever. One day, I promise you, you'll never be wanting again. 'We'll get a tram in a bit.'

When I can stop running. There's a whistle still screaming through the banjo and the fiddle in my mind, though they are well behind us. Screaming through my legs. God save Ireland? Jesus, God save Agnes O'Keenan and me.

Olivia

I wish we had a wireless, I sigh into my zigzag of silver satin. I'd turn some music on over the rather heavier metallic fashioning going on and on and on crash-thunk down at the bridgeworks tonight, bashing and grinding out the old adage that success is one percent inspiration and ninety-nine percent perspiration. To be gained only one stitch at a time. Or one hydraulic hammer smash at a time.

Crash. Bang. Thunk.

It's five after eight now, too. Must be another big bit of zig or zag going up tomorrow, or perhaps I'm especially bothered by it tonight. I don't know how the people at Milsons Point get any rest at all, I really don't. How long is this going to go on for? At least another two years, they say. I wonder if we might afford a wireless, sooner rather than later; they've got some models on special at Hordern's right now. Perhaps, with Min Bromley's final payment for the trousseau and with some Christmas sales –

SCREEEEECH. THUNK.

And I stab straight into the top of my palm with my needle at that one. Oh, for crying out – don't get a bloody smudge on the sisal, Ollie. I drop Glor's hat and press my handkerchief onto the wound, inspect it under the lamp and it's hardly there already.

BANG. BANG. BANG.

I just about jump out of my chair with this one — a bit closer to home. Indeed, it's the front door. A man calling: 'McIlraith's!'

Our McIlraith's hamper is here — I'd all but forgotten it was due — our box of festive goodies. Yummy yum yum: it'll be a task and a half not to get into it forthwith. I open the door to the man and give him a cheerful: 'Good evening, you're late.'

The man doesn't return my smile; he grunts, slaps the box down on the step at my feet and thrusts a docket at me: 'Sign there, will you.'

'Oh. Yes.' I sign the paper and give it back, presuming I've offended: 'I didn't mean you're late — I meant it's late, to be working.'

He grunts again, says something unintelligible and climbs back into his motor-lorry, putters off. Rude man. Obviously has no idea what a Parisienne muse is when he's looking at one, does he.

Crash. Thunk. SCREEEECH.

Or perhaps he lives at Milsons Point and hasn't slept for six months. I look out at the North Claw, in the very last of the light, black talons on indigo velvet. Striking, and I'm almost compelled to dart back inside to sketch it: a slouched toque with a random spray of girder-ish appliqué high on the upturned side. Crisp. Smart. A little theatrical. Winter, most definitely. A whole series of Bridge hats, by the season . . .

And fun for another day. I must stick to finishing Glor's tonight. Oh but it's turning out well; I look over my shoulder down the hall and spy it, toppled on its side on the tea table under the lamp, just as I dropped it. When I finish it off with the bronze ribbon bands round the brim, which will contain the silver zigzags, it's going to be *the* snazz. Snazziest snazz that ever there was. It's so Glor. I want to give it to her tomorrow at our lunch, and not only because I'm bursting to. We possibly won't get another chance before

Christmas. Things will most certainly be hectic for us both in the rush, and then the Jabours shut shop lunchtime Christmas Eve, when they all pile into their elderly Oldsmobile, off to Mr Jabour's equally elderly parents' place in Menindee, wherever that might be, in the Never-Never somewhere. So very odd, the thought that Gloria's a native, second generation and of bush pedigree, too – her grandpapa Jidi is a pioneer outback haberdasher from Broken Hill.

That returns my smile to me as I heave our hamper in off the doorstep: if there's such a thing as Levantine pioneer outback haberdashers from Broken Hill, then there can be such a thing as internationally renowned costumières from Sydney, can't there? And – oh dear God – there's always the Mexican chocolate cake, I see as I flip the lid of our box of goodies. How am I going to keep my hands off *that* till Christmas? Ritual yuletide torture. How cruel are the Mexicans to combine dark chocolate and cinnamon in the one cake and then smother it in a layer of cinnamony-chocolate shell? How cruel to have to wait six days to eat it? Think about prawns at Pearson's with Glor tomorrow. Mmmmm. Now, put the Mexican chocolate cake in the sideboard. Put it in the sideboard right this minute and lock it. Take the rest into the kitchen and unpack it: almonds and walnuts and cherry shortbread tarts, fruit mince for our pies, Paradise pineapple creams, caramel fudge bonbons, the real French cognac for our brandy sauce . . . oh dear God. All for Mother and me. Just the two of us – and we'll eat every crumb. After an appearance at the Christ Church morning service while the ham cooks, we'll race each other home to spend the rest of the day wallowing in fabulous, honey-glazed, chocolatey-cinnamon sin.

It will be just the same this year, won't it? I ask the depths of the pantry as I hide the tin of bonbons behind the Bovril and baked beans. Of course it will be, I answer myself above the whisper of doubt.

Darling Em . . .

What's she doing now? Whirling about with *Bart* to 'Blue Heaven' in the Jazz Room, martini in hand. A place as foreign as Menindee, to me. He's not going to whirl you away from me, is he?

But Mother is entitled to a romance, isn't she? A real one. Not a strategic liaison for a deal on felt supplies or a dancefloor fling to help pay the council rates by the frock orders of the envious that might or might not come of it. She's entitled to two dozen spectacular white roses. She's only thirty-nine, and she's so very delightful, and so very deserving of all good things. This is her chance, perhaps, now that I'm grown. I so very much want her to be happy, in a permanent whirl of happy, happy days. But I don't want a man in our lives; I don't want us to change. I can't remember ever having had a man in our lives. I can't remember our Christmases in London at all either. I only remember them here, by McIlraith's boxes.

In this little leaky-roofed house. Our house. I put my hand on the cool, solid stone of the wall between the kitchen and the sitting room. It's a good foot thick – not about to whirl off at any time soon. It used to be the back wall of the house, and I remember when it was, before Mother had this kitchen added on with the bathroom soon after we arrived, with the tuppence go-away money she got out of his Lordship. I remember it most vividly and permanently: I was terrified of that outside lavatory, the spiders and the spooky hoots of the ferries through the night. I'd been terrified for weeks, it had seemed, for the whole of the voyage here, terrified just looking at the sea, that endless sea. Mother had jollied me along, of course – *This is our adventure, Ollie. Grab your hat and coat.* Intrepid, Mother is, unfailingly chin-up intrepid; I've only ever seen her frightened once. Somewhere in London, out shopping, we saw a biplane in the sky: she grabbed me and pulled me along the street and into a lane so fast she hurt my arm. I can still hear the crash-bang thumping of her heart as she held me to her. Wasn't until years later I realised what had been going on then: the Germans, dropping their bombs in the summer of 1917. We left not long after that, mother not taking no from a man about travelling restrictions and submarines. *Does the name Ashton Greene mean nothing to you, sir?* Our passport out. Didn't say goodbye to Daddy, though; can barely remember what his Lordship looks like; he was still in Flanders at the time, with that woman called Marie, with whom Mother decided she didn't want to share a marriage, however fleetingly – such backward, colonial sensibilities she has.

She's a native, Mother, undeniably, and so is this house – indeed, it's a brief history of the nation. Convict hewn, *1847* engraved above the front door, built by her Grandfather Weathercroft, before he made his fortune in shipping wool along the riverways, so he could build a great big stone house on an estate at Windsor, on the Hawkesbury, where Mother grew up, with her beloved brothers, Archie and Alex. The Weathercrofts had a great big sheep station of their own in Mudgee too by then, but her father lost it after the slump of the nineties. Soon as she was old enough, no older than I am now, Mother was sent to London to marry well – *well-accomplished disaster*, as she says. Sent Home to Mother England, then all the way home again eight awful years later, and utterly alone but for me, as both Archie and Alex were killed in France, and her parents had gone not long after them, utterly ruined, in every way, the remains of the shipping company gone too, finished off by the railways. A wild colonial tragedy. Some wobble of the wheel of fate kept the creditors from getting their claws on this cottage, though. Or perhaps it was simply overlooked, it's certainly small enough: four rooms on a handkerchief-sized piece of East Crescent ridge top, lost amongst the great jostling argument of flats and great big boarding houses that range around us. But it's ours. My home. We'll always have it. Won't we?

And McIlraith's Christmas boxes.

And Mexican chocolate cake. No: don't think about that Mexican chocolate cake. Get back to my ribbons, my creation for Glor. Don't think about the cake. Don't. Thread my needle, settle to it, one stitch at a time.

Grrrr. Thunk. SCREEECH.

The Blue Mile

Good God, but remember how frightened I was when the bridgeworks first got under way? What was I – thirteen? School holidays and they brought the whole of the rock face at Milsons Point down to put the workshops there and move the train station round the bay: *BOOOOM.* That rattled the windows. The sound of the end of the world. Mother sang it away that night; she sang 'My Sweet Little Alice Blue Gown': *oh, when I had it on, I walked on the air* . . . I can't remember how the rest of it goes, though. I try to catch it as I stitch but it swims off and loops around into 'Blue Heaven'; that'll do, sing the blues away: *A smiling face, da da da da, a cosy room, a little nest that nestles where the roses bloom, tra la la la la, tra la la la la, so happy in myyyy bluuue heaven* . . .

Who needs a wireless when you can rattle the windows all by yourself? While you're not even looking at that sideboard, are you, Olivia? There is no sideboard and there is no cake. None at all.

Stop looking at that clock, too. Won't bring Mother home any quicker.

Yo

I've stopped running. Ag's given up on tea and fallen asleep. I can't find anywhere to eat, anyway. I've been the length of George Street now, down to the Quay, and nothing's open, excepting for a few hotel dining rooms with dance bands, and I can't take Ag in them, can't take myself in them, not as we are, so I'm trying our luck on Pitt Street now. There's got to be something. Don't people want a parcel of chips in this city after dark? Seems not. We'll get something back at the Haymarket. There'll be a Chinese cafe open, there has to be. I'm getting weary myself and the want of a smoke is starting to drag at my knees.

So is the wonder of where we're going to sleep tonight. I've got a little short of four pounds in my pocket; how long's that going to last us paying for a room? And not here. This is the big end of town: banking, insurance and trading companies, six and seven storeys high, and only words, to me, words you wrap parcels of chips in; can't sleep or eat in any of them, either. Maybe I should just keep walking and take Aggie right the way back home. But each time that thought comes to me it's a fist in the face. I can't take her there; never again. Not for all the tears our mother will cry over this, our leaving her too. They'll only be more tears. They didn't do anything for Michael. They don't do anything for her. Our mother will have to live with it. Or not. But the cruelty of that is another bashing. For all the failings she has, how can I do this to our poor mother?

'Evening there,' a fella says to me from the corner we're passing, bending over something under the street lamp – a trombone case, clipping it shut. I see the silver buttons of his Salvation Army uniform as he stands up straight again, and there's the rest of the band, five of them. All saying: 'Evening.' Friendly.

'Evening,' I say, and I almost stop as we get nearer, to ask where we might find a place to eat. But I can't trust them with the question. Do-gooders: they'll take Ag off me. They're as good as Welfare, these tambourine types, coming into the Neighbourhood to the sound of doors slamming shut and the silence of kids hiding under their mothers' beds. Keep walking past them. Heart jumping like I'm running again, but I don't run. Walk. Look normal. Normal as a filthy O'Paddy in the big end of town, looking for trouble.

And one of them, the tallest one, steps in our path: 'Lovely night, isn't it?'

'It is,' I nod, and go to step around him, get past the glare of the lamp.

But another says, stepping out too, to meet me there: 'You all right tonight, young man?'

He's an old man, and there's something familiar about the lines on his face, like he might be an old alco dragged up from the gutter. There's some kindliness in this face that puts me at ease enough to ask him: 'We're looking for somewhere to eat.'

'Oh,' he says, and all the Salvos look at each other as if conferring about it before he adds: 'There's not much around this part of town, not this time of night.'

There's helpful for you. I say: 'Thought as much,' and I go to keep on round them.

But the old man stops me again, his eyes gone bright with an idea. 'Hang on a minute,' he says: 'Do you like apricots?'

'Apricots?' I can't say I remember the last time I had one, and the strangeness of the question fixes me to the spot for a second.

'Yes, lad. They're a bit overripe,' he says, looking behind him and then back to me. 'But they'll be sweet. Barrowman passing earlier this evening give us a couple of bags.' And a couple of paper bags there are, sitting by the trombone case. 'The little girl might like a few, eh? She looks a sweet thing. Your little girl?'

'Yes,' I say, holding her so tight round the legs it's a wonder she doesn't wake and yelp with it. My little girl, and what do you reckon about it, you sly old bastard? Just you try it on with me – go on. I'll take you all on.

'It's all right,' another of them says, a short, fat one, fiddling about with the bags, slipping something from his pocket in one too. He's smiling as he hands the bag to me. 'You'll be doing me a favour, lad.' He pats his gut: 'I'm on a diet.'

I take the bag from him. I don't even say thanks. I've taken three steps back and sideways, away from them, and I'm running again now, off Pitt Street, uphill, as fast as I can manage, keeping to the shadows. On the next corner, there's this big-end hotel with all lights blazing, shiny motors along the road outside and a doorman out the front. A woman is getting out of one of the cars, I hear her laughing. I see her shiny dress caught under the lights and she's made of diamonds, and though my boots have got some lead in them now, I can't stop running.

I don't stop again until we've got to the top of this hill and I've turned left again, taking the darker alternative, back towards the Quay. And now I've got no idea where we are. Shame bashes into me again: this is my city, I've lived not five minutes from here since we come off the ship from Tralee, when I was two years old, and I've no idea where I am in it now. Not a fucking clue. How can I look after Ag when I can't even say where I am?

Jesus. I could cry. I could stand here and cry.

The Blue Mile

But Aggie rouses in my arms, rubbing her eyes. 'Yo-Yo?'

It's a crime that she's ever been denied the simplest thing: her safety. I say, 'Bet you're starving,' and I scrunch the bag I'm holding by her left foot.

Her eyes light up like Christmas as she holds my face in her little hands, and I could cry for that too. She doesn't know what's in the bag, only that I've got it for her. Promise her again: one day, you'll never want for anything. I look about for somewhere we might sit so she can tuck in, but there's not a bench in sight. Of course there's not. But as I'm squinting up the road and across it, towards the furthest street lamp I can see, I just make out a gateway – big high palace gates. I could fall on my knees with the recognition.

I know where we are. That's the Gardens up there, the gates to the Botanic Gardens. I tell Ag: 'We're off for a picnic, yeah?' And she's says: 'Can we, Yo?' as I start heading off again. I'm hoping so. I've only been here a couple of times and a long time ago, three or four years, it must be, just before I left Gibsons and we did some big deliveries of cupboards and desks and that, to Parliament House, which I realise we've just walked right past. We're on Macquarie Street. I could laugh with relief.

Almost. When we get up to the corner and cross the road, there's a cop, on the beat, on the path outside the Gardens, between the gates and the statue in front of them. I don't have to tell Ag to shush as I sneak us down behind a line of skinny-trunked trees that run this side of the statue, watching him all the while; she's watching him too. I take note of where we are: behind us, a big building that looks like a courthouse, with a stone triangle face and columns, but it's something else; I don't remember what. Yes, I do: it's a library. I ate a pie on the lawn here, looking across at them gates, the walls either side about ten foot high, and the gates even higher, keeping the mob out dusk till dawn. When I look at the cop again, he's moving off into the darkness, down the road behind the library. We watch him till he disappears, till the crunching of his boots is long enough gone.

Then we're across the roadway, quick as thinking it, and I'm following the wall down from the gate and into the dark, running my hand along the iron railings, looking for a break or some kind of leg-up so we can get over, but I find one railing that's bent out like a runaway lorry's smashed into it for us earlier, thank you, Lord, and we're through. Into the trees: fat trunks and great black billowing heads; they're fig trees. I keep on for a bit, through the trees, with the sweet smells of the earth and the softness of walking on the grass letting me believe for a few moments that we might be all right. We're together, we'll be all right; I'm just looking for a place to picnic, with my little sister, my starving, shoeless little mop-headed sister. I keep on through the darkness and the quiet until I think my lead boots are going to sink right through the softness of the earth, I'm that weary. But before they do, I trip up on a fig root and I ask Ag: 'This do us, then?'

'Mmm,' she says, with her chin on my head, she wouldn't care, and I can hear her smiling as I put her down on the ground, in the fork of these great big fig roots that rise so high near the trunk they seem made to harbour us. I pass her an apricot and I listen to her chomp that down, slurping the juice of it, and I listen to the rustling and squeaking up in the huge roof of the branches of this tree – bats, I suppose, big fat fruit bats, same as the ones in Victoria Park. And Aggie says: 'That was nice. Is there another one?'

'There is,' I tell her. 'There's another five of them.' There's also a sandwich in the bag, wrapped in paper. A big fat sandwich. She won't mind whatever's on it, and I say: 'You can have all the apricots when you finish this.'

I have half with her. It's ham and pickle, and it tastes just like what it is: a gift from heaven, from good strangers in the street, and for the first time in what seems forever, I think maybe we might be all right too. I will be giving us a fair crack at all right anyway. Somehow.

As she's chomping away, Ag sneaks back in under my arms,

making herself snug. She says, through a mouthful: 'Will we go on a tram tomorrow?'

'I don't know, Ag,' I tell her. 'Maybe. Got to get you some shoes before we get far anywhere, yeah?'

'Buckle shoes?'

'Whatever ones you want. And a new dress, too.'

'You mean it, Yoey?'

'Yes.' I'm counting out our budget now, and she can have the whole of our £3 17s 6d, if that's what buckle shoes and a new dress are worth to her. I'll get another job soon. Things will work out.

But for this moment, this night, weariness is finishing me. With my gut chomping round that ham and pickle, I've even gone past my want of a smoke, and my lids are already at half-mast as I ask Ag: 'Reckon we should stay here tonight or go home?'

'Stay here,' she doesn't hesitate. She pushes the back of her curly head into my chest: 'Promise me, Yo-Yo, promise you won't take me back there.' I do. She says: 'I like this tree.'

'So do I,' I tell her. 'It's a wonderful tree.' I look up into its branches, so thick with their leaves it's blacker than black against the starless sky, and I close my eyes and pray for our brother Michael, that he is at peace with you, Lord. Somewhere.

'There's fairies up there in it,' Aggie whispers. 'Can you hear them?'

'I can hear them,' I tell her, and I know her eyes are wide with it as she tells me all about the fairies that live in this tree and how apricots are their favourite thing and so she's going to leave one for them and if it's gone in the morning we'll know that Oonagh the Fairy Queen likes us. I hold her to me as she burrows round deeper inside my arms, inside the arms of this great fig tree, and inside her blue eyes, wide and bright, some kind of sleep claims me.

Olivia

Can't decide if it's the alarm clock gone rogue or the Bridge Monster resuming its din in earnest, but I do know it's dawn and it's screeching. Listen carefully: it's only the brakes of a tram plummeting down Blues Point Road. Good morning. Open eyes.

And see that Mother is not here. Her bed across the other side of our dressing table is untouched. She didn't come home last night. Not at all. Furious. And petrified. What has this Bart Harley done with her? Fling off the bedclothes. Furious. Petrified. Furious. Furious. Clock says five to six. I've had three hours' sleep, at the maximum. After I finished Glor's zigzags, I painted my white mary-janes, sketched out that indigo toque and then made us some bacon rissoles for breakfast, knowing we'd be tired this morning. Trying not to worry. Waiting. And waiting. And – how dare they. *Arrrrrgh!*

SCREEEECH! The workshops reply.

'Please!' I yell out at the harbour, at the nothing between the claws and at everything, before I begin stomping about. I'll give you two dozen spectacular roses, I will. Throw myself under the shower and into the wardrobe, where I rail at her liberally, and there's plenty of her to rail at here, in our wardrobe that is the entirety of the other front room. At least I have no trouble deciding what I'll wear today. Red. Box pleats. Severe. Angry. Black cloche with the red feather. Black stomping-cross double-strap mary-janes. There: this'll tell her what I think.

Before I realise I can't possibly wear this ensemble. I'm going to Pearson's with Glor today. Take it all off and re-ensemble in floral – the sage georgette with the white peonies. White split brim, fix it with a brooch of horsehair froth. That's quite a lovely effect. And an excuse to add my favourite gloves with the little heart-shaped buttons. White mary-janes still tacky but they'll do. I'll do. Glare at myself in the mirror for a final assessment: pity about the face and the knobbly twigs you've got for limbs.

Out you go, don't forget hatbox and portfolio. Remember I've forgotten bacon rissole halfway down the ferry steps. I turn to go back for it, but half of North Sydney is now descending on McMahons Point wharf, pouring out from the tram, avoiding the welter of the train connection by the workshops across the bay, as we all do, and it's not even peak hour yet. Fabulous: the ferry is already jam-packed as I step onto it, right into the midst of a tribe of sweaty schoolboys, already overheated for their last day of term. Good God but the Bridge can't come soon enough to fix this. Not to mention that you could virtually walk punt to punt with the vehicular traffic from Blues Point to the Quay this time of day, the stench of adolescent male body odour is going to kill me.

Transcend it, Olivia. Be elsewhere in your mind. Look up as we chug under the North Claw, and see that indeed a big bit of zig or zag is swinging off it on a hook. All eyes on this ferry are watching it, this girder being hauled up by the creeper crane, a spider reeling a catch into its web. Only it's men who will receive it. I look for them now – there they are, silhouetted in the golden light of the sunrise, four of them, lined up on a ledge of claw hanging out into blue space, waiting to receive this massive swinging girder, which has a man on it, too. Ceaselessly impressive to witness. Utterly heroic. I almost forget I'm cross. In fact I'm conjuring another hat for my Bridge series: an afternoon casual in sunburst yellow, a vagabond of plaited straw with froth of a deeper shade below a crown criss-crossed with slate satin. Nice.

'Oh geez!' one of the boys near me calls out, as the whole ferry gasps. 'Did you see that?'

No, what? I search the claw as we pull away towards the Quay.

'He nearly fell – geez, did you see? The other bloke caught him by the braces.'

Glad I didn't see that. Giddy enough as it is, and astonished, as ever, that it doesn't happen all the time. How do they not fall off? There have been some nasty things happen at the workshops, and there was that gruesome incident with that fellow being squished building the approach road, but no one's fallen off the claws. I reach across to the ferry rail to touch wood and see the box thing going up on the Dawes Point side, full of workmen, men in a pen. Please don't fall off, any of you.

But I could push a few schoolboys into the drink as I fight my way through them to get off the ferry. 'Move aside, let the lady through,' a gentleman commands by the gangway, and I can't even smile a thankyou at him. Head down and busy at the task of pushing my way through the pack at the Quay. Mad mob or what, surging up from the other wharves: men, hundreds of them. I stand at the kiosk for a moment to readjust the strap of the portfolio cutting into the crook of my elbow, and I watch them: a river of men, all heading round past this end wharf and up into George Street North. Towards the Rocks. An army of filing clerks, by the looks of them. How odd.

I ask the man at the kiosk window: 'What's going on at the Rocks?'

He shrugs: 'Another demo at the Labour Exchange, I s'pose,' and he reaches past me to take money for the paper.

'Labour Exchange?' I ask the air.

'The unemployment office,' I hear another voice say, below

me. It's the old blind digger, under the awning, so close he'd be looking right at my shins, if he could. He says: 'It's coming on fast now.'

'What is?'

'This depression. It's coming for us again. Happened just like this back in the nineties, putting men on the street overnight. Hard times ahead.'

'Oh.' I manage to find two halfpennies in the bottom of my handbag and plink them into his cup, as if that might stave it off. Unemployment has been creeping up and up all year, a matter of general grumbling, and now –

BOOM. THUNK.

Here are the faces of international catastrophe, all these middling men trudging round to the Labour Exchange. I shudder, and then I just about run away, up Pitt Street, fleeing the curse of them. Their middling wives and sweethearts won't be indulged with a new ensemble this Christmas, will they, and I'm mentally finishing Min Bromley's bebe roses as I scoot double-time to the Strand. Mother is bang-on right, isn't she: we must look up the ladder for our clientele now. As up as we can go.

When I reach the arcade, I look down the ground floor to see if the Jabours are in yet, for me to snap up the best of their new Fujis: no, the grille is still closed, and I'm taking the stairs around the lift well two by two as if our livelihood depends upon it. Perhaps it does. Perhaps it depends on this Bart Harley chap too. Hard times call for hard measures, and my anger is dissipating now as I reach the window of our shop, the gold lettering, the velveteen. Mother really does know what she's doing, doesn't she.

But in the next breath my thoughts are in uproar again as I spy the stockroom door is open. Just a crack, but open it surely is. Oh dear God, we've been robbed! My hand flies to my mouth.

Before I see the swathe of honey cashmere draped over one of the hooks on the coat stand. Mother's wrap. The one she took with her last night. Fling open the stockroom door.

'Mother!' I am so shrill I rattle the glass in the cabinetry. 'Where on earth have you been?'

She looks up from her beading, at her sewing table, squeezed in amongst the shelves of fabric bolts and boxes of bits – as if she's been at that all night. Butter wouldn't melt. She smiles, slowly, not even a hint of apology in her eyes as she says: 'Now Ollie, please, I –'

'No.' I put my hand up. 'Don't tell me. I do not wish to know.'

Mother puts her beading down and stands up. 'You look beautiful today, darling.'

'Do I?' I close the stockroom door on her, tempted to lock it.

But she follows me out. 'Ollie. Now, don't you get all imperious with me. You must know. Bart has asked me to marry him.'

'What?' Shrill smashes through the glass roof of this arcade. 'You've not known him a fortnight. That's insane!'

'Yes.' She smiles, an immeasurably happy sort of smile. 'It may appear insane, darling, but Bart and I have been acquainted a little longer than a fortnight, and you must know I'm considering saying yes.'

'No!' Atrocity of atrocities, and I could not sound more like a petulant five year old if I tried. Mexican chocolate cake stomped on and smashed to pieces.

'Yes.' Mother is calm. 'We must arrange for you to meet. I won't accept him if you truly can't. Please, Ollie. Tomorrow night, we'll dine at the Merrick.'

'At the Merrick?' Not that I've ever been there but it is presently *the* place to be seen, where all the beauties go, theatre people, intellectual people, and people who want to be seen with them. Not a place for me. A place where I can't hide under the brim of my hat. And I don't dance. Or rather I can: like a baby giraffe. How cruel are you, Mother?

'Yes, Ollie, the Merrick. Stop that face now. You're almost nineteen. It's about time you left this nonsense behind you. You're as lovely as –'

'You stop this nonsense.' I put my hand up again: 'I will not go, and I will not hear another word about it.'

'Olivia Jane Greene, you –' Mother is cross now too.

Saved by the screech of the Jabours' grille opening, I stomp out: 'I'm too busy for nonsense today.'

She doesn't follow me. Good. I hide on the landing of the stairs for a few moments, staring into the lead lines of the stained-glass window there, staring right into the big fat white rose in the middle of it. I will not accept him. I will never accept him. I'm not going to give this another thought until after Christmas. He's not ruining my Christmas. Steady my heart and my will as I go the rest of the way down: I have Fujis to choose.

And Mr Jabour's warm smile to meet me. 'Olivia, my dear,' he welcomes me into his Aladdin's cave of silk; breathe in the sweet earthy smells of patchouli and sandalwood. 'Gloria is dawdling this morning,' he says with the sweet earthy warmth of his affection. 'Late night, her cousin Sam announced his engagement to us at dinner, a great surprise.'

A great disease. I try to match his smile: 'Oh, how exciting.'

He's too shrewd. 'Oh, but I see something is troubling you, child – what is it?' he asks.

'Mm, nothing,' I reply, and I don't have to feign distraction: I've spotted the candy stripes, waiting for me on the cutting table behind him. I want to fall into a cloud of it and I haven't even touched it yet. I tell him, vaguely: 'Mad mob down at the Quay just now was a bit troubling, I suppose, a whole load of poor chaps heading for the Labour Exchange.'

Mr Jabour sighs: 'It is a terrible shame.'

'Yes.' Oh, but I want to buy the lot: the lemon one especially – so pretty, citrony, on an almond meringue ground, that's for Min Bromley's kimono.

'It is the Bank of England that should bear this shame, though.' Mr Jabour clicks his tongue as he unfurls one of the bolts for me, the blue one – a heavenly, powdery, cloudy shade.

'Hm? Shame...' I've gone nebulous with it. Matching pyjamas?

'Yes, my dear. The Bank of England is calling in their loans, and this whole country, as they say, is in hock to the eyeballs to them. But they are *war* loans.' He clicks his tongue again. 'They are calling in war loans, can you believe it? Sixty thousand boys we give to them and they are calling in the loans now – ninety days to pay or else. You would not do this to an enemy.'

That prompts me to look at Mr Jabour and pay attention: his brother was one of the sixty thousand Australian boys who died for England, just like Mother's Archie and Alex, and Australia had to borrow to send them over in the first place. I say: 'That is shameful.' Want to bite my tongue now with the shame of all of it, including mine, take back my childish shrieking at Mother. World doesn't necessarily revolve around me, et cetera. 'All the shops that are closing up,' Mr Jabour shakes his head, 'like flowers in the night – you should see Randwick, three businesses have closed along Belmore Road this week. You can be sure the department stores will do well out of it.' He sighs again, smoothing the candy stripes. 'And now we must do battle with cheap rayon, too.' He laughs, such a jolly laugh he has and he always rubs his ample waistline when he releases it. 'Promise me, Olivia, please promise me you will never buy rayon.'

'That's an easy promise to make,' I do match his smile now. 'May I have the whole bolt? This one, and the lemon, too? Please.'

He shakes his head again, but there's more mirth in it, as he reaches under the cutting table and pulls up another bolt. That makes me gasp: I've never seen anything like it. Fine stripes of navy and aquamarine on a ground of cerulean true blue. Stunning. Mine. Must be.

Mr Jabour laughs again, a great booming one for my silly face, before leaning towards me with a conspiratorial whisper: 'Just one bolt of this in all the world. Exquisite, no?'

The Blue Mile

I nod, and as I do I glance at the great teak sideboard behind him, where the most fabulous of the trims are kept, and I nod at the antique brass bottle that sits atop it too. It's rather the same shape as Mr Jabour, stoppered with a bulb of ruby and sapphire glass, and I no longer believe it's merely an Oriental decoration: it's where Mr Jabour keeps his genie.

He winks: 'But for you, Olivia dear, special price.'

Special Arabian one – tall as the tale. But I'm as yet unable to reply with anything apart from an awestruck caress of the invisible weave, as the words from that song, 'Little Alice Blue', come to me in Mother's sweet voice: *The little silk worms that made silk for that gown, only made that much silk and then crawled in the ground . . .*

I'm in love. I don't know what I'll do with this piece, my bolt of blue heaven, but I do believe I'd pay with my life for it.

Yo

'That's right, I'm afraid. You can't register as unemployed without an address,' this fella at the counter of the Labour Exchange is explaining. I look around behind me, as if I might check on Ag by doing so, but I can't see her from here. She's waiting for me outside, with a bag of grapes and a bun, behind the foyer door. Not that there's many here to see her: the couple of hundred or so registered unemployed that were here when we arrived have gone on a march up to Parliament House, to tell the Premier what they reckon.

I turn back to this fella at the counter. He's looking sympathetic enough but there's nothing he can do for me. Still, I have to say: 'But I need a job so I can get an address.'

'That's a predicament for you,' he nods; not his problem.

'Can I just look at the noticeboards, then? See if there's places I might try at?' There's three of these noticeboards all pinned with cards, fenced off along the side of the counter, I could almost touch the nearest of them.

'Well, no, I'm afraid not,' he says, and I hear the change of tune: he'd like to be clear of me now. 'These jobs are for the registered unemployed, and I must say that with all of the listings here preference is given first to returned servicemen, and then married men, men with families to support.'

He's supposing I am neither, of course. But I do have a family to support, even if I can't tell him that. Jesus, help me.

I start begging: 'Can you recommend *anywhere* I might start looking? Just doors to knock on?'

I think he's going to tell me to go to buggery, but he cocks his head for me to come nearer and listen, going to give me some under the counter advice. 'You could go across to Surry Hills and Redfern, there are a few factories there that have been putting men on, textile workshops, one or two which have lately got contracts with some of the big city stores, long hours and working for Syrians, but good enough for some. You said you have machine work experience, so that might be the ticket for you.'

Lebbo work. And it might well be the ticket for me if I could go back to the Neighbourhood. I can't go back there; I can't take Aggie back there. But I can't say anything about it to this fella, either; I can only ask him: 'There's not anywhere else?'

He rolls his eyes, thinking I'm some kind of bludger, too good for a Lebbo sweatshop. 'There's always farm work, for a *fit* young bloke. They're crying out for hands at Windsor and Penrith, Blacktown, and further afield – cherry pickers are needed most urgently at Mudgee for the Christmas crop, if you really want to know. But that's *hard* work, isn't it?'

Fuck you behind your high and mighty counter. I could grab him by the tie and smack his face into it. But I can't do that, either. I can only turn away from him.

And rip a card off one of the boards on my way out, just to tell him what I reckon.

Then clear off quickly, grabbing Ag from behind the door on the way through.

She says on my hip: 'Did you get a job, Yoey?'

'Not yet,' I tell her. I've got one voice in my head telling me to give this up, get myself to Redfern; while the other voice can't speak at all for showing me Michael's boots jumping on the kitchen table to the Devil's beat. I tell Ag: 'I'll get a job soon. After we go and have that tram ride, yeah?'

'Now, you mean?' she says, throwing her arms around my neck: *please*.

'Right now,' I tell her. 'We'll go to one of them big city stores, get you some buckle shoes now too, yeah?' Fuck this, let's go shopping, why not?

'Yeah.' She kicks my backside to make me go faster back round to the Quay, and I'm praying again: please, Lord, I'm not asking for myself. Get me a job for Aggie.

We get on the first tram we find, a Pitt Street one, which I'm supposing will take us past that biggest store, Hordern's, at Brickfield Hill. We won't be able to miss it: it's that big it's a whole block. Worth the price of the tram ticket already, though: when the bell goes ding as the tram moves off anyone'd think this was the best day of Agnes O'Keenan's life.

I'm still holding that card from the Labour Exchange in my hand as I set Ag down on a seat and I'm just about to scrunch it up into my pocket when I see what's written on it:

LABOURERS WANTED FOR SYDNEY HARBOUR BRIDGEWORKS. BOILERWORKER & IRONWORKER GANG ASSISTANTS. PERMANENT POSITIONS TO SUITABLE APPLICANTS. £4 /17/6 to £6/5/-. PER WEEK. APPLY IN PERSON AT PUBLIC WORKS DEPARTMENT, PUBLIC ENTRANCE, BRIDGE STREET.

I stare at it like it could well be £6/5/- there in my hand. Even less believable that it's for labouring. Too good to be true, and you'd have to be registered to go for it, wouldn't you, but I'll have to see about that for myself, won't I. After I've taken Ag to Hordern's, and taken myself to a barber. I need a shave and a haircut before I apply in person for anything. I could do with a new shirt, too, if I can stretch our resources, wasn't wearing my best when we set off yesterday evening: it's grey, and not originally that colour, missing a button and starting to rip through at the elbows.

I look out the window and past all the la-di-da arcades and restaurants I see the great shopping palace of Hordern's coming up ahead at the next cross-street, and I grab Ag up again: 'Here's the stop for buckle shoes.' And as we get near it I see there's a sale banner strung on the corner verandah posts.

'*BARGAINS ALL DAY FRIDAY – UNTIL 9 PM. LAST CHANCE BEFORE CHRISTMAS!*' Ag reads it out, almost shouting with the excitement of it, and I say: 'Isn't that lucky for us, then?'

As well as a good majority of the women of Sydney, I see. The place is swarming, and I stand at the doors for a moment, doubtful we can go in. Swarming with flowers: these women in their shiny shoes, their hats of every colour. They're all just people, I tell myself, ordinary people, wives and mothers hunting for a bargain, but it looks like another world. It is another world. We can't afford it here; this is not a place for us.

'Yo-Yo, see,' Ag is pointing at a sign inside the doors. 'Children's wear on the third floor.' She's a good girl with her reading, isn't she? And that gets me through the doors, knowing that Sister Joe will be missing Ag today, this last day of school, missing out on never giving Ag a prize for her reading, the sour old bitch. Ag's never going back to that shitful school. She's getting buckle shoes instead.

Up the escalators we go then, and I can say that I have never been so put off my stride in such a way as this in my life. The bright lights, and the noise, and all these women going everywhere, with all their perfumes enough to knock you about. Still, they are so busy at what they're getting on with, they don't seem to see us, the unshaven lout and the shoeless child. Who slept under a tree in a park last night. Please, don't let that be where Aggie sleeps tonight.

'Oh Yoey, look at the red ones! Can I get them? Please?' she says and we've barely stepped off the escalator.

'Near half price, those ones are, dear.' A lady comes up beside us, an older lady, small and slight with round eyeglasses, and a keen eye for a customer.

I say to her: 'We want a pair of them then,' and I hold her stare for second: *Don't you chuck us out.*

But she just smiles over them eyeglasses at us: 'What an adorable imp you have there, look at those lush dark curls.' Not clear if she's meaning me or Ag, or both. We're all the same to her anyway, I suppose, and by the time she's finished with us, Ag's got a pair of red buckle shoes, a dress with yellow flowers on it, a blue cardigan, and socks for a bob thrown in too. All for less than a pound and she looks something better than adorable. She's looking down at the new buckle shoes on her feet as I pay for them: this *is* the best day of her life. I don't care that we can't afford it. She looks like one of them rosy-cheeked little girls on a billboard for Sunlight soap. And she's not sleeping in a fucking park tonight.

We leave Ag's old clothes with the shop lady, and I hope she burns them too. 'Merry Christmas, sir, and little miss,' she says, and we say, 'Merry Christmas to you.'

Right. We're off to this Public Works place now, and I'm going to get that job. I get a new shirt from the ground floor for eight bob, good-looking white one too, and barbering of my own woolly head for four – with directions to Bridge Street for free. 'Public Works?' the barber says. 'It's just around off Macquarie Street, big building, can't miss it, across from the Gardens.'

'The Botanic Gardens?'

'That's right.'

Right. And I'm smiling, because this must be my job, I must have dreamed it into our tomorrow last night.

It must show in me, too, because not fifteen minutes later, past the crowd of the registered unemployed outside Parliament House shouting 'WE WANT WORK' against a line of unhappy cops, I'm being looked over by a fella at this Department of Public Works, and he's saying: 'Yes, there's one vacancy left, needs filling urgently – can't seem to keep a man at it. Ever done any heavy work?'

And although the honest answer is no, not lately and not much, I have to say, 'Yes, heavy work is my calling,' and he doesn't even ask me for references, never mind any registration. He looks busy; come out of an office somewhere beyond the counter and he just wants a man for the job so he can get back to his own. I am in the right place at the right time, thank you, Lord. Two pounds left in my pocket and saved in the nick.

He says: 'You look fit enough, I suppose. Get yourself to the loading dock by the Dorman Long workshops at the north arm tomorrow morning at seven-thirty – the wharves at the Milsons Point shops, right?'

'Yes, sir,' I nod; I'll find them wherever they might be.

He says: 'Speak to Mr Matt Harrison at the office there, he's the foreman in charge of the ironworker gangs and he'll give you a go.'

Give me a go at what I don't know, and I don't push my luck to ask. I'm that grateful, I could jump the counter to lick his boots. He gives me a piece of paper to give to this Mr Harrison, and I tell him: 'You won't be sorry you gave me a go, sir.'

'No, I'm sure I won't be sorry. You might be, though, lad. Six pound five a week and you'll know you've earned every farthing.' He's already turned away from me.

'Merry Christmas,' I tell the back of him: and no, sir, I won't be sorry, whatever this job might be. It's six blessed pounds, five shillings a week for me. I'm going to rent us a little house somewhere good and we'll live like kings.

I pick Aggie up from where she's waiting for me, picture of sunlight behind the foyer doors.

'Did you get a job?' She looks up at me with those big blue wondering eyes of hers.

And I could cry for happiness and all the madness of hoping as I tell her: 'Yes I did, Ag, I got a job.'

She nods, pleased, then she asks me: 'Can we have egg and chips for lunch, then?'

I tell her: 'You can have whatever you want.' I'll be having a smoke next, whatever I do, and not thinking about an ale to chase it. Jesus, I will not have an ale while I am alive.

My sister says: 'Could you put me down, please, Yoey? You might crush my new frock.'

And I reckon I could live for the next hundred years on that alone.

Olivia

Hm, what about a smart von Drécoll-ish coat-dress? I wonder as I drape my bolt of blue heaven over the back of the chaise. I'd ask Mother to come out and give me her opinion, but I'm still avoiding her. She's in the stockroom, running up the kimono to my specifications, and I'm truly sorry about my shrieking tantrum but I still don't want to face it: him. Marry him? Ludicrous. Dinner at the Merrick tomorrow night? No. Absolutely not. Can't think about it. What about contrasting collar and cuffs, then: white, or perhaps a purple? That smart shade of heliotrope that's everywhere in Milan at the minute? Or maybe just a simple Lanvin-ish shift instead – boat-neck? And then I decide no altogether – the fabric itself is too much for Min Bromley's going-away frock, it would swamp her colouring and her tiny figure. I'm not even going to show it to her when she comes in at four this afternoon. It's for someone else. Or perhaps not a frock at all . . .

The shop bell dings and I'm happy for the interruption: more busyness to avoid Mother with. It's been all hats this morning, my department, all middlings wanting a little something special for church, emphasis on the little, and fiddly, pernickety trims. I'll be cross-eyed with horsehair froth and spider daisies – cheap but very effective. Might do something a bit special for Mrs Ebbert, though, of Ebbert's Confectionary in the Royal – word is, they're not doing well at all, badly positioned there on the first floor, too, and she's such a pleasant lady. Like Mrs Wilton, of Wilton's Ladies' Tailor on the first floor here, middling of middlings, and she's losing hers to Hordern's House of Economy ready-made today. When I turn, though, it's not a customer.

It's Glor: 'Lunch now.'

'Oh? Is that the time?' My stomach groans. Audibly.

Glor clicks her tongue. *Yes*, that's the time. You're Christmas blitzed already, aren't you? Come on. You complain about being twiggy, and you don't eat properly. Hop it now.'

She starts dragging me out by the elbow, and I grab hat, gloves and handbag as I call out: 'Mother? I'm off with Glor – Pearson's. Might be a while.'

'Oh, is that the time?' I hear her wonder from the stockroom as I'm pulled out the door, only just remembering to grab special snazz-filled hatbox from coat stand. Glor doesn't even notice: too busy hurrying me along.

Into the lunchtime melee: the ground floor of the arcade is teeming. If it wasn't for Pearson's prawns, it wouldn't be worth the trouble battling through it. We've only got to get two minutes down Pitt, just over the other side of King Street, oh but the stench of humanity. So humid today too – *phlergh*, but is a little talcum powder really too much trouble? I could collapse from it, but that Glor is still pulling me along: 'We can't be late, they'll give our table away.'

They would, too: one of the waiters is standing at the door, turning a couple of chaps away, the usual Pearson's chaps, young lawyers and journalists, come here to rub shoulders with barristers and politicians, which is why Glor likes to lunch here: for the young lawyers. Hasn't found one she likes, yet. But they all like her: the pair at the door are so transfixed as she walks past them the waiter tells them to move along.

The Blue Mile

Oh, the stench of masculinity in here: powerful amongst the powerful. I pull my brim down as we're seated, and Glor says at my hatbox: 'What in whosiwhatsits, Ollie – you've brought some work with you, have you?'

'Oh? No!' I push the box across the table to her: 'This is for you. Ho ho ho, lovely one.'

'Oh!' Her surprise is a treat in itself and she hasn't even opened it yet. She lifts the lid off the hatbox and she cries out, for the whole cafe to hear: 'Olivia Greene, oh my! Olivia Greene, what have you done!'

So that everyone in the room looks at me. Including – oh dear God – there he is, bang on time, it's Mr Lang, Leader of the Opposition, walking across to his usual table at the back of the cafe, tipping his hat, granite jaw cracking into a grin – at me – on his way through. Mr Fabulous. Even Mother thinks he's fabulous, as most mothers do, for bringing in the Child Endowment when he was the premier – not that she'd ever openly admit to supporting Labor Party anything, or the raise in company tax that funds anything they do. Six shillings worth of well-earned justice, she calls the maternal pittance under her hat, and I call Mr Lang fabulous right now for taking the attention from me. People would look at him even if he wasn't Mr Lang, though: so tall and dark, and those searching eyes, soulful – for a suburban real estate agent, anyway.

'Oh, Ollie.' Glor couldn't care less if John Barrymore himself romped in as Don Juan as she lifts the zigzags up out of the box. 'I adore it. Velma and May are going to be crazed with jealousy.' Her older sisters. I grin. They will be crazed.

Our bubble of loveliness is restored, and just as the waiter takes our order, Glor leans across the table and whispers: 'Don't look now, but boy to the right, two tables across, maroon tie – what do you think?'

I think I want to run out into Pitt Street and scream. Why does everyone I love want a boy? I don't. They don't look at me, unless they're a bemused leader of the opposition, and I don't look at them. Glor's rattling on about this one: Paul Gallagher, he's so and so's son, who's a friend of Uncle George, and he went to Waverley College, the year below Cousin Sam, and her father approves – 'I'm thinking of letting Dad ask him over for coffee. What do you think, Ollie?'

Give him a glance from under my brim. He looks all right. Generic boy. Fresh-faced garden variety. Nice. Reasonably gorgeous blue eyes. Not handsome enough for her, though. I say: 'He looks hardy enough to withstand coffee at your house. But it's what you think that matters, Glor.'

He looks across the room and smiles at her, enchanted.

And my prawns taste of grit.

Glor doesn't notice; she's too busy making eyes at him, and trying on his name about a hundred times: Paul this, Paul that, la la la la la la la la . . .

Until I look up at the wall clock and, 'Oh dear God, Glor,' I deliver the excuse I've been fabricating these past five minutes: 'I've forgotten I have to pick up some fox trim from Barnaby's, for an appointment I've got coming in at three – I'm going to have to go.'

'Oh, Ol, I –'

I pop my share of the bill on the table and I'm off. I don't know where. Anywhere, pounding out this screeching resentment to the rhythm of my mary-janes, some grubby black mark on the left toe already. I've got to get clear of this stinking, cloying crush of Pitt Street, and I stomp round into Hunter, past the garish vermillion drapes of the Tulip Restaurant on the corner where Bart Harley took Mother to lunch the other day, past his wretched chambers four doors up. Bart stupid Harley everywhere. Oh look: there's a mob of them, flapping across the road on their way back to the law courts. What is the collective noun for barristers? A murder? They look like horrible crows.

I just about start to run, up to the Gardens, to be clear of all of it. Haven't been for a walk up here for months, not to mention a run. Too busy. Stop being busy now. For five minutes. Be calm. Stop being a baby. Breathe in the fresh, sweet air beyond the gates. Ah. There... Incredible, how instantly soothing that is, although it doesn't yet slow my pace. I take the path down behind the Conservatorium of Music and follow it right round towards Government House, to the water, to this most soothing of views out from Farm Cove: not a stupid ferry or a stupid Bridge or a stupid person in sight.

Just the water, and me.

And this colour – this gold-shot teal. And that's exactly it. I see it now: Min Bromley's going-away dress. Shantung and organza, in magic-carpet teal. Of course.

Yo

'I'm sorry, lad, but there's no room at the inn, as they say,' this woman at the Paragon says, and this is the fifth hotel we've asked at round the Quay. She's all pity for us, leaning over the counter at her private entrance window, with no reason not to believe our story, which is a sad and simple one, and true enough: that I've come into Sydney from out west for work on the Bridge, with my child who's lately lost her mother. The woman shakes her head: 'You could go round to the Loo but, love, always vacancies there, and then there's always them places a bit further afield towards Paddington, though I wouldn't take the little girl there, you know what I mean.'

I do, and I understand the warning. I wouldn't take Aggie into the filthy knocking shop that is Paddo all the way to Darlinghurst if paradise lay in the very centre of it; I'm not taking her round to Woolloomooloo either, for the entertainment of sailors bawling and brawling all night long. Not that they'd be likely to wake her. She's asleep, and heavy with it now, long past caring about me making creases in her frock, or failing her again, as I am.

I look at the woman for a second in want of pleading with her:

what in Jesus' name is a homeless man with a child supposed to do? But I know the answer: go back to the Gardens, for tonight. Blessed be our merciful Lord it isn't raining. And know that we are not alone in our plight; we can't be: from all the enquiries I've made this evening, it seems it's near impossible to find decent, cheap accommodation in the city even with a good job, unless you're after a room at the Australia Hotel – that big one on Martin Place we passed just last night, as it turns out. The rates there are very reasonable, apparently, only you have to own a dinner suit to get in the door.

'If you ask me,' the woman taps the counter with her finger, thinking, really wanting to help us, 'Balmain's not a bad place to look, lad – it might be a bit rough around the edges but they're good people, working people. Try for a boarding house over that way, you'll be right.'

'Thanks.' I nod. Balmain. That's the second time I've received that advice, but it'll have to wait till tomorrow now. The clock on the wall behind the woman's head says it's five after nine. It's too late to be going off somewhere I don't know. Balmain's not far – it's where those timber and colliery's wharves are, and that big electric power station, further down the harbour to the west, you can see it across the water from Pyrmont – but it might as well be another country. I've never been there.

I'm about to turn away when the woman says: 'Hang on a sec, there.'

I think she might be going to see what she can do for us by way of accommodation, but she comes back with a paper bag. 'Couple of pork pies for you, love. My Maurie makes them himself, they're very good.'

'Thanks,' I say to her again. 'That's very kind of you, I appreciate it.' And I do. Goodness. There is plenty of that about if you need it, isn't there. Just no room at the inn. Not tonight.

I hold Ag tight to me as we walk back into the street, don't look back at the great Tooths billboard lit up above the pub, calling all souls in for *SYDNEY BITTER,* wouldn't want to stay there anyway, would we. I walk back round towards the Gardens. Back through this empty city. You wouldn't know there were any homeless people about, not in the night, it's so quiet once you get up to Macquarie Street. Not even a late-opening department store round here. There's nothing but the trees and the bats that live in them. Those fucking fruit bats. I've got to try to get some sleep tonight; I'm supposing I only got about four or five hours last night, bits and pieces of it, thanks to the bats and the damp of the ground, and keeping one eye on Ag and the other out for a cop or a gatekeeper that might fall over us in the dark. I need a good sleep tonight. I've got a job to turn up to in the morning. What in Jesus' name am going to do with Ag tomorrow while I'm at it? On the North Shore, too. Somewhere I've never been, either.

At least the Gardens is safe. No luck getting back in until I've gone all the way up and round to where I found the bent-out railing last night, and when we're in, I keep walking, just keep walking, almost back down to the harbour again, as if by walking I might somehow get us further away from hopeless. I get us down to the tram sheds this side of the Quay, and they're lit up like hell's tomorrow, so I keep walking down to the seawall, away from the harbour lights, to where the sound of the water washing against the wall seems quieter than silence. It sounds like sleep. Even the figs here are quiet. The air is warm and still. This will be a good place for us tonight, I think.

And then a dog barks somewhere in the blackness ahead and a fella calls out: 'That you, Perc?'

I don't run. I couldn't run if it was Welfare after us. I'm far too past it now. I say: 'No, and I'm not looking for trouble.'

'Righto,' this fella laughs as he comes up to us. 'No one's ever looking for trouble, are they – poor lonely bugger, he is, that Mr Trouble.' I can't see him well, but I can smell him. On the metho.

Ag must smell it too; she wakes up and yawns: 'Yoey?'

And the old fella sees her; he says: 'Ah, you got trouble anyway, I take it. What you doing out here in the night then?'

'Not a lot.'

'Righto,' he says. 'Well, since you're not looking for trouble, let me tell you two bob's: you don't want to go into the Domain for not a lot tonight.'

'Wasn't thinking to,' I say, thinking about it. The Domain, it's the park along from the Gardens, behind St Mary's Cathedral, where there's a permanent hobos' camp and the soap-boxers preach their politics on Sundays, not that I've ever been to see or hear any of that steaming pile. I ask him: 'What's going on there?'

The laugh goes out of his voice: 'Listen, you can still get a good feed from the Salvos there, my word you can, but you have to get there before five o'clock. After sunset, no good. Lot of young blokes hanging about nowadays, warming Mrs Mac's Chair – like you, not looking for trouble, none of them. But they are – stirred up and it's worse than the last time, it is. It's no place for you to be taking a child.'

I don't need to be told that, and not by this old piece of shitbag. Keep going past him.

'Stay round the Gardens,' he calls after us. 'We'll look out for you – we're the Governor's new groundsmen!' He starts laughing again, wheezing like a dead man with it.

I keep walking, and Ag says when we're well past him: 'Don't worry, Yo-Yo. We'll find a place tomorrow.' Patting me on the shoulder.

Jesus, please: she's seven years old and consoling me. Have a heart, listen to her now as she chooses our tree for this night, telling me all about the fairies that live in this part of the Gardens, that they have white wings and pink roses in their hair, and they all have the prettiest names, like Nina and Lucy, and that they'll like the hard bit of this pork pie crust to dunk in their tea. 'Don't worry, Yoey, Queen Oonagh likes us, I know she does.' Telling me with it all that I haven't failed her a bit, and soon enough, in the warm still air, she's asleep again in my arms, in the arms of this tree.

I don't sleep, though. The more I will it, the more I can't do it, and the louder, beneath the quiet wash of the water, I can hear our mother crying for us. Telling me I should take Ag back to her; but I can't do that. Ag hasn't mentioned our mother once. Not once since we left. And I can't take her back for all the crying in the world. I can't take her back to that life. It is not any life to have. I need to sleep, to best take our chance at this next life, whatever it might be, but I can't sleep, not really. My gut chews around and around the shame in me for not taking Ag away from there sooner, doing it properly, in some orderly way – with a place to live, with a job. Not sleeping in a park. Not sleeping at all. Greasy in my veins from wanting a drink to bring it to me, and hating that want more than ever: days that come and go in the half-hour before closing, making that sly bottle of KB last into the night, until you don't care anymore, until you'd drink anything, anytime. Our mother crying and crying. I can only close my eyes over it and try to will the sun to rise, to bring me the new day, this new life, as fast as it can come for us.

And when it does come, the seawall is a ring of gold stone around us, and in the quickness of Ag's smile as she turns in my arms to find me still here, it doesn't seem to matter that I haven't slept, or that I don't know what or how we'll manage this next hour, never mind this day. I just have things to do.

Olivia

I can't do it. I've tried to reconcile it all in my mind, tried to be accepting, mature, calm, reasoned. Forced it into floral georgette. Be sweet. Unselfish.

Impossible.

I've continued this argument down the ferry steps, under monster claws North and South, and right through the gangway at the Quay: impossible. I simply can't go to the Merrick tonight.

And it's *not* selfishness on my part anyway.

How can Mother justify herself to *me*? Not coming home – again – last night. When I got back to the shop yesterday afternoon, I was met with a note: *Ollie darling, taken some work over to Bart's at Rose Bay, need the peace and quiet – see you in the morning.* The morning that finds me a ruin now, a frowzled and frayed scrap of ruin. And it's her fault. How do I know she's safe in Rose Bay somewhere and not met a bad end somehow, tossed in the harbour there? How do I know she's merely been making love all night long? Oh dear God – *merely*? Does she *want* to ruin me absolutely with this carry-on? Even without *that* humiliation, how can she conscience leaving me all alone, for two long nights in a row?

Leaving me alone to deal with Friday late opening five minutes to Christmas. Leaving me to go home alone to the torture of untouchable Mexican chocolate cake in the sideboard. And – the worst – pinching my bolt of blue heaven on her way out the door. While it may be true that she is unaware of my attachment to that fabric, primarily because I wasn't talking to her yesterday, she could have left it and *asked* me before taking it *for herself*.

I pull my brim down tight against my ears, to keep this rage and infuriation in. But it won't stay in – it's even escaping through my hair today. Which is only more and more reason I am not going to the Merrick tonight: I'm not taking this rebellious mess anywhere it might be hatless, not to mention the rest of me: it looks like it's been through the surf. It is the surf, at Manly, in a tempest. I'm a tempest. Competing with Medusa for ugly.

While Mother is . . .

I glance up Pitt Street ahead, along the bright riot of verandah posts of this busiest street, already a mad contest of carts and lorries and trams and people intent on parting with their hard-earned. The place my mother has delivered me my future. My business. My certainty. Myself. My mother. And the storm suddenly dies out of me. My gorgeous and clever mother who has raised me, loved me, sacrificed herself for me and cared for me in all ways for all these years. She can do as she pleases. She can marry Bart Harley, she can marry Don Juan.

So long as I don't have to go to the Merrick tonight.

But no. No, she can't do any such thing! The storm rails up again and I am a child lost and wailing in it.

Mother can't marry Bart Harley. She simply can't. And I can't hurt her by saying no to it either. To him. He must be made to disappear, then. Can't one of those razor-gang drug hoodlums shoot him in revenge? I'm going to unstopper that brass bottle on Mr Jabour's sideboard and command the genie to arrange it forthwith.

Oh dear God, that takes me by the throat: what creature am I to think such a spiteful thing? Take a sharp left along Albert Street, up to the Gardens. Now. I must cool myself down before I do anything else. I can't go into the arcade in this state. And I can't be so cruel to Mother.

Damn her, I send my cursing up into the mess of squiggling limbs of the fat old Moreton Bay figs that stretch across the foreshore here.

Stomp, stomp, stomp, beneath their million leaves of glossy indifference, doing nothing to soothe me whatsoever.

DAMN!

I slap my hands onto the cool, solid stone of the wall that edges this garden from the sea, and I look out across the cove here, asking it for a loan of just the tiniest fraction of its serenity, just a moment to see my way clear in this.

But all I see now is a claggy haze of humidity rising off the water with the sun, over a great grey expanse of *phlergh* . . .

Yo

'Look. Yoey – that's her.' Aggie points up ahead: 'That's the fairy princess from our tree.'

'Is it?' I say, not really looking, hurrying up the path now. We have to get across the harbour earlier than I'm due there, find a good safe spot for Ag to spend the day. I'm sick at the thought of leaving her on her own, in some place I know nothing of, but what else can I do? She'll be right, won't be the first day she's spent alone with a bag of grapes and a bun.

'Yoey,' she gets a whine in her voice now, and she's never one for whining: 'You're not looking.' She pulls at my shirtsleeve.

I look up to where she's pointing, at her fairy princess: it's a girl standing by the seawall, her dress is white with pink flowers on it, and she has a long scarf round her neck that's floating behind her on the breeze, of that see-through type material. I say: 'You might be right, Ag – she's got the same colours as your fairies last night.'

'She must become a real girl in the daytime,' Ag decides as we get nearer to her.

'Yeah.' I say, and I'm already past her in my head, counting the wharves along the Quay, to the Milsons Point one I checked for yesterday – *Milsons* not *McMahons*, we have to get to, the ticket fella at the Quay said, on the *east* side of Lavender Bay. Wharf number six, I count them off again, as if the little folk might have swapped them all around in the night just to entertain me. Then we're to keep to the *left* along the water to the Dorman Long wharves – don't go right to the trains or up the escalators to the tram, it's a confusion round there, the ticket fella said. I pick Ag up the better to start a run for it.

But as I do she calls out, 'Oh no – look!' and I just catch what she sees: the wind picking up and taking the girl's hat with it. A little white hat with a black band, it flies up and spins against the sky, till it's caught by the branches of the fig behind us.

'Oh dear God!' the girl shouts at the tree, high and loud like a tin whistle. 'Well, that's just fabulous, that is.'

And it is. I can see her face now, and it's stopped every other thought in my head, my feet as well. Her cheeks are the same colour as the flowers on her dress and her hair is as wild as Ag's, only it's gold, a wild halo of gold. She throws her hands up in the air. She's very upset about this hat being in the tree. But her arms, long and pale and bare, are all I'm interested in for the moment. Everything about her seems long. She's a tall girl, tall like a tree, a beautiful tree of a kind I've never seen before. She's a –

'We have to get the hat for her, Yoey,' says Ag, kicking my backside.

'What?' I return to our reality as fast as I left it. I'm not climbing up any tree to fetch a hat. We have to get to Milsons Point – ten minutes ago. I look back over my shoulder towards the Quay, the tall masts of some old sailing ship this side of it telling me to move it along.

'Oh, you wouldn't be so kind, would you?' the girl says and I look at her again. She's looking up at the hat in the tree, wanting, worrying, asking with eyes that are neither blue nor green, and her voice is like honey now she's not shouting. She could be a princess, she's got that type of bearing about her. She is without doubt a fairy: she has me in her power. I look at the hat in the tree, searching for the best way up.

'I can reach,' Ag says. 'You hold me up, Yoey, and I can shake it out.'

Takes a child to see sense sometimes, doesn't it, and the hat's tumbling into the girl's hands two seconds later.

'Thank you so much,' she smiles, and her hands jitter a little putting her hat back on her head, pulling the brim of it so low on her face all I can see is her smile.

And I can no more reply than move from it. A smile that has changed me into a spoon, powerless except for goggling – and being instantly convinced that this is the girl. *The* girl. The one who will be mine. I have the worries of the world on my shoulders today. I have my little sister on my shoulders for sure. And I've decided to take a wife on the way to the ferry to I don't know where, as if any girl would want me, never mind one such as this.

I laugh. Though it's not funny. This is why I've never been too orderly about my business: too easily diverted from it. Thinking about a girl, drinking about a girl, and getting nothing done about anything while I'm definitely not getting the girl.

But she laughs as well: honey winding round that tin whistle. Jesus. I'll bet she can sing.

She says again: 'Thank you so much.' And she smiles again: 'I needed that laugh, too – really I did.' She looks away, down at her shoes, as if she might have some terrible worry with them now too. They're white shoes; of course they are.

'I like your frock,' Aggie says to her, and I don't hear the reply.

I can only see the way this girl is smiling up at Ag now, this fairy princess smiling on my sister and talking with her about frocks, so that my own empty-headed spoonery now joins up with our need, and I'm asking this girl: 'You couldn't find it in your heart to do me a favour in return, could you?'

'Oh?'

I'm as surprised as she is at the question, and I don't know how it is I manage to continue with it when her eyes fall on me again, but I do; I ask her: 'You couldn't look after my little sister for a few hours, could you, today? While I'm at work. I'll pay you.'

Her back straightens at the question, and though I'm an inch or two taller, the look she gives me squashes me into the gravel at our feet.

Yes, I have intelligence enough to know that question was monkey-nutted enough to win me a prize, thank you, and we'll be on our way.

Olivia

'No – wait,' I call after them, and I'm not entirely sure what compels me to, apart from gratitude at being spared a walk back across town as hatless Medusa.

The man turns on his heel, scruffy work boots that have never known a polish, and two sets of impossibly blue eyes implore me, one above the other. Almost a cornflower blue, touch of violet; extraordinary colour. I glance away from them again, into the crook where the stone wall meets the path: why have I stopped them? Perhaps because the man is not much of a man but a boy, not much older than myself, and like myself he's in a spot of bother on his way to work. I look up at the little girl on his shoulders: impossibly lovely, from jumble of jet ringlets to Indian red mary-janes. And although the answer must be, *No, I can't look after your little sister, as I have to go to work myself, and you shouldn't have asked such an outstandingly insane question of a lady in the first place*, I ask the near threadbare knees of the man's trousers: 'Where do you work?'

'I've got a job on the Bridge,' he says, 'I start today,' heart on incongruously crisp white shirtsleeve, and the little one, her whole tiny person cuddling his head: *Please.*

Well, that's it then, isn't it. How can I refuse? A Bridge worker. He could be the dustman there for all I know, but he might just as well be a brave and heroic scaler of monstrous Bridge claws, mightn't he.

I look at him square on now, the whole of him, and when I do, something even odder strikes me. Whatever he might do for a living, he's been designed to inspire maximum giddiness in a girl – tall and dark, and those eyes – but I am not giddified by him in the least. The seething ball of nervous squirms I carry about inside me has utterly ceased. Perhaps because he is laughably handsome – original template of masculine beauty variety of handsome – I am somehow safe in his gaze. Such an intent gaze, he's not really looking at me at all, is he. He clearly needs this favour very much. A nice boy, obviously, looking after his little sister. Appealing for my assistance. Deserving of a good turn; as I might well be deserving of giving one.

And so, however impossible it might seem, I find myself replying: 'I can look after your little sister, but she'll have to come to work with me.'

'Miss,' he says, setting the girl on the path between us, his relief so plain I can feel his heart trip over it, 'you are a life saver, you'll never know how much I appreciate this. I'll pay you – whatever you think is a reasonable thing. It's just that we've been caught short today for help and we're not from round here, and –'

'No,' I assure him, 'you don't need to pay me.' His gratitude is as embarrassing as it is charming. Such a nice boy should not have to beg help of strangers in the street, all but on those threadbare knees, and I look away from him again. I look at his hand resting on his sister's head; surprisingly well-kept hand, one that might belong to a tailor rather than a death-defying dustman.

And then I almost smirk – with the realisation of the favour this will do me too. Mother will be put out by my kindness, won't she. A small and yet noble act of spite with which I might pay her back for all the madness she's caused me, and for pinching my fabric. If she can marry a strange man, I can bring a strange child to the salon for a day. Petulant but fair. And priceless. Mother has affection for one child only: me. And Mother, beneath all her cosmopolitan savoir faire, is also a terrific snob: wait till she hears this little poppet open her mouth – coarse as the weave of her big brother's shirt. Appalling bargain-table mercerised cotton, blindingly over-bleached and soft-collared. Dreadful. Lovely. I look at him square again and say: 'I had better tell you who I am then, I suppose. My name is Olivia Greene – with an e on the end. And you'll find us at a salon called Emily Costumière on the second floor of the Strand, do you know it – the arcade?'

'I'll find you,' he says, and the neat proportion of his shoulder-line has me mentally sketching him into a dinner jacket. 'But I'm not sure when I . . .'

'Doesn't matter – be as late as you need to be.' I dismiss his concern: with any luck, you'll be so late I'll have to give the Merrick a miss tonight. I don't suppose the Saturday Bridge shift ends at midday as it does for the rest of us. Good God but I'd taper the cut for him, snug on the hip and make it white, with a brocade vest, trousers in midnight. Very New York. Very nice. 'You'd better tell me your name, though, too, hadn't you?'

'Oh yeah,' he shakes his head at himself, and I shake mine at the outrageous dimples in his cheeks, and he says something that I don't hear properly – 'Owing Keenly'? – his speech is so quick and fluid, dancing over his words. 'Pardon?'

'Yo-un,' he says it slowly. 'It's e-o-g-h-a-n. Owen, but with a bit of a y at the front, or not . . . Eoghan O'Keenan.'

An Irishman. Of course you are. That'll annoy Mother even more. Probably Catholic, too.

'And I'm Agnes,' the little one says, working her hand into mine. And I don't mind a bit, she's such a dear, dear, perfectly scrumptious thing.

'You be a good girl now, Ag,' he says to her and he assures me:

'She's a good girl, Miss Greene, I promise you. Thank you. Thank you a thousand times.'

And so we wave him off. 'Bye-bye, Yo-Yo,' little Agnes calls after him.

He turns once more, and I think he's about to say something else – such as *Wait, no, this is not right, I have no idea who you are, or if you might eat my sister for lunch* – but he only waves back, and then runs off, towards the Quay.

How extraordinary.

'I like your scarf, Miss Greene,' little Agnes says. 'Is it made of fairy wings?'

Extraordinarily lovely. I might have to eat her for lunch after all.

Yo

'You've not got an issue with heights, have you, lad?' this Mr Harrison says, raising his voice above the noise coming from the shops, looking me over outside the door that says OFFICE. He's head foreman in charge of something to do with butting something or other, he said on introduction, and he's got arms on him that look like they're made of the stuff that's being pounded into existence in the sheds behind him.

'No,' I shout back, I've got no issue with heights, though I wouldn't know if I did. The tallest thing I've ever been on would be them escalators at Hordern's yesterday, and before that the ladder up to the leather stores at Foulds. I look at the workshops again: they are tall, they are the famous iron shops of Dorman, Long and Company, they are enormous, and there's a lot going on in them, a hundred men or more going all about and that much noise, but I don't get the feeling that's where I'll be labouring today. Mr Harrison met me right here, *Oi you, young fella,* he saw me looking lost as I came up from the ferry, and he doesn't look like he's about to invite me anywhere inside now. I don't look at the crane moving up near the open edge of the Bridge above his head; that's quite a bit taller than anything I've ever seen. A lot taller than it seemed at any view I've had from the south side. I'm not sure I want to go up there.

Mr Harrison looks at my paper again and he says: 'Boot-making before this, eh? Good eye for getting things right with that work?'

I nod and have no issue with that one: I'm particular at any work I do.

He looks at the paper yet again: 'Funny name you've got — how do you say it?'

'Yo-un.' I wish I had a penny for every time I've had to say it, and having to shout it here is even less entertaining.

'Ian?' he cups his hand to his ear.

And I say, 'Yeah, that'll do.' We can argue the difference another time.

'S'pose you will, too.' He shoves my paper into the front pocket of his leather apron. He's got no more time to waste on the matter and he points behind me down the wharves, to what I suppose is the loading dock, as another crane is moving a great beam of iron onto a barge there. 'You're with Adams — Wal Adams, boiler-maker, sub-foreman,' and something I have no idea what he's talking about, then: 'See on that rear punt, bloke with the grey shirt, red braces. Get over there now, and do as you're told, or you end up dead, right.'

That's not a threat, that's a fact, it seems. I look at the punt, but I can't help seeing the crane behind, with that beam, which I can now see has a man balancing on either end. Jesus, what have I got myself into? A job. Six pounds a week. A home somewhere for me and Ag. If I ever see her again. Now that I'm here, now that I made it on time to these wharves at Milsons Point, I can't believe I've left my sister with that girl — she could be anyone — and I can't believe I told her Ag's my sister, either. She could be taking her off to Welfare now. No, she's not. Why would she do a thing like that? She's Ag's fairy anyway, and Ag'd not have gone with her otherwise. Have faith, for that's all I can have. And don't look up, and don't waste any time doing as I'm told getting over to this last punt, to this Wal Adams fella with the red braces. When I find him I see he's not a big fella and he'd be forty or more, but he's built from iron too, and he could slice the lid off a tin can with the bastard look in his eye, for me, as I step onto the punt. I'm about to tell him who I am, when he says to the six or seven others standing with him: 'Won't see out the day, this one.'

A big ginger-headed fella takes a notebook out of his apron and says, 'Right now, what's your call for pretty boy?' and they start taking bets, it seems – on me. Pretty Boy. 'A week?' Wal Adams says to him: 'Why don't you put your five bob in the poor box and save wasting the lead there, too, Tarz?' And at that I've just caught in his accent that this Wal Adams is an Ulsterman, with possibly a natural disregard for my skinny Kerry arse right there. I wonder if I can avoid telling him my name altogether.

'Don't mind Wal,' the ginger-headed one says to me, and puts out his hand: 'Clarrie McCall – but you can call me Tarzan, and you'll be my follow-up, not Mr Adams's, right?' I nod, for whatever a follow-up might be, and shake on it. He's wearing an apron too, but none of the others are; he must be a boss of some sort as well; he says: 'What's your name, then?'

'Keenan,' I say, swallowing the O, and it's all swallowed by the winding up of the punt engine anyway.

'Keen, ay? Good for you, Pretty Boy,' says this Tarzan, and we're moving out from this dock, back out into the harbour a bit and under this making of the Bridge that looks like a great big wall of ladders going all ways from here.

I'm going to a big crate below it, hanging by a hook and chains, that a couple of the other fellas catch. One hops over the rail of it and in. And they're all getting in.

'Pick up that bucket and broom. What are you – decoration?' the Ulsterman yells at me from behind.

I pick up the bucket and broom he's pointing at and it's all I can do not to cross myself when the crate pitches with my weight as I fall lead-footed over the rail and in myself – and it's not six inches off the ground yet, hasn't even started taking us up.

'Don't look down is the trick,' Tarzan says to me as it does start upwards. 'Look out.'

I do as I'm told. I look out as we go up, out across the water, and the breeze is cold on my face. This is not difficult, this looking out. One of the other fellas is sitting up on the rail opposite, arm round the chain there, rolling a smoke, not difficult at all. I look out past him, across this blue mile of harbour to the Gardens, fix my eyes to the point of the land where Ag and I slept last night, to keep the rest of me from swaying, and it's not difficult to keep looking out. What a beautiful city it is from here – a million trees worth of it. Merciful Lord, thank you. Whatever this day brings, it'll be worth it, it'll be better than yesterday, it has to be. And at the end of it, I'll get to see the girl again. Olivia Greene. That smile, under her hat, lets me forget for a moment where I've left my guts and my sister. I know I can't have the princess, I know I can't have any girl as things are, but I ask the little folk in the figs anyway: go on, give me a chance.

The breeze has a different plan, though, as it picks up now to a gust and has a more enthusiastic go at throwing me into the sea. Mother of God, all I can see is blue as the crate swings, the world seems to turn upside down. I drop the bucket, and a hammer that was in it slides out across the floor of the crate, Tarzan stopping it with his foot, and me by the scruff.

'Hold on to the rail when it rolls, you crack-headed faggot,' the Ulsterman is giving me a gobful over the hammering of my heart, repeating it in his own Irish that I have no issue with understanding here, no doubt informing me that I am as useful as a sack full of crack-headed faggot farts, an inch from my ear, in case I didn't understand it in the English: 'There are no accidents in my gang. None of any kind. Hold on to the rail or you go back down to the ground – now – go home. Fuck off. Is that clear?'

I might nod; I don't know. I've just been told off by the Devil and he's from Dungannon. Who else would use that language outside the Neighbourhood? That's almost as stupefying as being where I am.

'Fair go,' says Tarzan in my defence. 'At least he didn't spew.'

I hold on to the rail as they all have a laugh, and I look down at my boots, and down through the cracks of the boards to the sea, and I pray, with all my faith: please Lord, if I am anything at all to you, let me just see out this day. I won't think about the girl again. Let me just see out this day.

Two

Olivia

'Miss Greene?' Little Agnes squeezes my hand as we turn into the Strand and the answer is already yes. 'Can we go in the lift?' she asks.

'Of course,' I reply, and wave at Velma – Glor's sister – rushing past the other way, no doubt on some errand between her father and her husband, Eddie Nasser, whose Tycoon Clothing factory in Redfern has gone absolutely hectic lately with orders from Gowings for business shirts and ties.

'Hidee, Ol,' she waves back, a querying eyebrow for the child at my side, but too rushed to stop, court heels echoing on the tiles through the pre-rush hush.

I look down at Agnes as we step into the lift – she's looking straight into Jabour's Oriental Emporium, eyes wide with amazement at this cave of many colours, as if she's never been inside a shopping arcade before, not to mention a fancy draper's. Perhaps she hasn't. What an awful thought, and a curious one. She's impeccably turned out. New frock from Hordern's – I checked for a label, the pin tucking at the bodice too precise for your average homemade. But there's something about her that's . . . not exactly of this world. Or my world, at least.

She asks me as we judder slowly upwards: 'Will we really go to the Christmas Tea Party today?'

'Oh yes, we shall,' I assure her. The children's morning tea on at David Jones, at the new Elizabeth Street store – they always have one, and I've never been. I want to be amongst the tinsel snowflakes hanging from the ceiling and see the mechanical Santa display, too. I also want to abandon Mother to the five-minutes-to-Christmas Saturday morning super-rush for an hour or so, see how she likes that herself.

She's on the telephone when we arrive at the door of the salon. Frowning into it: 'Oh, I see.' And looks up with a frown for me, and the child: *What is that thing you've brought in with you?* 'Of course, Mrs Bromley, I do understand. Absolute confidentiality and discretion, yes, you may rely upon it, and your kind offer of settling the account as agreed is most appreciated.' Mother closes her eyes with concern: 'Yes, Mrs Bromley, thank you. Goodbye.'

She places the telephone back on the cradle, a pained expression; rare display of crow's feet, wincing. For Mrs Bromley, Min Bromley's mother, who's telephoned to settle the account, at eight-fifteen Saturday morning, when it's not due until Monday. Oh, no. I think the Bromleys have found out about Mother's illicit liaisons with Bart Harley and withdrawn their custom. My world is in ruins. I demand to know: 'What, Mother – what has happened?'

'Poor Minerva; poor Bromleys,' she sighs, and she looks tired about her eyes, too much concern, too late at night. 'The groom must delay the wedding – Samuels have gone into voluntary liquidation.'

Oh dear. Right. Samuels, wheat merchants and family company of Min's fiancé, Bryden, have gone under. My first thought is an uncharitable one: good. Cousin of my Pymble Ladies tormentor Cassie Fortescue takes tumble from high horse. Serves her right for entangling her heart in a boy. But this is quickly followed by: good God, we've lost our best hope of entrée into the upper circle via Commonwealth Bank board of directors. Not ruin exactly, we're clearly going to be paid, but our business has just taken a trousseau load of backwards. Min Bromley will not be wearing my bebe roses; going-away frock not going anywhere. All my work – mothballed.

'Damn that,' I say, and stomp my foot: damn them.

And Mother chastises: 'Swearing and stamping will not alter the situation.' All her work mothballed too. That's business. Live with it. She glances at Agnes and back to me: 'What's this? Lost child?'

'Lost? Ah. No. Hm . . .' I search the perfume cabinet for the answer. Why have I brought a child to the salon today? That's right, the bottles of Number Five remind me: I am a fool sabotaging my own best interests. 'I'm minding her today, a favour for an acquaintance.'

'What acquaintance?' Mother glowers. I don't have any friends she doesn't know of – indeed, as the Jabours don't really count as people as such to her, I don't have any friends at all.

And, the situation having altered as it has, there is no triumph of preposterous payback in my announcement now: 'A young man, the girl's brother –'

'*What* young man?' Mother's impatience is sharp as her pattern cutters.

'A young man I met this morning. Ah. I went for a walk in the Gardens, and I . . . ah . . .' I am shame-faced and resentful at once. 'Well, he was desperate, he needed help, for someone to mind his sister today – hardly a criminal offence. And he's a Bridge worker. I thought I would be kind, and –'

'Kind?' Mother's not in the least convinced of that, nor sympathetic: 'You met a workman this morning, in a public park, and you have brought his sister here. To mind her. What – all day?' Her face is sculpted of cold alabaster contempt. 'Of all the vindictive and wilfully infantile things you could do, at this time. I should telephone the Department of Child Welfare – and turn *you* in as delinquent.'

And at that, little Agnes's hand slips free of mine, and the whole of her tiny person slips right out the door.

Yo

Mother of God and every saint that ever drew breath, no, it's not possible.

'Don't look down, look out, Pretty Boy,' Tarzan is smiling at me from the scaffold he's standing on. It's suspended off the side of what they call top chord, the top line of the arch – and it's the highest possible place you could be on earth, not including that fella sitting on top of the crane above us. Tarzan is trying to coax me off the Bridge construction itself and across a plank that's attached to the scaffold. There's a gap, though, only about a foot, but it's the gaping chasm of death as far as I can see.

'Come on, mate,' this other fella, Clarkie, shouts from behind me, getting itchy at me. He's the 'cooker', heating the rivets in the oven that's suspended on its own scaffold on the curved upside of the chord, that's not made of curves at all but straight lines, and each one of them called a chord, too, just to keep me from confusion. I try to keep my mind fixed on that to get me across: these are all straight lines, flat surfaces, not curves, firm, flat, straight, and this particular joint of the chord I'm standing on is the size of a tramcar. I hold my breath. It's only a step to the plank, to the scaffold which is also the size of a tramcar. Hold on to the upright of the scaffold and look out across the blue at the Gardens and I do it for Ag. I take the step.

'There you go,' says Tarzan. 'Now give yourself a minute, till your knees stop shaking.'

He gives me about two seconds before he hands me back my bucket: 'Don't worry if you miss one – it'll only hit a ferry.'

That is a joke, I'm sure, and it does nothing to lift my confidence. I'm to catch the hot rivets with this bucket, which Tarzan will fix into the wall of holes in the chord here, with the contraption he's holding, a gun he's called it, which is attached to a hose that's attached to . . . somewhere. I follow the hose with my eyes to see where it goes, but my eyes go down the great curve, and my guts go for another swim. This job is not possible. This Bridge is not possible. Defying the laws of nature. Straight lines or no, how does this curve not keep on curving to fall off the edge of the land and into the water from its own incredible weight? How can it be that I am standing on the side of it? I will not catch a single one of these rivets. I want to get down on my hands and knees on the bottom of the scaffold and stay there. And I would, too, if I could let go of the upright of the scaffold.

'Aye-o,' Clarkie shouts from above and I look up to see a rivet screaming down at me.

It's white hot, and the size and shape of a cock. If I don't catch it, I will get it in the face.

I find the power to let go of the scaffold and raise the bucket.

And I catch the rivet.

Jesus fucking Joseph and Mary, there it is. In the bucket.

I'm looking for some congratulation from Tarzan, but he's busy picking out the rivet with his tongs now. Then quick about ramming it into the wall with the gun, with another fella, one called Dolly, ramming it back from the other side with him, and I think my skull will split in two with the noise.

Olivia

'Agnes!' I call out for her again, across the empty expanse of the second floor, my alarm ringing along the apex of the roofline, threatening the glass. I look over the railing, down through the void to the tiles on the ground floor, which will be teeming in a minute. She could be anywhere, the little rat. Three floors of arcade. Big city. I've lost her, and while the majority of my conscience says, *That's no good, is it,* the small but insistent remainder of it is shouting: *Oh my God, no!*

What am I going to say to that nice boy when he comes to collect his sister?

What should I do? Call the police? What would I say to *them*? *Erm, yes, that's right, officer, I picked this urchin up off the street; no, no idea who she is. Pretty little thing, though.*

Oh, how could she have vanished so utterly two steps out the salon door?

Damn. I peer hard into the window of Boston Shoes, as if she might have flown in there through the crack in the transom and hidden in a pair of satin pumps. Nothing's open yet but I cast my eyes across the void again anyway: to the lace drapes of Madame

Marjorie's Hair and Beauty Art, the floating damasks of Loughton's tableware, the banks of phonographs in the Challis showroom, and stacks of travel luggage at Blayney's . . . all silent and soulless.

I don't know what to do, apart from return to the salon. To Mother. And her disgust. Oh, but I could have a jolly good turn at her for this, couldn't I. This is Mother's fault. That's what I'll tell the police: Mother frightened the poor girl away. Never to be seen or heard of again.

I'm deep in planning the opening lines of my next tantrum as I see Mr Monty, the photographer from next door, querying over his spectacles at me on his way from the lift: 'Morning, Miss Greene.'

I smile: 'Hello!'

I am not a wanton loser of small children. Not me. Why indeed do I have a small child in my care to lose? *Of all the vindictive and wilfully infantile things you could –*

I'll go and check the stairwells – now. Oh God. Start with the Pitt Street end.

I dash back past our shop, and don't so much as glance at the window there as I do, nor at the permanently closed blinds of Mr Solomon's, the optometrist, on the other side, but then, just before the stairwell, I do glance up – up the small flight of steps that lead to an office there, of an accountant, or it used to be, not sure it's occupied anymore – and I just catch sight of the little white socks in their little Indian red mary-janes, right at the top, sticking out of the shadows.

'Agnes?'

She doesn't move; so still, she must be holding her breath.

'Agnes,' I try again and some instinct tells me not to call her a naughty little rat as I might like to; instead, I gentle my tone: 'It's all right, you know. Mother was only cross with me. Please don't run away – your brother would be sad if you did that, wouldn't he?'

Still she doesn't move; but she might well race off again if I take the steps up to her, mightn't she, so I stay put, try yet again and more firmly: 'Agnes, please stop this nonsense and come down from there. Don't you want to go to the tea party with me anymore?'

At last she steps down, one step, into the light, but still she doesn't speak, and her eyes are wide with fear. Not a skittish sort but a dread sort of fear – one that this situation doesn't seem to call for. Mother wasn't *that* horrible just now. But then, this little girl doesn't know Mother, does she. Strange people, strange place; she must be terribly confused. I hold out my hand to her: 'Poor little sweetie, I'm sure you just want to go home, don't you?'

But at that the fear in her eyes seems to deepen, and she shakes her head. If she could disappear back into the shadows, she would. Something calamitous has happened at home, I suppose, something to make them *short for help,* as her brother said. I should find out, shouldn't I, see what's the matter, so I ask her: 'Where is your mother today?'

She frowns, surprised and suspicious at once, and then she finally speaks: 'Don't you know?'

'No.' I shake my head. 'Why should I know where your mother is?'

She doesn't answer that; she asks me, barely a whisper: 'Do you know the Welfare people?'

'No,' I tell her, and I'd smile if she wasn't so clearly afraid of them. The Department of Child Welfare: an old and empty throwaway threat of Mother's I've heard a thousand times before; but perhaps not so empty for this little girl. Speculations race with the facts: the child is poor and Irish and something awful has happened to her mother, who must therefore be a criminal, a gangster's moll, in childbirth with the thirteenth, or dead from TB. Alternatively, Agnes's own mother's threats of getting rid of her are merely much more convincing than my own mother's. I hold out my hand to her again in comradeship against maternal cruelty: 'I wouldn't know a Welfare person if I tripped over one in the street.'

The Blue Mile

She puts her hand in mine, but she doesn't move from that step; she stares at me for the longest moment, searching, measuring me up perhaps, and then she fixes me with the clarity of those huge blue eyes, telling me: 'My Yoey is the best brother that there ever was.' A plain statement of fact. 'Don't let them take me off him, please, Miss Greene.'

'I wouldn't do that,' I assure her, against another instinct shouting at me to telephone Child Welfare immediately. She squeezes my hand, as if to make me promise; but I can't do that either. Something awful *has* happened. I ask her: 'Where do you and Yoey live?'

'Don't you know?' she frowns, doubtful, searching my face again.

'No, I don't know where you live, Agnes – you'll have to tell me.' And I'm supposing Surry Hills, Paddington, Glebe, some slum or other where the enunciation of individual words is not required: *dontchaknow?*

But she tells me: 'Under the fig trees,' her rosebud lips curling into a smile. 'In the Gardens.'

'You live in the Botanic Gardens, do you?' I don't believe her, of course, and I do smile, with some relief: this is all just a childish nonsense, isn't it. Look at her pin tucks and ringlets, her new shoes, her perfect peaches-and-cream complexion; she even comes complete with missing one and a half front teeth and a lisp. They probably live in a flat in Randwick, just moved in and truly caught short amid the muddle of it, or something like that.

She nods, of course it's all a nonsense, and her eyes are bright with fun again: 'Oh, it's beautiful under them trees, miss.'

'It is indeed,' I nod in return. What an intriguing little girl you are. I won't be telephoning Child Welfare, no, but I might be having a word with your Yoey, to find out exactly who and what you really are. I squeeze her hand in return: 'Now, are you ready to come back to the salon for some hard labour before our morning tea? I've got a great big tin of buttons that need sorting – will you do that for me?'

'I will,' she nods again, bright and earnest. Thoroughly edible again. If this child is not ordinarily spoiled stupid I want to know why not.

Drama of lost child thusly concluded, I'm searching for something suitably terse to throw at Mother about petrifying little girls, when I see, through the salon window, through the open door of the stockroom, her mannequin, and on it what's become of my blue heaven.

I am a small child stunned by injustice and disappointment, both of which cut deeper and deeper with every step I take towards it. If there is selfishness in me, I know where it comes from and I'm no match for the original. This gown Mother has made for herself, from *my* fabric, undoubtedly to wear to the Merrick this evening, is her most fabulous creation yet. Bias-cut to the hips so that the blues will swirl around her before she even steps onto the dancefloor and, when she does, the skirt, with the stripes set on the opposing diagonal, will flute out from three rows of clear crystal drop beads over panels of palest aqua chiffon. Ingenious. Now I see why she looks tired about the eyes – nothing a bit more powder won't fix. Good God, but I hate her at times. Such as this time. I want to run and hide on the stairs.

Agnes won't be joining me: she's stunned with wonder, but for a reverent: 'Ohhhhhh.'

Mother smiles up at me from where she's snipping the last of the squiggles from the chiffon hems and asks, smugly and rhetorically: 'Don't you like it?'

'Like is not the word.' I am terse as I say it, but terse with my own tiredness. Defeated. Mother will do what Mother will do; I shouldn't try to fight it, any of it. *But that was my fabric*, the little girl inside me protests. Her voice is so small, though, so irrelevant, no one can hear her.

Mother hasn't noticed my dejection, or she's not bothering to acknowledge it. She's going to marry a barrister; the magistrate's hammer descends and smashes my Mexican chocolate shell, smashes the whole sideboard to smithereens, and blows up the house and the business too, as she gets blithely up and goes over to the jewellery cabinet. 'The crystal choker should set it off perfectly, don't you think?' She picks it out from the top shelf and holds it above the gown. 'See? These blues, so fabulous, the crystal could be genuine against them – Viennese. Luscious and yet so simple. No other embellishment required.'

No. Are all people who are born both beautiful and clever so stupid to others' pain? I know I've been petulant, but I don't deserve this.

'Nothing except this.' She steps over to me and removes my hat, scrabbling her fingers through my hair: 'Good God, Ollie, what a bird's nest.'

That makes me feel so much better, Mother. She makes a side part with a fingernail, scraping along my scalp, and pins a clasp into my hair; one from the cabinet, one of my favourites, a line of baguette diamantes on a silver slide. That makes me feel utterly ridiculous.

And *now* she notices my dejection: 'Olivia Jane Greene, you must stop this silly game this instant.'

And *now* I retort: 'How about you stop sticking silly pins in bird's nests?'

'Oh Ollie,' she sighs, annoyed. 'Yes, it might look a little more stylish when we've got some warm oil into your curls. I've made you an appointment with Marjorie for three-thirty – she's got some jasmine-scented in that's just gorgeous.' She detaches Agnes's hand from mine, no more than an object to be removed, and she shoves me in front of the cheval in the fitting room. 'Now I need you to try it on, see if the neckline is sitting well.'

'Try what on?'

'The *gown*, Ollie.'

Oh. Cross purposes uncross and at last I see: 'You made this gown for *me*?'

'Yes.' Mother's exasperation turns to amazement: 'What did you think you were going to wear this evening – a chaff bag?'

I can't answer her. Mother made this gown for *me*? She's been up all night going blind with diagonals and crystal drops for me. This is too lovely by far, but the hairs stand up on the back of my neck, anguish clashing against any joy. I'm not going to the Merrick in it. I'm not going to the Merrick at all.

'You truly don't like it?' Mother is aghast at the thought; she is hurt.

'I like it, Mother. I do,' I say, turning away, stepping between her and the fitting-room drapes.

'Ollie . . . ?'

I step round her again, step round the gown on the mannequin and into the stockroom, all these conflicting emotions whirling, surging through me so that, if I were that light globe hanging up there from the ceiling, I might explode. I can't explode. There's a little girl watching me from the end of the chaise. Why is there a little girl in the salon? That's right: because I'm not going to the Merrick tonight. Don't look at the gown. I reach up for the biscuit tin of odd buttons on the middle shelf above Mother's machine table, and almost bring down one of my old hat blocks on my head with it. What am I doing with this button biscuit tin? That's right: stepping back round past Mother to place the tin at my work table for the child; she'll be a picture in the window today, won't she, making rainbow trays of buttons for me. Don't look at the gown.

'Come and sit here, Agnes,' I say and she climbs up onto my chair.

And when I bend across her to take out the first tray of buttons, she places her little hand on my wrist and whispers, conspiratorially: 'See, I knew you were a fairy princess. But I won't tell no one.'

Remind me again, why is there a little girl in the salon? That's right: because I'm lost in a dream. There's no little girl, no boy in the park, no gown of blue heaven, no salon, no mothballed trousseaux, no buttons but imaginary ones. The alarm hasn't even gone off yet. Has it? I'm still in my bed. Either that or my nerves have gone full pitch and I'm delirious.

And the little girl is a persistent illusion; she lisps as she pats my hand: 'Your secret is safe with me.'

Yo

There is no fear like the fear of getting a four-inch white-hot iron cock in your face and that takes over all other sense as the hammering of the rivet gun takes over the hammering of my heart. After catching the first dozen or so rivets, my shoulders start aching from holding the bucket up, and a while after that the ache becomes white-hot skewers through my bones, until it becomes nothing but not getting it in the face. I don't know what time it is or how many rivets have come down, but I know I've caught every one, and that becomes everything. I am the task. And I've done this before. It's what I do. I could be stitching on soles and passing boots up the line. No room for thinking in it. Just the job, and I am just another bit in the machine.

I am a machine.

Until the hammering stops and Tarzan lays down the gun and yells at me: 'Smoko.'

It's a sound from far away, though he's not two yards distant, and as I put the bucket down, I look back along the curve to the rooftops of the workshops and I don't lose my guts at all this time. I look down through the boards of the scaffold floor to the water and I see it for what it is: miraculous. I'm hanging off the side of the Sydney Harbour Bridge. Fucking miraculous. I smile at Tarzan. I did it. I can do this job.

He shakes his head and shouts something else but I don't catch it, apart from the word 'deaf'. Yes, I must be deaf, from that riveting. He waves at me to hurry up, back off the scaffold and onto the Bridge itself. All right, I think, I can do this now: I got on here, I can get off. But when I'm standing up on the plank looking across at the bit of rail at the edge of the chord, it seems too small and too far away.

'Come on, Pretty, I want me cuppa,' Tarzan says and I hear that clearly; he's getting itchy about it, too.

And it's all too clear again: the water rears up at me from that foot-wide gap. But I can fight it this time: it's just a gap, no different than walking across a storm water grate. Several hundred feet above the ground, with the breeze gusting up at your back.

Chasm of death.

Dolly, the fella who was round the other side of the riveting, leans down over the rail: 'Here.' He grabs me by the elbow and pulls me across.

And the nails of my boots slip, metal on metal, and on the slant of the chord, so that if it wasn't for Dolly holding me and the rail, I might have slid off.

'Bloody hell, kid, get yourself some sandshoes,' says Dolly, still with a hold of me, though I've made it onto the level surface of the chord joint now, into the shelter of it, out of the wind, and only now do I notice that they're all wearing sandshoes, rubber soles. That fella at the Public Works office might've told me: get yourself some sandshoes. Slipped his mind. Too busy. Jesus, I could be dead.

Clarkie, the cooker, shoves a hot tin mug of tea into my hands: 'Monday, this is your job, right?'

Whatever that might be; making the tea, I suppose. I say, 'Right.' I'll find out Monday, won't I.

I take a sip of the tea, hot and sweet, and I'm taken away again by where I am. I'm sitting here having a cuppa on top of the Sydney Harbour Bridge – fucking miraculous. My hands are shaking so that I can hardly roll my smoke, but I'm hearing myself asking: 'How high up are we here?'

'About three hundred feet now here,' says Tarzan. 'She'll be four hundred and forty at the top of the arch when she's finished.' He says that with pride, as if this is his Bridge.

He opens a beaten-up old lunch tin and says, 'Help yourself,' and I don't mind if I do, as I haven't had anything to eat since that pork pie last night. And so I sit in sky chomping on fruitcake listening to Tarzan and Dolly talking about pneumatic something or other in regard to some issue with the riveting gun pressure that is lost on me, excepting that I work out that the tool Dolly holds up round the other side of the wall against Tarzan's hammering is called a dolly.

Then they're quiet again, eating their cake, enjoying the view, until Clarkie's off back to his oven and Tarzan and Dolly are getting back to their feet too, wiping cake crumbs into the sky. This is just another job; in a strange place. A beautiful place: look out at them trees all across the city. Sweet, sweet Jesus. I asked for a miracle and I got one. And I'm not going to let the fear of falling get me this time; I will think across it, talk over it, following Tarzan back to the plank, looking out across the great space between the two halves of the arch: 'What's the trick that's holding the chords up?'

As my heart is belting again: fucking hell, how can it be that we're not toppling into the sea?

'You're full of questions,' Tarzan says over his shoulder as he steps across the gap, not even looking where he's going, he's that confident of where he is, and I keep right behind him, my footsteps in his, it's just a step and no congratulations for it, and then, when we're back on the floor of the scaffold he turns around and shows me, pointing back down this curve of straight lines: 'Tension cables,' he says. 'Beyond the abutment, you can see them. More than a hundred, north and south, anchoring each of the two sides, deep into the rock on either shore. They won't budge for anything.'

I can't see these cables from here and I don't know what an abutment is, but he smiles at me and my question, this ginger-headed Tarzan, and I believe him and his confidence in this Bridge, as Clarkie shouts, 'Aye-o,' from the oven and the gun starts up again.

Olivia

'Oh, look at that, aren't they fabulous?' I say of the reindeer in the David Jones Santa display, their hooves raking the air as they fly above the rooftops of Sydney. 'Magical.'

'Hm,' says Agnes, studying them as she slowly and daintily devours her vanilla cupcake, cracking off the pink icing crumb by crumb to make it last. Then she looks up at me, studying still, and she says: 'It's not magic but, is it? It's just a wind-up thing in them that makes them go. Magic is when things happen just by themselves, isn't it?'

'Hm,' I reply. Such a bright little girl but so fixed on her fantasies; querying frown in want of confirmation from her fairy princess. 'I suppose so,' I tell her, and rather than squish her ideals by confessing that the only magic I believe in is the one that inspired the board of directors at DJs to get in a mechanical display to pack in the kiddies for Christmas, I say: 'If it really rained tinsel snowflakes over Sydney – now *that* would be magical.'

'That would be silly,' Agnes giggles. 'You are funny, Miss Greene.' Grinning, with that conspiratorial squinchy-faced grin which says she will not be dissuaded from her conviction that I am somehow magical too.

I say: 'You're funny.' And I consult my watch: 'But we should go, or Mother will turn us both into pumpkins.' We've only been gone half an hour, but we really should be back at the salon; I shouldn't have left. It's been hectic all morning, not with serious purchasers but with expert pernicketers: I abandoned Mother to a woman after a pair of gloves, wanting the buttons of one swapped to the style of another, wasting time in lieu of money. Couldn't have been a more perfect payback for Mother's abandonment of me last night, if such an idea didn't seem to belong to some other realm now. God, how are we to make up for the loss of the Bromley follow-on clientele?

Agnes giggles again: 'You won't turn into a pumpkin – your *carriage* will, and that doesn't happen until *after* the ball.'

'Silly me again.' I take Agnes by the hand and, possibly grasping it a little too hard, lead her through the throng of kiddies, past the reindeer, past the cake table, guilt nipping at my heels. I'm not going to the ball. My stomach lurches and spins, grasping for reprieve: if there is magic in the world, then make it so that I won't have to go to the Merrick, Mother will stop this business with Bart Harley and we'll all live happily ever after. As if Agnes might be a conduit for such a plea, I squeeze her hand: 'You're a clever little girl, aren't you?'

'Your mother is very clever to make that gown for you.' Azure eyes look up at me, unblinking, crystal clear as her wonder. 'I never seen such a magical thing as that.'

'Hm.' *Ding*, here's the lift, 'Oh good, look at that,' but Agnes is unimpressed by lifts now; still in her rapture over the gown, she says as we descend: 'Your mum must love you very much to make you such a special frock as that.'

'Hm.' I would change the subject to enquiring further about Agnes's own mother if I weren't so thoroughly caught up again in tortures over my own: the look of hurt on her lovely face. My lovely mother. I must make it up to her; I must, with no more than ordinary daughterly obedience, simply do as she asks and go to the Merrick. It's only stupid dinner at a stupid restaurant. People do this sort of thing *all the time*. But each time I imagine this all I can see is my gangly frame mocked by that gown, and right in the midst of the snazziest place in town. Stares. Whispers. Who does she think she is? Trumped-up milliner. *Sticky sticky stick insect, is she a bug or is she a boy?* Or a baby giraffe, tripping over too-big two left feet on the dancefloor.

I trip up the gutter crossing Castlereagh into the Imperial to prove that there is no such thing as magic at least, for if there were, I'd have sprained an ankle just now, wouldn't I. We don't even come close to being run over crossing Pitt Street either – traffic parts as if Moses were in town – and we're back in the Strand. Dawdling slightly outside the Jabours' but I see they've got a queue, Glor's got her head in the sideboard, amongst the metallic laces, too busy to so much as look up to wave, while Mr Jabour's genie ignores me from his bottle above.

As does Mother when we return to the salon; she's too busy to so much as look up and scowl. The glove pernicketer is still harassing her and she's got another one umming and ahhing over the style samples across the hat tree, and yet another on the chaise flicking through the *Vogue*s. That one I recognise.

Fabulous: it's Allison Palgrave. Friend of Cassie Fortescue, and if there is magic in the world it is naught but black.

'Olivia,' she looks up from the magazine, all dazzling white teeth deftly concealing her forked tongue. 'You remember me, of course – it's Ally. Ally Palgrave. How *are* you?'

She couldn't care less. I glance over at Mother, and in one twitch of an eyebrow she confirms what I instantly suspect. There is only one reason Allison Palgrave is here: to get the torrid details on Min Bromley's wedding catastrophe. She's not here for couture, judging by the atrocity she's got on. It has the floaty fey lines of a Vionnet, but the fabric is all wrong for the design: ghastly wallpaper pattern of lotus flowers, elegant as the back end of a brewer's cart. Bet she bought it in London: walking advertisement for Duped Colonial.

'Ally, how lovely to see you,' I say, as her evils against me tumble one over the other: smashing her tennis racquet into the back of my knees to make me buckle, pushing me into the trophy cabinet in the hall, always pushing me aside for living in lowly Lavender Bay in my tiny old cottage, with all the dirty trams and the trains and the workshops and the wharves, always sneering at my darned stockings and my bacon rissoles. *Never give your tormentor the satisfaction of a reaction* was the advice Mother gave me then, and it holds as well now: Allison Palgrave won't be getting anything out of me today. Especially not here: my territory. My smile could get me arrested it's so counterfeit: 'To what do we owe the pleasure?'

'Oh, I'm just browsing around.' Allison tosses my Paris *Vogue* onto the table as so much rubbish. 'Thought maybe I'd like a bunch of summery things – for May-ish, though. I'm going Home again next year. May as in late spring at Home, of course. Wondering what to take, as usual.'

Such a liar, as usual. 'What sorts of summery things did you have in mind?'

'Oh, I don't know,' she throws her hands up in the air: oh, the ennui of being a paper mill heiress with nothing to do but contemplate your wardrobe and betray your friends. She says: 'You wouldn't have time for a coffee this afternoon, would you? We could have a good old catch-up, throw around some ideas.'

I could have a good old throw-up. Every fibre of my being is screaming: *Get out of my salon, you horrible bag of spiders!* Liar, liar, liar. The last person Allison Palgrave would want to be seen in a coffee lounge with is me – or any working girl for that matter. But if a private ladies college education is good for anything, it's good for this: 'Oh, Ally, I'd love to but I'm so sorry, we're terribly busy just now, as you can see. You wouldn't be able to reschedule that coffee for sometime after Christmas, would you? Say, mid-Jan?' Perhaps circa 1980.

'Of course,' Allison Palgrave continues the pretence too as she stands but her eyes dull: rebuffed and she knows it. Oh God, but I wish I could tell her who I really am, have her cringe at my feet and call me by my rightful name, the Honourable Miss Ashton Greene, more London and more entitled than she will ever be. But I can't do that, no more than I would divulge a client's confidential wedding catastrophe. Matters of scalding hatred and common decency aside, betrayal of the Bromleys is out of the question. The Bromleys – and the Fortescues and who knows who else if we play our cards well – *are* our customers; Allison Palgrave will never be. All money and no sense of style, and Commonwealth Bank director trumps filthy-stinky paper mill any day. 'Goodbye, Ally.' I see her out. 'Hope to see you soon.' Good God, but she is as broad as the chaise is long in that ensemble – overstuffed and ill-upholstered.

'Well done, darling,' Mother whispers as she swishes past behind me. 'Very well done.'

But when I turn around again, I see only Agnes, sitting over there at my table, returned to folding and colour-sorting the little pile of remnant scraps I gave her when she finished the buttons, before we left for the morning tea. I didn't instruct her to go back to it; I don't even recall letting go of her hand. Seen, not heard, perfect picture of a perfect little girl. I wonder if any nasty B torments her at school: undoubtedly. I ask her, 'Agnes, if I give you my little wooden mannequin, will you make her a gown for me?'

She looks up at me with crystal-clear delight: 'Oh, can I, please?'

Oh, can I steal her and keep her always, please? I could sit and watch her play dolls with my little mannequin all day. But not this day.

'Now, miss, here,' the ummer and ahher at the hat tree summons me and the next four hours is a blur of horsehair froth and spider daisies. Don't even stop for lunch.

Mother doesn't pop the closed sign round until quarter past three, in fact. 'Shush, don't tell the Minister for Industry,' she winks at the coat stand in respect of our illicit trading, before she says to me: 'Where's this chap for the girl, then?'

'The who?' I'm tired and half-blind and I want one of those vanilla cupcakes with pink icing – seven of them.

'The girl's brother.' She waves a hand at Agnes. 'This Bridge worker chap. Don't they finish at three or the unions go out on strike and what have you?'

I wouldn't know; Mother does: union people are Reds who go on strike and make the price of coal and everything else go up, forcing us all to hell in a handbag with a Labor prime minister – just look at the state of the economy, all his fault, though he's not been in the job two months. Everything that goes wrong is Labor's fault, and the unions' – including the New York stock exchange falling into the sea. I look at Agnes, still working away diligently at my table, now pinning a length of raspberry rickrack zigzags to the hem of a skirt she's made from a scrap of the lemon Fuji. She is me at the same age. But now, and for the first time, I wonder if I haven't made some untold mistake bringing her here; this strange, otherworldly child, with the Bridge worker brother I met for all of about three minutes, in a public park. What exactly have I invited into the salon? What if they *do* live in the Gardens – like tramps? Sundowners. Drifters. No, that's ridiculous: childish make-believe living under *them* trees. And he seemed such a nice boy, so concerned for his little sister. I tell Mother: 'I'm sure he'll be here soon.'

Mother taps the face of her wristwatch. 'You won't be, Olivia – your appointment with Marjorie at half past, yes?'

For my hair; for tonight. That sends me buckling and lurching and spinning again at full speed. I don't want to get my hair done; I don't even so much as want to look in the stockroom at that gown. I don't want to look at Mother; I turn away, bend down and busy myself picking squiggles and snips of spider daisy off the rug. I've always loved this floor rug, its beginning-less pattern of Florentine swirls, curling off into lily trumpets.

'Olivia.' Mother is tired too; tired of my resistance. 'This nonsense ceases now. *Your* nonsense. These anxieties, these confabulations of dread at coming out – it must stop today, this minute. Bart or no Bart, I'm not going to be around forever to progress our business socially – and it *must* be progressed if you are to become who you deserve to become. If you want this business, you must grow up – today – and accept all the responsibilities of it. Or, if you must remain closed in and shut up, accept Miss Greene's Hat and Frocks in Homebush. Is that what you want?'

No, I do not want: lonely suburban coffin lined with easy-wash, easy-fade poplins. Death by a thousand bolts of gingham. But still I can't look at her. Still I resist.

Mother gentles her tone: 'What are you so afraid of, Ollie?'

She knows very well. *Sticky, sticky, stick* – damn Bs – and the Merrick is *their* territory. In here, I'm the one holding the hatpin; out there, in this place I've never been, I will be exposed, alone, sneered at, rejected. Ugly. I'm terrified.

Mother persists, 'You can't worry what that Palgrave girl might think of you, or what anyone might think of you. I know how much it hurts, Ollie darling, and I know what a waste of time it is to dwell on such things.'

She does: she knows what it is to be sneered at and rejected, packed off and erased from Ashton Greene history, no less. But I know her story by heart; I dwell in its disaster, and lavishly. It was the spring of 1910. They met at the Savoy, quite by accident, as she was dining with old wool trade acquaintances of her father's. She was wearing a gown of satin-banded bisque organza, copy of a delectable wasp-waisted Worth she'd seen at Hanover Square, every stitch her own, when amid the spangle and swirl of the grand banquet hall she was accosted by a tall and dashing stranger in finely tapering swallow tails. He was Shelby Ashton Greene, then a viscount's honourable son, and he asked her to dance. By the end of summer, they'd eloped to Paris, where she wore genuine Poiret. I arrived the following spring in his London digs, and there she stayed. While he resumed his dashing. She was trapped, albeit in a rather pleasant Grosvenor Place prison, wondering how to work a nappy. Alone. No society, no friends, as if she didn't exist, though every detail of his every peccadillo followed her in stares and whispers from Covent Garden to Belgravia. Girls called Penny and Edith, his valet's niece, a restaurateur's daughter, his whole battalion in Flanders, and then Marie, whoever she might have been. *But do cheer yourself up, Emmy – I'll always love you, too. Why don't you change the drapes?* He was ever honest with Mother, as were his family: the Ashton Greenes refused to acknowledge her at all, and my grandparents never laid eyes on me, not once in my seven years there. As if I am illegitimate. Why? Because self-stitched Emily Weathercroft was not the right sort. No breeding and no cash in the bank. Australian and sheepless. No good reason to despise a girl, force her to beg for her own divorce, beg for the fare back to Sydney, but that the Ashton Greenes are not the right sort in themselves. They can't be, can they: look at my father – mean, arrogant, selfish, lion-hunting Don Juan.

And I'm half him, aren't I. I am a sparkling princess-cut pebble of shame every way I look at myself.

'You are better than all of them put together.' Mother places a finger under my chin to make me look at her. 'And revenge is in your grasp.'

'Revenge?' I half-smile at that: Mother, for all her sharp edges, is far too lovely to play a convincing wicked witch.

'Yes,' she says and she smiles; outrageously lovely: 'The only revenge worth having. And I want it to be yours.'

'And what's that?' I sigh, not giving up forlorn.

'To live well, darling.' She says, her fingernail pressing the point into my chin: 'Live well. Be happy. Become *you*. Nothing annoys a bully so much as success – *your* success. You shall have it – please, trust me.' She releases my chin, enough said about it, on with the show, and she consults her watch again: 'Now, if this Bridge chap isn't here by – well, soonish – I shall have to telephone Bart about the girl. One of his chums is a magistrate at the Children's Court, he'll know what to do. And we must –'

'No, please, miss!' Agnes leaps up from the table, suddenly and desperately klaxon-loud: 'Please. Please, don't nark on us.'

Yo

'You get yourself a hat for Monday too, right?' Tarzan says on the crate back down, or the 'cradle' as they call it. 'Sandshoes and a hat. The back of your neck is a beauty, sunshine – that's going to kill tonight.'

Sunburn. I don't doubt I'm sunburned. I'd reach round to see how bad it is but I'm not letting go of the rail.

Adams, the sub-foreman and likely the Devil from Dungannon, has his bastard eye on me to see that I don't. I take a good look at him now, half to help me ignore the feeling that my kneecaps are going to slide down my shins and off the end of my toes with the swinging of the cradle as we descend. Adams looks like one of them British pit-bull terriers: bastard-faced Ulsterman. If the cable above us snapped, he'd take it in his iron jaws, no big issue. Or rip your guts out.

He keeps that bastard eye on me and I think he's going to give me another gobful for staring, but instead he says: 'You get here early, too, Monday. You go back to Mattie Harrison at the shops and you tell him I said you're to join with the IA – the Ironworkers Assistants.'

No idea what he's talking about but my face is so busy trying not to look ignorant I can't get a word out to ask.

'The union, lad,' he says, casting his pig eyes heavenward up the cable, like he's in want of asking the crane driver if he could be sent someone a bit more ignorant next time. 'You'll be with the FIU – Federated Ironworkers – under the Assistants with them. Right?'

'Right.' I don't know the first thing about unions; never got my invitation to join one.

'It's important – listen.' He starts barking on, in that way as he might be telling me I'm a scruttery waste of breath, et cetera, but he's only explaining: 'You're not looked after by us in the gang up here – we're all United Boilermakers or Ironworkers or Engineers. You're with them down there – and as a labourer associated with the shops you're with the FIU. If you were a labourer associated with any of the other trades, you'd be with the BLF – the Builders Labourers. See? It's important you know who you're with and who your delegate is. There's nine different unions on this Bridge. Right?'

'Right. Federated Ironworkers.' If you say so.

'Right. Under the Ironworkers Assistants Union.'

'Right.' Jesus. He can't talk without yelling, this fella; maybe he's permanently deaf from the rivet gun.

'If you're not with the union, you'll not get paid. Like working for nothing, do you?'

I'm not expected to answer that, I don't think.

'And if you're not with the right union, you'll not be looked after. Right? There'll be a fine from the Industrial Court, too, if you don't get on to it, a fine to you, two pounds or more – get that paperwork in Monday morning. Right?'

'Yeah righto, Wal, lay off,' says Tarzan. 'Now where's my five bob, ay?'

Wal Adams turns them devil-pig eyes at Tarzan: 'I made no bet with you – if he lasts the week, I'll give ten to –'

The Blue Mile

I don't hear what he says as they start arguing the odds on Pretty Boy, and Clarkie, the cooker and chucker of hot cocks, winks across it at me: 'You did all right, kid.'

Yeah? Did I hear that right? I did all right? Clarkie nods. I did all right. My heart flies out across the water and back into me with the realisation, and the relief. I've got a job. I've got to join a union. I did all right. And I got through this day. Thank you, Lord, for looking after me. I look across the harbour at the Gardens and thank the little folk too, and as the cradle comes to a rest on the barge my hand comes off the rail and goes straight to my forehead, to make the sign of the cross. I just manage to stop myself, turn it into a scratch as Tarzan elbows me in the ribs.

'Come for a dive with us this arvie, ay Pretty?'

'A dive?'

'Yeah, off the southern abutment – it's a beaut day for it.' I still don't know what an abutment is, but he's pointing across the water, at the other side of the Bridge. He says to my disbelieving face: 'I'm joking.'

'Right.' Forgive me for not rolling about laughing.

He has a good one, with everyone in the cradle, seven of them having a good old wheeze at me, then Tarzan stops laughing and points west, away from the city: 'We dive round Balmain – off the coal gantry at the wharves this arvie. Got a bit of a competition going. North and South riveters. We get a crowd. Drink at the Opera House after.'

That sounds so much more reasonable, doesn't it? But the laughter's stopped and I hear in that I'd be well advised to attend this activity of diving and drinking. He's just said Balmain, too, hasn't he – I could ask around for accommodation there. But besides not ever having learned to swim, never mind hurl myself off something the height of a ship, I can't be in sniffing distance of a pub, not today, not now – I might go a keg – and I have to get to Ag. It must be heading for four o'clock, as we finished at half-past three, and I've still got to find this Strand Arcade place. And I've got less than two quid to my name, with no idea when I might get paid. I say: 'Ah.' As I play at being distracted rolling my smoke.

'You don't want to be going round with them,' Adams says as the barge gets going back to the workshops, but I don't know if that's said to me, and I don't look up from my smoke.

'You don't want to lose another bet,' Tarzan says to him.

'I haven't made a fucking bet,' says Adams. 'But if I did, I'd put my money on Kelly and I wouldn't lose.'

Everyone in the cradle goes in at that, all arguing about their favourite, and the names are all Irish, apart from Tarzan McCall and you wouldn't say for sure he's not; there's this Vince Kelly who they call Ned, and a Flanagan, a Murphy and a Mick Doolan; a Sean someone. It's not that they're Irish that grabs me, or that they're all Irish and obviously monkey-nutted enough to chuck themselves off coal gantries, it's that they're all Irish boilermakers: tradesmen. I want to be one, I see, as if the idea has been sitting here on this barge waiting for me all this time to see: I want to be one of them that drives the rivet gun. Ticketed. Respected. How do I do that? The only ones I know that have got out of the Neighbourhood, or out of poverty at least, are knocking-shop proprietors, publicans, dope smugglers or cops. Or SP bookmakers. Never tradesmen.

'So, you coming, Pretty?' Tarzan nudges me again.

I have to say yes, don't I. But I can't. Not today. I have no trouble looking troubled about it as I say: 'I've got to get away today . . . family . . . obligation . . .'

I watch the idea of getting a trade disappear into the wake of the barge as quick as it came. An opportunity missed. I'll never be one of this lot. I'll never drink with them. I don't drink at all, do I? I do not. It's a whole boat missed as I'm too old to learn a trade anyway – they only want boys straight from school for indenturing and that, don't they.

But that Adams claps me on the shoulder, 'Good enough, lad,' and nearly knocks me into the water with the surprise of it. An

Ulsterman *not* calling me a faggotty old nana for having an excuse to avoid the pub. He's looking at me with what I think might be a smile; it looks painful. 'Some of us have families need looking after, don't we.' That smile; Jesus, is there a wife that loves that face? Seems so. But he's got more in store for me; he says: 'Now, you don't happen to play cricket, do you?'

'Cricket?' I'm smacked. This is just about the least believable thing I have ever heard: an Irishman asking me if I play cricket? Do they play cricket in Belfast? I didn't think them from the North were that odd.

'Yes, lad.' Adams is a cricket-playing grog-forgoing freak potato. 'The UBU are short a couple of bats for tomorrow,' he says. 'We don't expect to do well against Sheet Metal anyway but we'll give it a go. Birchgrove Oval – midday. It's a hat-around for the Ambulance Fund.'

If I wasn't so smacked, I would be rolling around on the deck of this barge with it. I drag hard on my smoke, thinking: this is an opportunity that's not getting away from me. Take it. Take it now. But I don't play cricket, not unless you can include the couple of Friday afternoons I was made to stand on the pitch at Redfern Park at the beginning of sixth class to avoid the attention of the truant officer. I don't play any sports at all, besides darts, which I do not play anymore, do I, because I've only ever played it pissed. What do I say?

I say: 'I could give it a go, Mr Adams.' Don't I. And it's at Birchgrove. That's near Balmain, isn't it, where the colliery is over there? They probably all live round that way – where else do you get a job load of boilermakers and ironworkers but round where there's wharves?

'Good on you, then,' says Adams, a freak potato but not a devil of any kind at all; he says: 'I'd not have picked you for a family man.'

I give him what I hope looks like an affirming smile in reply: I am a family man. Family of two that we are.

He asks me as the barge starts churning up the water, pulling in: 'You have far to get home?'

'No, ah . . .' Think. Opportunity. A more important, and urgent, one. We need to find a place to stay: now. 'Um, yes, actually . . . it's a fair way home, from out west . . .' I give him another hopeful smile: 'I'm looking for somewhere closer. Round Balmain, as it happens.'

He shakes his head, not hopeful. 'Not easy these days, is it? Not easy at all. I don't envy anyone looking for any affordable housing nearer the city today.' He folds his iron-hard forearms across his chest and turns up his lip: 'But I might know someone who could help you.'

'True?' I sound like Ag on the tram to Hordern's. This could be the best day of my life. Please.

'True. Ha!' He barks a laugh at my disbelieving face. 'As it happens, I know of someone who's just had a tenant do a flit on them – little old place, round behind White Bay, but it's good enough and might do you, if there's not too many of you, that is. Three rooms, only nineteen a week.'

'That sounds exactly what I'm looking for.' Nineteen shillings a week? You can't get anything under twenty in the Neighbourhood – not a house. Can't be worse than the one we've come from. A broom cupboard will do us. I say: 'We'll take it.'

'Hold your horses,' he says. 'You come round, in the morning – Fawcett Street, on the corner with Gladstone. Come at eleven o'clock, after Mass. We can go across to Birchgrove after then too.'

'All right.' Saints alive, and he's Catholic, too? Can this get any more promising? Keep my head on; thinking: might have to try a pub round there after all, for a bed for me and Ag, for tonight, get us to Mass, somewhere . . . 'See you tomorrow, then.'

'Tomorrow it is.' He nods, and he's got one more surprise for me as he does: 'Eoghan, isn't it?'

The Blue Mile

'Yes.' *Yaw-in*, he just said it; more than near enough, he knows the name. My name. 'Eoghan it is,' I say. 'Eoghan O'Keenan.' And my kneecaps want to slide down my shins again at that: he's known my name all along? Mr Harrison must've said, I suppose, but – ? But the clock on the wharf says it's half past four – horseshit. The girl said never mind how late, but – sweet Jesus, I'm going to see that girl again. Don't think about the girl. I've got to find Ag. Find them kneecaps, O'Keenan, and get running first.

Olivia

'Olivia Jane, I must,' Mother hisses, whispering in the fitting room, buttoning me up. 'Before he leaves to meet us.'

Must call Bart at Rose Bay to nark Agnes in to the Children's Court at Surry Hills before you nark your own child in to an evening of misery and humiliation at the Merrick.

'No,' I hiss back. 'It's only five – perhaps they don't finish until five.'

'It's ten past and they don't finish at five – I know they don't. They went on strike about it – their shift hours and what have you. One of Bart's associates is an industrial lawyer. The unionists – they won.' She says that as if victory entailed finding a typhus-infested bag of rats on the doorstep.

And doesn't Bart just know everything and everyone.

'Wait until half-past,' I insist.

'*We* have to leave at half-past,' she insists.

'We do *not* – don't have to be there until six, do we? And you're always *late*.'

'Ollie, you are impossible.'

I peep out the curtain into the salon: Agnes is still there, at my work table, daintily and slowly eating the cheese sandwich I got her from the Aristocrat just now. So quiet and dainty, she'd turn herself into a Florentine lily and vanish into the rug beneath her if it were at all possible. She's not going to the Children's Court. Whatever she is, whatever her brother is, she's not a criminal.

Mother hisses at my ear: 'You've been had. This child is unwanted. Ollie, these sorts of things are happening with increasing –'

'No,' I hiss back; this child can't be unwanted. *That* is impossible. Look at her: she is a perfect and perfectly dear little human being. I don't know what to do about her, though. What could have gone wrong? A kind of panic starts to bubble up in me. The boy has fallen off the Bridge. Or been eaten by one of the big machines in the workshops: I saw a picture of one in the paper: a wheel of torture. Spitting out hot metal; they're always getting burned and cut and packed off to the Royal North Shore, shop siren going *waaa waaa waaa* across the bay in the middle of the night. And my hiss now is shrill as a kettle about to boil: 'If we telephone anyone, we must telephone the Bridge people.'

'Bridge people? Who, where and what for? Don't be silly.' Mother yanks me back into the fitting room by the crystal choker, fixing the clasp. 'Now, put the shoes on.'

The shoes. Heels. Navy satin sling-backs, pointed toes. 'No.' I will look eight feet tall and my feet will look enormous: clown feet flapping on the end of my stick legs.

'You are not wearing mary-janes with this.'

'My black ones – why not?'

'Because I said so!'

'But I don't want –'

'Put them on!'

Rattle the windows with shrill.

And a *thunk, thunk,* knocking at the salon door.

As a little voice cries: 'Yo-Yo!'

I dash out of the fitting room to let him in, telling Mother behind me: 'Told you.'

And then I see him – it's him all right. Good God, look at that shoulderline. Male mannequin. Live one. Smiling eyes for his little sister. Perfectly dear, sweet boy. Sunburned too. Laughably gorgeous nevertheless, and I am laughing as I open the door: 'We'd just about given you up.'

He looks at me and something in his expression changes; his words dulled, not dancing: 'I'm sorry I'm late, miss, I missed a ferry and then I went to the wrong arcade.'

'Oh dear, not to worry,' I assure him, 'honestly,' but he's already looked away. He must be embarrassed at his lateness.

'Come on, Ag,' he calls her over to him. 'You look like you've had a good day. Say thank you to the lady.'

'Thank you, Miss Greene.' Agnes smiles up at me as she attaches herself to her brother's side, her hand in his. 'Thank you for a very nice day.' Oh, but I do want to steal her back.

'It was a pleasure,' I assure both of them, but the boy doesn't look at me. He's deliberately not looking at me, isn't he.

Ah, I see. My reflection. In the window. I am a great glamorous vision of multi-blue catastrophe. Shoeless one.

Embarrassing all round, really.

Yo

She is no lady, she is no girl. She is a jewel risen up from the sea. Jesus, what are you doing to me this day? I promised I'd not think of her again, and I didn't. Are you having a laugh at me with this?

What do I say to her? 'Ah . . .' I can see out the corner of my eye she's gone straight-backed, disdaining me down her fine long nose. Done her good turn for the season, now clear off so she can get to the theatre or wherever she's going. No wonder she didn't want paying; look at this place, all this finery. I knew she was a lady, and I knew she was a beautiful girl, but Jesus, spare me. I can't look at her; I say, to Ag: 'Thanks again. We won't keep you further.'

'No. Well. There you go.' She says it quick and sharp: hurry up, clear off.

'Yeah, there you go.' Can't lift my eyes from Ag to her; start turning back to the door: 'Wherever you go, there you are, ay, Ag?'

Ag rightly frowns at me: monkey-nut, what are you going on about?

The girl says: 'Well, goodbye then, I suppose.' But softer now. Jesus, her voice has me wanting to throw myself on my knees at her feet again. I'm still away with the music of her laughter, caught in her smile as she opened the door. That song is not for me, though, is it. 'Right, yeah,' I say over it. 'Goodbye. Thanks. Sure. Bye. Yeah.' Or some such string of bejabbering spoonery.

I look round my shoulder with a nod, so I don't seem completely lacking in manners as well as brainless, and I see her again, just for a second.

Jesus, but she is blindingly beautiful. Her curly blonde hair has been made into these ripples around her face, shining ripples. And what a face. Her eyes are the same colour as the waters of the harbour, not blue, not green, but exactly in between. As I look away again, though, I see the face of this other woman, by a curtain in the back corner of the shop, same eyes, maybe her sister, but with the blank stare of hatred in them: *Get out.* I'll oblige her.

'Bye bye,' Ag waves as we leave, and she says to me as we near the stairs: 'See, I said Miss Greene was a fairy princess, didn't I?'

'You did, Ag. Yes, you did.'

And I don't know if I'm thankful or shattered that I'll never see her again.

Olivia

'I forbid you from having anything to do with that young man ever again.'

'Forbid all you like, Mother.' It's hardly likely we'll cross paths ever again. A sadness sweeps over me at that, swiftly followed by relief. The way he looked at me: couldn't look at me. I'm used to boys not looking at me, but that one . . . that was rough. I'm not that much of a Medusa. Not as though I didn't do him an insanely enormous favour today, either; he could have been a little kinder. Why would I ever want to see him again? Who is he to not look at me like that? Some dustman. Some stupid sunburnt dustman.

I look at myself square on in the cheval now: I'm not that bad. The gown does compensate somewhat. I can almost vanish into it, it's such a spectacular creation, and this fabric is . . . it is a little slip of heaven, nothing less. I am wearing air. And you have to be a bosomless stick to carry off these diagonals or you'd look like a house – lopsided one. My hair looks nice, too; Marjorie knows what she's doing. My face might remain all schnonk, but I'm no Medusa.

'What's his name?' Mother asks behind me, holding those navy heels, and wanting a name for nark purposes.

I'm not going to tell her. Eoghan O'Keenan. E-o-g-h-a-n. Owen. Yoey. Yo-Yo. I'm not likely to forget it. And another strange sort of panic bubbles up at this: I don't care for boys. I never have. Why should I care about this one, or what he might think? I don't know who he is. I don't know anything about him. He's just a mannequin. For hideously cheap mercerised work shirts.

I don't care who he is.

God, but I see us meeting in the Gardens again, along that path by the wall, and my stomach flips.

No. I never want to see him again.

I won't see him again.

This is merely residual intrigue. That I'll never know anything about them. I'll never see dear little Agnes again or find out if she lives in the Botanic Gardens or a flat in Randwick. Never know if he's a death-defying dustman or . . . But there was something about him, something heroic – those fine, long fingers . . .

'Put your shoes on. Please, Ollie,' Mother says.

I take them from her. Resigned to whatever the evening holds for me. The future. *Phlergh.* Grow up and thank God Glor never saw him; I'd have to hear her go on and on and on about his gorgeousness, how Lebanese girls always fall for the Irish boys. She's plying one with her mother's coffee cake in the lounge at her house right now, that Paul boy. It's all in the eyes with Irish boys. All in the deep blue sea of their eyes, and everywhere else. So gorgeous, and I'm the only one who saw this boy. It was just a dream after all. Little Agnes a sweet dream. Half a cheese sandwich is all that remains. And her rickrack and Fuji creation on my miniature. Oh but I meant for her to take that home.

Mother mists me with a fine cloud of Number Five, never mind that I always wear Coty's Lily: 'Pout all you like, darling – enigmatic on your features. Smoky.'

She pencils my eyes, powders the schnonk. A coat of plum lipstick, grab handbag and wrap.

'Out you scoot, darling, our cabbie awaits.'

Yo

'Will we visit Miss Greene again one day?' Ag asks me as we're walking back down to the Quay.

'No, I doubt that,' I tell her. 'But we will have egg and chips for tea.' While we're waiting for the pubs to close and the streets to clear. I doubt that six o'clock Saturday is any different in Balmain than anywhere else for fucked-up: maybe worse with a job load of wharfies.

'But I don't want egg and chips for tea,' says Ag, that whine getting into her voice.

'But I do,' I tell her, over the pointless want of saying to a seven year old, don't ask me how my day went, will you? I went up on the Sydney Harbour Bridge today, if you want to know, didn't miss a rivet. First go. I did all right. Never mind. I'm that tired and that hungry now I could eat a buttered frog through a flyscreen.

'Miss Greene bought me a cheese sandwich,' Ag says.

'Did she?'

'She did.'

'That was nice of her.' Miss Greene doesn't give a silver-plated shit about you, Aggie. But how do you tell a kid they're not good enough for some and will never be? I'm not about to.

'Miss Greene let me play dresses with her little wooden mannequin.'

'Did she?'

'I made a skirt that was red and yellow. I sewed it all by myself, and Miss Greene said it was very good.'

Ag'll run out of things to say about Miss Greene. With any luck in this lifetime. Keep ignoring it. I'm not thinking about the girl; she's gone, a lifetime behind me. I'm thinking about getting my tea, and my bed, please, we need a good bed tonight, and I'm otherwise thinking about what I should say to Mr Adams about Ag when we meet him tomorrow. Should I tell him the truth? Or tell him she's mine? Should I take her to Mass with me in the morning or not? She's got to start her Holy Communion lessons in the new year. Somewhere. Don't think that far ahead; it's too much to consider. On more practical and immediate matters of salvation, how am I going to get my hands on a pair of sandshoes, never mind the hat, for Monday? All the shops are closed from now until then. And what will I do with Ag come Monday? I'm not leaving her with some strange sheila again. Got away with that once; never do that again. But where will she go for all the weeks of school holidays ahead? Somewhere . . .

'She took me to see the Santa display and she bought me a pink cake there, Miss Greene did.'

'Right. Shush for a minute there, will you, Ag?'

She does. She doesn't say another word, right down to the grease traps at the Quay. Her Yoey is a mean bastard. I'll make it up to her, get her an ice-cream for the ferry. After I've had my egg and chips.

Olivia

'Don't speak, then,' Mother says as we get out of the cab. 'Suits you too. Every fault's a fashion if you wear it well.'

We've only travelled a block and a half up Elizabeth Street, not a long enough trip for me to have let go of anything but the tight clasp of my hands, hanging on to each other as they were all the way, awaiting the call to the gallows. Which is here: the Merrick Club. It doesn't look like a place of execution; it looks like a small bank, wedged between Studebaker Motors and the Manchester Unity Oddfellows Society of the Secret Handshake, minarets of the synagogue beyond. Establishment but slightly shady.

A strip of red carpet at the threshold, less vice-regal crimson, more folly rose; the celluloid spike heels of these stupid satin pumps squish into it, as my heart and soul begin their inevitable squish into . . .

An empty foyer. It's only a dot after six; I don't suppose the fabulous people arrive until after eight. So they can't see me struggle to negotiate spike heels on the parquet. It's a fabulous foyer, though: elliptical columns like ships' funnels clad in silky oak veneer inlaid with bands of turquoise and bronze, the walls too. Snazz as. The oak is honey-coloured watermark taffeta. But as the girl at the cloakroom counter greets us with a cool, 'Good evening,' lids so heavy with paint and the tedium of her own fabulousness, I can't help thinking: welcome to the *Titanic*.

As a tuxedoed man emerges from behind one of the columns and makes a lunge for Mother. 'Em, hello, you naughty little minx,' kissing the air either side of her face and just about startling me back out into the street. He is obviously not Bart Harley. I am aware that barristers are notoriously theatrical, but possibly not quite this theatrical. White spats, maroon cravat, and I'm sure he's pencilled his brows.

'Arthur, darling.' Mother kisses the air around him in return, as he makes a lunge for my hand, and just about shrieks the silky oak veneer off the walls.

'Em – oh Emily, is this yours?'

'Of course.' Mother is droll and dry and utterly triumphant: 'The girl and frock both, yes, all mine.'

'Superlative,' he says to me and he looks right into my eyes as he does; something warm-hearted about him, puckish, dropping his voice to a whisper as he kisses my hand: 'Superlative.' Before he shrieks at Mother again: 'Oh but I must fly away, precious Em – got to go pick up something before the show. Nudgy nudge – you want some too?'

Mother's laugh is a soaring glissando of gaiety, but I catch the deadly daggers she looks at him as she waves him away.

So I have to speak – I have to know: 'You want what too?'

'Nothing, Ollie, shush. Up we go.' She waves me towards the staircase past the columns: 'Bart'll meet us for a cocktail in the Library Lounge.'

'Who was that Arthur man?' I pester as we take the stairs, 'God Rest Ye Merry Gentlemen' tinkling on a piano somewhere.

'Arthur Spence – he's an actor. The ringmaster of the cabaret here, the supper show.'

The Blue Mile

'Oh? You seem close in with him.' She's never mentioned anyone called Arthur to me before.

'He's close in with everyone,' she says, shooing me up again. 'Theatre people are always good to know – sequins, darling.'

Millions of hours of work, yes, and the last sort of work I'd ever want to do. But I wouldn't mind seeing a show, though; I love a good show, not that I've been to that many. You can disappear into the theatre, lights down, another place and time. I want to disappear right now as the chandelier above the staircase shimmers across the band of crystal drops at my hip. Dear God. I ask Mother, beg her: 'Are we going to see this cabaret tonight?' Immediately?

'Perhaps. If you grow up quickly enough,' she says as we reach the landing, where she waves ahead, her face divine in the glow of the late sun streaming through the windows above. 'Oh look, wonderful, Bart's beaten us here.'

She is transformed in this moment, as I've never seen her; alabaster yielding to the softest silken flesh. A blush that finds its way through the powder on her cheeks, and I see: she loves him.

At the top of the stairs, I see him: soft grey hair, black-tie debonair, a crooked smile, raising his glass to her: he loves her too.

He is sartorial perfection. His jacket is a semi-formal cutaway in-betweener for an early soiree; distinctive and precisely tailored, possibly Savile Row. He is the Well Dressed Man: he will have an array of twenty suits to his wardrobe, one dozen hats, eight overcoats and four pairs of shoes, not including sports attire. She is wearing an old favourite tonight, her pewter lamé tunic, with long strands of jet beads, and when they meet, when they touch, with their silvers and blacks and superlative loveliness, they are two halves of a whole.

I knew it. I knew it would be this way, didn't I.

I look out at the gilt-edged figs of Hyde Park across the road, and the world as I know it shudders and disappears.

Yo

'You're fibbing to me, you are – you didn't go up there today.'
Ag's looking over at the Bridge from the ferry rail. It looks amazing, side-on like this, going across from point to point, from Dawes to McMahons and back again now, with the sky going every colour there is as the sun sets.

I say: 'I did, Ag. I was right up at the top there, and I don't believe it much either.'

She reaches up her arms to me, for me to pick her up. I do. She's tired, her body's asleep already; she smells of perfume and ice-cream, as a small girl should, and she says, over my shoulder: 'It's made of liquorice sticks.'

'What is?'

'The Bridge.' She laughs: 'Silly.'

'You might be on to something there, Ag. Liquorice sticks . . .' I laugh back, at Ag and the black liquorice lines of the Bridge, light-headed, asleep too. 'Them rivets are made of fruit bullets then, ay?'

'Yeah,' she says. 'That why there's a big piece missing out of it – see in the middle? Some greedy gorgy's been eating it. He's in them workshops – that's what all that banging is. He's getting hungry. He comes out in the night and gobbles up what you done in the day.'

'Of course he does – I had been wondering about all that. You're a cracker, Ag.'

'What's your favourite flavour?'

'Of what?'

'Fruit bullets. *Silly.*'

'Blackcurrant.'

'Mine's orange.'

'I know it is.'

'You know everything – every silly thing, Yoey Yo-Yo.'

'I might just do.'

'I could listen to you two all night,' this fella beside us joins in, a rough old voice, sharing the laugh with us. I turn around but I can't see him well for the sun in my eyes. He says: 'She'll make you proud, that one. You're a lucky man.' And he tips his hat and walks off, before I can tell him I couldn't agree more. He's in a hurry to be in his home, I suppose, with all the other hats and lunch tins gathering to bolt off the ferry as it pulls in to the wharf.

Here at Balmain. Not that I can see it too well either, the sinking sun is that harsh. I look the other way for a second and it's hardly better with the glare coming off the water, but in it I catch the shadow shapes of Port Jackson, see this town of Sydney for what it is: a string of a hundred points and bays with a wharf or half-a-dozen sticking out of every one of them. Exhausting just to look at, and Ag, little as she is, has got heavy in my arms, arms that have never felt so heavy from work.

I start walking up from this Darling Street wharf. There are a dozen wharves on Balmain alone, as I learned getting the ticket for us here: besides the colliery and timber wharves, there's the Thames Street ferry, Louisa Street and Some Other Street. This one is the main one, and this Darling Street is the main road. When I asked what the pubs were like from the fella at the ticket counter, he said: *There's twenty-six of them, take your pick.* Twenty-six pubs in one suburb, full of wharfies, on a Saturday evening. I hold Ag a bit tighter to me, expecting the worst: Chippo by the sea. It's half-past six, so I'm expecting a hundred women are getting bashed in here somewhere, something to do between the pub and the knocker.

This Darling Street, though, as far as I can see, is empty, smelling of roasts in the oven, and if anyone's getting bashed, they're being very quiet about it. Even the tobacconist across from the ferry is closed. Maybe there's a hundred Wal Adamses round here, keeping the bastards in order. *Good people, working people,* that woman at the Paragon said last night. Was that only last night? Maybe that's the difference round here, though: good work. Men's work and only men's work. Trade depressions might mean you put off buying them new pair of boots, but it won't stop the need for coal steamers to be coming and going, will it? The houses along this street seem to say so; they're terraces but mostly wide and double-storey. There's a pair of them set back with a garden at the front, and a little wooden one next to it needs a coat of paint but it's got a window box full of bright red flowers. This is a good place.

A few hundred yards up the road, the first big pub we come to doesn't have a name on it, excepting a sign for Star Ale across the front tiles: not Tooths, at least, and it looks tidy enough, too; even the couple of fellas having a smoke in the lane by it, pretending they're not waiting for sly, are tidy-looking. The last door along the front of the pub says *PRIVATE ENTRANCE* and I say to Ag: 'Reckon this'll do us.' But she doesn't answer; she's already fast asleep.

The fella who looks up from the evening paper at the counter, switching off the wireless beside him as he does, is fat and happy looking: 'Yeah, g'day mate, what can I do for youse?'

'We're looking for a room, just for the night. One bed'll do.' This freshly polished hallway will do.

'Well, I can give you two beds, fella,' he says. 'Seven and six the double, that's the only one I got, and that's breakfast as well, bath up the end of the hall.'

The Blue Mile

That's a bit expensive; that's a lot expensive, that's nearly as much as some of the pubs in town, and possibly explains the vacancy, but I've got my hand in my pocket before I tell him: 'We'll take it.' I'd take it for a pound.

'Good-o.' He grabs the key and comes out the door of his office, showing me up the stairs. 'Welcome to the Commercial. No grog in the room, mind, but you can have an ale with your tea till nine.'

'No worries,' I say; I'm not going to be awake long enough to even think about the want of a drink in me; I can hardly get one foot past the other on these stairs.

'You're travelling light,' he says, checking us over, as he should.

I give him the horseshit I've been rehearsing: 'We come in to go to the zoo – missed our train home, out west.' Don't ask me where west, or where the zoo is.

'Big day for your little one?' he says at the top, a nod at Ag; not being nosy, just nice.

I nod. Big day all right.

He says: 'My wife's sister is out near Bathurst – right pain if you miss that evening engine, isn't it?' He opens the door of the second room along this hall and I see Paradise. Two beds, and I can smell the soap in the linen from here. There's a washstand with a sink too, a white flannel on a hook by it. This will be the cleanest place my sister and I have ever laid our heads.

'You had your tea?' He's asking after Ag, not me.

'Yeah, thanks.'

'Leave you to it, then,' he says. 'Breakfast seven-thirty Sundays, all right?'

'Couldn't be more, thank you again,' I tell him as he closes the door, though we won't be eating again till after Mass anyway.

I lay Ag on the bed nearest the window and go over to the washstand, soak the flannel and put it round the back of my neck. It just about jumps back off me with the heat of the sunburn there, but it feels good. Sweet Jesus, it feels good.

Kim Kelly

    Everything is good.
    We're going to be all right.
    I get down on my knees by the washstand and I stay here for a long time: thank you.

Olivia

'Olivia, might I recommend the pea salad for entree? Sounds terribly humble but wait until you taste the minted mayonnaise.' Bart Harley is so at ease with himself and his world, I want to hate him. I desperately want to push him out the great arched window beside our table. Watch him go splat on the footpath below. But he's so charming. Suave and urbane, and all the same, there's nothing arrogant about him. 'Isn't it a tasty dish, Em darling?' he says, as if the future turning of the earth depends upon Mother's approval of his opinion of this minted mayonnaise. He's no Don Juan. The only thing desperate about him is his desire to win my approval too.

I look back down at the menu. It's all festive fare: devilled oysters, lobster tartlets, turkey and goose with all the trimmings, cherry pie, plum pudding . . . everything but a partridge in pear sauce and all mouth-watering, but I don't think I can eat a thing.

Still, I say: 'Yes, please, that sounds lovely.' And good God, but I think I might be going to cry. Stare harder at the menu. How am I going to get through three courses of this? Glance at my watch: five to seven. Longest almost hour of my life so far, much of it spent listening to Bart Harley going gooey over this frock, toasting Mother's design with French champagne; he's completely in awe of her and freely admits he has been since they first met a year ago. A *year* ago? She's had her design on him going for a whole year. Of course she has. And when he is not going gooey over her, he's a King's Counsel Crown Prosecutor putting razor-gang thugs in prison, presently going after some doctor who's been doing unseemly things at the behest of that infamous mobsteress Tilly Devine. He plays jazz clarinet and goes sailing in his spare time. He's forty-three and never been married. Never found 'the One' – until now. Bart Harley is too fabulous.

'Oh look, there's young Warwick.' Mother is calling someone over to the table now: 'Ollie, Warwick Bloxom is Bart's new clerk – his baby lawyer. What a pleasant surprise.' Her too-casual tone suggesting that this Warwick's appearance is no surprise to her at all.

I look up quickly and see a pleasant-faced boy, fresh from the pleasant-boy factory with his long fringe neatly brilled back and dinner jacket cut high at the waist, Oxford style, the type you wouldn't see at Pearson's because he lunches at the Australia Club, possibly with his father, who is possibly a stockbroker, a wheat merchant or member of parliament for the Nationalist Party, or all three. Much monied, evening dress every night type, all fopsy accoutrements present and accounted for but a topper, and I must force myself to be pleasant in return to him: his mother or sister might possibly want a bunch of summery things for Home one day.

'How do you do?' I manage, before burying my face in the menu again, and Mother digs her heel into my toe to make me look up again.

'Miss Greene, isn't it?' He bows slightly, and he's slightly awkward about it, too: he's been put up to this, I know it. He holds my gaze for so long he's being paid by the second for it, and what I wouldn't do for a brim to slide under, or for the chandelier above us to come down and send me through the floor.

'What brings you in tonight, eh, Rick?' Bart Harley rescues the moment, as fabulously avuncular as he is smooth.

'Oh,' and Warwick gives a light chuckle, rather be elsewhere now: 'I've brought Mother in for dinner, sir, with my aunt up from Melbourne, proving to them that this is not the den of iniquity they imagine. But never fear,' another phony chuckle, 'I'll ditch them after we've eaten –'

Bart Harley laughs at that, a genuine and jolly laugh. 'You two must have a dance later,' he says, and he is referring to me.

Mother adds a glissando trill and they're all laughing.

We two must have a dance?

Ha ha ha ha ha ha. Ho ho ho ho ho ho.

When hell freezes and the earth stops turning, but I think of his mother and his aunt and say: 'That would be lovely.'

The pea salad is, at least, when it arrives, and I give it my full attention. 'Oh dear yum, Mr Harley, you were right about this minted mayonnaise.'

'It's Bart, please.'

La la la la la la, listen to the string quartet in the corner playing 'Angels We Have Heard On High', very prettily too, tinkling over whatever lovey-dovey gushy mush from Barty Woo I'm not listening to next. Chatter is rising round the dining room; it's filling up, and I dare a few more glances about, to find a few more distractions from my anxieties confabulated and otherwise. The business opportunities here do indeed appear to be abundant. Mother spake the truth, and so does the regular assertion in the women's pages that Australians do not know how to dress after five. Half the men in drack sacks as if they've just come in from the office, and far too many dowdy dowagers in dreary unmitigated crepe atrocities like matrons from the Anti-Liquor League – which is not likely judging from the quantity of wine being consumed in here. I've never seen so many wine bottles in one go.

'I'll have the shiraz with the beef,' Bart Harley tells the sommelier. 'And you, Em dear?'

'I think the riesling for the goose, don't you?' Mother replies, and I'm tempted to ask if her consumption is legal. This will be her third glass – after the champagne cocktail in the Library Lounge and the chablis she just had with her lobster entree.

'Would you like a glass of something, Olivia – perhaps a spritzer?' Bart Harley asks me.

And I decline: 'No, thank you.' I'm not going to be carted off for a drunken giraffe when this place is raided after nine. I have been drunk, just the once, on our cognac last Christmas Eve when Mother was out – I tried it, retched savagely on it, don't know how anyone does it, not to mention Mother, and she hasn't even got to her martini yet.

I glance away, across the room again, and imagine I catch a glimpse of a dark-haired boy in white tux and midnight trousers. Wanting to find him here, and not merely for another pathetic glimpse of the heroic dustman, but because, even to the utterly untravelled, this is clearly not New York: did that chap over there truly just blow his nose into his napkin? Glance the other way at the sound of a party coming in through the doors of the dining room, the sound of barging gaiety: a small flock of funsters has arrived. My kind of clientele, at last.

With Cassie Fortescue in their midst.

There she is. My nemesis and Min Bromley's cousin, and as sincerely, edibly, hatefully gorgeous as ever. Petite and perfectly proportioned, I hope her overbeaded headband slips off her glossy auburn bob, down her minuscule nose and strangles her. *Sticky, sticky, stick.* How I despise her, this girl who first composed that taunt. Still, I mentally redesign her boxy shift, lengthen it a little so she doesn't appear so dumpy in it, and so last summer, one tier of flouncery too much at the waist. Her beau, whom I instantly recognise as Denis Clifton, looks like he got his clobber off the rack at Gowings – you would not know his father is Director-General of Customs House, but there's Sydney High old boys for you. How I could clothe this city, and how I betray myself.

I should design Cassie Fortescue a trousseau entirely of rayon. Flapper.

Mother's heel spikes me again as the main arrives: *Eat your turkey and grow up, Olivia Jane.*

No, I don't want to.

So she leans across and whispers in my ear: 'Back straight, darling.' Not hissing. 'How I wish you could see yourself as I do – as we all do. You are the most beautiful girl in the room.'

You are my mother and you're drunk.

I don't know how she's not, as New Yorkers might say, utterly spiflicated by half-past eight, halfway through dessert, halfway through her glass of sweet muscat, when that Arthur Spence fellow appears at the dining room doors and announces: 'Supper time, ladies and jellybeans!' Pencilled eyes more crazed than puckish, and he's swapped his tux for a gold lamé vest. 'Show begins in ten minutes!'

Mother looks at her wristwatch and stifles a yawn. 'Martini time already?'

'You are insatiable,' Bart Harley remains gooey as the cherry pie. 'Shall we?'

'Ollie?' Mother asks.

'Yes, shall we what?' I'm watching Cassie and her pack flap to their feet and head for the doors.

'Shall we carry on into the Jazz Room for the show?'

No. Jazz Room: Cassie and dancing in there. And I'm tired, ghastly delirious tired now. But Mother must be too. I don't know how she does it. Three times a week. This show that's as much business as it is pleasure for her. Remember: this is all for me. Going blind with drop crystal beads and diagonals for me. Me and me alone it will be, as Mother is going to marry Bart Harley. The least I can do is walk into the room, and then disappear into this show, into this frock. Only across the hall . . . Stand up. Grow up. It's not hard.

Through the tables and there's a hand on my arm: 'Dear girl, come here and let us see your gown.' When my heart resumes beating I find two crepe dowagers smiling above their pearls at me – the dowagers belonging to that Warwick Bloxom, who's striding for the stairs, 'I'll fetch you a cab, Mama,' as the aunt from Melbourne clucks at me: 'I must tell you how becoming that style is on you. Those colours. Delightful.'

And it is somehow. I find myself actually smiling in return. There's no reason for her to lie; I'm sure she has no idea who I am, and possibly couldn't care less. I must be wearing the frock well; and that's the point, isn't it.

'One of our own designs,' Mother gets a sale in before they go. 'Our card.'

'Incorrigible,' Bart Harley's crooked smile says of Mother, and of me: 'Absolutely delightful,' holding the door of this Jazz Room open for us. Perhaps I might find that pleasant one day too. There aren't many men who would so enjoy a woman behaving as Mother does, not to mention handing out business cards under his nose, outrageous ones with gold lettering that look like invitations to a ball. But he's clearly thrilled by her enterprise, her joie de vivre, and –

Oh, but as I step through the doorway the stench of male odour in this Jazz Room overwhelms. Good God, gagging at it. The place is crowded already, a different crowd from the dining one, multitude of shoulder-to-shoulder tables crammed around the floor and a small stage, all surrounded by heavy velvet drapes, four walls of that folly rose, ingrained with endless nights of dancing sweat and tobacco smoke and some other awful, acrid smell. A trumpet screams through the dimness and the room starts spinning, I am feather-headed and the folly walls are closing in, and as I look at Bart Harley again, gesturing to a table in the centre near the dance-floor, all I can see is me eating my Mexican chocolate cake alone in the cottage on Christmas Day, picking the crumbs out of the bottom of the tin, and I've got to run away. I've got to get some air.

I yank Mother by the wrist before she whirls off to someone she's spotted across the floor: 'Ladies?'

She waves me away: 'Back out in the hall and up to the right.'

And I dash for it, celluloid heels skidding across the boards to the toilet rooms, to splash some water on my face, and while I'm at it I manage to smudge my make-up so that now I look like I've got a black eye. Startling under the bright bulbs surrounding the mirror. Damn. Always carry a phial of witch-hazel in your handbag for such unfortunate events. Unless you're hopeless and, like me, don't listen to your mother. I can't carry this off, I tell the chi-chi gold taps and the marble basin. Miss Greene Hats and Frocks in Homebush, here I come. I don't have the nerve for business. I make things. Beautiful, luxurious, stylish things. That's what I do, all I want to do, and I'm good at it. Can't I just do that and avoid everything else?

Mais non, Madame Chanel appears in the mirror, a vision of elegant insouciance: *Do you think I simply woke up famous and in Paris one day? I began with hats and frocks in Moulins, oui? The things I've done to get here. Pull yourself together, chérie. Find the woman in this dress – if there is no woman, there is no dress.*

I can almost feel her poke me in the ribs with her nail file. But that's the very problem right there, isn't it? There is no woman in this dress.

'Ollie? Ollie Greene – that *is* you.'

And that is Cassie Fortescue, trotting out from the conveniences to my left. This show couldn't be better for farce.

I sigh: 'Yes. Me.'

But I swear Madame Chanel says: *Look at her*. Finger under my chin, and so I do. I see Cassie Fortescue at my shoulder in the mirror, in her too-short dress and – oh dear – two black eyes. She is bouncing and smiling behind me, waving like a kitten after string. 'I thought it was you in the dining room. God, how the hell *are* you, old beanie beanster, old sticky – it's been *ages,* hasn't it?'

'Yes, it's been a long time.' *Sticky.* A flash of rage: I want to hold her face an inch from the lavatory water and see how she likes it. Or simply say: *That dress is so much more appalling at close range – God, where the hell did you find it? You look like a frilled cover for a dunny brush.*

I don't do anything but stare, though. There's something odd about her, beyond the frock. She's hopping about from foot to foot, already dancing, or like a child who's had too much cake. She says, grinning: 'Auntie called you this morning to keep shtum on Minnie, didn't she?'

I nod. Odder and odder, Cassie. Tell the whole ladies room what a shtumly devoted cousin you are, or put an ad in the paper: of the three compartments in here the doors of two remain closed and the occupants very quiet – no doubt so that they can hear every word.

Cassie sniffs – horribly, like a guttersnipe – and lights up a cigarette, or tries to. I can't believe this show I'm seeing now. Her hand is shaking as she strikes the lighter again: is she drunk?

She gets it lit and she puffs and prattles: 'I've been meaning to pop into the shop – Min is thrilled to the gills with what you've done. Was – ha, did. You know what I mean. Anyway, Palgrave says you're a tough nut. Thanks for that, always good to know who your friends are. Poor Min, though. Don't believe a word about Samuels going belly-up – that's just for them to lose a few shareholders, get the price down before they do some merger thing with their other company. You know what I mean. Poor bugger, our dear Min. Bryden's ditched her.'

'Awful.' Poor Min indeed, and Allison Palgrave was sent to test me? Somehow, that's the most disgusting thing these girls have ever done to me. But for the first time ever, finally, and at last, I feel superior, in many more ways than sartorially. I am a lady, actually, rightful title or not. I smile, steel in my spine, and speak to her ill-chosen flouncery: 'Truly awful. But yes, Cassie, yes, you must pop into the salon one day.'

She over-giggles, 'Oh yeah-o, I'll say,' then she snorts, and I'm altogether unsure now what a Ladies College education might've done for her. She's behaving like a flapper on some lunacy-inducing drug. Perhaps she is. Who are you, Cassie Fortescue? *No one,* says Coco. *Only a stranger on the road – the road to Paris. The road to you.*

A breathy laugh escapes me: 'Toodles.' And I'm past her. Easy as that, a little ladies room revelation, to hold my fears up to the light: and then go past them. I am past them. Cassie Fortescue is no one. A phantom fear. A puff of smoke. She disappears.

I go back down the hall and into the Jazz Room where the smells are just smells somehow now too, the smell of people. Just people, having fun, all singing a song with that Arthur Spence ringleading them, a risqué burlesque. 'Ta-ra-ra boom de ay! Ta-ra-ra boom de ay!' they chorus and clap in time. All of the lewd jokes go over my head, but I know some of the words, and I don't know where from: 'Though fond of fun I'm never rude. Though not too bad I'm not too good.' And I start laughing with the crowd, finally, at last. 'A queen of swell society as freely gay as gay can be . . .' They roar at that and I stand at the back of the room and I laugh: loud and freely. Not quite gay; but it's not so bad.

It's five past nine now and there's no hold on the liquor either. One rule for the rich and one rule for the poor; I know the contradiction well, but I've never seen it demonstrated quite so flagrantly as this before. I clap along with the next song too, but as I do I fancy I see Eoghan O'Keenan again, shoulderline on the edge of the empty dancefloor in that white tux, and I dismiss him as quickly again: there will be no white tuxedos this side of the stage in the Merrick any more than there'll be a liquor raid. No riffraff in this place, private club, members only, do what you like here and do it till dawn. For a price.

There's a round of applause, a shuffling of chairs, a clarinet soars up through the thick smoky air. Mother and Bart Harley stand to take the floor. To 'Blue Heaven'. Of course: well, it is the song of the year, after all. I laugh again, to myself, as I watch them step into a foxtrot. And I see that Bart Harley is not a fabulous dancer: stiff-gaited and a little hesitant on his feet, he is, but then no one's perfect, are they?

And Warwick Bloxom is beside me as the tempo changes again: 'Miss Greene, would you care to dance?'

Yo

'There's a bit of dry rot at the back of the kitchen here.' Mr Adams is showing me a hole in the floor Ag could hide in if she had to, but I'm not bothered about it. The place is still a palace to me. A stone cottage of three rooms, a bed, a sofa and a kitchen, all older and damper and colder than anything in the Neighbourhood, and it's nothing less than perfect. It's got the gas on for light, and a good-looking fuel stove in the hearth here – a proper range type of stove.

'You can fix that up and I wouldn't raise the rent on you,' the landlord, a Mr Sturgess, says of the hole in the floor. 'It's a permanent tenant I want, one who'll pay the rent – and on time.'

'That's me,' I say. I'll pay the rent on time. I almost always have. I'll fix the hole in the floor too, though I know as much about that sort of thing as I do cricket. I'm pretty sure I'm being told I'm expected to fix it.

'We'll see – see how we go,' Mr Sturgess says to Mr Adams, wary, but we're in. I'll prove to him I'm a good tenant. I couldn't be standing straighter if I tried, as his rough head over his stiff Sunday collar and tie turns back to me: 'Well, at least you're not a miner, I suppose.'

'Miner?' I ask; what's wrong with them?

Mr Adams says: 'Last lot here was miners, never got the rent – if they're not striking they're planning one, or the council's got the workings shut down with some old crank complaining about what the dust is doing to the worth of their property. Ay, Alf, all ten bobs' worth of it.'

Mr Sturgess lets out a laugh at that so powerful I think he's going to bust his collar with it; but he goes grim again as quickly, for me: 'Ten bob is ten bob, right? Those who don't pay their way pay the consequences.'

'Right, yes sir.' He will find me and break parts of me and doubtless enjoy it.

'So it's just you and the kid?' He doesn't look at Ag, where she's hiding behind my leg. I reckon this Sturgess might be the type who wouldn't even look at his own kids, not unless they were mucking up.

I tell him: 'Yeah, it's just the two of us.' We're not going to rip up what's left of your floorboards for the stove, don't worry, and I couldn't lie about us in the end, to Mr Adams or anyone. When I got us to Mass, finding a St Augustine's only two streets away, I realised horseshitting now would be pointless. There was not one face that didn't take a good look at us walking up the street, never mind at the font in the door. Word will get around eventually. If the Devil is looking, he will find us; and what authority other than his would say Ag's welfare isn't best with me? I have a job, a house now. The Lord is looking after us, because I'm in the right. I told Mr Adams that our parents had left us: a lie only in that I doubt they've ever been with us. He said: *That is a tragedy*. And there is no greater truth.

He says now, to his mate Sturgess and in pity of me: 'They've no other family, as I told you. How many lads you know would take such care of a child on his own?'

Mr Sturgess stares hard at me, and then he says again: 'We'll see about him, Wal.'

I give him the nineteen bob for the rent, agreed as starting from last Thursday, just about all I've got left, and he gives me the key.

'Thank you. You won't be sorry, Mr Sturgess.'

He says yet again: 'We'll see.'

And Mr Adams says: 'Lay off, Alf, the boy's all right.' I'm grateful for that, more than grateful, but I don't know why he should be so sure of me; he turns to me now and he says: 'We'll see what you're like with the bat, though, won't we?'

We will. We're going to go and have a game of cricket now, aren't we. It's only a social game, for some charity fund they have; I only have to give it a go. Jesus, but I don't want to fuck anything up with it. I'm not going to, though, am I. I'm not going to put a foot wrong for the remainder of my earthly life.

Back outside, I look down this Fawcett Street, this skinny lane of cottages behind the timber dock at White Bay, some stone, some wooden, all sitting under the bell tower of St Augustine's, with a stretch of scrub down the waterside end, a good view of the electric power station stacks beyond that, and it's now I see the tree. In front of the place opposite. It's small, with white flowers on it, and it looks to be struggling. But it's a tree. I want one in front of our place too; I'm going to get one.

'That's the Opera House up there,' Mr Adams nods down Gladstone Street as we start walking, pointing out the pub verandah rising above the rooftops that way. 'The pisser Tarzan and them go to – he lives down that corner, Stephen Street, at rolling distance; his poor mother. I'm another two streets that way, Adolphus Street, the first house next to the corner shop there.'

I look at him, set on being such a help to me, taking me under his wing, telling me which shop is best for groceries now, and I have to interrupt him to say: 'Thanks, you know, for getting us a place. I don't know what we'd have done.'

'You needed the hand,' he shrugs.

And the Devil in me makes me say when I should just keep it shut: 'You've gone well out of your way.' I'm asking: so, what's the bargain here?

'Nothing out of my way,' he shrugs again. 'You're all right, and I'm a good enough judge of that. I see you work well, you're no time-wasting fool and you know the language. That's good enough for me.'

The first one is true, the second depends on the circumstances and the third has me smacked again and asking like the little folk might have been in his ear: 'How do you know I know the language?'

'Look on your face when I let it go at you.' He laughs, recalling it, and it makes me laugh too: if I recall it correctly, I shat my soul into a tin cup, more fear of him than the height and the swinging of the cradle for a second there.

He's wheezing across the road with it, back on that main Darling Street and then onto another I can't see a name for, and when he stops laughing he asks me: 'Where's your family from, then?'

And when I say, 'Tralee, mostly,' he looks at me with greater pity than ever: 'Oh.' But he's still having a laugh with me, not unkind, and that's unheard of: a North–South not unkind laugh? Is there such a thing? There is for him.

I have to ask in return: 'What about you? Where are you from?'

'Originally, Arranmore, off the coast of Donegal, but Lifford is where I left from.' He's there now, staring at some emerald hills.

In Donegal, and that makes some sense of him: he's from the North but not from Northern Ireland; even still: 'I didn't think they spoke Gaelainn up there.'

'We don't,' he says, and I know that by now of course, he speaks his Ulster type of it, before he tells me: 'It's all Irish, though, isn't it?'

Yes, I nod: 'It is.'

'Never lose it, whatever of it you might have. Don't let the Sasanaigh have that too; they've thieved enough off us.'

Haven't I heard that a thousand times. He's an Irish Revivalist; like Father Madigan, pounding it out of the pulpit of St Ben's, calling for the language to be taught in the school, and when the government said no, he declared it an Imperial conspiracy.

But I have to admit to Mr Adams: 'I don't have much more than the worst words in me.'

He shrugs: 'Good enough. As long as you can tell the King where to go.' He's serious; but even more so now he says: 'I see you didn't bring a hat, though, nor shoes for playing.' Unlike himself: he nipped home from Mass to change before meeting me at the house – he's even got a white vest on.

'I don't have any gear for sports,' I tell him. 'Haven't been able to get to the shops.'

And the pity is genuine here: 'It's been hard for you, hasn't it?' I shrug.

He says: 'Well, don't worry about it, you're on your way up now.'

We are. Ag's skipping along beside me and she's smiling at this Mr Wal Adams: more than a nice old fella; somehow, he's a friend, this cricket-playing Irish Revivalist pit bull: freak potato.

And just for him I'm out for a duck on Birchgrove Oval, busy looking at the pitch that's black from coal dust instead of the ball, and looking out for Aggie, where she's sitting on the fence rail, not looking at me, but at another friend she's made in five seconds, another little girl belonging to someone from the Sheet Metal Workers Union.

'Well that was a short innings,' Mr Adams shakes his head as I walk off the pitch again, back among this crowd that's congratulating me just for turning up to enjoy the sun and buy ginger ale and lamingtons for their Balmain Ambulance. There's kids running around everywhere, hanging off trees, and a dog stealing the ball every five minutes, and as the shadows get long Mr Adams is slipping a pound note into my pocket and saying: 'For Christmas – don't say nothing about it. I mean it – say nothing to no one.'

I can't say anything about that at all, don't worry, and not a lot more when Ag and me get back to the little stone cottage, our house, and there's this woman on the front step not five minutes after we've got in, with a cake tin in her hands, saying: 'Hello there, Nettie Becker, next door – welcome to Fawcett Street.'

She might be about thirty, I suppose, something motherly about her but something else too: lipstick, on a Sunday, don't think I saw her face at Mass or I'd have remembered it. She's good-looking, all over. She just walks right past my goggling and into the house. 'Now if there's anything you need, you just shout over the fence.' Poking around the bits and pieces of furniture in the front room. 'Oh dear, but look at this place, didn't they leave it in a state, filthy animals,' and then to Ag, 'Aren't you a darling thing,' and to me, 'How old is she, your little one?' Not waiting for an answer: 'You don't look old enough to have a child that age but you can never tell these things, can you?'

This Nettie Becker could talk underwater with a mouthful of pebbles, and she's past me again before I can correct her and say Ag's my sister, poking her head round into the next room: 'You're not staying here tonight, are you? Where are your things? There's no linen on the bed. Disgusting people. Where's your linen?'

'Ah . . .' I think this is the first sound I make.

'Never mind, I've got spare you can borrow. Won't be a moment. It's Johann, isn't it?' She finally stops to draw breath, back at the front door.

'I'm sorry, what?'

'Your name – they said you had a funny name.'

I don't know who they is apart from pixies, but I tell her my funny name: 'It's Eoghan.'

'Ian?'

'Yo-un, or –'

'Is that foreign?'

'Irish.'

'Never mind.' She bats it off for a blowfly, and says to Ag: 'And what's yours?'

'Agnes.' I tell her on my sister's behalf; Ag's gone wary, trying to disappear altogether round the back of me.

Nettie Becker doesn't notice: 'Aren't you just darling?'

A bit scary she might be, but in no more than ten minutes we've got sheets on the bed, a blanket for the sofa, a clean frying pan, a jug of milk and a bowl full of eggs from her chook run and she's saying: 'My wash day is Wednesdays, don't mind throwing yours in too for a shilling, and as well of course the child can come to my house tomorrow while you're working, if you need her to. Agnes, you can come and help me with my little Johnny. Would you like that? He's only three, but he's a handful and seven-quarters, I'll say.' She puts her hands on her hips and gives me a look that's a bit scary too: 'Any time after six – that's when John's off, up at the Glebe Island silos, lumping. Six till six, that's what a ten-hour shift round there is – and anything goes between six and six round here. But no other time, right?'

'Right,' and that's my final prayer answered, our new life set up; it doesn't seem enough to say, 'That's very kind of you.' But that's all I can say.

'Oh, I don't know about that,' she says, in a sarcastic sort of way, making a sour face, but I don't know what she means by it and can't ask her because she's turned on her heel and gone back out the door.

Take a moment to scratch my head and then I ask Ag: 'What do you reckon?'

She shrugs; not too keen on Nettie Becker.

But I am. She might be a strange sheila, but she seems ordinary strange; and she's right next door, in this place full of decent working people, who obviously all have an eye out for each other even if they can't get a story straight, and she is probably genuinely wanting help with her baby. It looks good all around. I tell Ag: 'You might get a headache from her, but she might be some fun, too, yeah? She seems to like you.'

Ag doesn't want to know about it. She goes out to the kitchen and pushes the chair in here up to the sink so she can reach the tap. She turns it on, inspects the flow, and she turns it off. Her skinny little arms are then lifting the old black kettle the flitters left on the side of the sink, telling me she's more than capable of looking after herself, once we work out the stove at least; and she says, filling the kettle now under the tap, with her back still to me: 'Why can't I go and help Miss Greene?'

Because she wouldn't want you to, you're not good enough to, is the truth I won't tell her, so I say: 'Because you can't,' which is no reason at all; so I say: 'Because we live here now. And that's a pretty good thing, isn't it? What do you reckon?'

She turns on the chair and gives me one of them smiles that make the angels sing. 'It's the best house ever, Yoey.'

It's our house. It really is. We have landed on our feet.

We have landed on our feet so surely that when I get down to the ferry the next morning Tarzan's there waiting for me, 'Hey, Pretty,' with his sore Monday head and the sandshoes I couldn't get for myself before now – and by another miracle they fit, too. I lose my guts all over again going up in the cradle, I know I will never get used to this height, but I as I look out this time I see the points and bays for what they are today: a tear in the emerald hills of my country, with a river of silver pouring through it from the sun. I will never get tired of this looking out either. I don't want to catch white-hot flying cocks forever, though, nor scald my hands daily getting the billy off Clarkie's stove, and like the Lord of Balmain has dreamed up a plan for that too, Tarzan says to me as I hand him his tea at smoko: 'You should think about getting into a construction trade – you're good on them feet when you get going.'

Should I? Am I? What I wouldn't do to get into any trade. But I don't get too excited at the idea; I tell him: 'Yeah, but I'm over twenty-one, bit old now, aren't I?'

'Old?' he says. 'Age doesn't do you any harm up here. Any

foreman working at height wants a fella he can trust above another any day – sixteen or sixty-six.'

Trust. He trusts me? I am as tall as the top chord we're standing on this second.

'Keep kissing my pink hairy arse, kid,' he tells me, 'and one day you too might be on your way to sixteen quid a week.' Because this Tarzan McCall can't breathe if he's not bragging.

And I am disbelieving: 'Sixteen what?'

'Quid. That's what you get riveting at height, from the increases we got last month.'

'Shit – yeah?' So that's what I'm going to be, a riveter, like Mr Adams and Tarzan. I will make a point of finding out how.

He says: 'Yeah, I'm buying me mum the house with it now.'

Good on you. One day, I'm going buy Ag a house, too.

But for now, for Christmas, I'm going to buy her a little tree for the front of the one we're renting. I get it from Paddy's on Tuesday afternoon, and I have to fight for it, all the way down George Street and into the Haymarket, through the Christmas crowds. There's a lot of happy faces here, trays of cherries and peaches flying everywhere, but mine is the happiest, finding what I'm looking for when I see it. 'That's a gardenia,' the lady at the flower stall tells me. 'Lovely choice but she's a fusspot. Not too much sun, not too much shade, lad. Not too much water and not too little. But the flowers will reward you for your trouble with their scent.' They already are: big white flowers that smell like some memory of summer I never knew I had.

I carry this pot of summer under my arm back along George, back through the la-di-da end of town, back past that Strand Arcade, where I look up at all its gold trimmings and tell that Miss Greene in her ivory tower there: *We're just fine, top of the world, thank you.*

It's all working out for us, it is. When I get back to the house, Ag's telling me again, as she did yesterday, how she loves little Johnny Becker next door, his fat little face and his funny little laugh, and if she doesn't think much of his mother she doesn't complain, while Nettie thinks Ag's nothing short of a miracle herself: 'I've never seen him so still as when she's telling him one of her stories – spellbound, he is. Oh, why, what have you got there? A gardenia?' Nettie Becker knows all about them, for at least ten minutes; while Ag knows the petals are really the finest linen prized by the little folk of White Bay.

Christmas morning, we go round to Saint Gus's, and all the children are invited up to the front of the altar to sing before the solemn high Mass gets going. I've never known anything more heretical, and when they start singing the 'Bird Song', I have to hold my face in my hands as they do, 'Full many a bird did wake and fly, curoo, curoo, curoo . . .' as I'm taken by a river of gratitude I've never known, and it's a river of golden light. 'On Christmas Day in the morning . . . The lark, the dove and the red bird came . . .' they sing and I pray for our poor mother, that you might find it in your heart, Lord, to do something for her suffering, to help her, wake her up to this light and mend her somehow, keep her from the Devil's worst. And I promise you again here and forever that I will keep off the grog myself, that I will keep my sister as happy and well as she is this day. I will keep from all sinning, and keep my trust in you, Lord. For all you have given us.

And when I look up again I see Mr Adams, looking at me from across the aisle; he's with his wife and his son, a boy of about twelve, a sunny-faced kid who by some good fortune looks more like his mother than his father, but there's something not right with him, something touched and unmendable about him, rocking on his soles, singing to himself, some different tune. Mr Adams knows something about hard times and rivers of gratitude too; he nods at me: *Merry Christmas*.

Then after, into the sun, Ag and me go back to our house and plant our little tree, or our shrub as Nettie Becker said it is. And after our dinner of tinned ham and spuds and the pudding we found on the front step, Ag and me go for a walk, up to the park near the Darling Street ferry, where there's a dozen or so kids running around, playing tip. The friend she made on Sunday, Gladdy Hanrahan, waves her over: 'Aggie!' And she's in.

I roll a smoke and watch Ag running around, across the grass, and tripping up over the roots of a scrappy old gum, laughing and squealing and getting tipped. I look at the Bridge of liquorice sticks across the water: *Merry Christmas.* And I don't think life gets any better than this.

Olivia

'I'm calling for the doctor, Em – this is not some trifling thing,' says Bart from outside the bathroom door.

I'm on the inside of it, with Mother. It's Christmas night and she is terribly, unglamorously sick – just as she was twice yesterday, as well as the evening before that, and this morning, keeping us from church. I can only agree with Bart as I wring out the face washer for her again: 'I think it's for the best, Mother – you need to have a doctor see you.'

'No. No, Ollie.' Mother dismisses the idea even as she's not yet letting the edge of the lavatory seat go: 'I know what this is.'

'What? What is it?'

'Never mind. I know what this is, and it'll pass in a minute.'

'Mother, I –'

'See – it's finished.' She gets up from her knees and takes the washer from me, the band of her engagement ring clunking against the porcelain tap handle as she turns it on. As if Bart's adoration weren't obvious enough, he's given her this gigantic table-cut trapezium diamond set in platinum. Unboxed it just now, under the gigantic tree. Nothing smaller would fit in this bathroom, not to mention this Rose Bay mansion, up the Vaucluse end, which comes with its own jetty, private sea bath, and yacht, and an undisclosed number of staff – for the yacht, never mind the house. Prime view of the Bridge from the east but we're not bothered about the effect on real estate values round this way, not when we're inclined to give our future stepdaughter just a *token* Christmas offering of a sable shoulder wrap – a deliciously chocolatey, practically weightless Russian sable wrap – when I'd have been as content with Mexican chocolate and the sweet silver gypsy hoop earrings Mother bought for me: *Thank that divinely long neck of yours that you're one who can wear – oh dear, excuse me a moment, would you?*

Mother inspects her face after splashing and smiles at me now, smug: 'See – it's nothing.'

'It is not nothing,' Bart's voice booms barrister-stern from the other side of the door.

And he's quite right. A doctor acquaintance is called from up the road and, after rather a lot of hissing behind the closed bedroom door, I hear Bart declare: 'March, then – we'll bring the wedding forward to March.' And he calls for a toast of French champagne. Which Mother ominously declines: 'Better not.'

'Why?' I ask when I'm called for. 'What's all this?' I'm confused but I don't want to know either.

Mother's smile is sparkling table-cut joy: 'Darling Ollie – I must tell you now – you're going to be a big sister.'

'What?' No. Insane. This is beyond scandalous.

No, I am not going to be any such thing. I am the only child. I –

It takes every ounce of self-possession for me not to run screaming out through the gigantic plate-glass picture window in the bedroom here and throw myself into the sea.

Impossible!

But it's true, as undeniable as it is inevitable; it's written all over her beautiful face. Luminescent. As neon.

'Yes, darling, you're going to be a big sister. Come here . . .' Mother holds her arms out for me to join her on the gigantic bed, headboard a wall of genuine mahogany, where she's reclining on a gigantic ivory brocade bolster. And I do embrace her. My mother, breathe in her stale perfume and all her loveliness. She's such a slip of a woman, nothing to her; tiny, bird-slim ribcage, or my arms are so long around her it just feels that way. All too flimsy.

She whispers as she holds me: 'Won't it be wonderful having a wardrobe to yourself at last?'

'What?' I pull away.

'Here,' she's smug again with her smile, her triumph. 'You'll have your own suite of rooms. Room to create. Room to *move*.'

'No.' I can't help that escaping and once it has I can't help letting the rest of it go: 'No, I'm not living here.' The realisation stings and whirls around me: I can't live with Mother and Bart. Baby makes three, not four. This is not my Blue Heaven. This is not my anything at all.

'Don't be silly, Ollie, of course you'll live here. With me.'

'No, I won't.' I've never been clearer about anything in my life. I intend to remain at Lavender Bay. It is my home.

'Olivia Jane!'

And so begins the argument, one that threatens to rage on up till the wedding and beyond as the days unfold and everyone joins in.

Bart is gently cajoling: 'Don't you think you'll be lonely, Olivia? And won't it be better to be here, away from the bustle and noise of the bridgeworks?' *Be a good girl and comply with the pretence that you are your mother's chaperone in this house up until the wedding and I'll buy you a full-length mink.*

Glor, back from her grandparents' in the bush, is direct as always: 'Ollie, you can't. WOMAN LIVING ALONE – that's a headline usually ending in ATTACKED, BURGLED or FOUND DEAD. I don't want you on your own all the way over there – come and live with us in Randwick. You know Mum would love to have you.'

My mother is rapidly plumping infuriation: 'I forbid it, Olivia Jane. You're not twenty-one. You're not even *nineteen*.'

I give her an imperious dismissal: 'You're the one who's been insisting I grow up and hurry up about it.'

'Yes,' she hisses her exasperation, 'and not a week ago you were dragging your heels like a mule at coming out.'

Aghast at the shocking irrelevance of that now, I can only say: 'I've grown up hurriedly then, haven't I?'

'You can't afford it,' Mother appeals to reason, creasing her forehead with it. 'The rates and the bills.'

So I stomp: 'I'll demand a bigger allowance from Father then. I'll threaten him – threaten to tell everyone what sort of a man he is – if he doesn't give it to me.'

Shrill glissando of disgust: 'That'll hurt you more than it might ever hurt him.'

I know that. I know that too well: to expose Viscount Mosely, Lord Ashton Greene, would only mean humiliation, exposure of my own rejection. He will merely continue to ignore me in every importance sense, continue to remit his pittance from afar, absolving himself of me. He doesn't have to give me anything at all; unless he has a son, the whole estate will go to one of his cousin's sons anyway, whether I exist or not. Oh how I want to hurt him equally. Unfurl all this hatred and resentment coiled in my fist and one day . . .

But for now, I can only respond with another imperious dismissal: 'I don't care. I'll manage.'

And I will if the post-Christmas business at Emily Costumière is any indication. First in the door is Mrs Bloxom, Warwick's mother, with the aunt from Melbourne, after complete ensembles for the midsummer garden party at Government House, and collectively they pay for the balance owing on chaise and cabinetry. They are quickly followed by one of Cassie's funster pals, Liz Hardy, after a New Year's party frock with a bit of twirl to it, which then brings in half of Mosman, and I manage it all on my own because Mother's too ill to do anything but loll about in her sunroom at Rose Bay, sewing twirly panelling for me and telephoning the salon twice a day to remind me not to let slip to anyone that she's lolling about in scandal over there. Thirty-seven pounds, eleven shillings clear I end up with, after fabric and everything else. That's almost a yearly wage for a shop girl – in less than one month. And in the midst of retail arcade catastrophe, too: by mid-January Wilton's Ladies' Tailor has a discreet *For Lease* sign pinned to the blind drawn on the door; there's a whisper that Duke's Men and Boys on the ground floor is going too, gobbled up by the department store trade; and Cynthia Designs in the Royal, purveyors of fine crepe atrocities, won't be seeing in this new year, either. While I haven't had time to be lonely or burgled or murdered or anything but busy. Indeed, I'm studying my receipts and outgoings again to see that I haven't made a mistake with my adding-up.

And I haven't.

My smile is quite possibly smug, triumphant and something approaching rather excited about my future, and I'm gazing at the backwards *EMILY* on the window wondering if I might change it to *OLIVIA* one day, when I see someone wave at me over the lettering. A man shape.

It's Warwick. I wave back and smile at him too. Haven't seen him since that night at the Merrick, getting on for a month ago now, where he took great steps towards curing my fear of public dancing – at least two of them. Leading me onto the floor, first he trod on my toe, then, as he leapt back in dismay, he knocked a drink off a table and into a lady's lap, all with the aplomb an Oxford cut affords a man: you might be a fool but you'll never look like one. Once he got going, though, he dutifully led like a dream, and all eyes turned to the frock. Just the one dance, tripping over a quickstep for 'It Had To Be You', laughing through it just as I would trip about with Mother in the squeeze of our lounge, laughing with the whole room.

I'm laughing now as he comes through the salon door: 'Hello, Warwick.'

'Miss Greene, hello,' he says in his cheerful yet awkward way, as if he's just forgotten where and what he is while in the midst of fumbling his hat off his head. There is something endearing about him, that high Oxford waist just a little too high, half his fringe flopping across his face, a new lyric for our song: *And though your hair slips from its brill, with all your faults I love you still . . .* like the big brother I never had.

I say: 'It's Olivia, please.' Your mother and aunt just spent twelve guineas here — you can call me Dolly Dumpkins if it suits — and I must presume that's why he's here: to pick up their parcels.

But he says: 'Ah, oh, yes, of course. Um. Olivia. I was wondering if I might. If you might. Like. Ah. Oh confound it. What are you doing for dinner Saturday evening — this one coming?'

'Oh?' There's a surprise, and not an altogether pleasant one. *Oh confound it.* He's not awkward here, I see; he's dissembling, isn't he, looking up at the light fixture, now down into the Florentine lilies, everywhere but me, and I know what's afoot here: Mother. She's put him up to this just as she put him up to that dance. Sent her minion to illustrate that a girl can't live alone any more than she might dine alone. I'll show her. I tell Warwick with a shrug: 'Perhaps I'll go to the Merrick; perhaps I won't. You can join me if you like.'

He nearly chokes on his own surprise: 'Ah . . .'

And while he's thinking about that, I try catching him out in this charade: 'I say, while I've got you here, Warwick, I've been collecting opinions lately on a particular subject, and I wonder if you, as a more worldly sort of chap, might add a thought. Tell me, what do you think of working girls who live independently?'

He chuckles, nervously: 'Ah . . . well . . . what? Bachelor Betty types?' His voice cracking on the inflexion: well caught out.

'Yes,' I say, spider to fly: 'Bachelor Betty types. Go on, what do you think of them?'

'Well, it's a very popular thing in London, for the girls.' Hand in trouser pocket, going for authoritative nonchalance. 'Not all working girls, either. Some, um. Just. Ah . . . like it. I suppose.' He drops his tone a full octave, with what I suppose is dislike, and shifts his weight from foot to foot with what? Impatience? 'But. So, ah, dinner at . . . ?'

'Perhaps.' Imperious dismissal.

'Shall I telephone?'

'If you like.' Take your mama's parcels now and out you go. I'm so furious myself I can barely say good day to him. How dare Mother meddle like this. As if Warwick Bloxom could be seriously interested in sweethearting me: his mother attends private vice-regal garden parties; his father is Sir Whitney Bloxom, Federal senator and Chairman of Colonial Oil Refineries, among a string of other like and lofty positions; Warwick could well be prime minister one day. What could he possibly want *me* for? A dance-floor fling? Flop. I could laugh at that too, not very gaily.

By dinnertime I've turned devious; dropping some fabric over to Mother at Rose Bay I drop her minion in it with my own authoritative nonchalance: 'Warwick popped in today, to pick up the parcels. Had a chat about things, we two did. He said lots of girls in London bach. Didn't seem to trouble him a bit.'

Mother sighs; pushes her vegetables round her slice of poached chicken wearily. She knows I know what's going on.

So I go on: 'This is 1930, after all. Girls are allowed to do all sorts of things. Even walk down the street on their own. Spend endless nights *alone*. As I already have – haven't I?'

Mother ignores that remonstration too, even if it's damn well true; all those nights I've spent alone, lying awake listening to the ferries tooting the loneliest sound in the world across the water, to me, into my heart, as she wined and dined and danced, and she waves it all away with her napkin: 'You're turning into a flapper. From wallflower to flapper in five minutes.'

'Flapper?' I give her a piece of my condescension: 'Flappers are terribly last decade, Mother. Get with the times. Or . . .' She won't be getting so much as to the Merrick for the next little while at least, and this spider grows claws: 'Or *don't*. At least I'm not the one living in sin with –'

'Do not say another word. After all I have done for you . . .' I have hurt her: she stabs a piece of carrot on her plate but doesn't eat it; she tells it: 'You really can't see past the nose on your face, can you?'

Bart conciliates, touching her hand: 'Oh, let her have her way, Em.' He glances at me: *Speak to your mother again like that and I might stab you with this fork.* 'We'll always be here when things don't work out to Olivia's liking.'

Things will work out, though. I'll make them work out.

I'll have to now, won't I.

Yo

'But I don't want to go to St Gus's school,' Ag says as we're coming back from the park, the last Sunday of the holidays, and there's that whine in her voice. Ag wants to go to Nicholson Street School, because that's where Gladdy Hanrahan goes. I want her to go where she's happy to go, but how can I let her go to a public school? It's heavy on me – how can I not send her to St Gus's? She can't not go to a Catholic school.

There are good reasons not to go to St Gus's, though. They play sports against St Ben's – football and athletics, if I remember my non-attendance rightly – and although it's unlikely that Ag will be any more talented than me in that regard, I don't want her going near the old neighbourhood for any reason. There's also the cost. I won't have her being the charity case the O'Keenans have always been, but by the time the rent has come out and the union fees and groceries and the gas and the coal, and the caps I'm losing at the rate of one a fortnight and Nettie's shilling for the wash, I've not got much change out of my wages. I could do with that Child Endowment, it would go a long way towards the school fees, but I can't ask for that – I can't take the risk of Welfare deciding I can't have Ag with me. I don't know if they'd yet know that I've even got her; it's doubtful our mother's let them know – she needs that Endowment for her Royal Reserve. And that's a fact that makes me think Welfare won't take Ag off me; it's been more than six weeks now, and we're settled. I've fixed the kitchen floor, a black and blue thumbnail attesting to it. We've even bought linen for her bed, Egyptian cotton, from Hordern's, marked down fifty percent; Ag saw the sale in the paper.

'Yoey?' Ag's wanting her answer about school.

I could toss a coin in the morning, or ask Nettie what she reckons – she said she'd take her the first day and pick up the form and what-have-you for me – but I haven't had a spare ten hours lately for listening to Nettie go on. Haven't had a spare ten minutes, I've been too concerned with schooling issues of my own: when I'm not losing my guts catching hot cocks three hundred and two feet in the sky, I'm losing my mind over taking the examination on Monday week, on the tenth, to see if I can get into Sydney Tech to start them classes for the Black Arts, as the metal trades are called, which I have to do if I'm going to get a look-in at a boilermaking apprenticeship. If I do get in it'll be Wednesday nights starting from the twenty-sixth of February, and Saturday nights extra hours on dog shift in the workshops, and a weekly pay decrease of £1/6/- for the privilege. I have to talk to Nettie about that too, or maybe Mr Adams, see if Ag might have tea with them Wednesday and Saturday nights. If I get in. Jesus, but I'm getting sick about that exam. I've got a letter from Mr Harrison, the foreman, recommending me to the classes, but I have to pass the test to say I'm up to third form standard of learning. I didn't finish sixth class. I know I can do it, Mr Adams has given me all the books and that, it's dead simple, and I will pass it just for all the trouble he's gone to on my account and how miraculous it is that he reckons I'm good enough, but it's all looking too hard at this minute. The tech is at Ultimo, on Mary Ann Street near the tin pressers on Hackett our brother Michael was working for, before . . . Is it even worth it?

Losing that £1/6/- wages, just for the first year, but it's five years of studying for the journeyman's ticket. I don't know if –

'Yoey!' Ag raises her voice at me, pulling on my hand.

So I raise mine back: 'Oi. You –'

'Oi Yo!' Someone calls out ahead of us. 'Yo O'Keenan, that you?' A lanky stride and hair sticking up like straw. It's a Finnerty, but I don't know which one of them till he's just about in front of us. It's Jim, one of the middle brothers, and he's got a big smile on his head, happy to see me.

'Ay Jim,' I say, not all that happy to see him. 'What are you doing round here?'

'Working,' he says, explaining the smile. 'Me and Luke both – we got work at the power station, on the coal.'

Too close to where we live; I don't want him to know that, but he might know anyway. Ag's recognised him as well, and slipped round the back of me. I tell him: 'Yeah? Good on you.'

He says: 'What you doing round here, then?'

I shrug: 'Not a lot.' I'm not telling him anything.

And he doesn't ask. But he wants to tell me something. He starts rolling a smoke and he says: 'Good on you, for getting out, you know. The cops got called and that – there was a bit of a barney on at your place. Your mum went right off in the street, yelling and carrying on. But they never come after you that night. They won't, the cops. You know, everyone's sorry about what happened to Michael.'

I just nod. Are they? Tell Michael that. It's good to know the cops didn't look for me and Ag, though. We have police approval; maybe Welfare won't object to our having left the Neighbourhood either. Bit of a barney on at our place, yelling and carrying on: business as usual. Jesus. One day I will hear our mother is mercifully dead, too; half of me wants that, for her to be at peace, in your protection at last, Lord.

Jim shakes his head as he tells me more: 'Jack's gone in with Hammo, if you haven't heard. They're up at the Cross now. Some new swy joint Tex has got going.'

The Blue Mile

That's not good; I say: 'The spoon.'

'Yeah,' says Jim, and we're both shaking our heads, lamenting like we just found out Jack's got TB. He might as well have.

I'm inside a prayer for him too, as Jim says: 'See us for a drink at the Merton, on Victoria Road, if you're around here? Saturday arvies we knock off at three.'

'Maybe.' But I'm shaking my head: not a blind or bleeding chance. Drinking with the Finnertys, losing half my pay down my neck. What a pity I won't have Saturdays free. I've already opened my Mathematics textbook to Practical Applications of Geometry, and I'm applying it to Jim's face: he's not two years older than me and he's got the hollowed-out cheeks of forgoing food for grog already. He's been drinking since yesterday arvie, I reckon, and he's only just heading back to Chippo now, eyes on the road looking for lost tuppence to get there. Walking advertisement for Saturday arvie closing. I tell him: 'Say hello to Luke for me. See you.' And we're walking; I don't ever want to see any of them again.

'Yoey?' Ag's pulling on my hand again ten seconds later. 'Can I go to Nicholson Street School with Gladdy?' Desperate; she'll die if I don't let her: 'Please?'

I say: 'Yes, Ag, all right. You can.' Catholic school didn't do anything for any of us, did it.

'Oh Yoey, you're the best big brother in the world.'

'I'm the only one.' All my worries bite round my guts again with the reality of it.

'But even if I had ten thousand and fifteen of them you'd still be the best.' She swings on my arm and I lift her up and onto my shoulder like she's made of nothing.

I say to her: 'What have you been eating to make you so light, then? Dandelion seeds?'

I've got strong and my sister's laughter is all that matters. I'm never looking back again.

We get back to Fawcett Street and Nettie's out the front with her ciggie: 'Hello there. Lovely evening, isn't it?' Waiting for us;

waiting for anyone to say hello there to, her John's such a shitfully grim bastard. He's not a drinker, but he's one that could probably do with a loosening ale; he's that caught up with himself, you're lucky to get a nod from him to acknowledge your existence. Nettie's lonely as they come, and always got a frown on over her pretty smile; head full of worries, I reckon. Maybe I won't ask her about looking after Ag evenings; she's got enough on her plate trying to keep the baby quiet and everything *just right* for Mr Shitful.

But I do interrupt whatever she's jawing on about now to ask her about the school: 'What do you reckon about that Nicholson Street Primary, is it all right?'

'Oh yes.' She takes a long drag; she knows all about it. 'It's the best school in the district, from here to Leichhardt, better than the Superior near St Augustine's, don't send a child there – you know they throw stones at each other across Eaton Street? I've seen the little beggars – *Catholics, Catholics ring the bell, Protestants, Protestants go to hell.* Butter wouldn't melt on a Sunday. Anyway, that Nicholson Street school, yes, it's a very good school – more kiddies going on to high school from there than anywhere, and not only because Jack Lang got rid of the fees for secondary. Oh, we can only hope and pray he gets back in, can't we? That Jack Lang . . .'

Here we go; now she's mentioned him, we're in for the long haul: her Jack Lang. You'd think they were on together before she married Grim Shitful, the way she goes on about him. He's brilliant, and so handsome, and he has such a bearing about him that women faint in the street just seeing him walk by. According to Nettie Becker: 'With that strong jaw of his, like Moruya granite itself . . .'

I don't know much about this Jack Lang, except that he's a hard man and someone once said he looks a bit like my father, like he'd drive your teeth through the back of your skull if you crossed him. He was the premier before this one – Bavin, is it? I should pay more attention to politics. Mr Adams is hoping Mr Lang gets back in too; in fact the entire nine unions on the Bridge are hoping that. They want the Big Fella, as they call him, to do something with all the coal disputes going on – there's a stoppage at Birchgrove over wages right now, miners scabbing on engine-drivers like chooks fighting over a button – and the Bank of England has said it won't give any more credit to New South Wales if it keeps up, and that could mean a stoppage of the bridgeworks. I don't know what this Jack Lang will do about wage disputes or banks robbing people. I remember when he brought in the forty-four hours week, when I'd just started at Foulds, and everyone had a laugh: no such thing as a forty-four hour week in a non-unionised shop – you're praying for nearer fifty just for a decent wage. But if there's not money to pay wages, there's not money to pay wages, and you lose your job, don't you, and I wouldn't give my money to a bank if you paid me. Balmain is different, though: everyone's political in Balmain, specifically Labor Party political, as it's here, up at the Unity Hall pisser, that the party started, says Mr Ad –

'Eoghan?' Nettie's got her sour face on, tapping the ash off her ciggie at the gardenia. 'I said, so why don't you come in here for your tea?'

'What? I'm sorry, I –'

'Sometimes I swear you're not listening to a word I say.'

'I'm sorry, I –'

'John's taken the dog shifts now,' she explains, with her smile back on. 'Only be home Mondays and Tuesday nights, and the rest of the time he'll be sleeping, the poor thing. I don't like being on my own at nights, as you know. I'm so thankful I've got such a good neighbour in you.'

She puts her hand on mine, on the low fence between us.

'And being such, would it be too much to ask for us to be at your house during the day, so that Johnny doesn't wake him, while he's playing?' she says, letting her voice go up, like a girl's.

'That'll be fine . . .' I look at our hands. Hers on mine.

I know I'm being asked for more than the use of the house in the day. For the life of me I don't know why her John wouldn't find her appealing enough to keep her happy in that regard. If you look past the unceasing chatter and the know-everything horseshit, she is definitely a good-looking woman, takes care of herself, lipstick on and her hair always nice. I'm not that sort of fella, though. I've never been with a woman; not that I haven't devoted an unreasonable amount of my time to thinking about it. But maybe, if it keeps everyone happy . . . maybe I should think about it now.

And I catch that thought just in time: maybe Sister Joe and Madigan never did anything for me at St Ben's, maybe Catholic school is a steaming pile along with the Church in its entirety, but my God, my religion, has done everything to get me here. It's the roof over my head, every week I've paid the rent, every job I've ever had, every meal my sister's eaten, every bashing I've got through, since I can remember and never more so than now. My faith is the only thing that's mine that can't ever be taken away; the only thing that can set me apart from the rest, from my family, as decent. As good for something. I won't be going with Nettie Becker. Even if there's a part of me with a different opinion, insisting on it right now. Ignore it. It's not going to happen. Not for me. I'm aware of the earthly consequences of it, too, should faith ever fail me: Jack Callaghan went with this girl a couple of years ago, Mary Lightfoot was her name; she had an abortion at that doctor's on Bourke Street, he gave her the money for it and that, looked after her, and she fucking well died.

No. I move my hand away.

'Lamb roast almost done, love – and it's just me on my own. Little Johnny's asleep now too. What do you say?'

I say no.

I'm smelling that roast, though. Lamb and pumpkin. It smells good.

But Ag shifts round behind me; she doesn't want whatever Nettie's got in mind for us. We've got a tin of beans and mash for our tea, and all the butter we can eat. Just that butter itself is daily feasting to us. We've always got butter in the cupboard now. We've got everything, everything we need.

I tell Nettie: 'No, no thanks.' But I can't put her off altogether, can I? Can't put her offside: we need her, too. I tell her: 'Not tonight; I've got books to be getting on with. My exam's tomorrow week. Maybe another time . . .'

Olivia

'The boy is in love with you,' Mother spits through pins as I tack the lace train to the back of her wedding gown in her sunroom at Rose Bay. 'What must he do, throw himself on the ground in supplication to have your attention?'

'No,' I say, moving round to the front of her to check the pull on the charmeuse. Baby is starting to show, and if I keep my mind on the technical problem of its concealment then I can almost forget it's there, and that it will be born by the time they return from London – in a year's time. How convenient it is that Bart managed to organise a sabbatical at the Old Bailey? How convenient, too, that he convinced you to indulge me these past few months so that I might become accustomed to living alone. Working alone. Being alone. As if I'd never had a bit of practice at being not quite the most important thing in your life. How *in*convenient is this charmeuse, though – the shimmer in the weave is hitting exactly the wrong spot.

'Ollie, I must have dropped you on your head when you were a baby.' She sees the sheen herself, hand smoothing over it. What to do? 'This isn't turning him down for a night at the Merrick, you know.'

The Blue Mile

'I know.' Apart from the first time, I haven't deliberately turned him down, three times in all now – I have genuinely been too busy to go dancing or dining. With three gowns for this very event Mother is referring to. The farewell dinner for the Governor, Admiral Sir Dudley de Chair, and Lady de Chair, tomorrow night. Warwick's invited me – or rather Mrs Bloxom has, in place of her niece, who couldn't attend. I don't know if Warwick – or Rick as he's known to his chums – is in love with me or what, but I don't want him to be. He is a nice boy, superlatively nice, really, and his attention is flattering, more flattering than anything I've ever known – barely believable, in fact. The bouquet of riotously delightful dahlias he sent me for my birthday, *Dearest Olivia, For You, Warmest regards, Rick,* was just about the warmest thing ever – a veritable blaze of autumn sunshine. But I don't love him back, and I won't. I'm not one for boys and being in love and that's that.

Mother turns to the cheval to look at the problem front-on. 'Hm. Lace panel, down the centre. Three inches – distract the eye.' Then she looks up at me behind her again, thinking, sizing me: 'If you're worried about matters with his Lordship coming out to ruin things, don't be. Leona Bloxom only finds you more attractive for it – any aristocratic connection is better than none to them.'

'They *know*?' Oh dear God.

'Bart mentioned something, yes, to clear the way, sound them out about the . . . unusual circumstances – but the Bloxoms are discreet. Grown-ups – they know these things happen.'

I could stab her in the backside with my squiggle snippers for things *happening*. 'What have you been doing? Marrying me off behind my back?'

'No, darling, no – I would never do any such thing. Warwick is in *love* with you, you silly girl. The boy is in torment for you. Honestly . . .'

'Well, honestly, I'm not in love with him.' And I certainly won't be going to the Governor's dinner with him now, torment or not. They *know*. My torment. My Father: whom the entire English-speaking world now knows is in Kenya – on safari with a Hollywood film actress by the name of Gigi McAllister. There's a newsreel just come out, apparently, dead lions and zebras, luxurious tent facilities, native slaves, the whole grown-up atrocity, and I won't be going to a picture theatre anytime soon to witness it. Won't be going to the Governor's dinner as a sad little aristocratic pelt for the Bloxoms either.

'You should go with him then to be *seen*,' Mother insists: 'Think of your business if you can't think of him.'

My business. Yes. OLIVIA COSTUMIÈRE. I am mentally scraping off that EMILY right now, with my fingernails. But I am not so mercenary, not as she is. I tell her: 'I'm doing all right as it is, thank you. I don't need to *go* to the dinner. I'm an artist, not some dilettante. People come to me at my salon – I don't chase them.'

Glissando of hilarity: 'You are becoming arrogant, my daughter.'

'You made me,' I retort, unbuttoning the gown, and as I do glance out of the windows of this sunroom, across the water, and I see the Bridge, the arch almost finished. From this distance the arms of it seem only a couple of inches apart, and I see that boy up there, in my mind, skipping across the breach, dancing over his words, turning to run, light on his feet, over the span. The sun on his face, in his eyes; the only boy I seem ever to have seen. The Christmas dustman boy. Deep blue boy who cares so for his little girl. *You couldn't find it in your heart to do me a favour in return, could you?* Figment boy. And I tell the Bridge: I'll go to the ball if you send me *that* boy – in a white tux and midnight trousers.

'Come to London with us, darling,' Mother changes tack. 'Won't you reconsider?'

No. I'm not going to London, despite Bart's offer to have me set up there. London is not where I want to go, where this upcoming summer season promises fifty-three and a half shades of beige wallpaper with contrasting trims of Ashes of Roses, a bloodless pink inspired by that infamous scent of *phlergh* especially designed with a base note of musky Parisienne contempt for the English. Nothing original, nothing inspiring comes out of London. I don't think I'd fit in, and if I ever were to go, I'd want to set myself up, thank you.

I kiss Mother goodbye and take the ferry home, my carpet bag heavy with wedding gown, and my mind stuffing itself full of events and busyness beyond this week. There's the April racing carnival coming up, and then the welcome party for the Games in May, the new Governor, Air Vice-Marshal Sir Philip Game and Lady Game – and that'll be a daytime event, too. I think it will be a perfect time for my Bridge series of hats to appear: purples, teals and bronzes, some winter drama. Min Bromley should be out of post-ditchment mourning by then too – I think I might send her a cheering note, tell her I've designed something especially for her. Perhaps I can put Warwick on to her, too, kill two birds . . . hm, they would look quite good as a pair, sketch them into matching tweeds and stitch them up together. *Voilà!* By the time I've switched ferries for the north side I've solved all the city's problems and my Bridge series is such a hit I'm waving away streamers, tooting out of the Quay for the Parisienne summer in a whirl of my old-favourite flame-red cape.

Dreaming. Dreams that are as delicate as Mother's champagne charmeuse. Let the water at it and it'll shrink and warp to rags. I hear a woman cry out as I take the steps up from the wharf: 'No, please. Please, no!' and I look up to find her at the top, outside the flats above the vehicular punt ramp. Men are lugging her furniture and effects into the street. She's been evicted. The third I've seen in as many weeks. I look away, ashamed. Why do they choose the evening to turn them out into the street? Why not the morning? Why are people cruel to each other?

I hurry home, with the chill breeze at my back, and bolt the door behind me, keep my dreams shut in and safe from harm. Stitch by stitch, I fix my wishes into Mother's lace panel, get it done, out of the way, not thinking unkind thoughts such as *Why don't you make your own stupid wedding gown?* but rather seeing her walk radiantly down the aisle of St Andrew's Presbyterian a week from now, with a supper reception at the Royal Sydney Golf Club, before casual farewell drinks at the Tulip Restaurant on Wednesday afternoon, the day they depart. Streamered away by the uppest of up crowd, people I don't know and don't particularly want to know. So long as they continue to buy my hats and frocks.

Money in the bank for my own ticket . . .

Tooooot.

I know I've fallen asleep, my head on the table by my lamp, my hand still holding my pincushion, but I can't rouse from this dream. The woman from the flats is climbing the North Claw towards the breach. She's going to jump off. I know she is. Everyone is watching her from the wharf, pointing, but no one can stop her. She hits the water with a great big smash. Echoing across the harbour.

Hammering. From the workshops, of course, and it's not quite dawn. Roused now and compelled blinking into another day, I'm on the ferry again, beating the rush, and yawning up at the Bridge, into the breach. Good God but it's breathtaking now it's almost done: what's the industrial equivalent of haute couture? There is sadness in its beauty, though: what'll they do, all the men up there, when it's finished and there's no work to go to? Engineering Wonder of the World complete; move along. Women cry, *please no*; men walk the streets, dragging their shame to the Labour Exchange. My mary-janes clipping double-time through the hush of Pitt Street, so early I've even beaten the barrowmen.

But not Mr Jabour. The grille slides open on the Oriental Emporium, and he looks up from his keys, surprised: 'Olivia, dear.' Smiling his fond sleepy smile: 'It is too early – you are working too hard. Gloria is worried about you, so am I. We never see you.'

'I'm all right.' I glance up the ground floor at all the sale signs in all the windows; Electrolux is throwing vacuums away for March, if you want one; Loughton's Tableware is closing down up in the gods. Only the Jabours seem untouched by catastrophe. I spy the brass bottle on the sideboard in there, the ruby and sapphire glass of the stopper glinting in some shaft of light coming in from somewhere I can't see – that'll be the genie that's looking after them. Or more likely that they only deal in the finest quality and most fabulous things – never out of style – and Mr Jabour, I now remember, has a new shipment from Iran just arrived, which is why he's here at this hour too. And why I'm now peering harder as if I might see through the boxes stacked by the cutting table to spy the treasure within.

'I suppose you are all right,' he chuckles softly. 'The young are always right. I was, when I was your age. I was exactly the same. Rushing around, working, working, working. I would hawk out on my own, from Broken Hill right down to Adelaide, and then go all the way back up to Sydney to buy. If I missed one sale, one bargain, one train, I thought: This is a disaster. It was the middle of the depression in the nineties then – and I went and opened my first shop, up on Flinders Street. It was madness. I don't know what I was trying to prove.'

He looks at me shrewdly for a moment, and then adds: 'That shop: it burned down to the ground in my fifth week of business. I don't know why – someone didn't want me there. But it taught me a good lesson: don't want things too much. It's better to slow down, be happy with what you have before you want anything at all. Then, what you really want – it will come. It is a riddle, this life.' And now he asks the riddle of me: 'What do *you* want, dear, from all this hard work?'

'What do I want?' I don't know. I want my ticket to Paris. To the world: New York. Then Madrid. Cairo. Shanghai. I want my designs to be famous across the globe. Infamous. And on my afternoons off, I want to be muse to Matisse, the maestro's odalisque swathed in nothing but midnight velvet chiffon, lounging on a magic-carpet spun from lapis sky. With a copper fringe. Balancing a cherry on the end of my aquiline nose. I want articles about me appearing in *Vogue,* in French, to wipe the self-satisfied, stupid smile off Cassie Fortescue's face and all like her – if they could manage to read an article that length in any language. All things fantastical is what I want, and I don't know anything beyond my fantasies, my delicate and secret fantasies prone to shrinkage, warpage and utter devastation if subjected to a rainy day, and Mr Jabour knows I don't.

He says again: 'Be happy.' And then he rubs his round genie belly, changing the subject and not changing it at all: 'So, what is it about this boy Warwick I've been hearing about? He is a lawyer, yes?' Which means he has met the first criteria of Mr Jabour's prospective husband list, thanks for sharing that confidence with your whole family and half of Beirut, Glor.

I tell Mr Jabour: 'Yes, he's a lawyer, but he's not my boy.'

'Why not? Gloria says he's going to be a barrister.' *What more could you possibly want?* says Mr Jabour's face. Gloria's Paul Gallagher works for the firm that negotiated Mr Jabour's son-in-law's Tycoon shirt factory contracts with Gowings, so he's two rungs up the criteria list already. The road to happiness is paved with lawyers, especially if they are also going to become good sons-in-law from respected Eastern Suburbs Catholic families that religiously vote Labor. It's true: Gloria has won the happiness jackpot and knows it with all her heart: Paul is going to give her half-a-dozen beautiful Irish-Lebanese babies and a house in Dover Heights: they've already picked out the plot, new estate off Military Road, ocean view.

Just as I know – the one thing I *do* know – that happiness doesn't include any of that sort of thing for me; I tell Mr Jabour: 'Warwick is a nice boy, but he won't make me happy.'

He gives that idea an ambivalent shrug, and as I turn to the stairs, he laughs me up them: 'I will find you a nice boy to make you happy.' Great booming laughter thundering around the stairwell and all through the empty arcade.

'Run, Olivia!' I do: laughing too, but scooting up and round the landings as if the genie's after me.

'Come back down in an hour, though, my dear!' he calls. 'I will have Persian tussahs for you! Special price!'

Yo

The first I hear of it is the quiet, some kind of stillness, even before Tarzan drops the gun as the workshop siren goes. Clarkie's calling up to us with some word that's come along from the phone: 'Stop work! All men down!' Something's happened below.

In the cradle going down, Merv, Mr Adams's holder-up, says, 'Reckon I seen a splash, to the northeast,' but no one says anything else. No one knows anything except that the whole bridgeworks have stopped, even the shops. It's something bad.

'Addison,' we're told on the barge by Mr Harrison, who's telling us especially. It was Nipper Addison. I don't know him, except that he was a Pom and married a couple of months ago, not long after I started, and I had to put in a couple of shillings I didn't have for his wedding. He was a boilermaker's assistant. He was twenty-five. He could have been me. He fell a hundred and fifty feet, from the bottom chord, near where the road will soon be hung.

'Nah,' Mr Harrison is saying, 'it's not the fall that killed him. It seems he's drowned, poor lad. He came up – half-a-dozen dived in for him but he went under again before anyone could get to him.

They're still looking for him now.'

Then there's just quiet. Just the water splashing against the barge, then the engine winding up. Someone calling out off a pontoon a hundred yards away or so, still looking for Nipper Addison.

'You go home, Eoghan, if you need to,' says Mr Adams as we pull in to the dock; they're sending everyone home that works at height, should they need to get home, get to a pub, get away.

But I can't move from the dock. No one can. Everyone from the shops has come out into the sun. There's nothing going on, four hours of the shift to go, but no one can do anything but roll a smoke and not say much. My mind is charging, though, mostly with the thought: that could have been me. And the other thought: I have to get off working at height. I have to get into the shops full-time, dog shift every night if I have to. What would happen to Ag if I was killed? I can't dive; I can't even swim. Tarzan and them lunatics – Sean Lonergan, Mick Doolan, Vince Kelly – they chuck themselves off coal gantries bare-chested and drink their winnings afterwards. I'm not one of them.

Neither was Nipper Addison. Not reckless, nothing monkey-nutted about him: he was double-checking a bolt when he slipped, I've heard several say. Just slipped. No reason for it. 'Just bad luck, poor Nip,' I hear someone from his own gang say now. 'He was that slow and careful he couldn't keep worms in a tin. How could it happen to him?'

'All right, come round, come round!' The blacksmith, Tom Canning, who usually calls a union meeting, calls a meeting now, as Mrs Daly, the lady who does the pays, comes out of the shops and gets into a cab; they're sending her to Mrs Addison, in Naremburn, to tell her before the rest of the world does. Naremburn: I've never been there, but I've seen it from the sky, every day. The suburbs to the north: all the tin roofs happy in amongst all the trees, gum trees and oak trees; all sorts of trees. Making a home there, they were, the Addisons.

Jesus. I'm shivering with the question still: what would happen to Ag if I was killed? I miss most of what Tom Canning is saying as I think round and round it, while my hand goes into my pocket with everyone else's for the collection, for Mrs Addison, in addition to what she'll get from Dorman Long and the union. Whatever she ends up with, it won't be enough; it won't bring him back. But it will be something; she will be looked after. Jesus, but would Ag be?

Mr Adams has got up now to speak, standing on top of a diesel drum, and he calls out to us in his no-horseshit way: 'No man is replaceable.' He stops there and the quiet returns, the stillness, and it stills my mind as well; there's no man here not listening as he goes on.

'Every man who leaves hearth and home daily to go to work is a soldier, make no mistake about that, gentlemen. Each and every one of you standing here, each man across this city and across this world, labours for his sustenance, his family, and for his country. You are soldiers who do not kill and destroy but who create our world for us. Like a soldier, the worker does not know whether this day will see his death on the job, or if he will survive. Unlike a soldier, the worker is not revered, nor celebrated. Every day he comes home safe to his family, it is a day like any other day. The rubbish is collected, roads and bridges and buildings are constructed, our coal is mined to light our homes, to warm our hearths, the trams and the trains and the buses run, shop doors open and close. Let us this day remember him who will not go home.'

There could not be a man here whose head is not hung in prayer.

'Each one of you is irreplaceable, to your families, your communities, to your mates and to your union. Be proud, gentlemen, even in the grief of this day, that our safety record is the envy of the world. Our Bridge is the envy of the world. When you come back to work tomorrow, in every strike of the hammer, we will remember Sydney Edward Addison. We will remember those who have died before him here: Robbie Craig, Tom McKeown, Ang Peterson, Perc Poole, Ed Shirley, Nat Swandells, John Webb, Bill Woods. We will remember them today and every day we behold this Bridge of their creation, and may there be no more leave us in such tragedy.'

Amen.

The drinking will begin at the Rag and Famish on the corner of Miller and Berry, with the Engineers picking up the tab. I'm not going. I've gone straight back to prayer, shivering now with some strange relief: thank the Lord it wasn't me that fell.

I start walking away, away from everyone, and I doubt that it'll be noticed I'm gone, not today. I walk round along the back of Lavender Bay, down the path by the rail line, and, Lord, I'm praying with every step. I don't ask for much. I don't ask for impossible things or for anything a man doesn't need. I don't ask why you took Nipper Addison from his family, just as I don't ask why you took my brothers Michael and Brendan and our mother and father from mine. I only ever ask you that you let me live. Let me get on.

My eyes are suddenly full. With strange tears. For my family. Not until today have I grieved. Why today? I don't know. Maybe it's because no one has paid for the loss of my family and no one's ever going to. The brewery won't pay; no hat around up at the Sandringham for the death of my brother Michael either. But the company and the union and all Nipper Addison's mates will pay his family, to see that they are all right.

Mrs Addison will be looked after.

But my brother Michael was never looked after. No one in the Neighbourhood is sorry for what happened to him, not truthfully; only sorry for themselves, and what his life and his death and his sinning says about poverty. Michael won't be remembered by anyone, barely even by me. Grey and scarred and fucked rotten, on the kitchen table. He was an arsehole is the truth, but I'm not too certain that was wholly his fault. Nothing was Brendan's fault, either. Where's he, my little brother? Is he dead too? Brendan never gave anyone any trouble; you'd hardly know he was there at all. He was a good kid, but he could never get a look-in for a job: wrong time, wrong place, wrong horseshit trade depression. Or they just didn't like the look of him. Didn't see him. I didn't either. Some kid I was yelling at to get up to the shops for bread, for our tea: *What the fuck have you been doing all day?* Until he didn't come home at all, I didn't take in that he'd left the Neighbourhood until I hadn't seen him a fortnight.

I have to stop, lean against a lamp pole near me, near the public baths, closed up now summer's finished. I roll another smoke. Look down as I do and see there's a piece of broken glass on the path right by my left foot, the sun catching it. It's green, a muddy green, like the water washing up against the rubble stone of the shore here. I kick it with my toe, and it falls away somewhere down into the stones. Disappeared. What happened to my family? My mother and my father, they must have hoped for something better once, mustn't they? They got on a ship across the world for it, didn't they? Why did they come here then? What for? I don't know.

I see a ferry heading in towards the wharf across the bay, and I run for it.

I am not my brothers. I am not my family. It's just me and Ag, and when I woke this morning I was still smiling, still thinking I was something special from having been picked out of the class last night to demonstrate the planing machine. I've only been at Tech a week. I'm a fucking hero there, among the young fellas, and the teacher Mr Simpson, too, just for breathing: because I work on the Bridge. Jesus, I can still hardly believe I got eighty-seven out of a hundred in the Maths test.

I'm not going to fall. I'm going to get up tomorrow morning and catch hot cocks, because that's what I have to do, to keep on this path, up off the rocks. I will spare a thought for Nipper Addison as I do, but I'll be doing it for Ag. Lord, just let me see through a year at this: then I know she'll be looked after by them. By then, maybe Mr Adams would adopt her if I was killed. Would you do that for me? Would you give Ag to the Adamses? They'd love a daughter. But would they? Mrs Adams has her hands full with their Kenny, on twenty-four-hour shift for his needs and his moods. I don't know that they could take another child. Anyway, I'm not going to get killed, am I. If I make this ferry, I'm not going to get killed. Jesus, round the back of these endless jetties and boathouses here, I catch sight of the ferry tying up: if I make it, I will see out the year, I will see out my training, I will be a boilermaker and Ag will go on to high school and she'll become a teacher one day. She'll get a scholarship to the university, she's so smart with all her reading. She will be happy, and I won't get killed.

I make the ferry, it's going straight on to Balmain too, and by the time I've got there I've made that many bargains with God and whoever else might be listening I'm wretched from it. I'm so tired I could just lie down on the street and be done with it. I could do with a drink. For the first time since the night we left the Neighbourhood, I really am in want of an ale, to feel the cleansing cool down my neck, the warm nothing in my head. Just one schooey; I'll just have the one. But before I even see the awning of the Commercial, I find a friendly face looking at me: it's Mrs Buddle, blessed Mother of Darling Street Wharf, outside her little wooden house watering her flowers.

'Hello, dear!' she waves. Eighty if she's a day. She gave Ag some of her geraniums last Sunday, in a pot – waiting for us to come by, as we do on our way back and forth from the park here. They have a chat just about every time we go by. Because this is home; our home. I'm going to fix the loose palings on Mrs Buddle's front fence this Sunday coming; give them a coat of paint one day too. I could lie down on this footpath just to claim it as mine. She says, sharp as a tack: 'You're early today.'

I tell her: 'There was an accident.'

'Oh no, poor love.' She looks at the Bridge behind me, rising up over my shoulder, and she sighs for the thousand tragedies of it, asking me: 'Do you want a cuppa, my love?'

'Not just now, thanks.' I don't want to look at the Bridge for a bit, or talk about it; I tell her: 'I have to get home.' Wait for Ag to get in from school and then we'll go to the pictures, I think, that Charlie Chaplin one is on, *The Circus*, at the National. Just . . . get away.

She nods: 'You go and have some peace and quiet.'

I won't be getting that: little Johnny Becker will be tearing round the house while his father sleeps next door, and I'll be glad of it: he's a funny little kid. There's his mother, Nettie, out the front, having her ciggie as I come round the corner. Always alone with it, and I've finally worked out why: no one can stand her and her know-all gibbering.

'Eoghan,' she smiles when she sees me, still hopeful for it. 'What are you doing home?'

Before she can talk over me I tell her: 'There was an accident, someone drowned.'

'Oh my heavens, you don't say. What happened?'

She doesn't really care; she just wants the details so she can take them up to the shops, telling everyone she's the first to know. I shake my head; I'm not giving her anything.

She follows me into the house. Johnny's playing with his tin train, filling the truck with coal chips from the bin by the fireplace: getting filthy, having a great old time, and I'd like to join him. I look at the bin: I made it from an old pallet after Ag found the idea for it in the paper; good as a bought one.

Nettie's saying: 'Why don't you go and lie down; I'll bring you in a brandy.'

'No,' I say to both. 'Thanks.'

'Sometimes it helps, you know . . .' She puts her hand on my face and leaves it to trail down my neck.

It stirs me so that I grab her by the wrist, not gently, and I tell her again: 'No.'

'You don't have to be mean about it,' she pulls her hand away.

'Not mean, Nettie. I just don't want that, right?' It's the wrong day for her to have pushed the issue, and I have to tell her now what I've been wanting to tell her for the last few weeks, tell her today because life can be too brutally short for horseshit: 'I don't want you in my house anymore. Right?'

However meanly that might have come out, I don't want her near my business anymore. I don't want her near me.

Her eyes go wild: the look of a banshee.

I reckon she's going to smash me, but she says, as if I'm filth: 'I can have better than you.'

I say: 'Well, you'd better go and get it then.'

She gives me a last look of hatred before she drags Johnny up by the arm, leaving his train smash on the hearth stone, leaving him screaming, leaving this house. Slamming the front door.

Slamming this and that inside her own home, that's how much she cares for peace and quiet for her man. Telling me by all this carry-on that there will be consequences. I don't care, whatever she does or says. No one listens to her anyway.

I lie down on the old sofa and wonder if the previous tenants had to leave it here in their rush to get away from her. I close my eyes. Wait for Ag. She'll be pleased Nettie won't be here anymore when she gets home from school. She never did warm to her, only little Johnny and she'll survive without him tipping coal dust all round the floor. She'll be eight in May, on the tenth. She's old enough to get herself to and from school. She can go and help Mrs Buddle on Saturday and Wednesday nights, give her a shilling for the wash if we can't manage it all ourselves. Or Ag can stop with the Hanrahans – her and Gladdy, giggling Gerties having the stay-overs they keep whining for. If Mrs Adams doesn't grab her first: Ag is always welcome round there, and she'd only ever be a help with Kenny, he's always that happy to see her – she marches round the yard to his strange beat, making up songs about castles built of cheese and great armies of possums and rats, making him laugh along like no one else does. We have other friends. We'll be looked after.

The Blue Mile

Nettie Becker can go and do herself a favour.

Nipper Addison died today.

I cover my face with my hands and I pray for him; for him and for his new young wife and all her hopes come to nothing. No amount of being looked after can do anything for that.

It's just luck. Brilliant one minute; horseshit the next. Nothing personal. Just a test of faith.

I am alive.

I did not fall.

And when I open my eyes again, Ag's flying through the door: 'Yo-Yo!'

Light of my life. How could I not have faith? I might go and see about getting me some swimming lessons, though . . .

Olivia

'Lady Game is partial to a fine hat, so I've discovered.' Leona Bloxom gives me a scheming smile, as she signs her cheque for her own vice-regal welcome ensemble, as if Lady Game had cabled her personally from the ship when it docked yesterday in Fremantle, to tip her off. 'She is particular, however. Low-brimmed and modest, the style of which you yourself are fond. Her outfits are always of a certain simplicity. A continental elegance.'

'That's interesting,' I say, practising my poker face – not imperious but hopefully more nonchalant – covering my surprise: an upper-class Englishwoman with taste? How extraordinary. Gwendolen Game, whose imminent arrival is all any woman who walks in here can talk about, is the daughter of a long line of beknighted British bankers, a forty-four-year-old mother of three who's also partial to ball sports, so simplicity and continental elegance could well mean corduroy tunic and fleecy-lined bloomers. But, partial to a hat or not, a hat is what she'll be getting: a welcome gift from Miss Olivia Greene. A bold gesture, risky too – and one I dreamed up myself, well before Mother's letter arrived from London suggesting the very same, with the advice:

Gwen Game is long-limbed and lithely built; why don't you style her a smart jacket for the harbour chill as well, one that suits yourself, so that it's ready when she can't resist your invitation to the salon? Send her a small sample of sketches too, my darling – just a dozen or so. I can see you sketching into the night now as I write, oh how I miss you, Ollie – terribly. I do wish you'd recon–

No, I'm not going to reconsider London. Don't want to. Don't need to. The wedding of Mr and Mrs Bartholomew Harley was superb, down to every detail – half-page splash across the Monday's *Evening News,* and the Thursday's *Herald* at the dock of the RMS *Oberon*, both displaying the frockery of *talented daughter, Miss Olivia Greene.* Thank you, Mother. When I get a moment to write back you'll be pleased to know that I refused to be a pitiable figure lingering on the dock as the ship pulled out. *Tooooot.* I went home and watched you vanish from the front steps; then I stank up the house frying eggs and onion for my supper, for old times' sake, listening for the traces of your horror ringing off the stone walls: *Ollie, close the wardrobe door!* What's the difference between London and Rose Bay anyway? Just a bit more sea. And eight standard weeks for a letter, not a telephone connection to speak of. But honestly, I've barely had time to think about your abandoning of me. Really.

'I don't know how you're managing all this on your own.' Mrs Bloxom's smile shifts from one scheme to the next, folding her chequebook back into her handbag: she's still after me for her Rick. Mystifying but true, she's holding on for my aristocratic connections: dubious as they are, her intentions are as plain as the schnonk on my face. She is especially fond of likening me among the vice-regal set to Lady Ursula Woodridge, whose West End salon in London is becoming quite the place for beige wallpaper at present. *Poor little war waifs,* Mrs Bloxom calls us, for the circumstances of fate that have led to our need to earn a living by hats and frocks. Never mind that Ursula Woodridge's father actually *died* in the war, rather than having had his sense of morality removed and the fact distributed throughout the Empire by Cinesound. Or perhaps Mrs Bloxom is simply grateful I've got her out of brown crepe and into mauve georgette, with a mid-calf hem – she does have a decently turned pair of ankles, for a dowager. She chastises me affectionately: 'I don't know when you find the time to sleep.'

'Oh, I manage.' I stifle a yawn, slipping the cheque into the drawer and sliding my eyes over the figures scribbled across it as I do. One can't be too careful, I have managed to learn quickly enough: in the past few weeks I've had Mr Trumble, from Barnaby's Furs, short-change me *accidentally* by two yards of chinchilla trim, and I've had a pair of gloves disappear.

Mrs Bloxom pulls on her own pair now, gathers her bags: 'Now, Olivia dear, you won't reconsider and come with me, will you?'

No, not reconsidering this one either – attending the welcome garden party, for the Games. Hoorah for them. I smile, my gaze lingering at the bags on Mrs Bloxom's arm, *Olivia Couture* printed on them, as it is now printed on the window and on my cards. Black on white, tootling-smart as a Sydney ferry; I've even reupholstered the chaise thus in crisp, wide taffeta stripes, and *Couture* is so much more sophisticated than *Costumière*, mais non? I'm a personal designer, an artist, not a seamstress who takes instruction from her clients, and I'm still smiling as I meet Mrs Bloxom's gaze: 'I'm sorry, no, I won't be able to attend.'

And it's not merely my usual social reticence speaking here, but some strategy and one based on the example standing before me. The more aloof and yonderly I have become, the more Mrs Bloxom seems to buy. It's happened with a couple of barristers' wives I met at Mother's wedding and then at the Tulip farewell, too – I've turned down invitations and they've turned up at the salon, following some commercial law of scarcity I don't quite understand and am certainly not about to question.

Mrs Bloxom replies now, feigning cross: 'I am most disappointed, young lady. This famous shyness of yours . . .' She shakes her head at me knowingly and not knowing a thing about it. 'You really are a wonderful girl, every last bit of you. I'll get you along to something one day . . .'

'You might just,' my smile deepens, genuinely, as I wave her good day out the door; whatever I might think of Mrs Bloxom and her grasping at status, she and her friends, who think nothing of spending thirty of forty pounds an outfit, are doing wonderful things for my business. My plans. My visions. Letting me dare to believe that they might be realities, one day. Truly, Mother, I have not stopped for weeks now – months, God, is it? I've not had time to take a full breath since you blew me your kisses and tossed me your streamers from the promenade deck, and it seems I've caught every one . . . I will catch Lady Game, too: I will have her as my top client, and from there I will go triumphantly to London, to show you what I have made of myself *by* myself, and to steal Ursula Woodridge's clients, on my way to Paris, where I will somehow steal an invitation to meet Madame Chanel. Alternatively, I could go via New York with *vice-regal couturier* embossed on my card, couldn't I? Rich Americans love that splashy sort of thing, don't they? Make my fortune first. I am beginning to taste it already.

See my success, here in the salon. Look: all that's left of my Bridge series, one lonely little aeroplane grey vagabond among my batch of new samples that range across the hat tree, and this one remains unpurchased, I would say, only because the grey is a little severe, perhaps too severe given the times. I'll snazz it slightly for my next series, another Bridge series – they walked out the door; honestly, what a thrill. Everything to do with the Bridge is exciting: the arms are almost touching now, truly only a few yards apart, and there'll be parties galore all across the city when they finally meet, with their great big clanking steel kiss. But – roll the drum – will they meet? Or will the whole thing fall into the sea when the restraining lines are let go? So, so very exciting. I'll simply have to do a special one for Lady Game, won't I. Hers, I see now, is the moss stocking cloche on the topmost branch above the aeroplane vagabond: softest cashmere, which should fit her so long as she comes with a head, and its only embellishment shall be a small gilt buckle, left of centre. I see her jacket against it, masculine pea-style, double-breasted, but cut from rich buttery gamboge tussah. Quilted. That will look superb in the window, too – an advertisement of pure luxury – and Lady Game shall have the colours of the harbour at dawn. With taupe gloves and shoes . . .

Shhhh. Wait until she's here, for the details. Get in with her private secretary if possible: I have her name too, a Miss Isabel Crowdy. But for now, I'd better interrupt my dreaming and get cracking on the practicalities, draw up the pattern for that jacket. Reception's on Saturday. The streets will be aflutter with hoorah bunting and flags as their ship comes in. The thirty-first of May. Really? It will be June on Sunday. No . . .

I release the yawn, a great big lion yawn, and look out the window, to the sliver of sky I can see through the glass roof from here. It's not yet half-past four, but it's getting dark, and I don't know how I'm going to get everything done that needs doing. I've got Glor's engagement frock to finish before I cut any jacket pattern. Only the collar to do, on the floatiest copper-shot chiffon chemise, gaspingly backless, but it's a pernickety thing, bands of bronze and lapis and scarlet baguette beads. Worth it, though: she'll look like Queen Nefertiti gazing out from her barge on the Nile. Or the lawns of Waverley Tennis Club, at least. And I won't be able to get out of that party – tomorrow night – that'll be at least four hours' interruption to vice-regal jacket enterprise. I'm yet to go through my sketchbooks too – or should I design entirely new creations for Lady Game? *A dozen or so . . .* I should most certainly get a sandwich down at the Aristocrat before I do or think another thing – before they close for the evening, too.

Don't know how I'm managing at all, in fact. I look at the stockroom door as I grab my handbag off the coat stand and wonder if I might slip a little trundle bed in there, don't tell the Jabours I even thought that. But even the ferry to and fro seems a loss of time I can't afford. And I can't afford it: who knows how long these charmeuse dreams will stay afloat? I'm stitching myself an ark against it. Most nights I don't have time to remember I'm alone to even miss Mother. Which reminds me: the baby is arriving sometime around August – God, I should make it something, too. Shouldn't I. Perhaps not; it'll have plenty of attention otherwise, won't it. Regardless, if things keep up, as I surely hope they will, I'm going to have to start thinking about getting a girl in to help me here. Who though? I don't want to work with a stranger, or some middling thing waiting for marriage. I don't want to work with some – some *seamstress*.

I laugh aloud at my own snobbery. As if every great designer doesn't start out slaving over the nuts and bolts of their craft. Perhaps I'll find a girl who wants to be inspired. I'll word my advertisement somehow to attract one, an apprentice of some kind . . .

Someone like me . . .

I catch sight of my reflection in the window as I look up from the clasp of my cape: same neglected crop of tempest on my head in need of a hat, same schnonk in need of a low brim, but how far I have come otherwise, and in such a brief time. I have more than six casually crumpled pounds in my purse, for a start. I don't even need our Lordship's pittance. I can ignore him back: that is so very satisfying, it makes my fears of having his disregard for me exposed for all the world to see seem small, some forgettable unsnipped squiggle on the hem of my life. Makes the opinions of Cassie Fortescue and the Ladies College set seem laughable, whatever they might be, some long ago, little girl insecurity.

It's incredible to me now that I could ever have felt inferior to a girl who spends her Saturday nights sipping fizzy gins at the Merrick cabaret – which are fizzy not from soda, Liz Hardy let a whisper slip to me, but from cocaine. She told me that the funsters threw a mammoth party in the Jazz Room after one of the Randwick races – some horse called Phar Lap won it, taking in almost twenty-five *thousand* pounds, who would believe – and Liz said wild was not the word: they danced so hard they almost did tear up the floor. They get this fizzy 'snow' through Customs House, right under the Commissioner's nose – a nose which belongs of course to Cassie's Denis's daddy. She's leading Min astray, too. Poor Min: her response to her ditching appears to have been to make herself as silly as her cousin, and they both look like showgirls, satin and sequins from some faux bohemian designer of haute catastrophe in the Imperial. *La Boutique*, it's called.

I open the salon door and a blast of chill air shooshes up through the arcade as I step out. *La Boutique* – whoever heard of anything more revoltingly chi-chi? Revenge: it really can best be served with one's enemy entirely oblivious to it. But good God, isn't the Imperial going downhill –

Going *what*?

Something small, dark and fast hurtles towards me. Wanting to get *through* me.

And I just about sail head over celluloid heels.

Yo

'You don't play rugby, do you, Eoghan?' Mr Adams asks me as we're heading home up Darling Street, just as he's about to turn off before me down Adolphus. 'League?' he specifies.

I don't think I'll ever believe that he asks me questions such as these. It should be more than plain to him by now that sport is not my strength: can't bat, can't bowl, don't care, and no, I wasn't interested in getting struck out or whatever it is I did at that game of baseball last Sunday afternoon either, but I did it anyway, just to disappoint and prove I am shitful at any sports. I have to tell him this time, a bit more forcefully: 'Sorry, I've got two left feet there.'

Not that I'd know about rugby league; I've never played any kind of football and I am not about to be talked into it now, regardless of what it might be raising funds for on this Sunday. Not football or boxing or any of them sports that require bashing, or getting one, and the Irish do it more convincingly than most. When you've been employed as a punching bag regularly, I suppose some just aren't inclined to want to do it of a weekend for their entertainment. I've never hit anyone, as much as I might find myself wanting to at times; I don't think I ever could.

I think Mr Adams picks up something of that, my never wanting trouble of any kind, and he doesn't press the point this time, thankfully. I don't ever want to say no to him. He waves: 'All right then, good enough. Slán then, goodnight.'

'Yeah, see you. I'll go hard on the lamingtons instead, yeah?' I tell him and he nods. I shove my hands deeper into my pockets as I walk on, somehow hoping this action might do something against the wind. Jesus, this wind is into me today. It's been that bad over the last few weeks, six have thrown it in, more than what quit after Nipper Addison fell, they just don't turn up for shift: sorry, this job is too fucking monkey-nutted. Why am I never one of the lads sent dollying on the inside of a chord, ay? That's supposed to be the worst place to be for the lack of air, but I'd like to try it. Just the once, never mind the few bob an hour extra for confined spaces. I'm too fucking good at catching, aren't I. At least I can say I am learning, though. I am learning well the principle of physics that says the trajectory of a flying white-hot cock will remain steady while other forces of nature are attempting to lift the skin off your face. When I get in, I'll be smothering this face with Ponds Cold Cream, like a woman. Ag thinks that's the funniest thing in the world. It's not funny. A half-skinless face: it fucking hurts. And this jacket is shitful: more than a pound it cost me, naval surplus, and it's doing fucking nothing for me.

Less when I turn down Fawcett and the wind picks up like it's come tearing in off the ocean, through the heads, down the harbour and found this one little lane in Balmain is the best place to go.

And there's a woman standing in the middle of it. Outside my house. Grey coat done up to her ears, she looks about as happy as me.

'Is that Mr O'Keenan?' she says as I near.

'Yes,' I say, wary. There's something about her, like an undertaker or some other grim thing, though I can't see much more of her than her eyes, sharp and brown and wrinkled at the edges.

'Mrs Merridale,' she puts her hand out for me to shake it. A black glove; leather.

I don't take it; I say: 'What can I do for you?' But I'm looking at my front door, hoping Ag's got the fire on.

'Your sister, Agnes . . .' this Mrs Merridale starts and I look at her: *You are not going to tell me something has happened to my sister.* She says: 'I am an officer of the Child Welfare Department.'

I don't know how it is I remain standing upright: *They've taken her?*

This Mrs Merridale goes on: 'Your sister has, I'm afraid, run away.'

Thank you, Lord: not taken. 'Run away?' I say: that doesn't seem possible: 'Why would she run away?'

'Hm.' This Mrs Merridale bites her lip. 'May I come inside?'

I show her in; show her I've got nothing to hide. The first thing I see are the cushions Ag made for our sagging old sofa: they've got a pattern of red and yellow chickens on them. This is a happy home. Clean and tidy, food in the cupboards, and we have a bookshelf, with books on it, fourteen of them: Ag is reading *The Wonderful Wizard of Oz*, she's nearly finished, Dorothy's following the soldier girl in to see Glinda the Good Witch. She reads it out to me when I get in from not being blown off the Bridge. She's done her Communion: look at the print of her there on the bookshelf, smiling proud in her white dress and veil, with all the other girls at St Gus's. Jesus, but the anger bites me with the stinging of my face: 'You'll see there's nothing to run away from here.'

'I'm sure there's not, Mr O'Keenan,' this Mrs Merridale smiles above her collar, with some apology in it. 'This is a good home, I can see that. And Agnes is a good little girl. You have done nothing wrong – no need to be alarmed.'

'No need?' I nearly yell it at her: 'You're telling me my sister's run away. Why has she done that, then?'

'Well, er, I was called to the school today to observe her condition and to interview her, on behalf of the Department.'

'What? What for?'

'There was a complaint made, of child neglect –'

'Who by?'

'I am not at liberty to say, other than to tell you that it was a concerned member of the community.'

'Concerned?' I'll bet I know who it was: that Nettie Becker, always keeping an eye on me, through her front curtain, through the back palings. I would like to show her a bit of concern, right through the fucking stone wall between us.

The Welfare woman's face goes as red as mine. 'Well, perhaps an unnecessarily concerned member of the community. I'm terribly sorry, Mr O'Keenan. It has become clear to me that this was an unwarranted complaint. I have since interviewed Agnes's teacher, and the Hanrahan family, and several other members of the community, to ascertain that Agnes is a well-cared-for and healthy child.'

'So why has she run away?' And where to? Not with the Hanrahans? Maybe she's gone round to Mrs Adams, or she's with Mrs Buddle, and I've just walked straight past her. But: 'Why? Why would she run away?'

'Hm.' The Welfare woman bites her lip again. 'Well, er, it's difficult to be absolutely certain, but when I introduced myself to her this morning, she just went whoosh,' she waves her hand at the hearth as if Ag might have slipped up the chimney, 'right out of the room – ran for her life. This did of course seem rather odd, until my further investigations, with the Department and other members of the community, including Father O'Reagan at St Augustine's, revealed to me your previous and less fortunate circumstances. I'm afraid I might have frightened her off.'

Might have? Why wouldn't she have run away from you, you fucking Welfare witch? Jesus, Aggie. I tell this woman: 'Now you can go and find her.'

'Yes, er,' she says. 'We have two policemen searching the locality as we speak.'

And Ag won't run for her life again when she sees a cop coming for her, will she. I look at the door and tell her with my silence: *Get out.* Thousands of kids starving across the city and the government spends money it doesn't have on wages for this horseshit, when it could pay the dole in decent food and put a tax on grog to cover it. A bolt of something ice cold goes through me: if it hadn't been for those standing up for us, Ag might have been pinched straight from school, and I'd now be banging on the courthouse doors at Surry Hills begging for her back. Mother of God, but she'd better be all right.

The Welfare woman says: 'Yes. Well. I'm sure there will be a satisfactory resolution. Ah . . .' Her steps are quick ahead of mine: 'Good evening, Mr O'Keenan.'

I slam the door behind us both and I don't stop to kick her up the arse. I start running back up Darling Street. Jesus, Ag, please be safe. Please don't have fallen off the rubble wall down at the park, or from under the ferry wharf, if that's where you're hiding. Please don't have been pinched by someone even less interested in your welfare. Please be where I think you are . . .

Olivia

'I couldn't . . . find the . . . right . . . shop,' Agnes gulps through her tears when I finally get her to speak to me.

'Oh . . .' I see, looking behind me at the salon, its change of name, change from gilt to black and white. 'You didn't recognise the shop. Oh, you poor little sweetheart.' That doesn't explain why she's here, however, and in such distress. When I caught her and shrieked: *Agnes?* I thought she might tremble to pieces with shock. I ask her: 'Tell me, what's frightened you?'

'The Welfare lady,' she wails, but so softly, a tiny kitten wail. 'And then I got . . . lost. I went round and round and I couldn't find you . . .'

She is as edible as ever, in her navy serge tunic, boots polished to a shine and a red ribbon in her hair, which has grown, tempest tied back in a little fat plait: Wynn's Family Drapery would want her in the window for *Back to School* orders. But why does she want me? 'Agnes, you're quite safe now, it's all right, but why are you here?'

She mewls again, so that I am compelled to hold her to me, and as I do she sobs over my shoulder, for the whole arcade to hear: 'Don't let them take me away from Yoey.'

'I won't let them do that, Agnes. I promise you,' I say, rubbing her little shoulders, 'Shhhh,' as if I could possibly have fairy princess powers enough to erase whatever dreadful thing has happened.

When she's finished sobbing, she sniffs, and raises those glorious blue eyes from the ground. 'I like your shoes, miss.'

God, but I could eat her up; I say: 'I like yours too, Agnes.' I even remember your surname: O'Keenan. Like it was yesterday. Eoghan O'Keenan: what's happened? I stand up and hold out my hand, and my head spins a little as I do. I really must eat something. 'Sweetheart, shall we go and sort this out over a sandwich?'

She nods, takes in a steadying breath, 'Yes, please, I'm hungry too,' and she takes my hand.

We take the stairs, her clammy little hand in mine, and my mind boggles at this odd event, this strange stopping of time. A tingling up and down my spine, and Glor raises an eyebrow as she spies us going past the Emporium. Her eyes follow us, with the question, as she pops a bolt of her father's finest bebe pink lingerie Fuji back up on the shelf above the sideboard. Where I spy the brass bottle, glass rubies and sapphires winking at me, as Mr Jabour's great booming laugh releases at some joke his customer has just shared with him.

The gilt bands on the turnings of the verandah posts outside spin like carousel poles, and I know in this moment, mad with honking horns and clopping hooves and thousands of rushing souls, that the wheel of my world is wobbling once again, magic-carpet laughter carrying us out into the street.

Yo

I shouldn't have sent her to the public school, should I. Desperately spoon-headed as this notion is, it's a good measure of how desperate I am.

'She will be found, Eoghan,' Mr Adams says, and his firm hand on my shoulder is doing nothing to ease it.

'Don't you worry, lad, I won't cease praying until she is safely home,' Mrs Adams's kind sunshine face assures me too. 'Not for a second.' Their Kenny is banging something in his room upstairs; but it's true: she won't stop praying for a second.

'Go back and wait,' says Mr Adams. 'There's no good you being here when she gets in.'

'No.' That's true, too. Everyone's out looking for Ag: Tarzan and Clarkie, and Brother Francis from St Gus, the whole neighbourhood of Balmain East, and her teacher, Mrs Shipley, she's got her brother going round in his car, up as far as Iron Cove bridge. Plus the two cops knocking on doors everywhere in between. I can only go back and wait, and pray ceaselessly. Jesus, but it's nearly six o'clock and it's moonless black out there. Please, look after her.

Mr Adams sees me back down his hall and lowers his voice as he assures me of something else: 'Don't go near the Beckers. Shut your door, forget them. It will be taken care of.'

He adds something in his Ulster Gaelainn to the promise but I don't know what it means, and I don't want to know. Stupid woman. It was her: took her a while but she found someone to listen to her, and that Welfare woman told Mrs Shipley, who's friends with Clarkie's sister, and now it's all over town, from Birchgrove to Rozelle and up the Parramatta River. Whatever's coming to Nettie Becker, it's a lesson against spite, and it won't be nice. It'll be the long arm of Mr Sturgess, her landlord as well as mine, taking the care of it somehow, I'll bet. How could she be such a . . . Such a stupid bitch.

I step back out into the night. At least the wind has died. But it's still cold. Freezing, and Ag didn't take her coat: it's hanging on the back of the door. Down Fawcett Street, I see the shadow of Shitful Becker heading out, towards the timber docks, on his way round the foreshore to the silos at Glebe Island. She's alone then, but for the boy; I see the lamp on in there, strip of yellow down the gap of the curtains. A bolt of something evil chills me from the inside, and I shut it away: you'll get yours, you fucking bitch, but not from me. Keep my eyes and my mind on what is mine: our little tree here, our gardenia, its leaves shiny even in the dark, twice the size of when we got it, from all Ag's care. Ag will be all right. She has to be.

But this house is terrible without her in it. Terrible. I don't even want to get the fire going. But I do. I light the coals and all the lamps because she might be home any minute. She'll be home tonight. She will be. She has to be. Please, Lord. Tonight. Or I will go mad. I will certainly run out of tobacco, if I keep rolling at this rate. I light the stove now, too, put the kettle on, for another pot of tea I don't want.

I look at the picture hanging on the kitchen wall, above our table: Ag's drawing, a garden full of flowers spreading out under a great fig tree. She did it at school, with paints. She's pretty good at this sort of thing too. The ideas she comes up with. The colours. We got an old frame from the fete at St Gus's, and I nailed it up here. She works so hard, Lord: you must see that. Please. Please let her be safe.

There's a knock at the door and the kettle screams with my desperation: please, Lord, please let this be her.

Olivia

'Well, isn't that funny,' I say more to the air than to Agnes as we wait for the door to open. Uncanny: even in this dimness I can see the house is almost identical to mine, but that it's single-fronted, one of a pair, with a little patch of garden here, and mine has only three steps up from the street, all on its own. But the stone . . . it's just the same. I'm searching above the door for a date, some sign to say Great Grandfather Weathercroft made this house too, but I didn't bring my magic lantern with us for me to see through the dark, and the door flies open now anyway.

And there he is.

The figment boy, exactly as I remember him. Even with the sunburn across his nose. I laugh aloud: such a laughably perfect boy, throwing a tea towel over his shoulder.

'Sweet Jesus!' he shouts as he kneels, and little Agnes throws herself into his arms.

That was worth the trip around to Balmain, worth stopping time I don't have for: they are lovely. His joy for her is the loveliest thing I've ever seen. He might be her brother but he's what a father should be. Who would ever want to break them apart? I'll talk to him in a minute about this Welfare business. I'm certain Agnes is not making it up. It must be a mistake, though: this Welfare business and my wilful embroiling of myself in it both. Discussion will come. Thought will come. As will the equally laughable realisation that the glimpse of sitting room I can see behind them appears to be in far better order than mine.

For this minute, I must simply look at him.

Look into his deep blue eyes as he looks up at me, mystified: 'Miss Greene?'

Three

Yo

The conviction comes to me again and with a greater power, as if it's coming by divine instruction now: *This is the girl.* The one I will marry. My girl. And the bald, blinking idiocy of this idea comes to me again with just as great a power: she's a lady. She's not come here for me. And there's something different about her this time; something taller, something surer in her smile, her eyes. Her honey laughter, telling Ag: 'Home again, there you are. Isn't this good?'

And now she's saying something to me: 'I have promised Agnes I will help sort out this Welfare business with you and I mean to honour that promise. Shall I . . . ?'

I'm still giving her the spoon-faced goggle, still on my knees on the doorstep, and I'm not altogether sure I've taken in what she just said: 'Shall you . . . ?'

'Come in and discuss it,' she says, frowning under her hat, her green hat, and all my attention is taken by the little curl come free of it by her left eye, her gold hair against this green hat.

I say: 'Discuss what?'

'This business with the Welfare people, and Agnes having run away today . . .' You idiot, she looks down that fine, long nose.

Her face is . . . She's a . . . With her skin so pale and her golden hair and her eyes seeming so green by the hat . . . She's no fairy princess. She is Queen Oonagh herself. Jesus. And she's wanting to discuss the Welfare people. Right.

I say: 'Ay? Yeah. No. It's all right now, it was a . . . misunderstanding.' And my sense returns enough for me to raise my voice a bit for Nettie to hear me add: 'It was someone making some mischief, that's all, and the Welfare people are well aware of it now. It's sorted.'

Miss Greene looks at me as if I might be a bit touched; because I am, I'm sure I am: *This is the girl, Eoghan.* It's Oonagh telling me this, for sure, and there's nothing divine about it. I'm looking at the collar of her coat now, a type of golden fur that's almost the same colour as her hair, and I would give anything to be that scrap of fur just to touch her there where it's touching her cheek. Just once, just for a second.

Ag's pulling on my sleeve: 'Invite Miss Greene in for supper, Yoey.' You silly spoonhead, she's frowning at me too: 'I want to show her my sewing things.'

'Right. Yeah. Yes.' I get to my feet and look down at Ag again as I do: the relief nearly sends me back down on my knees again. This Miss Greene: she's brought Ag home to me. By what spell I don't care; I look at Miss Greene again: 'Thank you. Thank you for bringing Aggie home. I can't thank –' Thank you and half the world that's still out looking for Ag right now. I've got to call off the search. 'Can you wait?' I ask Miss Greene, and I can't believe I'm doing it. 'Wait here – please. I won't be a minute. I mean – inside. Wait. Not here on the doorstep.' Idiot. 'I – please?'

'Ah –'

Don't give her a chance to answer before Ag's dragging her in and I'm tearing up Gladstone to the Opera House, banging on the windows like a madman: 'Ag's home – call the cops. She's come home!' And Mrs Malone, the publican's wife, sticks her head over the verandah rail above to cry out: 'Oh mercy, yes, lad, thank the Lord!' Thank you, Lord, all right. I keep tearing on down to Adolphus, to bang on the Adamses' door: 'Ag's home! She just walked in.' Mrs Adams's rosary goes flying up in the air with the mercy of it, and Mr Adams is smashing a fist into my shoulder: 'Good news, lad, and where was she – did someone bring her?'

'Er . . .' I don't know what to say, what to think, but what comes out of my mouth is: 'Lady from a shop.' And I'm tearing home again. To Ag. To Miss Greene. Miss Greene is in my house? Please. I really was just a minute, maybe two. She has to be still there.

Yes, she is.

'Oh, look at that,' she's saying to Ag as I come down the hall. 'These are your chicken cushions you were telling me of, Agnes? How sweet they are . . .'

That tin whistle of hers goes off, this sound sent straight from the angels, and as I'm catching my breath in the doorway she and Ag are chatting about cushions and where she's up to with the *Wonderful Wizard*. 'See, and there's forty-two full-page illustrations,' says Ag. 'Oh yes, I see, Agnes, aren't they snazz ones.' Chatting away like old friends, so that if this girl spends a minute more in my house, there will be no getting away from her, not for me, not this time.

The minute goes past and Ag's pulling out the placemats she's been stitching for the table to show her Miss Greene. Whoever it is doing this – be it Oonagh or you, Lord – the job is done: you've got me.

Olivia

'The kettle, I'd just boiled it, before –' he says from the hall, just returned from wherever he dashed off to. 'Yeah? Yes?'

'No.' I stand up from the sofa. 'I shan't stay for supper, thank you. I really must be going.' And I must: baguette beading to do for Gloria, and our Mr Yoey O'Keenan is clearly uncomfortable at my being here, having trouble stringing two syllables, never mind two words. That strange hurt swishes through me: fantasy over. No one's fate is about to change here. Figment boy has a real life, and a crucifix glaring down at me from the wall above the fireplace. He sleeps every night on this tired little brown sofa so that his sister can have the bedroom to herself, her window tacked around with a length of red gingham as she's not quite up to making curtains yet. I add as I turn to depart, 'I'm so glad you've sorted things out with the Welfare people.'

'Yeah. Good. Yes. That is good,' he says, looking at Agnes, stepping into the room now. 'A great relief it is. Thank you again for bringing her home. Hm, yeah. Ay, Ag?'

Good God, but I don't want to leave. He steps further into the room to stand beside his sister, and as he does he notices the tea towel slung over his left shoulder. He looks a little startled at it, brushing it off, but then he trues-up the edges of it as if he always dashes about with a tea towel over his left shoulder for that very purpose. His hands, his beautiful hands folding the old linen square so precisely, carefully, placing it on the mantel as if it weren't a rag but a thing of value. Over the other side of the fireplace, an exercise book lies open on the middle shelf of the bookcase with some sort of technical drawing in it that looks like a pattern for a three-quarter raglan sleeve. I want to know this boy. I want to know this real figment boy whose words dance even as he's stumbling over wishing I *would* leave; I want to find out what on earth this business with the Welfare people is about, too. Fish around in my handbag: 'If you do have a problem again, please don't hesitate to contact me . . .' I hold out my card.

He looks at it, a little startled again. Of course he is: what could a couturier possibly have to offer him? He possibly doesn't know what a couturier is.

'I have some legal connections . . .' I say.

And he looks at me with such astonishment, I am appalled at myself. *Legal connections.* I might as well have said I don't believe him, told him that the nasty woman who came to the school was in fact on to something untoward here and he's a Welfare-offending crook. I open my mouth but no sound comes out: I am bereft of explanation.

He looks at the card again. 'Miss Greene?'

I say: 'Yes?' Perhaps he's wondering if *Couture* is my stage name.

'Er,' he says and when his eyes meet mine again he appears to be as uncomfortable as his sunburn looks.

And I remain such a graceless, clumsy lump of a girl. What humiliation am I compelling him to here? I don't need to know about the Welfare people. None of my business. I don't need anything from this nice boy at all. Just tell him good evening and *leave.*

But I can't.

'Ahhh,' he looks back to his little sister now and he says: 'We should thank Miss Greene properly, shouldn't we, Ag?' Agnes nods and looks to me. And then so does he: 'You wouldn't care to come out to the pictures or something with us some time? In town? Or a picnic or something. I mean, would you . . . ? I – ah . . .'

Did he just ask me –? Would I what? Oh yes I would indeed, but I'm too stunned to respond for a moment, and in this moment my own practicalities squish the idea: I don't have time to go to the pictures or picnicking. I have too much to do, beading, pea-style patterning, order in that new Lelong scent as I forgot to, again, this afternoon . . . And I can't be seen anywhere with a boy who I'm sure doesn't even own a suit coat. Can't happen. But fantasy as quickly overrides all sense of can't happen and I'm telling him: 'Yes. Well, I . . .'

And he's turned to Agnes again: 'What's on at the National tomorrow evening, Ag?'

'The double is *The House of Horror* and then *Divorce Made Easy*.' Agnes giggles up at her brother, showing her two perfectly grown-up front teeth. 'I don't want to see them, Yoey.'

And I have to say: 'I can't go tomorrow anyway – I've a prior engagement.' Engagement party: and much baguette beading to finish off before then. I should go and get to it right now . . .

'Of course,' he says and he thinks I'm turning his invitation down, too far above him. 'It was just a thought. Well, we'll not keep you any further.'

'Ah . . .' I should turn the invitation down but I'm busily thinking past Glor's party, Lady Game's cashmere cloche and cutting that pea-style jacket pattern, until I come up with: 'What about Wednesday night?'

'Oh?' He looks surprised again, and then disappointed again; he says: 'I can't then either – I go to school, to the tech, the Technical College, Wednesday nights.'

'Oh?' That'll explain the drawing in the exercise book, I suppose. I have to know: 'What do you do there?' I have to know everything about this boy.

The Blue Mile

'Metal arts, for boilermaking,' he says, and he still looks half-surprised, half-disappointed. What's going on here? I don't know. Keep conversing, Olivia.

I ask him: 'Is that what you do on the Bridge? Metal . . . things?'

'I'm just a labourer,' he says apologetically.

No you're not, I decide. You're not *just* anything. That feeling of sympathy floods me again, just as it did in the Gardens that day half a year ago: why should such a good and decent boy apologise for himself? I ask him: 'What does a labourer on the Bridge do?'

He looks down at the floorboards, hands in his pockets. 'Mostly, I catch rivets. In a bucket. For the riveter. It's called . . . catching.'

'Catching, is it? On the Bridge itself?' I look at the floorboard he's addressing and I notice he's wearing canvas tennis shoes. Filthy, near black, but most definitely tennis shoes. How bizarre. Denim trousers and tennis shoes . . .

'Yeah. Mostly.' And when he looks up at me again, he smiles. Those dimples . . . those deep blue eyes . . . I'm mesmerised.

He's just asked me something and I have no idea what it is: 'Pardon me?'

'I said, do you have far to go home, miss? It's late; you shouldn't be out alone. Would you like us to walk you to the . . . ?'

'The . . . ?' I seem to leave for a good spin around the ether before practicalities drag me back again. I have to go home, now, I really do. 'Yes. The ferry, and no, I don't live far. Only across to Lavender Bay.'

'Really?' He laughs and it's a laugh that dances too. 'Isn't that something. I must see you every day, going across on the ferry. Look up tomorrow and wave.'

'Yes.' Insane. Our smiles meet, here in his bright, warm hall. I want to cut a pattern for that white dinner jacket. Now. Oh dear God, look away from him. Mother was right at a glance: I should never see this boy again. The way he places his sister's coat across her shoulders: such unthinking tenderness. Oh dear God.

I'll bet he plaits her hair himself too, and as tenderly, never pulling a strand too tight.

We step out into the night. We start walking back to the wharf, Agnes skipping along between us, her hand in his but she's looking up at me. Can she see this terrific sensation sweeping through me? A tingling, twinkling like the lights on the water before us. The shadow of the Bridge appears against the indigo sky: so huge, so nearly complete. Such a wonder. Dear God, he works up there. He truly does. My stomach trips and falls.

He says: 'You live only a mile away.'

'Yes?' What? Only a mile away? 'Oh yes. I do. Only across the harbour.'

'White Bay to Lavender Bay,' he says and I can sense his smile through the dark. 'It's only a mile, isn't it? Only a blue mile.'

A blue mile. And so you're a poet as well as an heroic rivet catcher. I have to see you again as soon as possible. Contrive a reason; ask him: 'So, what does Agnes do on Wednesday nights?' Fix her own supper, I suppose, as I used to do for myself.

'She stops with friends,' he says. 'Saturdays too. I work on the night shift Saturday nights. In the workshops.'

'You work a lot.' And I see it's not sympathy I feel for him: it's recognition. Something about us already entwined: I can feel it. That's what this tingling is. Isn't it? A meeting of souls.

'Yes,' he says. 'I don't have too much time for picnics or going to the pictures.'

I make him an offer with every wish known and unknown in my heart: 'Agnes can always keep me company on Wednesday or Saturday nights. Or mostly any ev–'

'Oh Yoey, can I please?'

The city-bound ferry is just pulling in to the wharf at the end of the street. One stop between us, that's all there is. How funny. We must get on and off the same ferries every working day.

I doubt my poker face is doing a lot to conceal my eagerness as I tell Agnes: 'You can come after school this Wednesday, if you like. You're quite sure where the salon is now, aren't you?'

She giggles behind her hand, outrageously sweet. 'I won't make that mistake again, Miss Greene.' And then she yanks her brother by the arm, demanding: 'Yoey, can I go, please?'

'Are you sure it's not too much trouble?' he asks me.

'Trouble?' Oh, hilarity, I know this is trouble. Eoghan O'Keenan. A fantasy upon a fantasy. He can't possibly be feeling this tingling too. He's only grateful that I brought his sister back, and I can barely hear my footsteps on the path, that's how high above him I am. In trouble. I tell him: 'No trouble at all. You can come and pick her up after your night school. I'm just near the top of the steps up from McMahons Point wharf, can't miss the house – it looks just like yours.'

Toot. Toot.

Yo

Heading back home, Ag says: 'You love Miss Greene, don't you, Yo-Yo?'

'I do not,' I say. 'I don't know her. You don't love someone after five minutes.'

'You do, though, don't you, Yoey?'

Yes, I might well do. Ag's skipping backwards ahead of me up the hill, happier than she's ever been. I might love Miss Greene. I'm still holding her card in my pocket, don't want to let it go if it might break this spell.

I see Mrs Buddle's front lamp is off as we pass her geraniums; she'll have seen us then, or heard already that Ag is home, safe and well. Good. I might love Miss Greene so much I can't stop in to chat right now because I don't know what to say.

Olivia

'What are you all dreamy Dora about?' Glor asks me as I button her in. 'You haven't stopped smiling since you got here. Are you unwell?'

'You are a terrible friend, Gloria Jabour. Can't a girl just be happy? I have a hundred reasons to be.'

'A hundred new clients?' she scoffs. 'Business isn't everything, Ollie.' She looks at me in the mirror, eyelids at half-mast: scornful. 'I don't like you being alone. Gives me the shivers you over there all by yourself at night. Dad's invited Hoddy Delmont to the party, especially for you – he's with Customs House, junior inspector, and yes, he's got a law degree. Be nice to him.'

'I shall.' Customs House? That gives me a shudder: I can only think he must be Cassie Fortescue's drug runner, briefcase full of cocaine-filled matchboxes – that's how they do it, isn't it?

'Oh, my. Oh, Olivia . . .' Mrs Jabour appears at the door of Glor's bedroom: 'Oh my, my, my, what have you *done*?' She inspects my beading at the neckline, shakes her head delightedly scandalised at the plunging backline. 'You are a maker of dreams, my girl, a maker of dreams. But Gloria,' Mrs Jabour drops identical eyelids at her daughter, 'you are too thin – I can see your bones.'

'*Mum.*'

Arabian princess eyeball-rolling contest ensues, with a backhanded smack to Gloria's copper-shot derriere and a: 'Hurry up, daughter, your father is waiting in the car.'

'Hurry up, Norma!' Aunty Karma shrieks for Mrs Jabour up the two flights of stairs, up from the kitchen, and over half of Beirut bustling in the hall.

'Where are my earrings?'

'It's going to rain – get the umbrellas!'

'No it's not – don't be stupid! Where is my coat – who took my coat?'

'Don't forget the tabouli, oh my God! It's in the red tin, under the eggs.'

The tabouli is found, thank God, and stuffed into the back of Eddie Nasser's Tycoon factory lorry with the rest of the seventeen tons of food Mrs Jabour and Aunty Karma have made for the party.

HONK HONK! HONK HONK! Mr Jabour presses the horn of the Oldsmobile every few seconds, the whole five minutes from Randwick to Waverley, just to hear Gloria wail each time: '*Dad* – stop it. Please – *please.* You are so embarrassing.'

'What, Gloria? Can't a father be proud?'

I'm half-ruined from laughing before we've even pulled up at the tennis club, where inside everything is a wonder whirl of beautiful: peacock drapes over the windows, a starburst of silver ribbon across the ceiling, everything twinkling with loveliness, with Mr Jabour's particular style and pride. Especially beautiful are Glor and Paul. Their eyes meet across the roomful of napkins embroidered with *G&P* and it is fact: their babies will be the most gorgeous babies ever made.

Hoddy Delmont isn't too bad either I decide when Velma points him out. He's at least six inches taller than me, with the most lush auburn hair, and quick about introducing himself with the line: 'I've heard so much about you, Miss Greene – most of it good.' Witty and a little debonair, he is. 'You're a dreadful dancer, too, I'm told – shall we?' He gives me his arm as a saxophone calls all to the floor, and I take it. Why not? I don't even notice my feet are moving, much less take a moment to worry about how I might be making a muddle of this first waltz, whatever it might be. Because I'm in a dream. I am dancing on air in a wonder whirl with Eoghan O'Keenan. My Bridge boy. I can't even think of the Bridge, much less look at it, without my heart tumbling and swooshing and waving for him. I quickstep across girders swinging off cable strings all night long and there's not a joke I don't laugh at, not a glint off the crystal that doesn't singularly thrill.

And when the cab takes me home under the arch on the punt, I look up and send my wishes right up through the tiny space that's left between the arms. I want our arms to meet. I want to kiss him. I've never wanted to kiss any boy. Ever.

I dream it through until dawn, until I'm back on the ferry and under the Bridge again. Looking for him up there. I don't actually wave. But I am wearing my flame-red cape in the hope that he will not fail to see me and I am indeed smiling as wide as I can smile. Like a lovestruck loon.

Yo

'You want to hit a ferry or catch one, Pretty Boy?' Tarzan shouts in my face after I've missed the rivet for the third time. I never miss and there is no excuse today: not a breath of wind and Clarkie is cooking not two yards away from us. 'What the fuck is wrong with you this morning?'

'Nothing, just a bit tired.' Just a bit looking for her on every ferry that passes under, looking across the bay at her house. It's easy to pick that out, right on the bend of the road, between a block of flats and a big old boarding house. I walked over there yesterday, telling myself I should check for Ag's sake. Jesus help me.

Tarzan does; he says: 'Miss another and I'll send you down.'

Not necessarily by the cradle.

'Right,' I nod, but I have another sly look at the ferry passing under now. I see a red coat standing on the stern of this one and I think it's her.

Olivia

*E*ven the welcome bunting for the new Governor at the Quay is beautiful. Customs House is a great big beribboned gift and I am so high I could twirl up to its top balcony, pop myself there like great big red rosette.

'Are they here yet?' I ask the man at the kiosk and he points out beyond the wharves: 'Almost. Ship's been sighted off the heads, miss.'

'Jolly good!' I toot. Everything is so sparkling fabulous I barely notice the blind digger has been shooed off from his post under the awning for the day. There are plenty of policemen about to take care of that sort of thing, I see, twenty or more strolling around through the morning crowd: move along poverty, move along unemployed unfortunates, only beautiful ones allowed around here today.

'Miss,' a policeman by the corner of Pitt tips his cap and smiles at me as if I might be beautiful too. Perhaps I might even dare to believe I am. I float up through the chaos of carts and cabs, up, up, up to the salon to complete my gift to Lady Game, and I know exactly what I am. I am searching amongst my boxes of bits in the stockroom for just the right gold buckle to place on the moss cashmere – when a masterstroke of inspiration takes me. This hat does not want a tame and dreary little sports-mistress buckle at all. It wants a small but festive spray of Sydney wattle. A few deft twists of some lemon and chartreuse satin cord and it's an elegant explosion of joy. It's so beautiful I could almost cry.

'That is absolutely darling,' Liz Hardy's mother says of my wattle when she calls in for some inspiration on a new winter coat. I float over to the chaise to show her my sketch for the pea-style, and by the time she leaves, I've got three patterns to cut, including the gamboge tussah for the window, to catch the eye of Lady Game. But before I get to that, I wrap the vice-regal cloche in tissue and, with the rest of my sample sketches, I pack it into one of my new white *Olivia Couture* boxes. I'm so pleased with these boxes, tied with a black ribbon, that is the signature of my salon. Mine. Tie the ribbon tight with wishes now: if I should catch Lady Game's eye, my life really will change. Even still, the thrill of this idea, this anticipation of dreams come true, pales in comparison to my waiting for Wednesday.

It's fortunate then I am so flat-out hectic over these next seventy-two hours, otherwise I might explode and etherise entirely before we get there. Before little Agnes's darling face appears at the window at twenty-two minutes to four. Waving, excited as I am: 'Miss Greene!'

Straightaway she spies the little mannequin I've set out for her, still with her own creation pinned on it, and she squeals: 'You kept it for me!'

I must have done, mustn't I. I've been far too busy to clear the stockroom of extraneous bits lately is the truth of it. Or is it simply fate after all? Kismet, as the Arabs say.

Agnes sits down at my table, and I watch her stitch another and then another row of rickrack zigzags to her lemon Fuji skirt, while I dress the big mannequin in the gamboge for the window. So like I was when I was small, such concentration with the needle.

Except that she is so full of chatter today. Was I ever such a chatterbox? She tells me all about her friends at school, especially her best friend Gladdy Hanrahan, who always brings the best sandwiches for lunch as her dad's a foreman at the soap factory, and she's the champion at jumping ropes in the playground.

'I love Gladdy, I do. I loved her the first second I saw her. I'm allowed to call her mum Aunty Fern. But Aunty Fern, she was so cross that I didn't run away to her house. I did at first, I told her. I ran all the way up to Rowntree Street to her house – it's so far and I ran so fast I thought my legs would fly off or go on fire. But when I got there, their dog Maxie was out the front barking, and I'm even more scared of him than that lady from Welfare – he's big and black and there he was snarling at me through the gate and I don't believe he wouldn't bite me even though everyone says he wouldn't – and so I had to run again. And that's when I knew the only one to help me was you.'

You knew. You darling, darling thing. I say: 'You're full of stories, you are.'

She nods: 'I am. I love stories.'

'Why do you love stories?'

'I don't know.' She shrugs and snips a squiggle. 'I think stories must be like the air – without them my brains can't breathe.'

'That's the most beautiful thing I've ever heard, Agnes,' I tell her, and in the smile she gives me in reply, I simply can't imagine ever being without her. I want her in my afternoon every day. Pick up squiggles and pack away to her merry chatter every day. 'Home time,' I say and it's another fabulous adventure to her. As we walk down to the Quay, through the spent bunting, all grimy and torn, I almost ask her why she's really here, with me. I want to know about her mother; what happened to her. But I resist; I'm sure it's not something good. Instead, I say as we head under the arch: 'Your brother is very brave to work up there.'

She shrugs, looking up at the box-thing of men coming down above us. 'Oh, he's scared out of his brains all the time. It's only the rubber on their sandshoes that sticks them on. But he says anything worth doing is scary.'

Like love, chérie, Madame Chanel whispers over the water. *Avoid it if you can.*

No. I don't want to avoid it. At the door of my house, I am drawn by another impulse thus far foreign to me: I have to tidy up in here. Good God, the place looks like a bomb has hit it – a rainbow bomb – half my wardrobe spilling into the hall trying to crawl itself to the drycleaners. Line of smalls across the kitchen window – the Flags of Slattern. His house was so neat . . . and clean . . . even the hearthstone was swept.

'Miss Greene! Look at all your special things!' Agnes is in little-girl heaven amongst a pile of scarves spilling out of their basket.

'You don't happen to want to help me sort all this mess out, do you?'

'Oh, can I, please?'

We tidy my house: scarves in basket, clothes on hangers, fabric scraps and magazines in orderly piles, all conspicuous bonbon wrappers and squiggles removed. We feast on scrambled eggs and tinned asparagus. And then we settle down on the sofa to wait. Agnes is in a world of wonder with a stack of old *Vogue*s, and I watch her: so like me, she is, lost inside the pages so immediately. I prattle silly into a House of Drécoll sketch across her knees: 'Did you know there's a designer called Agnes too? French, with a grave accent over the e and you don't pronounce the g – so you say Anyes. Madame Agnès Havet of Paris – she was very famous when I was a little girl, when I was just about your age. She was the designer to the Empress of Russia.'

Agnes looks up at me and through me to some sequinned splash of her imagination: 'An empress?'

'Yes.' My smile is the thrill of then and now entwined: 'Lots of crushed velvet and brocaded bodice panels, all Grecian goddess lines. A bit old-fashioned now, I suppose, on the wheel of fashion fortune . . . but I'm sure I've kept some of those old *Les Modes* of

Mother's somewhere. I'll show you . . .' I get up to look into the impossible mess under my bed for Russian empresses, for those days before the *Titanic* sank the world into a war and raised the price of hemlines.

I release a squeak of a shriek under the bed while I'm here: 'Oh God!' Eoghan. Eoghan O'Keenan. Oh dear God. He is coming here. I am waiting for him. I am waiting to explode.

Yo

Get it into your spooned-out head that Miss Greene is not in any way interested in you personally. She's fond of Agnes. Who wouldn't be? And she's obviously a kind girl. For a lady. She's a lady. A charitable lady. She's not interested in me. She's not interested in someone wearing a naval surplus coat of wool so mean the sheep wanted its money back, but the only union-labour approved one I could get without pawning my arse. Nor would she want someone who spends Saturday nights on dog shift getting deafer from rivet holes going into plate indoors and still can't afford gloves for the catching, because I'm still paying off the tool belt I had to get and it's only got a hammer and chisel in it yet. And even if she'd have a pauper, she'd not be after one come from where I've come from. Not this side of hell.

But she has to be wanting me, says that voice from the other side. It's the Devil. Made me get a haircut yesterday. Made me nearly take my hand off on the planer just now at tech to demonstrate a quick amputation to the class.

The steps are too steep and too few going up to her house. To her door, and I'm knocking on it, my heart filling my mouth

The Blue Mile

so wholly I won't be able to speak. Speak to her. I'll have to.

Jesus, and the door is opening, and she's saying: 'Hello there. Yes, good evening. No trouble finding us? Of course not. Er – Mr O'Keenan. Should I better call you Eoghan? Oh, I don't know. What's decorum here? Do come in, please. I have Agnes hard at work reading fashion magazines. She's had an awful time of it. Ha.'

This is the girl I'm going to marry, her hands fluttering all about as she talks, saying my name so it sounds like Yon, because that's how she says it, so that's what it is.

'La la la la la la la. I do go on, don't I.'

Don't ever stop.

I'm going to marry you, Miss Olivia Greene. Yes, I am.

Olivia

'Well, we won't keep you longer. It was very nice of you to have Agnes over this evening. Say thank you to Miss Greene, Ag,' he says, slowly, carefully, as if he might've been robbed of his personality on the way here.

And I know. I don't know how I know, but there's something in his eyes, something in his looking away from me as he does, that tells me now: he feels this too. This tingling . . . singing . . . swooping . . . sensation. Sensational, he is. The collar of his duffel coat turned up at the back of his neck; the flush of his cheek; his fair skin; his dark hair. Black on white, and those deep blue – ooh . . .

He's folding Agnes's magazine and placing it back on the pile. He smooths out the dog-eared bottom corner of the cover, unthinkingly respectful of the value in everything. I see his fingers again, such fine fingers on one who does metal things. Such pristine and particularly cared-for fingernails. These are tailor's hands. Hands for fine work; hands to make valuable things with. He has a grazy scrape on the back of his left one and I want to kiss it.

Agnes says: 'Thank you, Miss Greene. I've had such a lot of fun.'

I say to both of them: 'Please, call me Olivia.' And I retie the bow at the end of her plait, as much to still my hands, my damn nervy hands, as to slake the compulsion for tying untied bows. 'I suppose you do have to go home,' my attempt at a sigh comes out in little fly-away breaths and can't hide the plea when I add, 'so that you might come back again. Yes?'

'Can I, Yoey?' Please.

'Well, I don't know, Ag, I . . .'

He looks to be in a torment over it. Please be in a torment for me, and not some other thing, some other girl. My conscience says it should be another girl. Some nice girl from Balmain. But I can't help it. If it's cruel, it's cruel to us equally: *please*.

He says: 'All right, then. Next Wednesday will be all right, I think.'

'Hooray!' Agnes throws her arms around his waist, and I don't know how I'm going to last the week.

*

The romance doesn't last a day longer. In the morning, I find a note under the salon door.

> *Dear Miss Greene*
> *Thank you for your thoughtful gift of the hat and the sketches of your designs. Such beautiful designs, precisely my style, and I have already worn the cloche twice – I didn't expect that Sydney would be so cold! I shall telephone to arrange an appointment at your salon for our mutual convenience as I have found my wardrobe terribly short on warmth, I'm afraid.*
> *Sincerely*
> *Gwendolen Game*

Fantasy finishes here. I must keep my eye on the dreams that will keep me. Dreams of figment boys need losing in the back of the stockroom – forthwith.

Yo

I'm halfway through slapping the cold cream on my face at the mirror in the kitchen, not two minutes in from work, and there's a knock at the door. Jesus, I think it's her, unlikely as that might be. I call out, 'Hang on!' scraping it off my face, with Ag laughing at me all the while.

But it's not her, of course. It's that Merridale woman from Welfare.

'Mr O'Keenan. Good afternoon, I –'

I step out the door and close it behind me; she's not coming in my house again. She's not going to scare Ag again. The trouble these people cause. The least of it is that Nettie's had what was coming: even the chooks are gone from next door, and I'm not overjoyed at that. A mob of Sturgess's Waterside Workers 'bailiffs' had their furniture all up the lane when we got in last night, which might have been done at Mr Adams's bidding, but there should be a law against the government coming into your house and stealing kids on the word of a neighbour anyway.

I say: 'What do you want?'

'Oh, please don't worry, there's nothing wrong here – not with you and your sister's living arrangements. I'm here only to let you know that, ah, after some checking of records it appears that your mother has been claiming Child Endowment payments for Agnes, er, unlawfully, for quite some time.'

I say: 'I'm not surprised. She's an alcoholic. It's grog money to her. Nothing to do with me.' I wish. Our poor mother.

'Yes, well. The Department has put a stop to that. But, ah, given the circumstances of your mother's, er, incapacity, there may be grounds here for you to legally adopt your sister, without your mother's consent.'

That changes my feeling: 'How so? What would I have to do?'

'Make an application to the court. Such an application would be unlikely to succeed for a single man, in your circumstances, but if you were to marry, then I would say, although I can't promise it as fact, that it would be a mere formality.'

'Marry?'

'Yes – is that likely?'

Is it? No. It's a promised fact that it's extremely unlikely. I won't marry Miss Greene. I can hardly say her name to myself: Olivia. O'Paddys do not marry girls with names such as Olivia. I tell this Merridale woman: 'No, marriage is not likely for me.'

She says: 'Well, there is another avenue by which you might achieve adoption – have your mother sign consent. Is that likely?'

Is it? No. I couldn't ask that of our mother, not to her face: your daughter's not your own anymore, right? How could anyone do that? I know I may already have done it to her. But to front her with it? Rub her nose in it? No. I shake my head.

The Welfare woman says: 'It's worth thinking about, Mr O'Keenan. A legal adoption would protect you in future – protect you both – from busybodies making false claims against you. If Agnes is unsupervised after school and she is your daughter, then that is *your* affair. It might entitle you to claim the Endowment too. But while you're a bachelor, well, another Welfare officer might not be able to take the time to investigate your situation properly . . . Do you understand what I mean?'

'Yes, I do.' This horseshit could happen again, or worse, because Ag isn't lawfully mine. I say: 'I'll have a think about it.'

She gives me her card: 'If you would like to discuss it further, make an appointment with me at the Department and I'll see what I might do to assist you.'

That takes me by surprise: she's really only come to help us, gone out of her way. Making amends maybe, but I say: 'That's kind of you, thank you.'

'Good evening,' she smiles, and walks away.

I open the door and Ag's there, had her ear to it, and she jumps up at me: 'You can marry Miss Olivia, Yoey!'

I say: 'That's not possible, Ag, and don't listen at doors or the Devil will fly in your ear.'

'Will not. Silly. And you can marry Miss Olivia. She loves you back. I know she does.' Ag puts her hands on her hips like it's done already: 'Easy.'

'No, it's not, Ag. It's not easy at all.'

'Why not?'

'Because it's not.' We're not good enough for that. Shitful but undeniable fact of the matter. 'Now, enough about it – where's my tea then, girl?'

She shakes her head, eight going on eighteen, had enough of my idiocy, and goes back out to the kitchen.

I go back to the cold cream at the sink, and think. Think about a visit to our mother.

*

I wait till the following Wednesday, for that hour I've got between getting to tech and going into the class. I usually go straight to the library, head-down round here to keep from looking down any street or at any face I might know, but this day I keep walking up to the brewery. Let our father see me, if he's in Ryan's at the bar

The Blue Mile

now, come out and challenge me here. I'll fucking kill him, I'm that much stronger from the work and not drinking.

But no one comes out for me. And I can't get halfway past the convent behind St Ben's. I just can't go further. I can't go anywhere this side of George Street West. My hands start shaking and my breath is short and I want a fucking drink like no other want. I just can't do it. I can't look on our mother again. If she's even there. I can't look on Mrs Callaghan looking down at me telling me our mother is not here because she's already in the lock-up for her thieving from the government. Or that she's dead. Too. Dead for as long as I can remember her. I start running, back over to Ultimo. Running to stop from crying over it. I'm not crying for her again. If our mother should ever want us, she knows where she can get us: through Welfare. If she'd wanted us at all she could have got us with one word through St Ben's. She doesn't want us. She wants nothing but her misery.

'Hey, Yo.' One of the young fellas from my class, Teddy Moss, is waiting for me by the library door. He's sixteen, keen as, and wanting me to look at his book work before we go in, scared of Mr Simpson if he gets something wrong. I tell him, 'Sorry, mate, I've got something in my eye. Mr Simpson won't kill you.' I can't see straight.

I don't know what goes on at Tech tonight. Some fella who runs some big motor import business comes in to give us a talk on chassis welding, and then Mr Simpson goes on about the importance of economy and record-keeping, a nail is not just a nail, it's a ha'penny for two dozen to the boss or some horseshit of common sense. I'm thinking about Miss Greene, with a desperation I've never known before. Saying her name to myself: Olivia. Olivia. Olivia. Is it possible? Ag's always right about everything else. She says Olivia is definitely a princess name, even better than Nina, and she's our princess to keep. Oh, oh, oh live eee ya! Could I ever hope to marry her? Olivia O'Keenan she'd be. Could she be? Could she love me back?

No. Why would she do that to herself?

When I go to pick up Ag from her house, there she is opening the door: 'Oh, hello.' Half-smiling and half-frowning like she's considering the idiocy of that question herself. The dress she's wearing answers it well enough anyway: it's got lace going round the bottom of it and round the sleeves that's made of some silver type material, catching the light in the hall, electric light and silver lace, and as she's showing me in, she's telling me everything else I need to know about it: 'We've had a terrible time as usual. I'm afraid I forced your poor sister to consume half a family box of chocolate creams. But I'm also afraid the usual is going to have to be not so usual, though. I'm going to have to suspend fun and games with Agnes for a few weeks – I've had some marvellous news, you see. The new Governor's wife, Lady Game, has made an appointment with me to book me up for the next hundred years – she's going to order just about a whole wardrobe from me, and I won't have time to sneeze. But unfortunately that means not a lot of time for fun and games.'

She can't look me in the eye.

The disappointment burns through me like hydrochloric acid, and comes right out my mouth as such. 'Good news for you then, isn't it?' I tell this Olivia Greene. I'm already grabbing Ag's coat. 'Come on, mischief. Miss Greene has things to be getting on with.'

Miss Greene blocks the way to the door: 'No, I didn't mean, I – Oh.'

'Thank you for looking after Agnes again,' I say. 'Very kind of you. We must be getting on ourselves.'

'Oh but, I didn't mean –'

I give her a look: I know what you mean. Get out of the way.

That shuts her up. She gets out of the way.

We won't be seeing Miss Greene again for her bit of fun and games with the poor folk.

On the steps down, Ag pulls my sleeve: 'Miss Olivia said I could come over every month, on the first Wednesday.'

The Blue Mile

'You're not going.'

'I am. Miss Olivia said –'

'You are not, Ag. Forget about Miss Olivia. If you mention her name again you'll not go to Gladdy's Saturday, right?'

She gives me a look under the lamp at the wharf: bastard. And that'll just have to be.

Olivia

'Yes, how perfect.' Lady Game is poring over my portfolio drawings – each and every one of them I have here in the salon – and she's choosing everything I would choose for myself. Not the sports mistress I was half-expecting, though her beige suit is a little atrocious: far too dull for her. She's my living mannequin for the mature woman. Me in about twenty years' time. 'Oh, but do you think I'd look like an old broomstick in that?'

I look at the sketch she's pointing to, ancient one, almost a year old now, my 'Lily', a scoop-necked shift with an asymmetrical crossover skirt that drapes from the hip like an arum cup, almost trailing to the ground, and I say: 'No, not at all. But imagine it in perhaps a pewter, of a light but cosy velveteen. Subtly metallic. Dress it up with multiple strands, perhaps pearls, or dress it down with a contrasting chiffon scarf, a good style for travelling, if ever you find there's no time to change entirely between afternoon and evening. Something like that might take you to a few Bridge parties too.'

Lady Game laughs: 'Bridge parties! But you're all Bridge mad here, aren't you?' A sincere and happy laugh that astonishes me each time she lets it go. There are no pretensions about this Lady, either. Not one snoot of superiority – she even told me not to close the shop especially or draw the blinds for her. She laughed, too, at my little bob of a curtsy: *Please don't bother with that.* She's not that sort.

And I must agree with her now: 'Yes, we are indeed – man, woman, child and dog – we're all mad for our Bridge.'

She laughs again. 'Well, so shall I be, too, I dare say,' and then she stands, no nonsense: 'Measure me up then, Miss Olivia Greene. Measure me up. I mustn't take up your entire morning.'

Do what you like! Mrs Harrington at ten-thirty won't mind a wait in this company, not one bit. So fabulous. I have this all sewn up, as a seamstress might say to herself when she's trying to stop her hands trembling long enough to fumble the tape out of the drawer. As soon as my frocks start appearing on the vice-regal mannequin, I will be *the* new Sydney designer to go to. God, I will have to get a girl to help me; must do that now. When am I going to find the time to interview girls, though? Oh God, oh God. How fabulously fabulous. Despite my planning this right down to the finest detail, now that Lady Game is here, in *my* salon, I can hardly believe –

'Uncanny – you must have made that for me.' Lady Game is looking over her shoulder at the pea-style now draped over the back of the chaise.

She'll be taking that one with her today; thank you, Mother, for that suggestion. I smile as I rope her round the hips with the tape: 'As I said, I made it for my winter window, Lady Game – and now I'll have to make another one, won't I?'

'Yes,' she says. 'That style will be popular, I'd predict. It would be well received in London, too, I think. Practical and just a little glamorous. That shade of yellow, so defiant of the season, and you wouldn't get run over in it crossing the road, would you?'

'Ha ha ha ha ha . . .' *That shade of yellow* is not that bright and it's not yellow, it's gamboge. 'Ha ha ha ha ha ha . . .' but I laugh now too, for my best client and my nicest, warmest one. 'I should hope not, Lady Game.'

I'm sure she's as warm to everyone she meets, but she's just made me feel as if I am the only couturier of any note in the whole world, and now she's placing her finger on the ribbon for me as I package up her pea-coat, asking my advice on the best place for sturdy school things for her youngest, Rosemary. She even carries her own bag out of the salon, driver waiting for her down on Pitt Street. Just another ordinary well-to-do mother of three. Who happens to be married to the King's man.

'Toodles!' I wave.

Did I just say toodles to the Governor's wife? I did. And she smiled under her hat. At me. When she's safely away, I shut myself in the stockroom for a moment and scream: 'Oh my God!'

Then look at my watch: ten past ten. Time to scoot down to the Emporium to hunt and gather, and have a scream with Glor.

Only she's not there.

'Surprise luncheon with the future mother-in-law,' Mr Jabour smiles when he sees me. 'Will I do?'

'Yes,' I say. 'That pewter velveteen – do you still have a shift's worth?'

'For Lady Game?' he laughs, already reaching for it.

'Yes.' My grin must be a sight – it's stinging the tops of my cheeks.

'Aha! Here it is, Olivia dear. Just the five yards left – I must have known.'

'Must have . . .' I run my hand over the feathery nap. 'Perfect.' But just as I do, the light from the lamp above the sideboard catches the silk, like a silvery sea, and as suddenly I slip from this high to plunge into it: splat goes my heart. Eoghan. I look over my shoulder at the brass bottle there, as if I might stopper every mad thought of him into it. One in particular: that rude look he gave me as he left, virtually pushing past me. Did I deserve that? It's no crime to have a life to be getting on –

'Is something troubling you, Olivia?' Mr Jabour is frowning at me, concerned.

'No.' I try to reclaim my grin but it's not much of a one. I say: 'I've just realised how much I've bitten off, Mr Jabour. You don't happen to have a spare daughter or niece hiding somewhere I could have for an extra pair of hands, do you?'

'Ahhh,' he pats his round belly. 'Well, now that you mention it, my brother George has a friend whose daughter is just leaving scho–'

'Oh, Mr Jabour – you truly are a genie, aren't you?'

But not even his genie laugh can quite lift me back up. I feel the slump of my shoulders. I can't see Eoghan again, nor Agnes. The gulf between us is too wide for any kind of relationship to ever be appropriate, and he knows it as well as I. Pushing past me, pushing me away. I must forget them, and yet I can't look at the Bridge without splatting into this sea. This regret. This disappointment every day our paths don't cross at the wharf. It'll stop one day, though. Won't it? Some dreams just aren't meant to be. No kismet for figment boy and me.

'Are you sure you're quite well, Olivia?'

'Of course I am.'

*

On top of this fabulous world, I am, and my new girl, Coralie Farr, is everything I could have hoped for if I'd had the time to think about what I needed. She's fifteen, neat, sweet and petite, with the exacting hand and eye of a Levantine draper's daughter. 'Oh, Miss Greene, yes, indeed, wonderful,' she says, regardless of the task, be it sorting out the dark recesses of the stockroom, cleaning the lint brushes or cutting for me. She's from Cootamundra; she thinks everything is indeed wonderful, with the swooshy caress of her father's Arabic on the w – *whonderful*. By the end of the first week I don't know how I ever managed without her.

By the end of the month, I need two Coralies. After more than a dozen welcome luncheons, teas and dinners for the Games across June, I'm forced to break my one-off rule and allow exact copies of a couple of my designs – never the same fabric, of course, but demand for the Lily frock and another called Pearl is such that I simply cannot say no. The irregularly scalloped hem of the Pearl is blind-making in itself, though, and I don't have the waking hours or the unlimited imagination to come up with seventeen subtle variations on the theme anyway.

And then, one blustery, mizzling morning, bleary and yawning on the ferry, I squeeze in under cover inside and find myself pressed up against a newspaper to see my little wattle cloche immortalised in black and white on the vice-regal head. Lady Game has been snapped boarding a plane for a joy ride round the harbour, the last line of the article beneath the photograph proclaiming: *Lady Game favours local millinery, she says. Her hat of deep green cashmere today was designed by Strand Arcade costumière, Miss Olivia Greene.*

One hundred wattle cloches swim past my eyes. So exciting, what an honour, thank you so very much, Lady Game. I would have preferred *couturier* but I'm not about to be pernickety here. Good God. My heart skips a beat – actually. Coralie won't get anything done for answering the telephone today, I know it. How will we manage with the deluge of work that's surely coming our way? Oh, I need some air, some space to think. To breathe. It's suddenly too warm and close, hemmed in on all sides amongst the steamy tobacco-stinking business suits, so I push my way back out into the drizzle.

Take a deep breath and, as I do, I look up from under my umbrella, and see him, as I do every day. Right up the top today, striding along a beam under the north-side crane. Any man, every man-shape I see up there, is him. Stubborn fantasies not stuffing as easily back in their bottle as I'd thought. Slipping out like the threads of 'Blue Heaven' violins, making me look over my shoulder once or twice a day. Making me glad I'm too busy to think, and too stubborn myself to spend too long staring out the venetians at night following the fairy lights across that deep blue mile between us. Refusing to say his name to myself. If I were one of those girls with little to do, I'd have given in and somehow . . . done what? Chased him? I'd not do anything of the sort. This is only five minutes worth of a fading, shrinking dream. Ill-fitting, annoying. Like the scratch of an improperly finished seam between one's shoulders: impossible to reach; whip it off and snip it off in the fitting room.

That's all it is. An irritating squiggle. Reduced to nothing as the honking, clopping chaos of the Quay whirls me into life. This real life. My fabulous life. One day, very soon, I'll wake up and the Bridge will be complete. That chink in the sky between the arms will be closed, bolted fast with iron, and he simply won't be there for me to look up for at all.

Yo

'Stop work – all men down!' It's Dolly shouts it out today from the underside of this final cross-member we're on. 'Hold off, Tarz!' He has to shout it louder: 'Stop work!' Because Tarzan McCall is more than half-deaf lately; he didn't even hear the workshop siren go off. I saw an ambulance come round by the dock about a half-hour ago when we stopped for smoko, but I didn't mention it, and no one else did either: there's been an ambulance every week, it seems, too many getting sloppy with the race on to the finish. I'm not getting sloppy: I'm on my hands and knees here with the southerly picking up. Tarzan steps across to the west top chord as if he's just seen his tram. I crawl. I hate this job. I hate every fucking four-hundred-foot-high second of it.

'Jesus, you're a faggot, Pretty,' Tarz says, watching me crawl.

'Am I?' A useless old woman? I don't give a shit what you reckon, Tarzan ginger fucking monkey-nutted man: you are twice my weight. As I get to my feet, I somehow knock the chisel off my belt, and down it goes. 'Fuck.' There's three shillings for nothing. That is such a sloppy sack of shitful I don't feel the cradle swing as I step in. I roll a smoke.

The Blue Mile

'You right?' Mr Adams says to me.

I look out, I look at the way the trees of the Gardens cover Bennelong Point like a woolly head, how the city sticks up out of it like a load of rotted and broken teeth, and I don't say anything. The workshop siren is going off again anyway as we go down and I'm hoping the poor fella it's wailing for is not dead, but obviously he is, or some similar tragedy has happened.

'Bloke called Fred Gillon,' Mr Harrison says when we're down, wiping his forehead with a rag from his apron for the shame of it. I didn't know him at all, not even to look at; no one in our gangs did. 'Hoist collapsed on him, down on the approach, one of the tripod legs come away. All ten tons of it, come right down on top of him. Terrible thing, didn't stand a chance. His mates all jumped clear, but it's flattened the poor bloke, killed him where he stood.'

There's discussion about how fairly ordinary his mates must feel. Seeing something like that happen. Jesus. Imagination is good enough. I feel as if I may as well have seen it. I am seeing it, right before my eyes.

'Go home any of you who needs to,' Mr Adams is saying and this time telling me to clear off. I mustn't look too good. Because obviously I'm not. I leave straight from the barge. I'll put in what I don't have for Fred Gillon tomorrow. I don't go home, though.

I walk round Lavender Bay, and my blood is pounding in my head, pounding right through to the insides of my bones with a feeling I can't begin to name. I am alive. I keep walking round the jetties past the public baths, past them swimming lessons I never got to because they were on here too late Saturday arvos and at Mass time Sundays at Balmain and I've been too ashamed otherwise to ask anyone to teach me how. What is shame to a dead man? I am alive and I walk out along one of the jetties into the middle of the bay. I can see her ferry stop from here. I can just see one small corner of the tin roof of her house against the dark brick flats by it.

From here, life suddenly looks too brutally short for horseshit. The leg of a tripod hoist come away. There's not a lot you can do about that. No more than I can't stop thinking about Olivia Greene. Wherever I am, whatever day it is, Olivia Greene is here, with me. I have tried but I can't look at the harbour waters without looking into her eyes, can't feel the sun on my back without remembering her smile. Seeing the way her hands go when she talks, like little birds tracing her thoughts around her. Ag's not mentioned her again, not once, just a look in her eye now and again over our tea table that says: bastard. I don't know if I'm depriving my sister of a mother, but I'm depriving her of a friend. I've got to do something about that now. I'll go up and slip a note under her door, and I'll tell her . . . what?

I'm not going to be a boilermaker's labourer forever. I might be unemployed again in the next few months if I can't get on full-time in the shops, or on hanging the road deck. That's right, unemployed again. I'll lose my apprenticeship, lose my place at Tech, too, then. I'll lose everything. There's no other work to go to now; there's nowhere that's not putting men off in droves. That's all the talk will be of at the Rag and Famish today: five minutes for Fred Gillon and the rest on how they're going to get this Big Fella Lang back into the government of the state so we can keep our jobs. On a job that's just about done. There's nothing to be done about that, either.

What point could there be in me telling Olivia Greene how much I think of her? Of what I think of anything.

None.

So I keep walking, back along the path below the railway tracks, keeping my eyes to the rubble shore. With my blood pounding a note out to me, telling me I'm an idiot for not living while I'm alive.

*

'It's no lottery, Eoghan, no mistake about it.' Mr Adams's grip on my shoulder has his fingers just about driven through my flesh with his own relief, as well as mine. We've both got on the road deck work, all our gang has, for when the arch is done. He says: 'You can be sure now you're one of the best.'

I am a boilermaker's assistant now, officially, employed with the company directly and I'll have to get membership with the union now too, but I rub my eyes to hide the disappointment at not getting in the shops full-time. I'd have taken the drop in pay and the shorter hours. There are just as many accidents in the shops – more so even – but they don't happen at height in the shops, do they. I do not want to work at height anymore, even if it's a thousand feet less hanging the road. I want my feet on the ground. But what I want and what I've got often bear little relation. Swimming lessons will be back on in October, I will book myself in for some then; Ag too. In the meantime, I can be certain and well pleased that I am one of the best. I know I am: too fucking terrified to make a mistake.

'Good enough, lad,' Mr Adams shakes me by the shoulder. 'Good enough.'

I look at him. His pit-bull potato head. Without him, I'd have nothing. I do well to make something of whatever I've got, I know, but without good people to give you a hand-up, you've got nothing to begin with. I owe him more than I can ever repay and all I can tell him is: 'Thanks, Mr Adams. Thanks.'

He shakes my shoulder again and he laughs at my face: 'Ha!'

The whistle from the crane goes off above us and we both look up, here outside the shops, and watch the dog men go up on the hook with the final piece of the east bottom chord, and strange as it is, I'm almost regretful it's not our gang that will be among the ones to rivet it. To step across the gap. Only about three feet left between once this is in. Would I have the guts to jump across? I'll never know now, will I. We watch some photographer fella getting in the cradle, going up to take pictures of it all, doubtless shitting himself and nearly losing his camera as the cradle bounces about twenty feet up – that's Dave Anders up on them crane controls, nasty bastard, does that deliberately for any uninitiated passenger. I look over my shoulder, across Lavender Bay, as if she might be looking this way too, but all I see there is Tarz and Dolly deciding that they'll start at the Rag and Famish with all the rest of the north-siders but get back to the Opera House by five to finish themselves off, staggering distance from home.

'Come round to ours for tea to celebrate, Eoghan?' Mr Adams asks me as we head for the ferry across to Darling Street.

'Thanks, yeah. That would be good, if it suits Mrs Adams.'

He hasn't taken his hand off my shoulder. More relieved about our continuing employment than he's letting on.

A fight breaks out behind us, spilling out of the heavy shops. An industrial dispute, from those laid off dog shift. Single men, they are, all labourers employed with Public Works. That was me yesterday. There's nothing Dorman Long can do for them. There's just nowhere for them to go, even with the shuffling round of hours requested by the unions, there's just not enough jobs to go round here, best at it or not. Soon there will be no dog shift at all, if the rumours there are true. There's no other work going round, but the government relief work, if you can get it – slave wages for digging ditches for the Nationalists, breaking your back for the dole. That would be a reduction in pay to six shillings a week, for a single man, for me. You can't live on that. You just can't. It wouldn't pay one-third of my rent.

'Keep walking,' Mr Adams says, as much to himself. There's nothing more he or any union can do about it but see that their Big Fella gets back in. To do what? He's not God. How do you make jobs out of thin air? You can't; you need money. This state doesn't have any, and what we do have we owe to the bank. The Bank of England. How do you tell the Bank of England to lay off wanting their money back? It's their money, and as far as I understand it, it's their money that runs the world.

'Fuck you!' someone shouts, and he's crying: 'Five years I've been here – five fucking years. You fucking bunch of –'

'Keep walking.'

There's a wagon coming round to the shops now anyway. Not an ambulance. The cops will move them off in a minute. There's a lot of cops around the works anyway; they say some Communists have threatened to cut the Bridge cables in protest of the great capitalist swindle that's every trade depression. But that's not really why the cops are here: they're just here to keep a full-blown riot over jobs at bay.

Olivia

It seems only to get worse, this... I don't know what it is. Each and every wattle bobble twist in the cord is him, round and round the violin strings go, *Just Ollie and me, and Aggie makes three*... Wouldn't it be good if the mind could have a dial fixed to it like a wireless so you could turn it off? I'm thoroughly moony with it this evening. I'd just like to tell him I'd never have made the first of these wattles cloches if that one day hadn't been made so beautiful by thoughts of him. And perhaps Lady Game would never have looked at my designs, and I wouldn't now be contemplating having the hot water put through into the kitchen at home when I'm not otherwise wafting wistful for a boy who doesn't exist.

Mr Jabour and Glor are right: I must be lonely, being on my own every night, doing nothing but working all day every day. But I like being alone, don't I. In so many respects I've always *been* alone. A little yonderly. I like to lose myself in my work, in my dreams and schemes. But perhaps it is making me a little mad. It is mad, surely, that even though the work has stopped on the arch of the Bridge, I still look up for him every day. He's not there, in either figment or fact. He can't be. The cables are being let go now, on either side, one hundred and twenty-eight in all – *ping, ping, ping*, I fancy they go, streaking through the air as so many lengths of black knicker elastic, though they don't do any such thing. They are let go slowly, carefully, and the whole city is holding its breath in anticipation to see if the thing will crash into the sea or be the Wonder of the World it's promised us for all this time it will be. But what do I see when I imagine that moment? I see the north and south arms meet with a last gentle clank and my figment boy placing the final pin to hold them together forever. It's a great big hat pin. With a golden wattle bobble on the end of it. The entire nation applauds . . .

'Is there anything else, Olivia?' Coralie is asking me if it's all right for her to go. It's six-fifteen, on a Wednesday, and the Emporium grille screeches shut downstairs to tell me Mr Jabour is waiting and shaking his head at me. It's more than all right.

I smile: 'You scoot.'

'Toodles then.' Coralie's shy smile in return is a vision of real-life dreams coming true. I let it catch me up for a moment. *Toodles* . . . Imitation is the finest form of flattery, is it not? More than that, it's so lovely to watch such excitement unfold in another: she's so thrilled every day to be here, wrapped up in the thrill of creating beautiful things, and there's a look in her eye, a certain thinking-waiting-lip-biting look, especially when I have her tacking up on the mannequin, that tells me one day soon she's going to ask me if she can perform her own experiments here. And I will be thrilled, just to see what she comes up with.

I smile down at the tiny real-life wattle bobble in my hands, at what it truly means to me: my dreams coming true. The ones that matter. The ones that mean I'm going to need to have an accountant do the books this year, for the first time ever, or I might get myself into trouble with a tax bill. How fabulous is *that*? Featherlight and fluffy these little wattle cloches may be, but they are listed and numbered on the inside band, so that my clients can be sure of their exclusivity – that was Glor's idea, off the cuff, over coffee. *You have to make people think that they're special, no matter how common their taste may be.* So true. That's why Syrians are overtaking drapery in this country. *So, do fifty,* she said, *and charge double.* So here I am finishing off number forty-nine and thinking I should have the phone put on at Lavender Bay too, when I have the time to meet the phone man there.

When will that be? God, I always have too much to do. If the stockroom weren't so stuffed with stacked-up orders I really might purchase that trundle so I could sleep in there. And things just don't get more fabulous than that, do they? What more could any girl want than Lady Game telephoning this morning? *Is that my private wardrobe secretary Miss Olivia Greene?* she asked. That thrill swooped and sang through every thread of me. She wants me to design her something special for a fundraising event for the District Nursing Association. Her actual private secretary, Miss Crowdy, who has an OBE for her heroic war work with the navy, takes shipshape care that the vice-regal touch lights upon every aspect of feminine health and welfare in the state, and Lady Game wants *me* to take care that she looks the part. *I don't wish to look too . . . distant, Olivia. I wish to appear approachable, I think is the word. I do so wish to be amongst things and be made good use of while I'm here.* She couldn't not be amongst things if she tried – she's adored in every quarter already. But I do know what she means: she doesn't want to look too fabulous amongst the easy-wash, easy-fade suburban poplin hoi polloi. Nor too dowdy. I will conjure up something just right, a little burst of early spring sunshine. Mr Jabour has some divine georgette prints just in . . . hmmm, that softest lime one with the faint leafy geometric floating through it. Perfect . . .

Perfectly enormous yawn.

I let myself pack up and float home on that, on Lady Game's kindness. How special she has made me feel. She could shop exclusively at DJs, or go to Melbourne like those who find Home far too far to get to. She could simply not buy locally at all. But she's

The Blue Mile

my client. She chose me. I'm barely nineteen and I'm choosing the Governor's wife a gently fluting skirt for the District Nurses. Yes, and that soft lime georgette, teamed with that misted petunia clutch purse that's just appeared in the window of Strand Bags, across from the Emporium, and with that amethyst brooch I have, and perhaps a mid-brim of straw with a simple band of lavender . . . it gets me almost under the Bridge, almost lost enough to forget to look up.

But still, I look up. There's nothing to see, no Bridge to see at all, the night is so black, but still I must look up. *Toot toot,* the ferries call to each other and they're the only sounds out here on the water tonight. Listen. All smash-bashing has more or less ceased now the workshops have cut back on their night shift. All is quiet on the blue mile tonight. Shhhh. Let it be simply lovely here in the crisp cold air. *Tooooot.* No, the melancholy ferry calls won't quite let me. They whisper: poor Eoghan, he's lost his job. Like most other labouring men have. And I'm whispering back: perhaps we'll meet in the morning when he's on his way in to the Labour Exchange. Shhhh, I whisper over that: Eoghan O'Keenan is not your boy. There is no boy. If ever there was one, he's *gone* . . .

It's so quiet I can hear the water plashing on the wharf now. *Shhh shhhh.* My eyelids are so heavy by the time my key is in the door I almost miss the envelope sticking half out of the mail flap. Who could it be? Of course it's an invitation to a ball, where a man in a white tux and midnight trousers wi—

It's a telegram. From London.
From Bart Harley.

IT'S A GIRL. SOPHIA. ALL WELL. EM SENDS LOVE. LETTER TO FOLLOW.

My heart plummets. Crashes into the sea. I have a little sister. Sophia. Em sends love. Even at this distance I am cast off. Mother no longer. She is Em. Something inside me wails up from the centre of a storm. My storm. Some terrible loneliness I knew was there but didn't see the shape of till now. Here, in this house with me.

Oh, how this hurts. I want to run out to the cliff top and scream out how this hurts.

But I reach for the Christmas cognac in the cupboard instead. I gulp down a sherry glass full of it. It burns and scratches me, and it's precisely how I feel. So hurt. So unspeakably scaldingly angry, and scratched-up, smashed-up hurt. I gulp down another glass of this poison. And then I have to race to the kitchen basin gagging on it, but I refuse to throw it up. I gulp down a third, and I sit on the kitchen floor and sob.

*

And it only gets worse from here. In the morning, with my throbbing head and savaged throat, I'm barely back in the door of the salon, barely quarter past eight and the telephone screams at me until I croak into it: 'Good morning, Olivia Couture.'

'Oh Olivia,' it's Mrs Bloxom. Leona Bloxom. I think she's going to gasp on at me about how I should start attending more functions, because didn't I know so and so was at Government House for such and such, and I really should reconsider Warwick's Oxford cut for a spot of lawn tennis *la la la la la la la* . . . but she's not saying that. She's asking me: 'Are you all right, dear?'

'Yes, why shouldn't I be?' I sound like I have a heavy cold.

'You've not heard the news?'

'Of . . . ?'

'Your father . . .'

'My father what?'

'His mistress,' Mrs Bloxom says, relishing the distaste. 'That actress, Gigi whatever she is. She's been found dead in a hotel room in Nairobi. Your father has been arrested. It's in the paper – this morning – right here, under my nose.'

I have no idea who my father is but he has just destroyed my world. Utterly. Splutteringly. Olivia Couture is finished. All my work . . . Oh dear God. A scandal of this kind . . . I am utterly finished.

'He is innocent, of course,' Mrs Bloxom is going on about it. Viscounts don't murder Hollywood starlets in hotel rooms in Africa. Of course not.

I wouldn't know. But I do know he's not innocent. Not to me. He should go to prison, for all that he has harmed me.

But I keep my head, somehow amidst the crash-banging going round inside it, and say: 'Thank you, Mrs Bloxom, thank you so much for warning me.'

'Don't worry about any of it, dear,' she says, and so sincerely I almost believe her. Until she adds: 'There are far more tawdry tales to entertain those who are after them at the moment. Have you heard about what the Fortescue and Bromley girls have been up to lately?'

'No.' And I don't care, until the nasty streak in me makes me ask: 'What have they been up to?'

'The *boyfriend*, Denis Clifton . . .' She pauses dramatically, and I think, here we have it, they've been found out for their cocaine smuggling, but she says: 'He's taken the blame for Cassie, but it was her at the wheel of the motor car.'

'I'm sorry?' I can't follow, and not only because Mrs Bloxom's excitement is causing her to babble. The cognac is revisiting and I think I'm going to have to throw it up this time.

'She hit a hobo – in the street – driving home from the Merrick. Drunk – out of her mind, so I've heard through the Shadfords.'

'Was she?' I don't know how people drink, I really don't. I am so ill. Oh, God help me. But Mrs Bloxom's message is getting through all the same.

'Yes. They left him there to die. In the street. Poor old swagman, he was. Warwick says they should go down for manslaughter, but they won't. They'll get away with it, he said. The Crown won't appeal, no money to appeal against money these days,' she snoots, as if her money is any different. 'I don't want Warwick associating at that Merrick Club ever again, and he won't. I always thought it the most dreadful place. But enough of that, Olivia dear. You keep your chin up about the viscount's spot of bother. The press do like to make a to-do of things like this. It will all be over in a few weeks, see if I'm wrong.'

You are wrong, Mrs Bloxom. So wrong.

Suddenly the whole world is wrong. The world is so wrong that the wealthy get away with *things like this* – with damn murder. Daddy's on the Commonwealth Bank board, so it's all right. Daddy is a top-ranking public servant, so it's so all right it's kept out of the papers. Whereas the Viscount Mosely, Lord Ashton Greene, well now, he's a good salacious front-page story – but he'll get off too.

Whether my father has done it or not, he's bloody done it as far as I'm concerned.

And yet somehow I still manage to keep my head, such must be my training in absorbing the preposterous around me. I say good day to Mrs Bloxom and then I pen a note to place in the window of the salon door:

Dear Customers
Due to unforeseen circumstances, this salon is closed from today,
14 August, for one week, reopening next Thursday, the 21st. My
apologies for any inconvenience.
Olivia Greene

One week. To take a very deep breath. To see out this storm. Wait it out. Sensibly. Wait to see what the upper circle makes of it. Wait for my many emotions to settle, if nothing else. Take a break. Need a holiday. Under a blanket. Wait to see if I am merely experiencing a moment of final-straw hysteria before deciding my life is over. Wait for cognac convulsions to abate – please. I hope one week is long enough.

I go down to the Jabours and find Glor, who's only just in herself, handbag on the cutting table. She smiles when she sees me in the mirror behind it: 'Yes, Dad's down at Customs now with the new Shantungs,' then she sees how leached I am and turns. 'Ollie! What's wrong?' she flies to me.

'Could you please tell Coralie when she gets in to reschedule my appointments? I'll be back on the twenty-first. Let her know I'll pay her for the week, of course.' I put the salon keys on the cutting table: 'She can go in and play if she wants to.'

'Ollie, what's happened? Are you not well?' Glor is worried I'm out of my mind.

Because I might be. 'Not well, no. Read the paper this morning. Mother's had a girl, too – Sophia. Nice name, isn't it?' That makes no sense, but Glor will work it out. I add: 'Lord Ashton Greene – Viscount Mosely – that's my father,' because she wouldn't know. I've never told her. She's not of that circle, lucky girl, wouldn't have reached her good and kind ears. Oh God, I could throw up on my shoes right here. I turn to leave.

Glor follows: 'Where are you going?'

'I'm going to bed,' I say.

'Do you want me to help? I can come with you.' Glor is quite frightened for me now. 'Coralie could help Dad. Just wait until –'

'No, please. I'd like to be alone. But thanks.'

'But Ollie –'

'Please, Glor. It's all right.'

It's so not all right I'm sobbing all the way back down Pitt under my brim and I don't really care if anyone sees. No one would care anyway. A thousand sob stories on this street as it is.

MONSTER SALE!
CLOSING DOWN BARGAINS!
RIDICULOUS PRICES!

The bookshop by the Tulip Restaurant on the corner of Hunter Street has been gobbled up by newsprint entirely, the windows papered over, up to the awnings in grim black and white, while a murder of barristers flap away up the hill to the courts.

What is this world I live in? What am I doing making hats and frocks for the rich? Are they all criminals umming and ahhing over whether they'll have the moss, the taupe or the tan for their wattle cloche, while they step disdainfully over the khaki swags of those less fortunate? Those not in the club. I know there's one rule for the rich and another for the rest, I was raised to learn that lesson well – to be thoroughly frightened of failing at it, too. But murder? Murderers aren't only bred among the razor gang thugs and brothel madams from Paddington that heroic Bart Harleys throw in prison, are they? Just as thieves aren't all Irishmen. Murderers and thieves: I rub shoulders with them every day, up in the gods at the Strand. Murderers and thieves: all cold-blooded creatures who don't care.

What good, then, are all my beautiful things?

A spider is still a spider, in guipure-edged lamé or coarse marocain.

But what am I?

*

Apart from confused and overwrought, I am one who is indeed suffering from a heavy cold. Phlergh upon phlergh, I start sneezing and shivering like there's no tomorrow soon as I'm back home behind my damp and draughty stone walls. It's fortunate then that Glor is kind enough to refuse my request that I be allowed to wallow in my own black horribleness here. She doesn't last the day, knocking on the door at three: 'Ollie, let me in – Mum and Aunty Karma will come too if you don't behave yourself.'

So I let her in. She marches up the hall. 'Right. This Viscount Whatsit, whoever he is. Tell me every last dreadful thing.' She's read the newsprint, evidently. She marches straight out to the kitchen, bag full of groceries for meatball soup, and before my stomach can even think that is beyond kindness, she's attacking an onion by the basin, saying: 'Come on – out with it. Who is he?'

'I don't know.' I quietly begin my unravelling at the kitchen table. 'I don't know who he is. He's just some man my mother married – once.'

'I thought you said your father was dead.' Chop, chop, chop.

'No – lost in the war. There's a subtle difference.'

'Right.' A flash of something in her dark eyes as she glances over her shoulder at me: anger at my deception.

So I must confess: 'He was quite well lost before it, actually – never mine to have. He's just the man who paid my school fees and once a month sends an insultingly inadequate allowance to forget I exist. Mother wasn't so astute at gold-digging in those days.' My voice is as small with hurt as my knuckles are white with clenching, with hatred of him. Strange flashes of memories shudder through me: the hook of his nose, the man smell of him, and his putrid cigars, the swinging hem of a damp tan coat, Mother laughing at his jokes, the popping of corks, and her silence otherwise. Mother forever looking out the window at Grosvenor Place, across the Palace Gardens: *Shush, darling, I'm thinking.*

'He was never faithful to her, Glor,' I say, shame whispering and burning through me. 'He never had any intention of being a husband or a father, an utterly dishonourable man. I don't know why he married her at all, just another perverse whim of his. But Mother thought it was a good idea to let the Bloxoms know of my pedigree before she left for London with Mr Number Two, and now everyone knows precisely who and what I am.'

'*I* didn't know.' The flash of anger again, and then a sigh: 'Oh, Ol, I'm so sorry. That's a nasty lot of shemozzle, all right, and that poor actress – *dead* at twenty-three? Too dreadful.'

'He's ruined me.' *God, why?* I wail inside.

'Ruined you?' Glor waves the chopping knife dismissively over her shoulder. 'No he hasn't. No one who matters cares about people like him. Blood might be thicker than water but we're all more water than we are blood.' She lops the top off the carrot on the board and then opens the cupboard behind her, poking about for something. 'Lock him up, lock him out of your life and throw away the key – but you are *not* ruined, my friend. Far from it. I remain concerned, though . . . Pepper? Where is your pepper?'

'I don't know – somewhere . . .'

'Ollie,' she sighs again, 'I'm far more concerned about the way you live. Alone like this. It's not good for you – it's not good for anyone. How can you not know if you have pepper in your larder?'

'I know, I'm a mad old spinster. I really should get the telephone man in,' I say absently. 'I'll go up to North Sydney tomor–'

'That won't do. That's not what I mean,' Glor chides me. Fondly. 'A telephone won't put proper food in your cupboards. I mean couldn't you ever see yourself settling down? Forget the rotters, darling Ol. There are so many *nice* boys out there. You've broken two hearts already that I know of – it's a brave man that asks you to dance. Hoddy Delmont's the type that might even let you keep your business, too, you know.'

Might – not good enough for me. I snort at Glor, as if a good marriage really is the answer to everything, and then I sniff: 'I've only met one nice boy I like – and he doesn't exist.'

'What do you mean?'

And so I unravel all that too: 'Remember that little girl you saw me with that day . . . ?'

Gloria Jabour's Arabian eyes grow wider as my tale about this nice brave rivet-catching Irish boy on the Bridge grows taller and taller. 'Dirt poor, of course,' I say. 'They live in Balmain,' and she drops the knife on the floor: 'No.'

'Yes.' I think she's appalled. Appalled at the mere idea that I visited Balmain. At night. As well she should be.

Until she squeals: 'That's the most gorgeous, *gorgeous* thing I've ever heard of, Ollie Greene.' Then she puts her hand to her breast, scandalised again: 'Don't worry, I won't tell Mum.'

*

The Blue Mile

Don't tell mine, either, that I'm wandering round to the other side of the bay just after dawn, along the reserve by the railway tracks to the Dorman Long workshops at Milsons Point. Telling myself that I'm only going over to walk under the arch, as half of Sydney is anyway. To see that the arms have kissed. Are kissing. Forever. Magnificent. The pin locked them together sometime around midnight last night, the milko told me just now and I've never ensembled myself quicker. There's no discernible wattle bobble atop the great curve, though, not that I can see, just as there will be no figment boy, either. I only want to join the crowds, don't I, to share this moment in history, and to celebrate my personal resurrection: after four days' moping, and a medicinal amount of confectionery consumed, my cold has lifted. Whoop. Hurrah.

A glorious winter's day it is for it too, this day, the twentieth of August. The early sun is splashing gold all through the water and the Bridge zigzags are bold black against the golden sky. If you're not cheered to see this, you must be dead. Indeed, I am much more than cheered. I am this moment deciding that my father can go to hell, and that my mother is quite possibly a saint deserving of every heavenly happiness for having survived him. Must write her a congratulatory note one of these days, mustn't I, something with a little more affection in it than my last effort in which I implicitly detailed how much I don't miss or need her by the number and variety of shoes I purchased across July. But what else should you expect from one of my breeding? The daughter of a starlet-murdering lord and a wild colonial seamstress. And if any of this matters to Lady Game or anyone else, I'll pack up right now and go direct to Paris. I have enough in the bank, enough of a portfolio and a refugee's story for Madame Chanel's entertainment – the French got rid of their aristocracy some time ago, didn't they.

If I fail, I'll come home and set up a hats-and-frocks in Homebush, or rather Chatswood – that's a suburb set to do well from this Bridge and the highway traffic they say it will bring north. Or perhaps I could work for the Jabours – travel the Orient buying for the Emporium. I have options. I have excellent friends; they may be few and all named Jabour, but they share my taste in chocolate, sending great big red boxes of Mr Hillier's finest and Aunty Karma's orange and date slice with it. Hardly a tragedy. Quality that counts.

La la la la la la l–

Oh good God, but there he is. That's him. That black hair. Hands in pockets. Standing beyond the path, on the rocks, right by the water. His back is to me, but it's him. I know it's him.

Crisp white shirt: I'd know that shoulderline anywhere.

Before I can stop it, before I can think, I am running towards him and calling his out his name.

'Eoghan!'

Yo

I go to turn around, thinking I've heard someone call out my name, but no one calls me Eoghan here, apart from Mr Adams, and he's standing right by me. It must have been a ferry whistling or something.

'Will you look at her!' Mr Adams shouts as if he's seeing her, for the first time, shouting over the workshop siren going off now, all the crane whistles going off in answer too, to signal to the city that it's done. The two halves are a whole. Up there on the jibs the blue flag of Australia is unfurling and the Union flag with it, and here we are. Seven o'clock, come in to be told we've been given an hour and a half off this morning and she's letting everyone know about it.

Mr Adams grabs my shoulder with something more than relief. He says: '*Buiochas le Dia*,' closing his eyes, no blaspheming in his wonder. *Praise you, Lord*. What a miracle this is. Thirty-nine thousand tons of steel holding itself up since about four o'clock yesterday evening, and she's staying up. That is fucking amazing. There are a couple of more-than-relieved engineers around here today as well, no doubt about it. Smacked as much as anyone that it's done. That they got their calculations and the timing right, to stop it coming together with too great a power, and no easy thing with the expanding of the steel in the heat of the sun. Look at her, all right. The heaviest bridge in the world, holding herself up. We'll be back up there soon enough, going along the joins of the bottom chord, by the centre pin, we'll be up there for a month yet, at least, before we start hanging the deck, but I want to get up there now. Shout out the miracle of it.

'Yeah!' I shout out where I'm standing anyway.

We did it, and I was a part of its making. This Sydney Harbour Bridge. I've never been so proud and happy in all my life.

Every man and his dog is going off along the foreshore round the shops, dancing, waving, fooling around. The ferries and punts all across the water are pulling their whistles too, with a big ship coming under the arch now, flying streamers and blowing its stack, all making such a noise, such a sight of pride and happiness.

In all this, I catch the high whistle of 'Oops!' behind me and turn just in time to catch a girl by the elbow before she slips off the rocks.

I laugh: 'I've got you.'

Half-hanging over the wash, she looks up at me: 'Indeed you do.'

That smile. Oh Jesus, I have died and you didn't care to tell me.

'Miss Greene?' I test the reality.

She says, straightening herself up: 'Please don't call me Miss Greene. Not today. Not any day. Call me Olivia. Just Olivia, from now on.'

'Now on?'

'Yes. From now on.'

Olivia

He doesn't let go of my arm, and I don't want him to.
The stocky older man in the grey flannel shirt beside him says: 'I'd better be off to rope in Tarzan, and don't you forget yourself either, Eoghan – eight-thirty back here and in the cradle.'

Figment boy looks at him as I'm sure I do: with complete incomprehension. Tarzan, cradle, untuneful Irish growl.

When the man is gone we look at each other again, with no less incomprehension, and still he doesn't let go of my arm.

He says, finally: 'Olivia.'

'Yes?'

He says: 'I would like to kiss you, if I may.'

I might nod; I'm not sure. My mind has gone to water, slipped into the sea at our feet, while my heart has flown away, zooming and looping the Bridge overhead. Kiss me: yes. Eoghan. Etherise me utterly. Here. Now.

But he only smiles. Only? Those dimples – I will slip into the sea.

His hand slips into mine. 'Come on,' he says, and he watches my step up the rocks. We start walking, back towards the path that runs along the head of the bay, through the thickening tide of Bridge wonderers. 'And here's the other half of the city,' he says, smiling into them, so many workmen and so many suits pouring down the escalator from the tram and out from the station, all coming to have a look on their way to work. I can't reply. I can barely breathe. Eoghan. He is holding my hand. The essence of my being is singing between our palms, with some other sensation altogether: a raindrop sizzling on an ember. I can barely see. But I do understand now how it is that a girl might find herself in a faint from this sort of thing.

Oh God.

We keep walking, away from the crowds, and he leads me in under the railway viaduct up from the baths, but every housewife in North Sydney is trotting down this way for a look too, coming down through the reserve beyond with an army of small children, all jumping about to the madly tooting ferries on the harbour.

I look up through the scribble of trees towards the top of the reserve. My house is not two minutes down that way. I want him to come into my house. I want to be his odalisque there. In my room, in my sheets, with the sun streaming through the venetians. I want things I've never dreamed of.

I whisper: 'My house . . .'

He squeezes my hand: 'No.' But he pulls me along up the steps here and towards my house anyway as though he knows the kinks in these streets as his own, and by the time Bay View twists up into East Crescent I should have well and truly reconsidered what I am about to do. We walk right past my house, and as we do Great Grandfather Weathercroft's 1847 glowers at me from the lintel with the rattle of convict chains: *You will not kiss this boy.* But I can't hear that. An ocean-going ship gives out a great big bellowing toot and I find it on the water, strung all over with hooray festoonery, tooting again, tooting up through my toes. What is this city going to do when the Bridge is actually completed? What am I going to do?

'Blues Point,' he says. 'There'll be no one around there.'

The Blue Mile

I may whisper, 'Yes,' but I don't know. I am a whisper, slipping round under the cliff face, past the queue of punts at the vehicular wharf and the rust-bucket council depot stores, and into the reserve beyond that. There is no one here. It's always lonely here.

He squeezes my hand again, up the steps to the old colonial lookout on top of the point. He pulls me into the little stone gun turret there that smells of salt and sandstone and some windswept childhood laughter curling around the edges of now.

He takes my face in his hands. So close I breathe the smell of his skin as he does, that salty musky smell of a man somehow made new to me now, thrilling me now. He smells *real*. He says: 'You are the most beautiful girl in the world.'

And as his lips meet mine, I am. Beautiful. I believe it. I believe I am. I am the most beautiful girl in the world.

I am the only girl in the world. At last.

Yo

I know it's wrong, but she says yes. She keeps saying yes.
'Oh yes,' she says when I touch her cheek, and I touch her arm and I kiss her neck. Her perfume is so sweet, she is so sweet and soft everywhere I touch her, and my hand is well where it should not be, against her breast, and she is softer than anything I've ever known when she says: 'Ruin me, Eoghan. Ruin me.'

Four

Olivia

'No.' He stops. He steps back against the turret wall and looks away, out the gun slit. 'This is wrong,' he says, and a cold humiliation sweeps through me. I don't need to be told this is wrong.

I push past him, back out into the light of day. What a dreadful thing I have done. What a dreadful fantasist I am. Thank God there is no one around here to have witnessed that. *Ruin* me? I told him to *ruin* me? There's an aeroplane zooming over the arch now, with a banner flying behind it. It shrieks: *HARLOT.*

I shriek as I run down the steps: 'Don't you follow me. Don't you dare.'

'Miss Greene,' he says, following me. 'Olivia. Let me apologise. I didn't mean –'

'No. Don't tell me.' I know what he meant. How revolting. I agree. I just threw myself at a boy. A Catholic boy, who has a crucifix nailed to the wall of his sitting room. I am going home to wash him off me. His smell. His hands. Oh God, who knows where they might have been. Filthy, clanging, metal things.

'Olivia! Stop!' He tries to pull me back by my arm.

And I shriek again, pushing him away: 'Don't you dare!'

'Stop, will you!' He gets me by the wrist anyway, and drops his voice, pleading: 'Your dress is caught up at the back.'

'Oh?' I glance behind me, at my pleats bunched up like a tartan concertina. 'So it is.' Worked its way up under my belt somehow, giving a good show of petticoat. I really didn't need that humiliation as well, right in front of the punt just in, giving me a front row audience of two sparkling Rolls-Royce limousines rolling up the ramp. I stomp round towards the passenger wharf.

He continues to follow. 'I mean it was wrong for me to do that. I let go of my senses. I shouldn't have asked –'

'No, you shouldn't have.'

'I'll not do that again.'

'No, you won't.'

'I mean that. I mean—'

'What could you possibly mean?' I shove the words behind me, but I don't look back. Meaningless. Stupid. Kiss. Ruin. This is not real: this is head cold delirium. I haven't left the house. Oh God, please stop following me.

He doesn't. He keeps on as I start up the ferry steps: 'I mean to marry you. I'll not ask to kiss you again until you say you'll marry me, Miss Greene. Olivia.'

'What?' I stop and turn around at the stair rail. 'Marry me?' I laugh – at him, down at him. What sort of a silly girl does he take me for? This is what Irish boys do with their dancing words, isn't it: charm you out of your wits. Marry you, give you ten children, and then leave for the pub. Three full steps below me here, I give him my imperious best. 'Well, you'll be waiting a long time, won't you?'

But he's not deterred. His gaze remains as steadily on mine and those deep blue eyes seem as honest and plain as the water behind him. 'I know I will wait,' he says. 'I know I can't have you. But that's what I meant when I said no. That's all I meant.'

The Blue Mile

'That's all? You only meant to say you mean to *marry* me?' Insane.

'Yes.' He is emphatic, firm, but his deep blues search my face with that melting tenderness of his. 'And it's not just for seeing you here on this day,' he says, 'it's not just the occasion getting away with me, though it has. I've meant to marry you since I first saw you, in the Gardens that morning. You are the most beautiful girl in the world, to me.'

Outrageously charming. And yet I believe him again. I want him to kiss me again. Here, in the full light of day.

'Excuse me.' An elderly gentleman is shuffling down the steps beside us, and I watch the way Eoghan moves to let him past. Carefully, respectfully nodding an acknowledgement to the man. Nothing imaginary about that. He is a nice boy. Such a nice boy. This is dreadful.

He looks up at me again, with such pleading; he says: 'The lights are going to come on on the Bridge tonight, I'm going to take Ag out to see it. Would you come with us?'

Would I? The Bridge is a solid steel rainbow across the cloudless sky behind him. I look at his hand on the rail below mine, fine long tailor's fingers that do metal things. Such a brave boy, who goes up on that Bridge. The aeroplane zooms past from the west now, the banner I see actually says *CELEBRATE!* and I am a whisper again: 'Yes.'

This is dreadful. Dreadful trouble. Ruin.

He says: 'I should get back to the shops. Me and Ag'll come and get you at six o'clock this evening? Have something to eat with us, somewhere?'

'Yes,' I feel my smile grow with the sweet delight of this: I will see Agnes again too. 'Come and have dinner at my house,' I say. 'We can watch the lights come on from there. On my front step. It's the best view.'

'It is,' he smiles back, not referring to the Bridge, and I swoosh and tumble into his dimples again. So very dreadful, being held up swimming inside his smile like this, but somehow I come to my own senses in it. Looking into his eyes, neither of us looking away. This is good, crystal clear. Kismet.

'But I should get back to work too,' I tell him. Indeed I must: no troop of fairies magicked away the thousand and one things on my to-do list while I was indisposed. Foremost, I must cut that pattern for Lady Game's District Nurses, even if it ends up rebuffed thanks to his Lordship's wanton efforts to destroy me. The show must go on, as they say. And then, good God, I must get things for dinner. What things? I don't know how to cook proper dinner things.

He says: 'I will try, I have to warn you. I know I can't have you, but I will try.'

Fabulous. So shall I. Somehow.

Madame Chanel clicks her tongue and sighs: *You will not marry that boy, chérie.*

Won't I? Why not?

You are too young. He is too poor.

I'm not listening. I watch him dance back down the steps, and I don't know how any sane woman could look past a shoulderline like that. I watch him turn to wave at the bottom, where he calls out: 'I mean worthy – I will try to be worthy of you.'

And I know he already is.

Yo

'So, the bastard can't even turn up to say hello,' Tarzan says of the company boss, Mr Freeman, and the note he's had pinned here for us on the office door.

The arch is safely joined, it says. *Mr Ralph Freeman personally extends to all employees of Dorman, Long and Co Ltd, an invitation to join him in the toast 'Success to the Bridge'. Mr Freeman regrets it is impracticable to meet you all in person, but requests you to call at the office on completion of shift for the means of honouring the above toast.*

'And you'd want him to, would you?' Mr Adams shakes his head. 'Load of boiling King's own bollocks, that is. You're all invited to a toast that you're regretfully not invited to attend. Fuck off.'

'Pommies,' Clarkie shakes his head too.

And I start laughing. I don't care if Mr Freeman is the King. I'm having tea with Olivia Greene tonight. Olivia. I kissed her. I'm still tasting that kiss. Touching her – Jesus. Stop it.

'What are you laughing at?' Mr Adams shakes his head at me.

'Nothing. Just happy.'

'Right.'

Happy all day, I am. Grinning all across the city from the centre pin. From the top of this last panel we're on, on the first row of what will be twenty thousand or so, I'm smiling at each rivet as it hits the centre of my glove. Whack. I finally got me them gloves for catching, last Friday night. I got me Olivia Greene today. I love Olivia. I love rivets. I am just about broke from these gloves, and who cares? I am a happy rivet-catching machine, tossing hot cocks from right hand to left, where Tarz tongs them up to their holes and has to stop the gun after a while to ask me: 'What's wrong with you?'

I say: 'It's a beautiful day.'

He gives me a look: whatever you reckon. I laugh. I don't miss a rivet all day; and I can't keep from laughing all day either, even when the argument that's been brewing gets going properly on the way back down in the cradle at the end of shift. We've come down with half a south-side gang, all of them Englishmen, and the horse-shit starts flying over which engineer designed the Bridge: Freeman the Pom, or Mr Bradfield the Aussie. I'm no more interested in it than I am in arguing the toss of Don Bradman's batting average on any day, but this day I'm especially uncaring of the differences between the comrades.

'I'm off,' I tell Mr Adams. 'I don't want to be late getting home – bringing Ag back in for the light show.'

'Hang on a minute,' he says. 'Don't you want to see how you're to be honoured?'

No, not really. But I go round to the office with the rest anyway. To receive a two-shilling piece. 'It's a Canberra florin.' Mrs Daly hands them out, trying hard not to look too embarrassed about it. 'Limited edition, they are,' she tries harder, but they're not medals; they don't even have our names on the boxes, or a card or anything in them to say they're ours. That is a bit cheap. A thousand pieces of silver. Someone calls out: 'Where's me invitation to the Australia Hotel then? I want me two-bob worth of champagne.' No one laughs, not even me, but another says, 'And you'll bite the hand that feeds, will you?' and for the first time the politics reaches me as I look at the picture of the King's head on the coin. For the first time in my life I wonder at this King and Empire horseshit. I'm not British. I'm not Australian, either. I'm an Irishman. Aren't I? Whoever you think you might be, you are a subject of this English king anyway, that's the truth, but I've never been arsed to think about it before this.

'Afternoon, gents,' a cop noses in among us, sniffing out the barney before it's got going, and I look down at the ground as O'Paddy should. Waiting for the trouble to pass. More than half the men standing here aren't Englishmen of any type either – there's Welsh and Yankie riggers come over for the sunshine and grog respectively, a couple of Dutch painters, a Canadian doggie, and a lot of Irish ironworkers and boilermakers – and the only thing stopping their argument from reaching its natural conclusion is the number of cops still hanging round the foreshore this afternoon, not here keeping celebrations in order any longer but waiting for a fight. The one that's always threatening to go off round here. Probably especially today.

'Off you go, lad,' Mr Adams says to me, and there's something sad in it. Regretful and tired. He says, glancing down at the piece of silver in his hand: 'Don't let this ruin your day. You have yourself a good time with your Aggie tonight, ay.'

'I will,' I say, and two steps away I'm back to not giving a flying sack of silver monkey nuts about anything else but Olivia.

And the look on my little sister's rosy face when I get home and say to her: 'Guess where we're going tonight, mischief?'

'Where?' she looks up from her schoolbook at the kitchen table, excited already.

'We're going to have our tea with Miss Olivia Greene.'

'No!'

'Yes.'

Olivia

Chicken. How hard can it be to cook a chicken? Everyone can cook a chicken. It's an ordinary proper dinner thing to cook. Even Mother can cook a chicken. I know you have to remember to get one without the insides left in and then you have to baste it in something or other, but I can't remember precisely what basting is and there's certainly no cookery book in this house to tell me. Do I even have so much as a scrap of a recipe of anything from the women's pages in the paper? No. Mother used to buy the odd copy of *New Idea* to keep abreast of life amongst the middlings, always full of fabulous things to do with tripe and seersucker, but is there a single one under the bed? No. So, I am madly flicking through the *Vogue*s now, plenty of them, in two different languages, or three if you count Americanese, and not too many proper dinner things in them. Fruit cocktails. Prawn canapés. Goose liver pâté. *The Perfect Thanksgiving Turkey*. But no chickens . . .

Damn.

And then not damn. Not really. I look around my little home, as if I haven't been here for a while, see the slumpy chenille cushions on the sofa that once were scarlet and now are a dusky rose;

the lopsided shade on the lamp, its grosgrain trim beginning to come loose from the bottom edge; the merry print of rioting Matisse flowers above the hearth that is lifting from its frame on one corner, damaged from a drowning it received via leaking roof three summers ago; the jumble of crumbling spines on the bookcase: what on earth did Mother ever want with that copy of *The Rules of Golf*? And I laugh: who am I trying to impress with a chicken?

Would Eoghan O'Keenan care if we dined on Leggo's tinned tomato soup? That warm tingling feeling squiggles up the back of my neck and I know the answer. If I am to do this daring thing, this wonderful thing, I must begin as I wish to go on: as myself, stray bonbon wrappers down the side of the sofa and all. Be myself or no one at all. Be at home.

So, I walk up to Dean's bakery on Blues Point Road and buy the last lot of their Vienna pipe loaf, which we will have toasted with bacon and cheese and the tinned beetroot that's sitting in the cupboard. My favourite scrumptious circle toasties. And for dessert . . . hm, I can't decide. I ask the baker: 'What shall I have, the apple cake or the cinnamon roll?' He says: 'Have both!' I say: 'Jolly good, then I shall.' With custard. Custard I can make – the best custard ever. Need eggs. Yes.

And a bottle of Quirks fizzy . . . raspberry or lime? Both! And a bottle of beer? Wine? I wonder as I pass Bluey's pub on the corner. No. I wouldn't know what to buy – I'm not old enough to ask for it anyway, I laugh to myself, and a man leaning against the tiles tips his hat: 'Good afternoon, miss.'

Yes. Glorious afternoon, it is indeed, as golden as the day began, with the low sun blasting across the point. When I turn back into East Crescent Street, even the Bridge is dusted in gold.

Good God, but what am I going to wear?

Yo

'Yes, Yoey,' Ag's pulling on my coat up Darling Street, 'you have to get flowers. Flowers and chocolates. That's polite. That's the rules.'

'Rules?' Several of them that I know of are already broken. How do you tell a child that? You don't. I don't. She made me shave. What are they teaching eight year olds today? It's that public school. Jesus. How am I not going to kiss Olivia Greene again tonight? Because I'm not. I've got Ag with me. Get back in your skin, O'Keenan, it's all right.

'Look, sweetpeas – get them.' Ag is dragging at me to a stop at the shop on the corner of Adolphus, pointing at the bucket of flowers by the step.

'Aren't they lovely, dear,' Mrs Buddle agrees, coming out of the shop. 'They tell you it's the end of winter.' And she waves her stick at me. 'Special occasion?'

'Er . . .' I don't know what to say, but Ag just about shouts it across the harbour anyway: 'We're going to have tea at Miss Olivia's house. She's a lady. She invited us. She's so lovely, she's prettier than anything that's ever been written in a book!'

'Is she, dear?' Mrs Buddle thinks that's a cracker, and she looks at me over her eyeglasses: 'Well, I hope you both enjoy your tea.'

'We will!'

By the time Ag's done we've got the sweetpeas and a tin of chocolate caramels and she says to me when we're on the water: 'See – look, it's all matching. The sky, the sweets tin and the sweetpeas. Everything is all lilac and pink.'

It is. The sunset is a cracker tonight. I say: 'What, that's the rule, is it? The sky's got to match your flowers and your lolly tin?'

'No, silly,' Ag rolls her eyes. 'It's just nice. Isn't it? All lilac and pink. And in Lavender Bay, too!'

Yes, it is, even if it means we're stony now till payday.

And when Olivia Greene opens her door to us she is prettier than anything that's ever been written in a book, and the dress she's wearing matches the purple colour in the flowers too. Why wouldn't it?

'Oh!' she says, with her hands going all around like little birds. 'Oh, but you shouldn't have. Oh! Oh, but I'm so very glad you did.' She smiles over the sweets tin, a bit of wicked in it. 'Caramel centres? Yum, yum, yummy, yum. Come in. Come in. I'm making circle toasties for dinner – special speciality of this house.'

I'm going to marry this girl. I have to.

Olivia

He prefers lime fizzy to raspberry. So do I. He prefers pickles over chutney or sauce. So do I. As I make up the toasties, he chats away about their trip here. 'The sky, it was just about the same colour as your dress – did you see it, ay?' he asks and I answer: 'Was it?' Of course he has an eye for colour. Of course he does! But I'm not really taking in what he says. I'm listening to how he says what he says, the sounds and the shapes of his voice, the gentle lilt to his words. He says *them* instead of *those*, and *me and Ag* instead of *Agnes and I*. He says *ay* at the ends of his questions. It doesn't bother me. Oddly, not really. It only seems right that he's here in my kitchen and that Agnes is down the hall with her face at the front door ready to sing out if the lights come on before we're settled on the picnic rug she's laid across the steps.

'This all looks too good to eat,' he says as I slide the toasties onto a plate. 'But I'm hungry, I have to admit.'

'Good,' I say, and I wonder what he might have had for lunch, if he had lunch. Do they eat lunch up on the Bridge? Suppose they must, but I don't ask him; I'm not sure how to ask him anything. I don't want to appear rude. Or too silly. So many questions.

I start gathering our feast onto the tea tray and as I reach for the pickle jar, so does he and his hand touches mine. He doesn't move it away and the tingle deepens and sizzles out from somewhere in the centre of my hips and swishes right down to my knees. I touch the back of his hand with my thumb, not accidentally. His beautiful fingers –

'Yoey! Miss Olivia! Quick! Something's happening!' Agnes calls down the hall, and I fumble the pickles onto the tray, just about smashing one of the glasses as I do, lime fizzy sloshing everywhere. I laugh. So does he. Our laughter together, a ribbon twist of joy.

'Look, look!' Agnes is jumping about on the steps and I can see the sweep of searchlights in the rectangle of night around her. 'Hurry up!'

As soon as I place the tray on the top step, Agnes has her hand in mine and the lights come on over the arch, a double strand of pearls across the black.

'Oh,' I whisper as I sit down on the steps. 'Look at that. It's our gateway to Fairyland.'

'*Yes.*' Agnes climbs onto my lap. 'You are exactly right about that, Miss Olivia.'

Eoghan sits beside me and hands across the plate of circle toasties. I am so very happy in this moment. I'm so very happy I could cry. I want my dinner with Eoghan and Agnes O'Keenan on my front steps every night. I want this with all my heart. I make a wish for this, with all my heart.

Yo

'Can I go inside and look at the French magazines, Miss Olivia?' Ag asks when she's finished her tea. She makes a big act of yawning. She's not tired. She's had two cups of that raspberry Quirks – she'll be talking in her sleep. She's letting us alone, and I'm not disappointed about it.

'Of course.' Miss Olivia isn't disappointed either. She says: 'I'll get you a rug, though – it's chilly now.'

She stands up on the step and I'm eye to ankle with her for a second; her stockings are so fine I can see through to her skin. I spend the next two minutes wanting to, listening to her footsteps in the house, and the way she chats with Ag has me seeing through to her heart. She is as good inside as out. Jesus, what am I doing here, with her? Am I good enough? I can't be, can I? Am I sounding too much of a spoon to her; have I been too quiet or been talking too much? I don't know. Help me.

When she comes back she sits down beside me again and she says, looking out to the Bridge: 'I wonder if I would ever be brave enough to go up there.'

And whatever it is about her that makes me feel good makes

me feel good now, forgetting I have anything to worry about at all. I tell her: 'I'll take you one day, and we'll see. There's a walkway, right across.'

'No,' she says, making an act of pulling herself away from the idea, pretending to be shocked. 'I was only wondering.'

And all I want to do is kiss her again. More than kiss her. But I will not. I tell her: 'You'll never have to wonder, not with me, Olivia. I'll always think of you as I do right now, today. Whatever might happen.' That sounds like the greatest steaming line of spadework that ever was, for sure, but I mean it.

She doesn't say anything. She only looks back out at the Bridge. It really is the best view from here, not only of her. The way this house sits on the bend at the top of the cliff steps, it could be the only house in the world. We could be the only two people in the world. Up in the clouds.

I ask her: 'Are you not cold?' That sounds even worse spadework, but I mean that too. I'm not cold. You could hit me with a blunt axe and I'd not feel it. But she might be cold. I don't want her to be cold out here. I want her in my arms. Jesus.

She shakes her head, still looking at the Bridge: 'I think I might feel the same way, for you.'

There isn't a name for the feeling I have in return at that.

And now she looks at me: 'You know, I probably wouldn't object if you kissed me again.'

'No.' That comes out of me quick to jolt us both away from it. As much as I think I'm going to die if I don't kiss her in the next five seconds, I know I won't stop there. I can't stop there. I'm too scared to kiss her again for what it might lead to. What I know it will lead to, What it *is* leading to even without doing anything. Jesus, Ag is not ten yards away, up the hall behind us. I make myself remember Jack Callaghan's girl, Mary Lightfoot, dead after the abortionist; let myself remember her mother's wailing all down the street like a blunt axe to my head. No. I tell Olivia, 'I meant what I said this morning. I want to marry you. One day.'

She looks to be in some kind of pain at that idea. She says: 'You're religious, aren't you?'

'Yes,' I say, I won't deny it. Maybe I'm not the average Mick that fucks first and begs forgiveness later, but I am a Catholic, and one with responsibilities, one who's made too many bargains with God to count lately, and I don't suppose she is one at all. I'm dead certain she's not a Catholic. Lord, what are you doing, leading me here? As you must have done, because I haven't come here wholly of my own accord, have I. I never set out for this girl. And it's not wholly my religion stopping me from kissing her either. I tell her: 'I am religious, but I am practical-minded too.' I tell her again in case she's missed it: 'I mean to marry you, before . . .'

She only looks in more pain at that, and then I really let her have it. I tell her: 'I've given thought to it. In four years, I'll be a qualified journeyman, at boilermaking, and on building construction that's as much as sixteen pounds a week. I mean to earn that eventually. That's almost twice a schoolteacher's salary.' What do I sound like? Like she would want to marry a boilermaker. Wholly and desperately monkey-nutted.

But she doesn't point that out to me. She's more polite about it; she says: 'Eoghan, I'm practical too. My business is turning over at least twice that at the moment. But that may not be the case next week, or the week after, for either of us. It's all so precarious, for everyone. Who could plan to marry?'

True enough. And she earns *twice* what I might do at the top of the trade. What hope do I have here? She's not just a lady – she's independent. I've really picked one, haven't I.

She says: 'Oh, please don't misunderstand me. It's not a matter of money or class, not for me – believe me, I've given *that* some thought. And if you knew the half of my situation you might want to run a mile. I'm not of good stock.'

'Oh yeah?' I say. 'You'd have to try hard to beat my stock for bottom of the barrel.'

'Oh yeah?' she says. 'My parents are divorced, for a start.

The Blue Mile

Up until recently, my mother was a martini-swilling dance-hall socialite, while my father is always, *always* a philandering, reckless, good-for-nothing Don Juan, presently under arrest in Africa for the murder of a Hollywood actress.' She makes a face of disgust and closes her eyes as she adds: 'He's a viscount.' As if that explains all of what she's just said.

I start laughing, I'm not sure I know what a viscount is, or a martini, and she starts laughing too, that high tin whistle floating out over the night. When she laughs she's even more . . . there's no name for this either.

She says: 'My father will ruin me before you do.' And she nudges her shoulder into mine as if we might've been friends for years: 'What about you, then? How bad is your family?'

My father's fist smashes down between us and she must see something of that on my face. She says: 'I'm sorry. That was rude. It's a talent of mine.'

'You're not rude,' I say, 'you're honest.' And she may as well know the truth of it, if I mean anything I say. I tell her: 'My father is not a good man, violent and usually drunk, and my mother is feeble and always drunk, probably on account of him more than anything. I've got one brother dead from them by hanging himself, and another I don't where he's gone. I had to get Ag away from them, away from where we lived, in Chippendale. That's what we were doing when we first met you, that morning in the Gardens, getting away from them, getting away from Chippo.'

'Oh.' Her eyes go wide with something else I don't have a name for. Some type of wonder. She says: 'I see. You got away, in the Gardens. Good for you. That trouble with Child Welfare. I see.'

She doesn't see; she wouldn't know the first thing about where we've come from or what trouble we've had. But I say: 'Yeah. I win the bad family stakes then, ay?'

She says, 'No. No, you don't.'

She puts her hand on mine. Smoothing her fingers down over mine. She says: 'You're a good man, though. Admirably good.

You've also got lovely hands.' The shiver that sends through me is some sort of heavenly bliss, but still I don't kiss her. Her face is an inch from mine, I can smell the lime drink and apple cake on her breath and still I manage not to kiss her. There's a curl come free from the pin in her hair and there's never been a greater mastery of will than my resisting the need here to brush it from her forehead.

But my voice does crack a bit as I say: 'I should get Ag home now, it's getting late.'

She nods and gives me a slow, crooked smile as we get up from the doorstep: 'One way or another you will ruin me.'

I promise her: 'If it's the last thing I do.'

Please.

She lets her smile take me fully: 'But not if I ruin you first.'

Olivia

*I*t's the strangest thing, this calm. This warm, tingling calm of certainty. That yesterday, this morning, he was a dream, and now, here, as we say goodnight, he is a part of the fabric. My fabric. There is no going back from this.

'Can I come to the salon again after school? Can I, please?' Agnes looks from her brother to me, bursting bright with confidence that the answer must be yes.

And I look to him. 'It's Wednesday today, isn't it? Make it Wednesday again, then?' Begin again as we'd meant to go on in the first place. This time, with conviction.

He says: 'All right, then. Wednesdays it is, for ruining.'

'Ruining?' Agnes asks, wanting to share the fun of whatever that might be. 'What's ruining?'

'Never you mind,' he says, sounding worried at the prospect already.

Yes. It's going to be awful. Utterly dreadful. And I'm not waiting four years for it, either, I am confident of that. I'm already running up a new dream, one in which the three of us travel to Paris on the RMS *Fantastico*. We can't be together here, not in this world. It wouldn't be acceptable, not to the upper circle. Murderous aristocracy is one thing; wedding a tradesman is entirely another. I would lose my clientele overnight. Get thee direct to Homebush – where the middling matrons might not buy from me either, from one who is young and newly married *and* in business. A girl can't win, and I don't want any of that suburban phlerghishness anyway. I want us to be each other's inspiration, slaves to love and beauty, in our cosy magic-carpeted salon on the Left Bank of the Seine.

Mon Dieu, chérie, but you have eaten too much sugar tonight.

But how can I not love him? This rescuer and protector of little girls. They did sleep in the Gardens that night, didn't they, I know it now, and that thought does not appal me in the slightest. It only makes him more heroic. He is perfection in a man. Look at the particular and careful way he's unfolding his sister's cardigan now and tell me those hands wouldn't best be pinning and cutting silk. I want to *marry* him – *now*. I want to beg him to stay, beg him to have me – *now*.

He says: 'Well, we'll see you Wednesday, then.'

I almost groan. 'Wednesday, then.'

'Yay!' Agnes bounces between us, and just as they're leaving I reach for his hand and pull him back to me, into the hall. I brush my lips against his, to breathe in his smell, that salty man smell, and something else – is that Ponds Cold Cream?

He whispers: 'No.'

I whisper: 'Yes.'

I bend to kiss Agnes too, 'See you soon, poppet,' and when they've disappeared down the steps to the wharf, I close the door and I bounce around too. All night. I can't sleep a wink from scheming. How can I make it all possible for us? I finish cutting the lining for Lady Game's District Nurses and I keep seeing his hands as I do, those beautiful fingers. They're not boilermaking metal-thumping hands. They're tailor's hands. Surely. We shall go into business together. Surely. There must be a path for us . . . somehow. White tux and some elocution lessons, perhaps . . . but who would want to change a thing about him? A white tuxedo on that shoulderline, though – truly, what sane woman wouldn't want that? He wouldn't have to open his mouth at all.

Well past dawn, I've almost finished tacking up the vice-regal frock when I hear the mail clunk through the slot with the post boy's call: 'Telegram!' It's from Mrs B Harley, and I almost don't want to open it. Mother. Whatever is in it, I don't want to know. I don't want it to intrude on the whirl of my new dream. But it glares at me until I open it, and read, in her code: *Ignore Lordship drama. Not his fault for once. Accident with pills. Poor silly girl. All good here. Letter in mail. Please write again soon. Miss you darling. Love Mother.*

Poor silly girl. That slides down my spine like a bead of ice. Never mind, there'll be another along soon. More importantly, his Lordship's drama has blown over, within the week, too. How convenient. Ignore it. Finish the tacking and pack up my troubles in my carpet couture bag, it's time to reopen the salon.

Time to flick through a newspaper, too, *et voilà* I find one left on the ferry on my way to the Quay now telling me that the Viscount Mosely, Lord Ashton Greene, is upon his release from questioning reportedly heartbroken by the untimely loss of Gigi McAllister. He says: *The light has been extinguished from my world.*

God, how I hate him.

I look up at the Bridge, for Eoghan, for he *is* there. This dream is solid steel, crisp and clear, and I will have it all. I will be loved. I will be fabulous. Damn Lord Ashton Greene. I will never let him near my thoughts again; I will never let any stupid fears shake me from my path again.

My steps have never been surer. These Pitt Street shop windows are the galleries that line my way to happiness, this bright jostling of colour, of life, weaving round the verandah poles. Real life. Ned tosses me an apple from his barrow as I pass: 'For that smile of yours this morning, miss.'

I blow him a kiss. One for Glor, too, across the cutting table of the Emporium as I swing round the banister and fly up the staircase. To *my* salon. I snatch the note from the window of the door. I'm back in business this minute, and picking up the telephone, calling Government House, for Lady Game. I get Miss Crowdy on the line first, of course: 'Yes, who is it?' she says in her no-time-wasters way. On any other day I might have to fight myself not to stumble at it, but not today.

I say in my own no-time-wasters way: 'It's Olivia Greene. As promised, I have Lady Game's outfit for the District Nursing Association event ready for a fitting. When might that be convenient?'

'It is not at all convenient for Lady Game to break from her schedule at present,' Miss Crowdy almost barks. Impatient. Aha, I think. Here's my top client, putting the phone down on the end of our relationship. Too much of a scandal risk, that Olivia Greene. Bloody well damn you. Damn the lot of you – I'm ready to snarl.

But Miss Crowdy barks again: 'You'll have to come here, girl. Four-thirty and half an hour only – that's all you've got.'

'This afternoon?'

'Yes, of course,' she sighs: I'm such a waste of time, I am.

I say: 'I'll be there.'

*

Humble servant that I am. Lady Game is very much the Lady this afternoon: distracted. Busy. Cool. 'Oh yes. Lovely print,' she says of the georgette: whatever. No private wardrobe secretary intimacy for me today. I'm on my knees, repinning the hem to bring it down half an inch, when Lady Game says, as if she's returned to the warmth of herself: 'I'm sorry to put you out like this, Olivia, calling you over here in your business hours. You must've had an interesting week?'

I take a deep breath in through the pins before responding to that. I've had a very interesting week, and let's put the best of it at the top of this breath to steady it: I've fallen dreadfully and irrevocably in love with the man I'm going to spend the rest of my life with. There. Let that secret warm me against the other. The other is hardly secret anyway. Lady Game would know of my father. She would know of the scandal. But I'm unsure if she knows as yet of my relation to it – she wouldn't know I'm his daughter unless someone told her, would she? Which means she probably knows.

I take the pins out of my mouth: 'Yes, it's been an interesting week.' Say nothing more; if Lady Game wishes to pry, let her.

She says, with that distracted air again: 'I went to school with your aunt – well, your father's sister, who would have been your aunt. Poor dear Phoebe. Do you know of her?'

She asks that last so gently I sit back on my heels and look up at her, like the small, wanting child I am. 'No, I don't.' I barely know anything about the Ashton Greenes at all, ancient family pile in Cambridgeshire that Mother certainly never saw.

'Well, I'm not surprised at that,' Lady Game smiles as gently, and with some sadness. 'You'd never have met Phoebe; she died before you were born. The seventeenth of January, 1910, it was – strange how I remember the date. But perhaps not strange: it was such a terrible thing, a shock to everyone. She was so . . .' She looks out of this upper storey dressing-room window, across the crenellations of the balcony and the tops of the figs beyond. '*Vibrant,* Phoebe was. Then one rainy afternoon, she slipped getting out of a cab, hit her head on the pavement, and she was gone. Terrible, terrible thing. Made no sense, she was only fifteen. I don't think Shelby ever quite recovered from it. He adored her so. I think it hit him even harder than the war. I think it caused him to make certain errors of judgment. And now this awful business in Kenya, with that young woman . . .'

I think Lady Game is trying to tell me something about forgiveness, but my heart only hardens further. I don't care about his reasons. Everyone has *reasons* for their personal atrocities. But there can be no excuse for his rejection of me. None. I was only a child. Cast off. He deserves every blow that comes his way. I return my attention to the hemline and give Lady Game as much honesty as decorum will allow: 'I don't know my father.'

'No. I imagine you don't,' Lady Game says, softer still. 'And I want you to know, Olivia, that whatever happens in that realm will have no bearing on my regard for you – none whatsoever. Indeed, quite the opposite.'

I bow my head at that. I have to, at the kindness. I see why she's favoured me now: she's known who I am all along. So very kind, so discreet, and I am humbled: 'Thank you.'

'Excuse me, Lady Game,' Miss Crowdy knocks and enters at the same time. 'It is now after five. We must attend to the details for the women's hockey afternoon party.'

Lady Game sweeps quite another smile over me. Perhaps she's a little intimidated by her secretary too, or perhaps it's just a fond smile for me. Whatever it is, I should come to my senses at this exchange, be dissuaded now from my reckless path, my determination to have my Irish Catholic tradesman. But I am not.

When I get home, there's a postcard come through the mail slot for me, a print of the Bridge. A view from the top, looking down the arch to the south, over the city. On the reverse is written in a hand of plain straight lines:

One day you will stand with me up here, Olivia.
By some other miracle I made it through this day without falling.
All the same I fell a thousand times – for you.
Yo

Giddy. And sleepy. Oh dear God I could swallow the sky with this yawn. I fall onto my bed and I fall asleep. I sleep like a cat stretched out languorous in the sun.

Yo

I hear her singing as I get to the top of the ferry steps, coming out through the open window of her house and across the night. She can sing, all right, better than my best imaginings of it. So sweet and so high, I don't want to knock on the door to interrupt her.

'Just Aggie and me, and a cossie makes three . . .'

And Ag and her start laughing, having fun in there. How good is that? How good is all this? It's been five weeks of these Wednesday evenings and with each one I'm more convinced, if that could be possible.

I knock at the door, and she's not two seconds from opening it. 'Hello there!' Her smile, always looking a bit surprised I'm here again, before she pulls me in by the elbow and a quick sly kiss that only I can see. And feel. Jesus, I wish she wouldn't do it; but I can't imagine her not. I can't imagine not having this quick sly Wednesday kiss from her. Less than a second's worth, for all it might take all week to recover from it. It's just a kiss; that's all it is.

With Ag as sweet and high jumping around her Miss Olivia and this night jumping up and down behind her on her bed in some funny fancy-dress made of scarves and flowers all in her hair, and asking me: 'Yoey, can we go, please?'

'Go where?' I ask her. You can go anywhere you want.

'To the baths – the Fairy Bower baths,' she says. 'On Saturday.'

'Ahhh.' Baths for swimming? I don't know about that idea. 'What's Fairy Bower?' It could well not actually exist.

'Up between Manly and Shelly Beach – there are baths there,' Olivia says to me. 'At the rock pool, pretty spot. I thought we'd picnic – you can come out for a frolic Saturdays now, can't you?'

That's true. I've no dog shift to go to Saturdays anymore. Now we're on the deck, it's Monday to Friday, with the corresponding cut to our pay, again, and up until last week, unpaid Saturday mornings in the shops, for me, welding, for my Tech practicals, hanging out for my fifteen shilling increase for second year that I've just found out I won't get until March. And be thankful for it, too: another fifty were let go from the heavy shop yesterday. Don't know what we pay union fees for. We've got a political meeting about it coming up on the weekend – *You're to be there, no apologies accepted, or the Devil take you,* Mr Adams said to us all this morning – and that's not a way out of this swimming, either: the meeting is on Sunday afternoon. Shit, but I can't afford to go anywhere. I can't afford a picnic. I can hardly afford to buy Ag an ice-cream at the moment. I've never even been to Manly – doesn't everything cost twice as much there?

'Please, Yoey. We've *never* been swimming, ever,' Ag says, with that whine getting in her voice.

For a second I could say to them both, don't ask me how my day went first, will you; don't ask me how Tech went tonight. I'm getting the first year prize, I just found out. I'll get the certificate Friday week. Or some such horseshit thing fairies couldn't care less about between their la-di-da French magazines and eating too many lollies.

'But only if it's warm enough, Agnes,' Olivia says to her.

It'll be warm enough, though. It's only the end of September but it's been that hot it seems that summer is here already.

'What do you say?' Olivia looks at me: *Go on, say yes – what's wrong with you?*

I look at Ag. I should be ashamed that she's never been swimming. I am. I'm ashamed I can't swim, too. I don't want Olivia to know I can't. I can't afford whatever it is to hire bathers there, never mind drowning in front of her. I say: 'We'll see what the weather's like, won't we?'

'Yay!' Ag says, jumping up and down on the bed again.

As Olivia leans in to me: 'Wait till you see me flapping about in the water. I'm not much of a swimmer – you could die laughing.'

I doubt it. I will be looking at Olivia Greene in a bathing suit as I drown. Not all bad, I suppose. Except that we could all drown. No. I can't go swimming. In public. In a bathing suit myself. Jesus, no.

'I've already asked Coralie to man the salon for the morning,' she leans into me some more. 'I need a day of fun and sun, I must say. I've been yearning for it. A day with you – a *whole* day. I've already bought half the treats.' *Please,* her voice is saying to me: *don't say no.* That turns me round again: Olivia works hard, as hard as me, just differently, and with money left over at the end of the week, money for treats. I won't always be this hard up.

'Yay!' Ag yells, still jumping, and throwing her scarves around: 'Treats and sunshine! And my new pink cossies! Look, Yoey, look what we made tonight!'

It's a pink bathing costume, you wouldn't miss her in a crowd, and she's that thrilled about it. How can I say no?

'It'll be a great day.' Olivia works her hand into mine behind my back.

'Yeah.' I try for a smile. If we survive it.

*

Depth of water 2 feet 6 inches, says the sign this end of the baths. We'll survive. And the only public here to watch me make an arse of myself is kids. About a hundred of them, running around all over the rocks and diving in the deeper end of the pool. I step out of the dressing sheds with the word *MANLY* stamped across my chest on this cossie hired for tuppence and legs I never knew were this hairy. What could go wrong?

Ag is waving me over to where she's waiting by the steps of the pool, and I wouldn't have missed this day for a bucket of gold as I see Olivia there beside her. Her bathers are striped black and white and her hat is matching. Who else brings two hats on an outing to be sure they match her outfit? What else has she got in her bag of tricks? The brim of this hat is so big it falls right over her face. She lifts it up and pins it back and waves too. Then she dips her toe in the water, and there's something about the way she does that, something about the grace of her long arms and her even longer legs that has me wondering if she's altogether human again. She is made of hazel wands.

And now in she jumps, up to her knees. 'Oh!' she says with the shock of it and then she moves towards the centre of the pool, swimming with those long arms out ahead of her, no flapping about to it at all, until she stops and turns and calls back to Ag: 'Come on, Miss Fish, I'll catch you!'

Aggie runs up the side of the pool and jumps – right into Olivia's arms. Screaming. Safe. Having the time of her life. This means everything to me. I just stand where I am for a minute, listening to the kids screaming and the gulls screaming above them looking for chips to pinch, with the waves washing on the rocks and all the kids washing through the waves in this ocean pool and Olivia laughing at something Ag has said, and for the first time ever I believe I'm in a family. That's how it seems. Like our new life is completed. The past is behind me. I'm just a man at the seaside, like any other man here, watching out for his kid. Entitled to a future: a good one.

And then Olivia screams: 'Oh God! Oh my God!'

A terrified scream. Flapping about. And I can't see Ag in all the splashing.

Olivia screams again: 'Help!'

Olivia

'Oh my God. Help me!'

There's something caught around my foot. Dragging at me.

I shove Agnes back towards the wall. 'Oh God, hold on.'

The horror in her eyes is the horror in my heart. It's some creature from the deep. No, it's not. It's a shark. I haven't had a nice day's outing anywhere for how long? *Years*. And now I'm being attacked by a shark. I'm certain it's a shark. Eating my leg. Oh my God.

'Oh God, Eoghan – help me!'

Yo

I don't reckon anyone has taken to the water faster.
'My leg!' she's screaming. 'My leg!'
I don't know what I'm doing but diving down into this water to find what devil of a thing it is that's got her. I find her ankle. Then the other. Then something the likes of which I've never felt before. Slimy; weird; something waving through the water. Heavy. I pull it up to the surface, and somehow even I know what it is.

It's seaweed. A great big slippery mess of seaweed.

'Oh! No!' Olivia screams again when she sees it, but now she's laughing. Covering her eyes and laughing and saying, 'Oh God, how embarrassing,' and grabbing Ag from the side of the pool and kissing her head and telling her: 'I must have scared you half to death. Oh Agnes – look. It was only a silly lump of seaweed.'

'Yuck.' Ag screws up her face and then she tells me: 'Put it back in the sea, Yoey.'

I push it over the side and into the waves and only now I realise I just swam about ten yards. How did I do that?

'Our hero,' Olivia says and she gives me a kiss, on the cheek, here, in this public pool, with Ag on her hip and kids everywhere.

Just for a second I feel like a hero too. 'I fight seaweed monsters wherever I go,' I say, and I sink back in the water, to see if it's true that I can swim. I can float, for sure. Miraculous, and not at all. Of course I can float. I don't know what I was so worried about. I float on my back with my face to the sun and I listen to Ag and Olivia go off on some other story, about the pine fairies that live around here off the rocks.

Then we have something to eat, then we have another swim, then we eat again and all day none of us can look at each other without laughing ourselves to tears about the seaweed monster. This is the best day of my life.

We're packing up to go, packing up the half a house of tins and towels and hats Olivia brought with us, when she says to me: 'Thank you. I've never been so happy. So free.'

'Neither have I. Thank you.'

By the time we've got the ferry back to Lavender Bay, it's almost dark and Ag is half-asleep as I carry her up the steps. 'Ooh, it's chilly now,' Olivia says, 'I'm all sunburn shivery,' and when we get in she tucks a blanket round Ag on the sofa and she is asleep, and Olivia is pulling me out through the kitchen: 'Come on, you need some cream on those seaweed-monster-slaying shoulders. You can have some of my Ponds – you'll be a lobster under that shirt.' She starts laughing again, at the seaweed monster and my own Ponds beauty regimen I had to admit to her the other week.

I know I am sunburned, too; I can feel it against my shirt already. But I'm not laughing now. There's a look in her eyes, even before she's pulling me into the bathroom and saying: 'You can have a shower too, if you like – a hot one.'

I'm not sure what she's meant by it but I'm sure of its effect on me. I want to say, *Stop right there, you don't want to be leading me along, not now.* I say: 'I don't want a shower, thanks anyway.'

'Well, I might,' she says, and she pulls me the rest of the way through the bathroom door. 'Shhhh. It'll be all right, so long as we don't lie down together.'

'What?' I don't know what she means by that for a second, then I realise she doesn't know the first thing about what she's doing. Not that I know much more than what you get from one of them filthy American magazines, but I do well know that it doesn't matter if we lie down together or not. Jack and Mary would go round the back of Gibsons, two doors down from her house, to the low window ledge there, not a place for lying down.

I just say: 'No. It won't be all right.'

'I only want to see you.' She starts undoing my shirt. 'I want to see your whole chest. I want to see all of you.'

'No, you don't. That's not what will happen.'

'I don't care what happens.'

'I do.'

'But I love you.' She unties the side of her dress, making it fall open, and somehow the sight of her petticoat is worse on me than having seen her all day in those bathers. She latches the bathroom door behind us and lights the boiler, turning on the taps.

I say: 'No, Olivia, I –'

'Yes.' Her cheeks are pink as the tiles here, her eyes are wild.

The hot water is steaming up the room. I've never had a hot shower. I've never been in a house that had one. We don't have a bathroom. We don't have a bath. Ag has her tub by the stove Sunday, Tuesday, Thursday, and I save coal with a flannel at the sink every day. While this shower is – Lord, you are making this hell for me. I don't know if such sinning in love will send us into damnation, if such a thing could ever be called evil, all I know is that it's wrong. Creating a child in sin is wrong. I'm not going to test the power of God or his grace, see if he might take away this love He's given us if we break the rules. Take everything I'm hoping for. Everything I'm working for. Call that superstitious idiocy or cowardice, call that whatever you want. I am not taking this risk. No.

She pushes the shirt off my shoulders, laughing against my neck: 'If you don't kiss me now, I don't want to see you again.'

The Blue Mile

She holds herself against me. Right against the part of me that has no mind to tell her no. Jesus, can she really be so blind to what's going on here? The power she has over me?

Olivia

'*B*e careful or you won't see me again,' he says and his voice is flat. Liltless. Threatening. Buttoning up his shirt.

'No.' Oh no. Oh dear. I say: 'I didn't really mean to say I wouldn't see you again, I –'

'Well, you did say it and it's too far. What you want is not happening, right? Nothing is happening between us. I should get Ag home.'

'No! Don't go,' I beg him. I only wanted to kiss, properly kiss, touch him as I want to, and . . . I don't know. My mind and my thighs are swimming for want of him. Why is he so angry? 'What do you mean nothing is happening between us?'

'I mean now – this evening. This day is finished.'

'Oh.' Yes. I see. Humiliation number two for this day: a much more profound one. He truly is religious, he truly does mean what he says. No proper kissing before marriage, et cetera. I turn off the water and try to laugh but my voice is a quivery breath: 'I'm sorry. I wish we could just elope and be done with it.' And, bizarrely, I think I do mean that: some restitution for my own disastrous conception mindlessly achieved on the way to the Champs-Élysées,

The Blue Mile

I'd elope to Chatswood with Eoghan to prove to him all I feel. That this is real.

He's not having any of it; his voice is rough: 'No priest I know would marry us – you're not of age and you're not Catholic. Pull your dress round, will you?'

Pull my dress round? Not a Catholic. How dare you. I pull my dress round and say with all the condescension I can muster: 'There are other perfectly respectable ways to marry, you know.'

He looks as if that's the most astonishingly stupid thing he's ever heard. He says: 'There is no other way. Not for me.'

How did we take this turn so suddenly? We've had such a beautiful day. I'm in a welter now.

I say: 'Well, I'll become a Catholic, I'll convert.' *INSANE!* Mother screams at me from the other side of the world.

Eoghan appears to agree with her; he says: 'You can't just become Catholic because you want to get married – it's not that simple. You have to do lessons – on the liturgy, the sacraments, your Holy Communion. You have to go to confession first. As it is, I'll have to miss Communion tomorrow because of this.'

'What?' I don't know what he's talking about. I never even went to Sunday school with any regularity, only to keep out of Mother's hair when necessary, and just often enough to appear respectable.

He says: 'You can't just put on a pretty dress and have it done.'

That *is* insulting. Mightily. I say: 'I am aware of the seriousness of marriage. I am also aware that religion is ridiculous.'

'Perhaps to you, but not to me.' Now I've insulted him.

But I keep going with it: 'No less ridiculous than fairies in the garden and magic-carpet rides.'

'Will you keep your voice down?' he hisses at me, deep blues flashing some black anger. 'You want Ag listening to this?'

'No.' But I can't stop this train now either. 'I think you're the one who isn't serious. You're just toying with my heart.' As Irish boys do. Every foolishness I've ever felt rages through me:

'Religious objection? That sounds like backsliding to me. You don't love me. You're not genuine.'

'Not genuine?' He clenches his jaw, with some rage to match mine. He closes his eyes, taking a deep breath, and he opens them, calm again, his words deliberate: 'Listen, I don't expect you to share my faith, but I do expect you to be respectful of it. In four years, I will marry you. By then, I will have my journeyman's ticket, and by then I'd hope you will come to see what my faith means to me. We are too young now. I want to do things the right way, morally, old-hat as that might sound, and I want to be able to provide for you.'

'Provide for me?' My words are shrill with my objection to seeing anything resembling his point of view now. 'But you don't need to provide for me. My business –'

'That could go in a second,' he stubbornly maintains his notions of practicality. 'You've said so yourself. Anyway, how would we live, Olivia? How would you do your business when the babies come?'

'Babies?' Yes, babies: that word cuts through my infuriation. I have actually given this a good deal of thought: I'm not having the Catholic ten, that's for certain. I will have two, or perhaps three, our little curly-topped ones gambolling about in our salon on the Left Bank of the Seine. There are methods of preventing more – my French is good enough to have gleaned that much from Mother's old copies of *L'Amour et la Mode*. But, relentlessly stupid as I appear to be right now, I choose this moment to share with him the ultimate practicality of my own fantastical faith: 'Go into business with me, Eoghan. We'll do it together. Babies and business, all of it.'

He laughs at the idea. At me.

That crushes. That humiliates me more than anything. 'What? Why not?'

'Me? In the princess palace?' he laughs again, and not happily. 'Where will you hide me, Miss Greene? In your stockroom? What will you have me do there? Sewing beads on your frocks?'

'Why not?' I repeat, so hurt at this. 'It's good enough for me. It's good enough for Jean Patou. Gustav Beer. Christoff von Drécoll. Caret. Bulloz. Lucien Lelong. The House of Worth – hundreds of them. Men sewing beads. What's the difference between that and cutting and machining at Foulds Boots?' as I know he's done before this.

'A big difference, and you know it.' He says, flatly, intractably: 'Foulds make work boots. Cutting and machining is not a proper trade. And sewing beads is not for me. That's ridiculous.'

'That is *not*,' I protest. 'That is *not* ridiculous.' I look at his tailor's hands, those beautiful fingers, and I appeal to them: 'You want to *be* a boilermaker?'

'If that's what I have to be to have a good and simple life.' What is that in his eyes now? Sadness? Disappointment?

Disbelief in mine: 'But I don't want a good and simple life.'

'Then you don't want me.' He turns away, unlatches the door.

'Eoghan – don't you turn your back to me. Please.'

He closes the door behind him. I hear him wake Agnes: 'Come on, mischief. What you been eating today making you so heavy then – lead sandwiches?' She mumbles something sleepily and they leave.

Leave me dirty. I am ugly and ashamed. More ugly than I have ever been.

But mostly angry, and mostly because he's right. This isn't going to work with us, is it. Our worlds are far too far apart. *Pass me them crystal beads, will you?* That's never going to happen. No more than my taking up rosary beads. You can't make a dream come true just by wanting.

Plain as the schnonk on my face, and as burned. Look at it. Horrible.

This is the most horrible, most painful degradation of my life.

Lead sandwiches, I'll say.

Yo

The two cops coming down Darling Street take a good look at me as I head for the saloon doors of the Unity Hall Hotel. I'm still that fired up from yesterday I could almost stop and ask them if they want to cage me for it. A good thing that it's Sunday and the taps are off.

I'm sure the publican doesn't agree: the Unity is packed, the meeting brought inside from Loyalty Square by the rain. I see Tarzan's square red head through the crowd, this side of the bar, over near a fella that's already holding the floor. The meeting has started, I'm late, and I don't care. 'Hear hear,' this metal trades mob goes and the fella speaking goes on, his voice that sharp and hard it's carving his words into the walls.

'While there is a pinched and starving belly in Balmain, not a penny – not a penny – should go to the bondholders of London.' The fella smashes his fist into his palm to make that a promise. He's a big fella. He looks like he must be standing on a box at first glance, but he's not. 'Lang is right!' someone calls out and I see who this is: it's the Big Fella. It's Mr Lang. He does look a bit like my father, strangely. A fucking enormous likeness of Satan O'Keenan himself.

And there is a few pinched and starving among us here, not convinced of the Second Coming of this Big Fella Lang. 'Talk is cheap – won't fill no bellies,' someone calls from over the other side of the bar, at the back. I see who it is: it's a fella called Tommo, a blacksmith on the timber wharves, until recently. He's also a Communist. A lot of shouting goes on now, from one side of the room to the other. I stare ahead; roll another smoke I don't want. I don't want to be here. This is horseshit. This is the Labour Movement, as I understand it: Jack Lang is the Labor Party, but everyone in it hates him, especially Federal Labor – they reckon he's a dictator, and a Communist. But the Communists hate him more than anyone else, because he's really a Capitalist. He's an estate agent, of Lang & Dawes, with half of western Sydney owing money to him. And he hates the Communists back. Lang hates the unions too. And some wonder why I'm not too interested politics. They can't even spell 'labour' the same way twice. Only one reason I'm here: to see the Nationalists put out of the job of running the place so that if I ever have to work for the dole, I will get the living wage for it. Or two reasons: Mr Adams told me to come. For numbers. To make a good show against the Communists, so they don't upset the vote by scaring off those a bit less inclined to be kicking in the heads of their enemies. Jesus.

Lang is standing there talking to some fella next to him, not bothered in the least by the horseshit flying around. He doesn't have to be bothered. When he opens his mouth again, he says: 'Those in the Labor Party who know me best know that my word is my promise. It will be done. The bloodsucking bondholders will be denied.'

And everyone shuts up like schoolkids with the archbishop walked in. This Lang knows how to silence a mob even quicker than Mr Adams. He might well be a dictator.

'Return to me the premiership of this state and I will see to it that the interference of British bankers in our affairs is stopped.

The economic science of these Shylocks, and of the Nationalists who support them, is wrong. Their so-termed "sound" economy is crippling this state. You know this yourselves. But did you know, gentlemen, that the Bank of England has discounted its interest rates even to Austria – our enemy in the Great War – and yet no discount has been offered here? We must pay a full five percent while all other nations pay but three or four. No discount for a nation that has sacrificed sixty thousand of its youth and millions of pounds of its wealth to fight for the British cause. How can this be so?'

No one says a word. There are plenty here who have suffered the loss of a mate, a brother, a father. Even my own father went to Palestine, though I don't remember it as anything but some different kind of crying in our mother. I was eleven when he came back, and I don't know why he ever did. We're all waiting for an answer here.

'How, you might wonder, can the Nationalists not ask on your behalf for that discount? A discount of a mere one-quarter of a percent would provide the government with public money, which then can be used for the invigoration of our economy. The only invigoration the Nationalists are concerned with is that which lines their own pockets, as they force wages down ever lower, using this Depression as an excuse to increase their profits. But you know this also. My government, should you return me, will not be slave to Shylock, or to the mindless sheep of the Loan Council in Canberra, nor to the board of the Commonwealth Bank – cowards all of them. My government will put your needs, the needs of this great state of New South Wales, this great engine room of the Australian economy, above all other considerations.'

He leaves that to settle, and even I think I know what he's saying here: he'll go against the Federal Government if he has to, and the Federal Government isn't run by Nationalists. He'll go against his own party.

He goes on about what he's going to do for us if we vote for him – return the forty-four-hour week and minimum wages, more powers to the Fair Rents Court and a moratorium on evictions, and building roads from here to billy-o to make jobs, Lots of jobs. 'So that *you* – YOU, gentlemen – will be the invigorators of this state yourselves, as you and your families spend your well-earned wages in the many good businesses of your neighbourhoods. This, gentlemen, is sound economy. This is not a mere promise. This is common sense. And for it, a discount from the Bank of England will be and must be demanded!'

He smashes his fist into his palm again and the whole room goes up in calling for it to be true. It does seem to make sense, too, even to me. He's going to rob the bank, this Jack Lang. He's going to rob the Bank of England for us. Good on him.

A chant starts up: 'Lang is right! Lang is right!'

Even Commie Tommo looks impressed by what's gone on here. There might even be a moratorium on colliers and dockers kicking heads in tonight.

I see Mr Adams now too; he comes over to me through the crowd. He's happy. 'We will win,' he says, and his fist is tight with that. It's not just the Labor Party he wants to win, it's fairness, common sense, with the minimum of head-kicking.

I nod: 'Righto, then. I think I know who I'll vote for now.'

Mr Adams smiles and taps me on the shoulder with that fist: 'Don't you even joke about it, boy.'

The chanting has got louder, and I look over at this Mr Lang: he's smiling like a king amongst it. Putting on his hat, making himself half a foot taller again, getting ready to go. I see over the other side of the bar the Communist lot have already left out the Beattie Street doors. I should go too.

I tell Mr Adams: 'I've got to get back. I don't want to leave Ag alone too long with –'

But he's already turned away, started talking to someone else. I leave them to it, and make it quick back down the hill home, through the spitting rain. I don't want to leave Ag alone too long, it's true – we're expecting bailiffs at Number Four sometime today, actual bailiffs from the court, as the moratorium on rent defaulting will come too late for the Bardons that live there, and they're not going to go quietly.

The street is quiet when I get down there, though, and when I get in the house Ag's got something nice in the oven. Smells like a cake. I ask her: 'What you got cooking?'

She says, so proud of herself she's half a foot taller: 'I'm making them biscuits, the ones Mrs Buddle gave me the recipe for. They look nearly as good as hers.'

'Aren't you clever,' I tell her. She is, and newly every day.

She says: 'If they taste as good, I'm going to make some more for Miss Olivia, for Wednesday.'

Horse fucking shit you will. I don't want to have this discussion with my sister. I've avoided it through Mass and all the way afterwards with my head in the *Historical, Theoretical and Practical Text-Book of Steam,* busy not reading it, and then having somewhere else to be. But it has to be discussed now. I tell her: 'You're not going on Wednesday.'

'What?'

'Wednesdays are off, we're not visiting Miss Olivia anymore.'

'No, don't say that. Yoey? Why?' I've told her the sky has fallen in.

'I'm sorry, Aggie, but that's the way it is. There's no more talking about it.'

'No. But why?' She's not going to leave this alone, as if I ever thought she might. She whines: 'But you *love* her.'

I do. I did. But it's not possible to love her anymore. It's not reasonable. Why? I stop myself short of telling Ag we will never be good enough and I keep it instead to what she might understand; I say: 'Miss Olivia isn't a Catholic.'

Ag screws up her face at me: 'So? Gladdy isn't Catholic and she's my friend.'

'It's not the same thing, Ag.'

'Why not?'

'Because it's not, Ag. The Hanrahans are godless communists – completely different thing.'

'But –'

'Shush.'

'God doesn't care if you're a Catholic or not.' Ag shakes her head at me, disgusted at my idiocy. 'He only cares if you're good.'

She turns round on her heel, goes back out to the kitchen, throwing the tea towel across her shoulder, telling me I'm making a mistake.

Maybe so, but it's my mistake to make. Ag is eight years old. She is not standing in my shoes, and Lord, with your blessing and her own cleverness, she never will. Stand in my sandshoes, hanging off the edge of the road deck on a scaffold, hanging off the edge of the air, hanging on by my toes to this monkey-nutted job, where an ability to swim means nothing to the dive. The fall would kill you. Tell me then, when you stand in those shoes, that hanging on to my faith isn't worth it. I hear Ag sniff at the stove; she's crying about it. But I will not be led towards that particular way of sinning again. Five minutes of fun and a lifetime to repent fuck knows what consequences.

Olivia isn't worth it, not worth risking all I've done to better myself. She doesn't care how far I've come or how fast the return journey back to the gutter can be. What do I have without my God? Nothing without His grace. No roof over our heads. No fucking biscuits. And princess calls me ridiculous. She'd like to keep me up in her ivory tower ladies shop, would she? What, as her fucking pet?

*

'Alleluia, praise the Lord, and fuck me, yeah!' Tarzan holds his gun high in want of riveting the sky: 'He's alive!'

Someone's taken the dive, come off and down through the joinings of the deck above us.

'Told you I seen that splash,' Tarz says and he's said it a dozen times. He saw a splash, and we thought it must have been a length of pipe or rail that's going on round that side. But it's one of us. And he's come up. It's a hundred and seventy feet of certain death and I couldn't be less moved by the miracle. We've just watched him get pulled from the water, someone dived off the cradle to help him, and now the word that's come up the phone from the shops is that he's alive.

'Well, who was it?' Tarz is asking Clarkie, who got the message just now.

'It's Ned – course it is. It's Ned Kelly,' he says, shaking his head, having a laugh, taking the notebook out of his leather apron to write something down, like there might've been a bet on it being Kelly.

Vince Kelly, his name is, one of them that chucks himself off coal gantries, ships and any other construction of similar height for the fun of it. His boots ripped off their soles and ended up past his knees with the power of the fall, we're told at smoko, and he's cracked a rib or two. But other than that, he's all right. They reckon he dropped the hammer off his tool belt to break the water as he fell.

Dolly says, with something like envy: 'Jeez, he'll be famous tomorra.'

And Tarz McCall can't wait to start off the celebrations: 'Who's coming for a dive this arvie, then?' Because that's what you'd want to do, isn't it. Chuck yourself off coal gantries in your off hours – or, as Clarkie did last Saturday arvie, pull a motorcar across the yard of the shops, by his teeth. For a fucking monkey-nutted dare. Tarz says: 'Come on, Pretty – you never come along. What's wrong with you?' Telling me I've got no guts.

'Get fucked,' I tell him.

There's plenty of guts around here and I'm not celebrating it or joining your circus. I hate this fucking job, as anyone with half a brain should. This miracle of Vince Kelly, it's just the nightmare come to life. Your feet losing hold, your hand missing the rail. Or the rail that isn't there at all. It's all the luck of surviving the fall used up, and my sister will never look me in the eye again anyway.

'Get fucked yourself, you skinny-arsed little faggot,' says Tarz.

'Righto then,' says Mr Adams. 'That's enough from you both. All heads to be kept until after Saturday and that is an order, that is a union directive, that is law.'

Saturday. Saturday is election day: Jack Lang can get fucked too.

Olivia

'Coralie says you've been grumpy as a bear. Come on, Ollie – what's happened? You're up and you're down, you're round and around like a Ferris wheel.'

'Am I?' I growl through the pins in my teeth. Coralie has no business telling tales. When she gets back from the bank, I'll –

'Don't you be cross with Coralie,' Glor warns. 'She's only worried. So am I, now. What's wrong?'

'Nothing.'

'I've seen the little girl, you know, going up in the lift to you. Agnes, isn't it? Coralie says she hasn't been in for weeks now, and I've held my tongue for long enough waiting for you to tell me what's been going on. What's happened with this Bridge boy? Has he harmed you? If he has, I'll tell Paul and he'll see that the police get him for it. If he's laid a hand –'

'Don't be hysterical, Glor.' I sit back on my heels and look up at her, distracted again by how divine this wedding ensemble is on her. A vision in Chantilly over Shantung, ivory bebe roses round the crown of her veil: Gloria Jabour is really an angel. I'm not. Far from it. My cheeks are hot with the shame: I virtually demanded he harm me. I am my mother's daughter. No, I'm more pathetic than a whore – there was no advantage whatsoever in the affair for me. It's been a month since and this shame only squirms worse and worse. I say: 'No boy has harmed me. There is no boy.'

No boy. There will come a time, I suppose, when I don't gasp like I've stabbed myself every time I think it.

'Oh,' Glor says, a small thud of dashed hopes; but she wants to know all about it: 'Why don't we have Pearson's prawns for lunch?'

'We'll never get in there again,' I say. Not exactly a lie to avoid luncheon interrogation, either. You can't go near the place for the gaggle of journalists and young hopefuls who follow Mr Lang around like a line of puppies. They follow his car from Macquarie Street down to Pitt. What a show. Women worst of all – one fainted in the street on seeing him get out of the car yesterday, mother of three, wanting his autograph. Now that he's won back the government and he's going to save us all from despair. A landslide victory, it was. There's no one in this arcade who didn't vote for him, even if they can't admit to it openly. You can't get any business going without money in the till, elementary accounting, and as Mr Jabour says, it's not entirely our fault the money isn't there. In his opinion, the faceless men of London stole it and spent it on guns and killing the flower of our youth; got our wool at a discount rate, too.

'Well, a sandwich then,' says Glor. 'At the Aristocrat. Quick one.'

'Glor, I can't – truly, I've not got time to blink today.' Business has gone entirely the other way for me – never-ending orders, money stuffed in the till like so much kapok bursting out of a mattress. And here's Coralie back from the bank now, with her hands full of boxes of summer straw berets for trimming. 'Did you get the cellophane too?' I ask her – I'm going to experiment with some little fruit-salady sprays of the stuff. 'Yes, Ollie. All present and accounted for.' And as well the telephone is ringing. 'Sorry, Glor.'

It's Miss Crowdy on the line: 'Can you come at four?'

My head swims. Mostly with gratitude. I'm yet to finish the ribbon cloche for Lady Game's ensemble, for the parliamentary reception thing, on Friday. Oh, but I shall. I shall get it done, to the rhythm of this mantra: what a very lucky girl am I. Sad and ragged round the edges, but very, very lucky. Aren't I?

*

'Extraordinary man, this Mr Lang.' Lady Game is setting the short brim of the cloche just so, and it's perfect – metallics suit her so very well, this steely blue satin bringing out her pretty eyes. 'Philip is not so much impressed as intrigued by him,' she tells the mirror. 'He's never been abroad and sees no cause to go – "Australia is good enough for me, I never want to be out of it," he said, and proudly. He doesn't even own a dinner suit – deliberately so, as he's a wealthy man. Isn't that a bundle of contradictions?'

'Yes, it is,' I suppose. I'm distracted, holding the white peony brooch I've made for the cloche against her head to see what she thinks.

She thinks: 'A little too young for me, Olivia.' Waving it off with an abstracted frown.

It's not too young for her; it softens the aeroplane hue and it's lovely on her. Everything is: pretty face and a lithe sporty figure, you can do anything you like with fashion. But who am I to argue?

'Or is it this famous egalitarianism of yours?' she asks me with a little wry smile.

'I beg your pardon, Lady Game?' I've quite lost the thread.

'This pride in not going abroad and not owning a dinner suit.' She turns to me. Lady Game is sincerely curious, and she takes her vice-regal role very seriously, she does so want to be useful and to do the right thing. Do good things. I'm still in awe that my opinion means anything to her at all.

I say: 'I'm not sure I know, really.' Search my memory for Mother's disdain for all things working class, and tell Lady Game:

'I think the dinner suit might be a Labor Party thing.' Or a general Australian male sort of thing – there are so many stubbornly ill-attired men in this city it is embarrassing to wonder what outsiders must think of us. How must we look to the English uppers, never mind the Continentals? Like a nation of walking bargain-table drack sack atrocities.

'Hm,' she frowns, thoughtful. 'Some of them refuse to toast the King. That is terrible. I fear Mr Lang is going to put Philip in a terrible position one day. But there's something about him . . . Something . . .' She won't say and she waves the thought away as sillier than my peony, then smiles, a deeper shade of wry: 'Well, he *is* rather handsome, I must say.'

'Do you think so, Lady Game?' I laugh with her. I think Sir Philip is handsomer, especially in his brass-button military regalia. But what would I know? I'm not a forty-four-year-old mother of three. They do share something, though, I think, Governor Game and Premier Lang: something in their eyes. Something soulful. A searching, a blueness. That only brings Eoghan's eyes to me. I close mine for a moment, to let the swimming pass. The way he held me in the baths, in my distress: killed a seaweed monster for me . . .

'Are you all right, Olivia?' Lady Game's concern for me is as sincere as the rest of her.

'Yes,' I smile. 'A little woozy with busyness, that's all.'

A little monumentally heartbroken. I won't be doing this love thing again. Ever.

*

Must be one of those days, though . . . A letter from Mother is waiting for me when I get home, another one.

La la la la la la la la la, it goes on about London, how they've moved to new apartments in Mayfair.

Please write, darling. Please, please, please, I haven't heard from you now in weeks and weeks. What are you up to? How are things at the salon? Better still, come to London and tell me. You must. Come to London – and stay. Or perhaps I shall assert my parental right and compel you to, Olivia Jane. You know I don't mean that, but I do miss you so. Sophia is growing so quickly, becoming so like you.

That can't be true: I look like his Lordship. Beaky as Fagan's parrot.

But you see Bart looks to be settling in here for the longer term now. He's been offered chambers in . . . some place I've never heard of . . . our move could well be permanent.

What could I write to respond to that? Permanent abandonment. My page is utterly blank.

You would adore it here, Olivia. I know you don't remember much of your childhood when we were at Grosvenor Place, but I'm sure the loveliness of London would all come flooding back. The squirrels running about through Hyde Park ahead of winter, they bring back memories for me of you as a little girl, so delighted by them. There's a little place I have my eye on for you, too – it's in Piccadilly, right in the hub, and it would be perfect to set your shingle on. I know it's clichéd, but society here is so much more genteel, polite, and so blessedly cool, so much more your style, Ollie – I didn't know how much I missed it myself until I returned.

As if eight years of desperate loneliness there never occurred. Just where do I get my tendency to confabulate? And she goes on and on . . .

Things aren't nearly so bad here with all this financial catastrophe business, either. I've heard it's got to unmanageable proportions in Sydney – it's quite the talk at Australia House. Unemployment is what – twenty-five percent there? How appalling. That's even worse than New York, and it's less than half that here. You'll have no trouble with clientele in any case – little birdies are already whispering your triumph with Gwendolen Game . . .

I toss the letter into the drawer of the hall stand and close it. I don't want to read any more. Mother stepping over khaki swags to have the life she always wanted: London, money, position. She can have it.

While here we have twenty-five percent. Twenty-five percent of what? Men. That's awful. More awful that I've been too busy to take note of what is happening right under my schnonk. Murderers and thieves: that shame whips through me once more, a motorcar zooming through my soul, skittling hobos. What am I doing making frocks and hats for the rich?

In answer, a woman cries out from one of the top windows of the boarding house next door: 'No, John – no! What do we do now? Where can we go?'

She sobs and howls for almost half an hour solid. No one tells her to be quiet. Her cries call out across the harbour long after they've ceased, and no one answers her.

I should go next door and offer her a room here. I have a spare one: it contains my wardrobe. But I don't offer, do I. I don't do anything.

*

I do my best for the economy. I have new tin put on the roof, I have the hot water put through to the kitchen. I fill my cupboards with far more than I need, religiously. I have the phone put on and I contemplate the purchase of a wireless for myself, for Christmas, as I have a good solid cry at Glor's wedding. Not altogether miserable: she's so beautiful, such a beautiful angel amongst the white marzipan columns of Our Lady of Whatnot, her Paul almost cries too.

Mr Jabour puts his arm around me at the reception; he says: 'Be happy, Olivia, my dear – you're next, I promise. You know, you have probably already met him. Things tend to happen this way.'

Not this thing, not for me. I am a wilted bloom in this room full of flowers. In the Randwick Town Hall no less, trestle tables groaning under the weight of the Irish-Lebanese race to the middle-class wedding-gift competition. 'Paul's football team have bought them a crystal dessert service,' Velma whispers to me across the three-tiered cake of bluebirds and butterflies. That's so sweet, I think I might have to go and have a good lie-down.

I go home and wait for the McIlraith's man to bring my Mexican chocolate box.

And I am stunned by my aloneness. There is no boy. There is no little girl. All through this year's mad Christmas blitz I am stunned.

The Jabours are off to Grandpapa Jidi's in Never Never Menindee as usual.

Glor and Paul are quite busy with each other.

And Mother is in London.

London. That's where I was born. I am English. Perhaps Mother is right. It is where I belong. Not Paris, not New York, not Lavender Bay. But London.

Maybe I should . . .

*

Turn up unannounced at St Augustine's on Christmas morning. Halfway through the service I arrive, though as it's all in Latin, I have no idea where it's up to, really.

I stand at the back of the church, looking for him. No idea if he's here. Maybe he goes on Christmas Eve. Do Catholics do that? I don't know anything about it. He probably goes twice or seventeen times anyway, he's so devout, damn him. It's so crowded, though, stuffed to the stained-glass and gilt-arched windows. A pretty Russian empress style of church, and now all the children are going down the aisle, to stand before the fairy castle altar.

The Blue Mile

I suppose it's their Communion or something, but at a signal from the organ pipes above they start singing as they gather there.

It's a song I don't know. It's a language I don't know. It doesn't sound Latin, as if I'd know. Is it Irish? I suppose it must be. All the children wave their hands, making birds' wings as they sing, and the tune is somehow familiar . . . What is it? They sing me the English now, to tell me: 'The lark, the dove, and the red bird came, and they did sing in sweet Jesus' name, on Christmas day in the morning . . .'

And there it is. So beautiful, so very sweet, I can hear the threads of magic-carpet laughter tinkling through it.

And then I see him. His black hair; his white shirt. Three pews from the back, on the aisle, just about right under my nose.

I tiptoe down the aisle and slip in beside him.

He turns to me. Stunned: 'What?'

Something small, dark and fast hurtles towards me at the end of the song: Agnes, holding me tight, burying her face in my skirt.

She looks up at me and cries: 'I knew it, I knew you would come back. I prayed and prayed so hard.'

I look up at him. What's that in his eyes? What's he thinking? I don't know. But now he smiles.

And I am here, where I belong. Inside his smile. Inside my tear that falls with relief now at knowing solidly. This is where I belong. I am a native of his deep blue searching eyes.

Five

Yo

'You can't go away again,' Ag says to her out in the sun, here in the courtyard of St Gus's, holding her hand like she'll never let it go again.

'I won't go away again, not from you, Agnes, not ever,' she says, but she's looking at me. As half the parish is: wondering what I got for Christmas as they rush away to turn the roast. Mrs Buddle winks over her walking stick on her way through the gate: she'll get the story later, in detail, from Ag. 'Come to my place for dinner today? Now?' Olivia is still looking at me, in that way I can't say no. 'I've already made the ham. Basted it myself and everything. Whole leg – don't make me eat it all alone.'

'Oh, can we go, Yoey – please?' Ag will never forgive me if we don't.

'Yeah, all right,' I say, for all the grace lacking in that. I'm still not wholly believing Olivia is here with us – come *here* for us. To have Christmas dinner with us. She is Christmas: her dress is green with red ribbons going all around it, her gold curls set all around the edge of her little white hat. She's the best Christmas tree I've ever seen, and it's not like we were going to have much of a dinner this year ourselves anyway, taking some sandwiches down to the park. Mr Adams gave me a pound, as he did last year, but I spent all of it at Hordern's on Ag's new dress and shoes.

'I must warn you, though,' she says, that bit of wicked in her smile, and making no attempt to hide it: 'There will be dancing.'

'Dancing?' I'm already laughing. And worried.

'Dancing!' Ag reckons that's a top idea.

'Yes,' Olivia says to her. 'You'll never guess what Santa brought me.'

'What?'

'A wireless!'

'No.' Ag can't wait to get there.

'Yes.' Olivia looks back to me. 'Don't worry. I'll teach you.'

'You'll teach me what? To dance?' The bell starts going off in the tower, ringing all round this courtyard that's empty now, calling the overly faithful to the Solemn High Mass to come, and I don't hear what she says next. I'm just staring at her again. She came to Mass. She came to this particular Mass, and we nearly went earlier but that Ag wanted to sing more than joining Gladdy down at the park quicker; that's the hand of God. It must be. That Olivia Greene came to us at Mass at all. Yes, she did. She's here.

Holding her arms out to me, for a dance. Right here. Her laughter sings high above the bell: 'Dance with me now.'

So I do. I take her and hold her to me and dance her round this empty courtyard of St Gus's, with this bell ringing and ringing out and only the great stone windows looking down on us. She leans her head back, still laughing, laughing up at the sky, and she says: 'I knew it. I knew you could dance.'

Of course I can dance. How else do you get near a girl? I made a particular point of being all right enough at it to ask Lil Casey to a social at St Ben's, and I never did dance with her, because she said no to me. That was an age ago. I wasn't good enough for Lil Casey. But here I am, this Christmas Day, a year away, with Oonagh. Olivia Greene. I hold her closer, the tin-whistle slimness of her, and I put my cheek to hers: 'It's amazing all the things I can do.'

She squeezes my hand: 'Yes.' And she whispers, her breath on my ear at the finish of the bell: 'I'll wait for you, Eoghan. I'll do whatever it takes.'

*

She comes to us again on the Sunday after. It's only two days that have passed but somehow it's like the constitution of the air has changed. The look of everything is clearer.

'Hold on a second,' she says as we're leaving to walk round to St Gus's. She takes a little pair of scissors from her bag of tricks and cuts a flower from the gardenia bush at the front of our house and pins it on her straw hat. 'What do you think, Agnes?' They fiddle about with the flower on the hat and I watch them. Ag is so happy, so easy in herself, and I take a second to take stock of how far she's come in this past year. She won the junior story-writing and the handwriting prize at school; the headmaster shook my hand in the street: that's never happened to an O'Keenan. Ag's gardenia's doubled in size too, with all her care. The leaves of the bush are darker and shinier, the flowers seem whiter and the scent of them in this patch of morning sun is miraculous in itself. The scent of memories for our future, and I'm easier in my own self too. I can look at Olivia here and I'm not going to die if I don't kiss her now. Because, one day, I will kiss her every day, in some patch of sunlight somewhere, and I will cherish that kiss, every day, for the rest of our lives.

I take her hand, up the street as we walk, for all the parish to see.

'This is Miss Greene, my friend and Aggie's,' I introduce her to Mr Adams first, coming in the gate. He's on his own; Mrs Adams must be held up with their Kenny having another turn, to break their hearts more than is fair.

'How do you do?' Olivia holds out her hand to him and he looks at it for a second, and not only because I'm sure he'd never have shook the hand of a woman in his life. But he takes it up and his pit-bull potato head smiles: 'We're doing well, Miss Greene. How do you do?'

She looks under her hat in that nervous way she has when she's uncertain. 'Very well, thank you. It's a beautiful morning, isn't it?'

'It is, indeed.' Mr Adams shakes my hand too and pulls me down by the shoulder to say in my ear: 'Beautiful morning?' and some Gaelainn of his that doubtless means: 'Where in want of some new type of blasphemy did you find her, you lucky bastard?'

Mrs Buddle waves from the back pew as we go in the church doors, nodding to me that Ag told her every last thing yesterday when she skipped round to hers, so the rest of the congregation will know by teatime too. Clarkie, three pews down, gives me a look to match Mr Adams's Gaelainn. I give him a look back: *Believe it.*

Thank you, Lord. I watch Olivia watching all that's going on through the Mass, her hand on Ag's shoulder all the while, listening though she doesn't understand a word. You don't really have to. Beyond doing the right thing, you're here for hope and wonder, to be better than you are, that's my belief, heretical as it might be, and I let myself hope and wonder: would she convert for me? Really? That would be a new height for pride and for happiness. I'm grinning with it even as I kneel to take Communion, even as Father O'Reagan has a good hard look there for sin on me.

Look harder. You'll find none. Even my prayer is pure. I have only one prayer, and it's all I'm asking for: this family that I want us to be.

*

'Oh dear God,' Olivia is praying this Sunday, only seven Sundays later, on our way down to the Darling Street wharf, on our way across to the zoo for the afternoon. Or we were on our way. Now she is shaking like a leaf with fear.

She's just watched a fella get chucked up against the stone wall of the Shipwrights Arms. He's hit the footpath with the sound of something rending: not the wall.

'You dirty fucking little –' says one them who just chucked him. One of three.

'Shit – they're coming,' says another.

They are: there's about a dozen running full pelt down the hill at us. Hobnails smashing along the asphalt like it might be an army of twice more coming at us.

'Oh dear, God.' Olivia is not screaming. She's gone past terrified. She's grabbed up Ag to her but she's just standing in the road, shaking.

I push them both into the lane that runs by the pub, and then I stand at the corner and watch.

I see who they are. I don't know any of them personally but I recognise them as colliers. They all drink at the Dry Dock, round at Mort Bay. They're not drunk today. I don't know what this fight is about. It doesn't matter. The mine is closing down and they've only got each other to blame: it was a collective, all these fellas here shareowners or sons of. Not anymore. There's no bargaining of anything if there's no company to work for. Lang's bank-robbing for roadworks will come a bit too late for them. All they've got left is their Communism now: collective poverty, and they're not happy about it.

'What you fucking looking at?' One of them looks over at me.

I don't say anything. Just hold his stare, as I make myself ready to grab the girls and run. Where? How?

But I don't have to. The cops' whistles are coming down the street now, hanging out of a paddywagon coming down the hill, as they all take off across the park, disappearing before the wagon's got the brakes on.

One of the cops gets out and asks me: 'Recognise any of them?'

I shake my head: 'No.'

He looks hard for the horseshit: 'You sure about that? I think I might recognise you.'

No, you fucking well don't, you steaming streak of filth. I tell him: 'I'm sorry, I don't know any of them.'

That's not a lie, and I don't say it only to avoid getting my own head kicked in. My sympathy is with the colliers for all that they might be at fault themselves. Their collective was as mean as any boss, not paying their engine drivers properly, always in dispute, running the mine down, giving the council every excuse to threaten to close them down. And now it's happened. But the cops make sport of shooting at miners and waterside workers in this country when they dissent, and they don't always aim above their heads. You can't interrupt the lives of the rich with industrial action, can you. The rich that reckon everything happens by magic, and happens for them; if the rubbish bins aren't emptied on time you call the fucking cops, don't you.

This one is still giving me the hard stare. Not one of the cops is seeing to the fella on the ground yet. He hasn't moved. He could be dead for all they care about it.

The publican of the Shipwrights now sticks his head out the door by me: 'I know exactly who they are, officer.'

Of course you fucking do: they don't spend their money in your pub.

'Eoghan, are you all right?' Olivia's face appears next to his as she steps back round from the corner of the lane. She's still holding Ag to her, keeping her from grim death.

I say: 'Yeah, I'm all right.'

Something in me is not right, though. Something in me doesn't want to keep walking past this. I can't keep on to the zoo, carry on with my Sunday. I'm staring at Olivia now and all I can think is: you're one of them and you always will be. As I will always be No one O'Paddy getting stopped by the cops that want to have a word. Barely enough change in my pocket for the fare out of here. Wages that wouldn't cover her drycleaning bills.

But she's looking over my shoulder now, waving her purse

at the cop: 'Officer. Officer – aren't you going to see if that poor fellow over there is all right?'

The cop looks at her with a bit of surprise first before he realises who's speaking to him and then he nods: 'Of course, miss – an ambulance will be along.'

She's giving him a stare that says she'll turn him to dust if he tells a lie and it brings me back into myself, into the here of where we are. Olivia is like no one but herself. Class of her own.

She says over the top of the paddywagon, over all of us: 'Oh look, here's the ferry pulling in.' And to Ag: 'Come on then, poppet. Not going to let a couple of silly bullies ruin our fun, are we.'

Of course not.

We keep on to the zoo, to Taronga Park, across the water at Mosman. We've never been before, me and Ag; Olivia hasn't been for years. It's another beautiful day, all day long, and there's nothing like seeing Ag looking at a zebra for the first time. She's shaking with the wonder of it. Kangaroos. Turtles and fish. Squealing at snakes. Getting to feed a carrot to a giraffe and disbelieve its long blue tongue. See two baby lion cubs rolling around on the grass. See Olivia holding Ag's hand all day. A beautiful day, excepting that I paid for none of it.

It's nothing to her. She waves that purse around however she wants. We eat sausage rolls and fairy floss so dear they should be more plainly called stealing. And it's eating me.

'You all right?' she asks me. 'You've been quiet today.'

'Have I?' Can't imagine why.

Olivia

'Is that a peculiarly Australian thing too?' Lady Game asks me and I bite down hard on my pins with this sharp jab of embarrassment: no idea what she's referring to. Haven't been listening to a word. A little preoccupied today: that fighting in the street yesterday, it's playing around and around in my mind like a seaweedy newsreel, one the general public is never shown, for good reason. I'm frightened for Eoghan. I don't know why I should be, but I am. That he'll be set upon in the street; as if walking the streets is somehow more dangerous than fixing railings to the side of the sky. Perhaps it is. He was so withdrawn yesterday, all through the zoo – he's worried too, isn't he.

'Olivia?'

What? Yes, that's right, Lady Game is wondering about peculiarly Australian things, isn't she.

'I beg your pardon? I was deep into your hemline just then.'

'And you do such very fine work, too, Olivia,' she smiles, that gently wry one. 'Such attention to detail, you have, and I'm so grateful. I was only wondering, about that way Australians seem to have of speaking in a derogatory manner of those things of which you should really be most proud.' She looks out the window, over the crenellations and the figtops, at the glimpse of the arch there. 'Your Bridge – I've now heard it called the Coathanger three times, by an array of people, and this morning, at the Bush Nursing function with the Country Women's Association, one of the ladies called it the Iron Lung. I don't know quite how to respond when I hear these terms. Isn't that terrible?'

I don't know whether she means the derogatory terms or her lack of response is terrible, but as I look out over at the arch myself I must work hard to stifle the snort: 'Iron Lung? I've not heard that one before.' That's quite clever: great big metal thing and the only thing keeping the city alive, financially. Terrible, too, monstrous, but I tell Lady Game: 'I'm sure it's said affectionately.'

'But that's the thing – I don't *know*. The rural ladies this morning were quite critical of city attitudes and the priorities of the parliament. Their opinions of politicians are in no doubt, however – they call the parliament here the Bear Pit and the federal one is the Canberra Zoo.'

Takes me straight back to the monkey colony at Taronga yesterday, mad apes screeching and leaping about and shaking the wire of their cage and I do have to laugh at that: 'Country women are infamous for calling spades spades.'

'I'm gathering that.' Lady Game's eyes glitter with wry, but then she's as pensive again, looking out the window. 'It's impressive how interested and active in politics Australian women are, especially amongst these country women. Conservative and utterly loyal to the Empire, they detest Mr Lang, to a woman, and yet a very lively debate broke out, just as I had to leave – about all the roadworks the Premier has planned. They desperately need the highways properly surfaced out in the rural areas but they were concerned they won't get the roads done because the money will be wasted on high unionised wages. I wished I could stay to hear them all. Such well-informed women, really very impressive.'

Are they? My face burns with some other embarrassment. I'm not impressive. I make hats and frocks and I startle and hide like a silly little girl at desperate men fighting in the street. Agnes was far better composed; she comforted *me* while we waited in that lane: *Don't worry, Miss Olivia,* she patted my hand, *Yoey knows how to keep out of trouble.* The only thing impressive about me was the fingernail marks I left in the top of Agnes's arm, I was so frightened. I can't mention any of that here, not a whisper of it, and not because the details of my life are inconsequential to Lady Game. They are preposterous. Unthinkable. The burn deepens with that other persistent whisper: Eoghan and I can't be together. Preposterous unthinkableness aside, he's going to lose his job. Sometime soon. When the road through the arch is finished. There is not going to be another job for him to go to, and he won't work with me. This is a catastrophe in waiting. It doesn't matter how much I love him. Worship him. We will never be married, and this hurt, this fear, this grinding ache is –

'Cutting the heads off the tall poppies – that's what he said.' Lady Game pauses, waiting for my response. I was barely even aware she had been speaking.

I look up from my pinning: 'I do beg your pardon, Lady Game. This voile is slippery as a basket of eels in butter. Who said what?'

'Mr Lang.' I spy the frown that fleets across her mask of tranquillity. Definitely not an imperious frown; I've hurt her feelings, and that won't do: she is a sensitive and wonderful woman, as well as the linchpin of my livelihood. She is also ten times busier than I ever am – church fetes, hall openings, children's recitals, girls' athletics carnivals: I don't think there's an invitation she turns down – and these quiet moments with me I am certain are somehow a treat for her, a small haven of hats and frocks.

I sit back on my heels. 'Please, tell me. What did Mr Lang say about the poppies?'

'He used that analogy with Sir Philip the other evening – cutting the heads off the tall poppies.' She frowns properly: concerned. 'He means to prune the incomes of the privileged. That's how he plans to fund his roadworks. I know he's not a socialist, he's far more intriguing than that, Sir Philip is convinced of his good intentions and his genuine care for his fellow man, but cutting the heads off the tall poppies – that sounds quite violent to me.'

It does. It gets yesterday's newsreel going round my mind again. That man's head hitting the wall of the hotel: *CRACK*. Eoghan doesn't think those men were fighting about anything in particular: they were fighting because they are angry. Chooks fighting over a button, he said, dismissive of the whole thing. I'd say they appeared out of their minds with anger. Who wouldn't be angry? I tell Lady Game: 'Yes. There's a lot of anger . . .'

'Yes,' Lady Game nods at the figtops, searching her own thoughts. 'I think he might well be an angry man.' Then she looks down at me, something girlish, grinnish in her eyes: 'You mustn't ever repeat any of the nonsense I spout here, Olivia. Promise me.'

'Of course I promise. You can trust in my discretion always, Lady Game.' The Governor's wife tells me state secrets: you can't get more fabulous than that. She presses her lips together and I think she's going to tell me some more.

'It's only gossip, of course,' she says and I'm listening with both ears now, 'so I don't know if it's at all true, really, and it's come from a political opponent, too, but as a boy, Mr Lang sold newspapers on the street, at Brickfield Hill, on that corner where Anthony Hordern's Department Store is: he had to, to support his mother in some disastrous family circumstance – that's why he has such sympathy with the poor, and no sympathy at all for the indolent. Perhaps it's why he is so kindly towards women, too, why the education of the poor is so important to him – he wasn't able to complete high school himself. The man who told me this said it with no small amount of disparagement, explaining Mr Lang's appeal to the masses – his presidential-style self-made demagogy. But of all the stories there are about Mr Lang, that one seems to me to fit. He is an angry man and the anger is quite personal.'

And I do believe Lady Game might be quite smitten. Why wouldn't she be? Even Mother was partial to Mr Lang: tall, dark, dangerous and dreadfully kind.

'I must say,' Lady Game continues wistfully, 'it's Mrs Lang, the Premier's wife, who is the more intriguing and impressive, in her way.'

'Mrs Lang?' I've only seen her once, and from a distance. Velma Jabour called me down to the window of Electrolux to watch her purchase a new vacuum cleaner a couple of weeks ago. Infamous as the dreariest dowd in the land, or of the western suburbs at least – she manages to make brown crepe look not so much tired as on its last legs.

'She is a feminist,' Lady Game smiles with a hint of *now, now* in it as if she might have heard my unkind thought. 'And while I'm never entirely sure what that term *feminist* means apart from fiercely well read, I do consider her to be exemplary of the finest Christian qualities a woman might possess.' Oh dear, this'll be a load of dull guff, I suppose. Christianity: I would call for it to be banned entirely except for what Sundays does for frocks, shush, don't ever tell Eoghan that Mass at St Gus, as far as I'm concerned, is the one true most interminable hour of the week. But Lady Game now drops her voice almost to a whisper: 'This is the most terrible gossip, Olivia, told to me in the most terrible terms, by an awful bigot, too, but I must express it, for what it reveals of the utmost purity of spirit in the one it seeks to harm. Mrs Hilda Lang, as you'd be aware, is mother to nine children. But what's not generally known is that one of them is adopted and that this adopted one is in fact Mr Lang's own son – born out of adultery, to a woman called Nellie Anderson. He's about your age now.'

'Oh?' Now that's a piece of gossip, I'll say.

'Hm,' Lady Game concurs but her whisper is one of hushed astonishment, not scandal. 'The affair carried on over several years and almost ended in divorce for the Langs but that Hilda Lang resisted that awful measure. This is not the extraordinary thing about her, though. The extraordinary thing is, when this Nellie Anderson died – suddenly and tragically when the child was small – Hilda Lang not only adopted him, but in the heartbreak that followed for Mr Lang, Hilda found it in her own heart to reconcile with her husband. Not only *that*, but she named their next child Nellie. What does one call that sort of generosity? What is that sort of compassion but sublime?'

Gaspingly so. I nod: 'Sublime indeed.'

'It's the antithesis of anger, is it not? That turning of the cheek, with love.' Lady Game sighs and laments to the lampshade above: 'But Hilda Lang doesn't know how to host a dinner party or how to wear a decent hat, and so I dare say history won't remember her as anything at all.'

No. But I will remember this moment. This story and its moral: don't judge a book, not until you've got to the end and then gone for a good long walk to digest it all. I stand up to stretch out my knees, my spirit somehow replenished. And more: I want to be an impressive woman. I want to stand beside Eoghan, whatever comes for us. Whatever it takes, I will do.

Yo

'Lang is Right! Lang is Right!' You couldn't shout against it if you were monkey-nutted enough to try. This crowd in the Domain is a thousand strong, at least, and most of them have left their women at home. I've counted at least thirty cops, and Lang's not even here today. If he was there'd be ten thousand turned up and I wouldn't have.

I look at Mr Adams beside me: I'm giving up my Sunday afternoon to this? What for? A fight? The Labor Party can do that without my contribution, fighting itself three ways now, over this Lang Plan: New South Wales Bank Robbery Labor is breaking from Federal Labor, which is fucking itself up backwards on its way out of Canberra, and now there's this other new lot breaking off the main party and joined with the Nationalists, calling itself the United Australia Party. There's nothing united about Australia. And I'm just shitful about it. They're letting the Nationalists win, by whatever name they call themselves, and that means I'm not going to get a living wage if I get lucky enough to work for the dole when I lose my job. When, not if. But Mr Adams doesn't look at me. He's full of faith, pumping his fist in the air with the rest of them: 'Lang is Right! Lang is Right!'

The fella on the podium is waving for everyone to shut up for two minutes to let him go on. He's something do to with the Federal ALP lot, though he's a Bank Robbery supporter; I don't care who he is, going on again now: 'It is wrong to denounce the Lang Plan as too drastic. It is too mild by far. The time has arrived for Australia to demand the entire cancellation of all war debts in conjunction with other Allied Powers. The –'

'Lang is Right! Lang is Right!'

Righto. I'm having an epiphany: I see how it is the rich get rich now. They don't stand around in parks pointlessly shouting slogans on Sunday afternoons. When there are smarter things to do, such as studying for a Mechanical Principles examination that might become completely irrelevant to me when I lose my apprenticeship anyway. Another two minutes and we get another sentence: 'The war debts are discreditable and sordid obligations which should never have existed!'

'Lang is Right! Lang is Right!'

Or I could be at Olivia's. She's making Ag's costume for the school play today. Ag's going to be a girl called Elsie in something called *Make-Believe*. She gets to say: *What a lovely princess,* and wear a petticoat skirt. Olivia had me cutting the bits of material for it before I left them this morning, saving her some time. *I want to keep you in the sideboard and have you cutting for me always,* she said. *You've got a tailor's hand, I tell you – true and sure.* And a lot easier than cutting boot leather as I've done a thousand times before. I'd rather be at Balmain on my own today, though, finishing off the present I'm making her for her birthday, next Thursday, the sixteenth of April: I'm making her a shoe rack from pipe offcuts. Olivia has thirty-four pairs of shoes. I've done a pattern of flowers and leaves in tin up the sides, so it'll be her shoe garden. It's tall as a baker's stand, don't know how I'll get it across on the ferry. Don't know how it is she can be only twenty. That's almost as amazing as the fact of anyone having thirty-four pair of shoes. When we met, she only had two good pairs, she told me; now she's keeping the shoe shop in the arcade afloat. Things turn around, don't they; you just have to work hard and hang on. You can't let it eat you. You can't let the bastards have you. Listen to Mrs Buddle telling Olivia every Sunday she sees her what a lucky girl she is to have found me. Is she? How am I going to stay afloat? I got my fifteen shilling raise I was due, and it's taken the pressure off a bit. But for how long? I could just walk off forever for the wonder of that. I know my hours will get cut down again soon and then cut altogether. What am I going to do if I can't find another job? How am I going to pay my debts then? The gas bill, my credit up at the grocers, the milko . . . What will I do? Cut out petticoat skirts inside Olivia's sideboard? Not in this life.

The fella on the podium has his voice cracking with it: 'Is it just or even reasonable that our grandchildren and great-grandchildren should be condemned to perpetual servitude in attempts to pay millions annually to the chief beneficiaries of the war? Are Australian citizens truly expected to tamely and indefinitely tolerate preferential treatment to every country but Australia? These bankers are confidence men. Tricksters and highway bandits! Bankrupt of all morality! Support the Lang Plan!'

'Lang is Right! Lang is Right!'

Yeah. Yeah. Yeah.

'Come on,' I say under my breath. I want to get going so I don't lose the whole of the afternoon to this. I want to get to Olivia's to get the roast on, too. She's always late getting it in the oven if we have it over there and it's the only meat me and Ag get all week, *Don't tell Olivia that, Ag – she'd be 'appalled', wouldn't she?* The cops are looking to be of the same mind, after their dinner. But Mr Adams is still pumping the air. I look around the crowd again. Tarzan and Clarkie aren't here; neither's Dolly: because they don't do every last little thing Mr Adams tells them to.

'Lang is Right! Lang is Right!'

We've all got the idea, and the Governor's heard you now, too.

'Greater than Lenin! Lang is Right! Greater than Lenin! Lang is Right!'

For fuck's sake. I'm just reaching over to touch Mr Adams on the shoulder to tell him I'll be off when they stop anyway and he decides: 'Good enough, lads.' Shaking some hands, saying some words about nipping United Australia in the bud, and saying to me: 'Well, let's not hang about then.'

No, let's not. We walk up across the lawns of the Domain and we're almost up behind the big library, across from the gates to the Gardens there. I can't see them gates without thinking of that first night Ag and I spent there – *those* gates. Ag's started correcting my manner of speech, as if I don't know the right way to say things.

I'm wondering if that old bent paling in the fence might still be up there when I see this fella step in our path now, saying something that sounds like: 'You don't like paying your debts, eh?'

'What did you say?' I ask him innocently, because I don't know that I heard him right.

'Keep walking,' says Mr Adams to me, and I see it's not just one fella – it's half-a-dozen.

Another of them comes up beside the first one, saying: 'An honourable man would consider welshing on a debt to the King as treason.' He's got an educated manner of speaking, but his shirt collar is greasy and his suit has seen better times. He's maybe thirty and a big bastard, broader than Tarz even.

Twice my age and twice my size, he steps in front of me: 'Are you an honourable man?'

Mr Adams puts a hand up in peace, between us: 'No trouble here. Good day to you.'

I look behind me. Jesus. A minute ago we were a thousand. Now we are two. Against six – no, seven, as another steps out from behind the nearest fig.

'But you are making trouble,' the first one says, 'Irishman.'

'No. No trouble,' Mr Adams tells him plainly. 'But I can make some, if you'd like.' He looks the big bastard over, making a point of looking hard at some badge pinned on his coat, and he says to him in particular: 'I've learned a thing or two about trouble, most of it in the Connaught Rangers.'

I'm more surprised at that than the standovers in front of us. The Connaught Rangers? That's a military regiment, legendary, the only one I've ever known of: otherwise called the Devil's Own, ask Father Madigan why and you'll be told they're all saints and martyrs to Erin for their mutiny against the Imperialists. The pit-bull stare Mr Adams is giving these fellas back is enough to say it's true: have a go and I'll rip your faces off.

While the rest of his own face is smiling: 'I don't know,' he says, so steady and plain it's a threat in itself, 'it might have escaped your attention that we have our own parliament in Australia these days. We have our own laws and none of them say it's treason not to bend over and let the Bank of England give it to you up the arse.' He looks at the big one again, talking to that badge on his coat: 'Maybe you like it that way, ay?' he asks him, just as steady and plain: 'You like it up the arse?'

So one of the fellas behind can't stop himself from laughing. Then they're all put off.

'Watch yourself,' the first one says as we start walking. 'We'll be watching you.'

When we're a good distance off, I breathe out: 'Who the fuck was that?'

'I don't know,' says Mr Adams, but he'll find out. 'That bloke, the big one – he's ex-army. AIF pin on his coat.'

That doesn't mean much to me. I say, still in awe: 'That was a skilful performance.'

Mr Adams laughs with a big breath out too: 'Performance is right.'

I ask him: 'Connaught Rangers?' Can't be true; can it? When I was a kid, I'd have got on a ship to India to join them: Irish heroes. I dreamed I'd be a drummer in their pipe band. Got the job stacking bottles at Quirks instead, and I believe the Rangers changed their stripes for the IRA soon after.

Mr Adams shakes his potato head and waves it off: 'Mistake of my life, that one, and a summer in France I'll never get back.' Holding up his hand to the sun in peace: 'But we all do some arse-brained things along the way to learning, don't we?'

Olivia

'You're so good with that sort of thing – matching and knowing what goes,' Mrs Bloxom is imploring. Scheming: her gloved thumb pressed to the back of my hand: 'Warwick would be so grateful, dear.'

Warwick has just purchased an apartment at Point Piper, above Seven Shillings Beach. I'm gratified to know that it cost almost two thousand pounds: real estate prices are not suffering from close Bridge views. But I am not going to decorate Warwick's apartment for him. Because this is not about decorating Warwick's apartment. It's about Mrs Bloxom's pursuit of me for her son. It has turned from mildly and amusingly relentless to vaguely threatening now: the pressure of her thumb on my hand is making my skin prickle all the way up my arm.

I tell the fox trim at her gauntlet, and firmly: 'Interior design is not my sort of thing, Mrs Bloxom – I can't bear wallpaper, I'm afraid.'

'Oh?' she's sceptical, fingernails pinch through the heavy cocoa charmeuse with the squeeze. 'I'd be mindful not to pretend I was too far above anything if I were you, *dear*.' She almost meows it.

'Oh?' I reply. My poker face is set but my heart is racing. She knows something. My first fear is Eoghan. She's found out. How? Someone has seen us. It had to happen. It's all right; I straighten my back. I won't deny it. My heart lies with a Catholic tradesman, not your flop-fringed fop. Oh but dear God this heart is racing, Phar Lap in full gallop, thundering with panic. I haven't even told Glor of our engagement. Why haven't I? Because Glor is expecting her first baby in December and I don't want to over-excite her. What rubbish. It's now late October and I haven't told anyone because — Because we agreed we'd wait to see Father O'Reagan in December, making it a year, before making our intentions official. What rubbish. I've been keeping this secret so close to my chest, as if it were made of antique glass. Stand beside him? I've done whatever it takes to wrap him in tissue and box him in the stockroom. So careful, I haven't even had Agnes here at the salon after school. Too busy, I've said; too dangerous to be wandering around town in the evenings. Rubbish. Too dangerous for whom? Me. Because —

'Nothing lasts forever.' The fox trim sweeps up theatrically, releasing my hand, and Mrs Bloxom's gaze is cold on me as she declares: 'Don't be surprised if the Games are recalled to London any day, Olivia.'

'What?' I say, and I almost etherise with relief. 'Ha!' but it explodes from me. Mrs Bloxom is only being a catty old B about the Games: Sydney's favourite new sport — that is, if you're a Nationalist or whatever the conservatives call themselves these days. Mrs Bloxom is their chief mastermind — of course it's all Lady Game's fault that her husband won't dismiss that treacherous Mr Lang in the name of the King — and as well, she's still not forgiven me for breaking that appointment with her last April: she presumes I was running off to Government House, as I occasionally must do, but I was actually malingering: day after my birthday and I stayed at home that Friday to play with my shoe garden. So happy. I smile at Mrs Bloxom and her silly presumptions now, give her the full blast of almost a year's worth of mostly wonderful Sundays and sweet blue miles of dreams.

Mrs Bloxom snips: 'Not a laughing matter, dear.'

And I turn as quickly: 'No, indeed it's not a laughing matter.' I give her my imperious best, which is less than the Fickle Witches of Upper Sydney deserve. These women, Mrs Bloxom at their vanguard, who are obsequious sycophants one moment and snubbing Lady Game en masse the next. Lady Game almost let a tear fall telling me what happened at the art gallery function in June: every woman turned her back when she entered the room, and when she got home she'd found she'd been uninvited to some event or other with the Country Women's Band of Bigots. I say exactly what Lady Game told me that day: 'It's not the Governor's business to dismiss an elected premier, Mrs Bloxom. We live in a democracy – one that even the King cares to uphold.'

'Here we are.' Coralie emerges from the stockroom now, beribboned parcel in hand: the bottle of Lelong's N which Mrs Bloxom has come in for.

Not here for any of that now. Mrs Bloxom narrows her already narrow eyes at me. Her top lip quivers with her bile: 'You little upstart.'

'No.' I stand straighter than I ever have, and decency stands beside me as I let go of decorum, let go entirely at this nasty, grasping dowager of moral decay: 'You are the upstart, Mrs Bloxom. You criticise Lady Game? When was the last time *you* had the homeless of the Domain line up for leftovers at your back door? When was the last time *you* went down to the Happy Valley shanties to have tea and cake with barefoot children at La Perouse? Hm? When did *you* last visit a women's prison to see what might be done to help and heal? For this is what Lady Game does for this city as a matter of course – these are the entries in her diary. If the likes of you shun her back to London, I shall go with her.'

That last was perhaps a bridge too far, but the rest of it I heartily mean. Mrs Bloxom is lost to her outrage and I will not step away

The Blue Mile

from this. Gwendolen Game is the closest thing we have to a saint in this city. An exemplary Lady, ceaselessly at work and concerned for others. Ceaselessly damn well impressive. While it's her husband's job merely to put on his feathered hat and ceremonial sword and appear at official openings, be the subject of hooray bunting and otherwise stroll the Domain with his dog saying good afternoon to the hoboes his wife fed earlier in the day. What must Lady Game think of our egalitarianism now? That we are all equally cruel and stupid and mean? She is too polite to say. I shall say it for her. 'Alternatively, Mrs Bloxom, if you don't like the way this nation is run, then you could always go Home yourself, couldn't you?'

That's a skewering right to the bone for Mrs Bloxom: she doesn't have any such thing as a home in London, and she well knows it. That's the only reason she's ever been after me for Warwick, so that she can pretend she's connected. To Mother England. To a viscount. Any damn scrap of aristocratic flotsam will do. She has the senator husband with the knighthood, the son who will be PM, and she wants the Honourable daughter-in-law to make up the trifecta of confected self-importance. I seethe, most honourably: I hear the air suck in through my teeth and I am a breath away from demanding she leave my salon before I throw her out, and I don't care if she takes every fat overpowdered witch in this city with her. Oh, but if I were a different girl I'd tell her the Hardys and all of Mosman think her Warwick is a confirmed bachelor, because rumour has it on good authority he's a little more theatrical than a barrister ought to be, behind closed chambers doors – nudgy nudge, wink wink, have a banana.

Mrs Bloxom points her finger at me, head witch that she is, and she warns: 'The Premier will be dismissed. You mark my words, he will be dismissed.'

I snort as she turns: as if Mrs Bloxom has any power to do any such thing. Parliament isn't the Merrick Jazz Room: you can't squeeze it out of business because it's not to your taste. But my righteousness is already fading into fear. Damn. There goes Olivia

Couture. I want to say: You'll be sorry. Dowdy lump you were before I came along. I gave you your calf-length hem, those fox trims and sling-backs. If it weren't for me you'd still be wearing Bourjois' Ashes of Roses and a crepe chaff bag, like the common pile of phlergh you truly are.

And she will never appreciate it, chérie. Let her go back to Bourjois.

'Oh, Ollie,' Coralie touches my hand, consoling, and I turn to her. She's sixteen now, plumpness giving way to some gorgeous angles at her cheeks and jaw but the child remaining says we're just two little girls here, playing dress-ups. Rolling Arabian eyes: 'Who needs her?'

'We do.' I take the parcel of perfume from her and unwrap it. But I don't put the bottle of N back in the cabinet. I unplink the stopper and dab a spot on my wrist, and inhale, to force the calm back into myself. It's a crisp, dry scent, Lelong's N: jasmine, magnolia and a hint of freshly chopped firewood. Forthright. I should grow up and grow out of Coty's lolly-water Lily and start wearing N myself. Indeed from this moment I think I shall. So long as I can afford it.

Stop that thought: Mrs Bloxom has no more say over what goes in my business than the Nationalists do in the business of the King. I say what goes.

I say to Coralie: 'Let's start on the pattern for Liz Hardy's engagement, hm?'

'Yes, let's.' Coralie is all for that – it's mostly her design, a little fishtail kick, a little Hollywood diamante sprinkle, and Liz will adore it. The Mosman set will adore it: must.

'Clear the decks then and I'll go down and get that Fuji for it now.' Lush bolt of champagne that came in yesterday; we'll need at least ten yards.

Down to the Emporium I scoot against fears, and my footsteps clatter round the stairwell, echoing through the empty arcade. It's three o'clock on a Thursday afternoon, and although it's October and this month is always a little bit quiet, it's too quiet. Even the grocery shop that's taken over where Duke's Men & Boys used to be looks empty. Even Mr Jabour is down on ordering and he's sticking more with plains and standards. Something must be done to put money in the till, and urgently. Belt-tightening is not working; everything is only getting skinnier, except for the department stores, as Mr Jabour predicted. The state is broke; public servants unpaid. Are they meant to work for free? How can spending less on government solve that? Sack Mr Lang, and sack all the public servants, and then what? Have them work for the dole? Take the Child Endowment away and let babies starve? How will that generate money? How will that keep Eoghan in a job?

How can the Fickle Witches of this world not see all this happening? Too busy closing their eyes on the lift down, counting their savings on the ever-diminishing cost of hired help. *Never had so many servants, Deirdre, half a pound of peanuts each*. And they call Premier Lang evil. He's only asking for a reduction in the interest rate of some fraction of a percent, isn't he? Peanuts. America has asked Britain for the same sort of consideration, and got it. Because it's merely simple business sense, isn't it? How is that wrong? Questions jumbling over questions. Why can't the British bondholders damn well wait for their money? They can *afford* to. Why do so many in our government think paying this debt is more important than feeding a child? Don't they care that people are suffering? Where is the compassion? Gone up in a puff of Commonwealth Bank cigar smoke, or rather trapped in the ruins of the Bank of New South Wales: *Terribly sorry, Madam, your life savings appear to have been permanently misplaced*. But what would I know about any of this myself? What's the difference between the Gold Standard and the Goods Standard to me? Ten yards of your finest lamé. What is money anyway but an utterly fabricated squiggly wisp of magic-carpet fluff?

Of which I know the basic principles well enough. No money in the till: no business. No nerve to stick to your guns: no business. Too much nerve: no business as you've just shot yourself in the head. Oh dear God. What have I done letting fly at Mrs Bloxom? Mother will be so pleased to hear of the salon's demise: she might well exert parental rights and put me on a ship. I haven't even told her about the grocery shop moving in here: she'd be appalled. Raise wrist to schnonk: smell the N, Olivia: be calm. After this coming April, Mother can't do anything at all. I'll be twenty-one and free. Utterly. To fall on my face as I see fit.

I'm going to ask Mr Jabour what he thinks of all this mess, get myself a good dose of Levantine business wisdom. It's time I asked him about work for Eoghan, too. Beyond time. The road through the arch is all but complete, and Eoghan's been looking for a place, to no avail. Everyone he knows, at the workshops, and at the technical college, is keeping an eye out for him, and there's just nothing out there. The unemployment figure is creeping ever further up to thirty percent, for God's sake. But there *must* be something for Eoghan. If he can't find something suitable in the metal trades, he can't keep on with his apprenticeship, and if he can't finish that, I can't have him. There's a basic principle. And another: he won't work for me; that's just a silly stitching dream in denial of masculine pride. He won't even let me measure him for a new coat. But Mr Jabour, on the other hand – he has his genie fingers in all sorts of pies. Mr Jabour is going to be terribly shocked when I unplink this news of boy. Barrister or boilermaker. Hm . . . I don't know what it's like to have a father that cares about such things. I think I'm about to find out. And I shall: stand beside my man, whatever the future brings, beginning now. This minute.

But Mr Jabour isn't here.

'Hidee, Ol.' Velma smiles and turns when she sees me in the sideboard mirror. So quiet in here she's taken to spring-cleaning. She waves, dust cloth in one hand, stopper of the brass bottle in the other. The glass rubies and sapphires twinkle under the overhead chandelier but there's no genie laughter. Only silence today.

Yo

'You go to Mrs Adams if I'm not back by six – right,' I remind Ag this morning as I'm leaving. She gives me a look as if I'm babying her. She knows to go straight to Mrs Adams if ever I'm not home when I should be, but I remind her because something in me knows. I won't be back by six today.

'I'm sorry, lad, but we've taken it as far as we can go.' It's Mr Harrison that tells me when I get across to the shops at the end of the shift.

Mr Adams stares into the heavy planer behind me: it's out of a job too.

I knew this was coming, but it doesn't make the fact of it any easier to take. It's a hammer blow to my guts. I tried to plan for this, I tried to think ahead. There's just nothing I can do. There's nowhere for me to go. Nothing. They're only wanting qualified journeymen if they're wanting anyone at all, and returned servicemen and married men first. It's not a good time to be apprenticed to anything, not when you're my age. I've said I'll take kids' wages. Everyone's said no: the union won't have it. Fuck the union. Fuck this.

'Something will come up, Eoghan,' Mr Adams says. Hold on, he's saying. Don't let them get to you. Well enough for him to say. He's got work at Colgate, the soap factory; they're expanding their operations and I can't get in there even to sweep the floor. Tarz and Dolly are going to Glebe Island and Clarkie's going back to the slip shops at Mort Bay, working on the steamers. How am I going to pay the rent next week? I'm already a week behind from the ten shilling pay cut last month. Sturgess will have it pounded out of me with a two by four and we'll be on the street. I've already had to let the Gaslight account go, they cut it off yesterday, and coal's that dear . . . Fuck that: how am I going to get Ag's summer uniform – she's still wearing winter's and it's getting too small for her. Fuck that: how am I going to feed us? The only dole I can get is for a single man and it's not enough. The only work I can get for the dole is on a road gang, in camps that far west they might as well be in another country, one I can't take a child to. What do I do? Cadge off Olivia – for the *rent*? Take another don't-mention-it pound from Mr Adams? 'Keep your head on,' he tells me.

But my head is already gone.

What did I do wrong, Lord? What did I do? I just wanted to keep in work, keep a good home for me and my sister, give her a family. A life. Is it Olivia? Is that why I'm to be punished? It's you who kept sending her to me. Testing me? Haven't I passed that test? I haven't touched her but to hold her hand for more than a year.

Or is it just me? Useless, filthy O'Paddy. Should not have left Satan's arsehole. Where I belong.

'Eoghan, where are you going?' Mr Adams yells after me.

But I'm already gone.

I go to the Rag and Famish, with every intention of getting more fucked up than I have ever been. Probably won't take much, I don't reckon, haven't had a drink for almost two years. But I am going to have several now: see you in the morning. It's half-past five in the afternoon at present, though, and I can't get near the bar. I can't see anyone in here I know, either. A fella near the door looks sideways at me, and I recognise him. I don't know his name, but I know what he is: one of them New Guard standovers, this army of broke grocers and unemployed bank clerks that have set themselves up to pick fights with unionists in the name of the King – like those fellas that stopped us in the Domain that day, only now they're getting organised: making a show of themselves in public parks, parading around with their straight-arm salutes and clicking their heels like the Girl Guides brigade they are. I see this establishment is packed with them, and there's a celebration of some kind going on.

Cheering.

I want to kill someone.

The celebrating is something to do with the elections that have gone on in Britain. The Labour Party there has gone down, in flames.

'Lang will be next!' they're cheering.

Why? I could laugh. The Langites have just crossed the floor of the Federal Parliament to vote with the Nationalists, to bring down Labor here next. Hang your hat on that for horseshit. One fascist is as good as another to a blind man, isn't he?

'God save the King!'

'God smash Communism!'

'God smash democracy!'

These ones are lunatics. Olivia reckons that the Governor is more scared of this New Guard than he is of the Bank Robber. First rule of self-preservation: you should never pick a fight with a lunatic. But there doesn't seem much left of me worth preserving right at this minute and the fella by the door is still looking at me.

I say: 'What are you looking at, Pommy faggot?'

And then I run.

Olivia

'It all happened too quick for us,' Mrs Adams is explaining to me in the courtyard of St Augustine's. She is as daintily pretty as her husband is rough-hewn, but her face is scrunched hard now in anguish. 'That Welfare woman came round on the Friday morning, to the school, and only because the teacher had had a bit of a worry for the child, that money might be scarce for them. She was only going to see what could be done to help, but then, by the evening, when Eoghan couldn't be found, well, there was no choice for her but to take Agnes with her.'

'Where?' I whisper. I want to wail: *But I found you a job!* Or Velma did. The people who do something or other with the machine parts at her Eddie's shirt factory will take him on, and if that doesn't work out long-term, they've got connections at the woollen mills at Marrickville. I'm supposed to be surprising him with the news right here, right now, this Sunday. *Bring him over for coffee in the afternoon,* Velma conspired. *Mum and Aunty Karm will go crazy.*

'That will be for the court to decide,' Mr Adams says, for Mrs Adams has had to look away to dab at her tears. Over his shoulder

I can see Mrs Buddle's lace headscarf bowed, just in the church doors at the end of a row of nuns, all furiously praying. Too late. 'The hearing will be Monday morning – tomorrow.'

The hearing. As if Agnes were a criminal. She must be petrified. 'Where is she?'

'They wouldn't even let me see her,' Mrs Adams is openly weeping now.

'See her where?'

Mr Adams's growl is forbidding and defeated at once: 'In the shelter, at the court.'

In children's prison? Since Friday evening? I could cry too. But I am too shocked, and too angry – with myself. I was almost going to surprise him Thursday night with the news of the job, or the hope of it. Why didn't I? Why didn't I take the ferry over? I was trimming a raffia mid-brim with cellophane salad. What on earth for?

'Hello, Miss Olivia,' Kenny Adams chimes in brightly, shaking my hand. 'How do you do?'

'Hello, Kenny,' I whisper my rage for every unjust thing.

'It's not likely they'll let us have the child stay with us, we've already been told,' Mr Adams says, his sadness as solid as the stone beneath our feet. 'Welfare know . . . about . . .' Kenny. Of course. Mr Adams is telling me it's not likely the court would let Agnes stay in a home that has a Kenny, with his outbursts, which, although I've never witnessed one, are apparently quite frightening, shouting and banging that can be heard up the length of their street, Eoghan has said.

Oh Eoghan. Where are you? What's happened to you?

*

Mr Jabour accompanies me, or rather I him, and we go in his brother George's sparkling new Plymouth for extra gravitas, to the Children's Court, in Albion Street, Surry Hills, a location most convenient to its purpose as it is the city's pre-eminent centre of poverty and degradation. Mr Jabour sighs heavily as he stops the motor at the kerbside, before saying, as he and Mrs Jabour, and Glor, and Aunty Karma have all said to me a hundred times since midday yesterday: 'You should have said something before this.'

Yes. And so should Eoghan. How could he not have told me he'd got behind with the rent? The whole of Balmain knew, behind his back at least. Agnes's lunch tin packed with only bread and dripping these past few months, since the last cut in his hours, which I also had no idea about. No idea things had got so desperate for him. I love a bit of bread and dripping but not every day. Mrs Hanrahan sneaking an extra apple for Agnes into Gladdy's tin, not wanting to hurt his pride. What good is pride to us now? There should be a law against people concealing difficulties. Gloria almost had a heart attack and her baby at once: *That little girl? That little girl is WHERE? She's WHAT?*

Beyond the liver-brick edifice, the interior is dank and dark as a crypt, sending shiver after shiver through me. Poor Agnes, being hauled in here alone, to this place haunted by the worst of our inhumanity: that which we inflict upon the helpless.

Mr Jabour is not so affected. He bowls directly up to the desk in the foyer: 'Good morning, I am here for Agnes O'Keenan.'

'Sir?' the man at the desk looks up from some paperwork. 'The court proceedings begin at ten o'clock.' He glances over his shoulder at the wall clock: it's a quarter to nine.

Mr Jabour waves his genie hand as if this were all a nuisance: 'The girl, Agnes O'Keenan, I am here to adopt her.'

Because that's how seriously Mr Jabour takes his fatherly responsibilities.

The man at the desk is naturally a little startled. He says: 'Er . . .'

Mr Jabour is a busy man: 'Where is the child?'

'Ahhh . . .' the man shuffles the papers until he finds the answer. 'Yes, here she is. O'Keenan. In the shelter – she'll be brought up any minute now.'

The Blue Mile

Brought up? I imagine from some mouldy rat-infested cell.

My heart thuds in time with the ticking of the wall clock. These are the most interminable minutes of my life. The man has gone back to his paper-shuffling. How can he do that when Agnes is – Please God, if she's been beaten, I shall sue for cruelty. I shall cable Bart and have the best barrister in this city send the whole of the Welfare Department to prison.

There's a shuffle of footsteps up a side hall and as I turn a small voice calls out: 'Miss Olivia?'

My little curly-topped dear. Oh! In the midst of half-a-dozen others, poor urchins, being filed in through another set of doors.

She breaks from the line and runs to me, too quick for the matron with them, and she dives into my arms. She's still in her school uniform; plaits askew but ribbons perfectly tied. She doesn't say another word; she only sobs, almost noiselessly, trembling, right into my heart.

I hold her dear little head to my heart and I tell her, as if I could tell them all: 'I'm so sorry, poppet. I'm so sorry. I'll never let you go again.'

*

I have to let her go, though, while the Welfare officer, a Mrs Merridale, takes her back to the shelter to retrieve her bag and coat, and to wait there while the paperwork is sorted out. Mrs Merridale is so helpful and almost as relieved as I am; she says: 'I'm so very glad it was me who went to the school on Friday.' Suggesting things might have worked out very differently otherwise. 'Agnes and I are old friends, aren't we?' She smiles, a gentle smile under a stern grey fringe; and I return the smile that Agnes can't. 'Come along,' the Welfare lady says, and Agnes looks so fearful at the idea it's a crime in itself.

'It's all right,' I promise her. 'I'll be here when you return. Right here, in this foyer.'

'Shall we say twelve o'clock on the dot?' Mrs Merridale promises too, and then she assures me: 'We should have sorted out all our particulars by then.'

I suspect she wants a few hours to satisfy herself that Mr Jabour is indeed the fabulous agent of rescue he appears to be before informing the magistrate, and I'm glad about that. That she cares.

Meanwhile, the legal particulars on our side are sorted out in about two minutes. The clerk shuffles some more papers, stamps one and scribbles on another, before explaining that while Agnes can't be adopted straightaway by the Jabours, they can foster her through the Children's Relief Department, a process which appears to me to be so easy anyone in want of children could walk in and pick up half-a-dozen. Obviously not too many are. Every children's home in the state is full to overflowing. And while it appears that the state cannot risk Agnes going into a home with a mentally handicapped child in it, it is perfectly acceptable that she be whisked away by a complete but obviously wealthy stranger just now charged in off the street. The only question is:

'The current status of the child – it must be officially recorded,' the clerk says, his nib hovering over the form. 'If the child is orphaned or abandoned, then it will be a simple matter for you as legal guardian to adopt it later. If it's in need of temporary custody only, then that's another matter altogether. It'll have to be investigated in due course for verification, but you'd be better off saying abandoned, so that the past family can then have no claim on it.'

No claim on *it*? What is a child? Not a person. A piece of property. No, less than that – there's not even a solicitor here to witness the transaction. Mr Jabour looks at me with the only relevant question, and I pray as I never have: 'Temporary. Of course it's only temporary.'

'Temporary,' Mr Jabour confirms and then signs the bottom of the form. Agnes is safely in our protection, or will be at midday, with magisterial approval, please Mrs Merridale. Then he looks at his pocket watch – ten past ten – and he looks to me: 'Chippendale. You said this boy of yours grew up in Chippendale?'

The Blue Mile

'Yes.' I said that on the way here, glancing down a side street and not wanting to see what was down there at all. Not wanting to see these slum lands.

'Do you know what street?' Mr Jabour asks me now.

And I do know. 'Myrtle Street.' I remember it immediately because he made a joke of it one afternoon, the streets and the pubs around where he lived being named after trees – Pine, Oak, Rose, Myrtle – and not a single tree alive in any of them. But it can only be by some other power that I remember the number of the house: 'One hundred and twenty-two.' The dance in the number; the way he says hundred: *hondred*.

'Stay here, Olivia, I shall make some enquiries there.'

'Not without me,' I tell him. I have to look now. I have to see where this mess began.

*

One hundred and twenty-two Myrtle Street is not a place fit for human habitation. The worst house there, was all that Eoghan said, and it's no exaggeration, not now I'm looking at it. It's the only weatherboard in this part of the street, wedged between two rows of blank-faced terraces, and there appear to be more and straighter boards across the front window than there are on the house itself. The transom above the door is smashed, but unboarded, and the right-hand edge of the awning, minus its verandah post, is on the verge of collapsing onto what remains of the fence. The idea that someone claims rent on this property is about as close to evil as I want to get. It smells of something evil here too: a broken sewage pipe?

The street is empty – soulless – but I prickle all over as if a hundred eyes watched the motorcar crawl past. Watching us now. I don't need to be told to stay in the motorcar while Mr Jabour knocks at the door. While I pray that Eoghan is here, and pray that he's not.

The door opens. It's a woman. Pinch-faced, lines down her cheeks, but she's not an old woman; a baby on her hip, another at her skirt. She looks so tired and careworn she might give one of them to Mr Jabour if he stands on the doorstep for long enough. She's shaking her head: Eoghan's not there. Thank God. I hear her say: 'Nah. O'Keenans was here. The old woman, Kath, she's gone but. She died. Grog got her. She come out of prison back in, orrr, middle of winter it was, and it got her real quick. The old man – dunno where he went. Be round somewhere.'

Round somewhere. Rage rushes through me at that. These men, who just walk off, leaving trails of destruction behind them. One difference between Eoghan's father and mine, and one difference alone: real estate. This is a medusa rage: I would turn them to stone and smash them.

If it weren't for the wave of pity now smashing over me. Into me. For Eoghan.

Oh, Eoghan. Where are you?

'We will find him,' Mr Jabour promises. 'It is good that he is not here at least.'

I nod. And cover my mouth as I begin to gag: 'That smell – Oh God, it's putrid.'

'It's the brewery,' Mr Jabour sighs, as if that might account for everything. Perhaps it does.

*

I take Agnes back to Lavender Bay, just the two of us, as it's quiet here and she knows my house as well as her own. It would be too much for her to meet Mrs Jabour and Aunty Karma today; save that great wave of nourishment for another day. She still hasn't spoken a word, and I won't try to push her to. We cuddle on the sofa. She stares into a magazine, into a drawing of Jean Patou's latest evening whimsy, of bias-cut satin flutes and angel wings.

I promise her: 'We'll find him. We'll find Yoey.'

She stares and I make her bacon rissoles. She has half a mouthful before falling asleep with her head on my lap and then I tuck her into my bed and I write to Mother, not of any of this. I tell her simply that I love her, for all that she has done for me. Her faults disappear inside this night, inside this sadness for all those less fortunate, as I tell my mother how much I appreciate her fortitude and all her care in raising me: all alone. Her selfishness was never without some purpose, some thought for me – for some future for me. As Agnes sleeps on, I make my sister a funny little doll from scraps, a mop of turquoise boucle for hair. I have a baby sister. Her name is Sophia. For the first time I dream of meeting her. I shall, one day.

I shall see Eoghan again sooner.

Please.

Be found. Be safe.

Come home.

Be alive, be around somewhere, so I might hate you for being a horrible fool.

Please.

It's so quiet I can hear the ferry bell dingling at the wharf. So quiet I can hear the harbour sigh.

Yo

I've never been much of a gambler, despite being raised with the form guide always pinned to the noticeboard at St Ben's – first thing you see before genuflecting. Never had the right amount of spare change or delusion for punting, but I have just enough of both today. It's Melbourne Cup Day. There's not a lot left for me to do, apart from put a bet on. Apart from go back to Balmain and get my dole forms in, sign on at the Labour Exchange for relief, but I can't do either of those things, not yet. I have to be sober to do those things. Ag, forgive me.

'What'll it be then, mate?' the bookie is waiting for my bet, hurrying me up in this back lane in Botany. I look behind me at the line of other fellas come round here, line of no-hopers going from pub to sly tote, like ants we are, going for a worm that's got fried on the hot sandy path, and I wonder where the cops are with this. It's only Paddy robbing Paddy, who gives a – 'Come on, I haven't got all day.'

I tell him: 'Phar Lap.' Give him the three bob in my pocket. That's all I've got in shillings, and after this I have enough for one more beer and a tin of Champion. Probably not a lot more when

Phar Lap comes in. I'm too fucked up to work out the figures, but it won't be a fortune I'll win. That's not the point of this bet. Phar Lap – he's the Big Red Wonder Horse, he's the favourite by far. I can't afford to lose, but the cash is less important than the winning. I need a win, to turn my guts around. When the horse comes in, I will think that's good. I will think that something is on my side. Some luck? You, Lord? Get yourself home now, you spoon-headed bag of bollocks, you say, Lord? You can get fucked. Go and get a job yourself, Lord, go and make a commandment called Thou Shalt Not Drink, and then get fucked. Show me I'm worth something now, ay? When Phar Lap come in, I will go home. Aggie, I will be home this afternoon.

I start walking back to the pub, somewhere in Botany, to listen to the race. I don't know Botany. Three mile from Satan's arsehole and I don't know where I am, do I. But I might have work at the new port here. 'Come back tomorrow,' the fella on the dock said, taking pity. The first one to since Saturday morning, since I started following the line of no-hopers south, along the docks of the Hungry Mile from Dawes Point to Pyrmont, looking in every door for work, all through the warehouses round the Haymarket and then down through the Lebbo factories at Redfern and Waterloo, to the meat and veg railhead at Alexandria and then down here. It's only labouring, on the Mexican oil tankers, it won't pay the rent, it won't be enough for me to have Ag with me, but it's a job and it might lead somewhere. Maybe Mexico. If it will pay Ag's way, I will go to Mexico. I will send the Adamses all my pay to keep Ag for me while I'm in Mexico. Or Manchuria. The moon. I will go anywhere for a job.

Anywhere except the Neighbourhood. I went back there for a look the other night. I went looking for Jack, Jack Callaghan; thought I'd call in to the knocker at Strawberry Hills to ask for him through Hammo, maybe get a loan off him or something for the rent, I was that pissed by the time I got there. But I didn't find him. Only found Luke Finnerty at the bar of the pub next door telling me: *Your poor mum – yeah, Mrs Nash went in and found her. She wasn't there that long.* Fuck me rotten, but I started running again then. I was mad with running that night. I went round to Ryan's then, looking for Satan. Looking for Patrick O'Keenan. To kill him with a blunt axe, but he wasn't there and I got told to clear off by McKinley. Sergeant McKinley, who knows exactly what my father is. So I told McKinley to suck his own cock through a flyscreen, and had to get running again. What a night. Can't believe I didn't get my head kicked in after the Rag and Famish as it was. Six of them National Girl Guides chased me – right the way down to the High Street wharf, where I jumped the rail of the Neutral Bay ferry there and then ended up in the Loo, and that's where I started drinking.

I'm bound for Botany Bay. Pissed with the hot sandy sun on my head. Singing toora-li li-oorali li-aditty. Waiting for Phar Lap to come in.

Phar Lap comes in eighth.

Can't believe it. I look at my ticket ten times as if it will stop swimming long enough to say something different from the wireless. Phar Lap has won every race for the last hundred years. But a horse called White Nose has won the Cup. Who the fuck is White Nose? No one knows. Wasn't even mentioned in the form guide.

'You have got to be fucking kidding.'

No. It's not a joke. I check my ticket again.

Get fucked.

'Let me buy you a drink, mate,' some fella says beside me. Hand on my shoulder. A new chum, this is. I sway a bit under his hand, from the solid diet of vitamin beer I've been on. I recognise him now, though. His name is Ced. Red Ced: he's a Communist. Opening bowler for the Unemployed Workers Union, he only got out of Long Bay last Tuesday – chucking rocks at the cops in Newtown, he told me, at the eviction riots. I met him yesterday morning, at that pub near Rosebery racecourse. We slept in the scrub by the Chinese market gardens last night, somewhere round

The Blue Mile

here, and he congratulated me at having pissed almost the whole of my last pay away. I said: *It's only taken me three days, too.* He fell over laughing then. He said: *You are out of condition then, aren't you, mate?* He had half a bottle of Royal Reserve claret, his nightcap, he called it. But I don't drink that fucked-up poison, do I. It'll kill you, won't it, Kathleen. Hydrochloric acid, burning a hole in your guts. I'm not an alco. I only drink beer. 'Yeah, make it a Star, thanks.'

I only drink Toohey's Star. None of that Tooths shit, either. And I've had too much of it. I have to stop now. I have to get home for Ag.

I have to get where? The tiles are spinning. Spinning me round with my own stink. Sack of shit. She's better off without me, Ag. She'll be coming home to Mrs Adams right about now. Coming home to a family. They'll love having her stop with them; she's old enough that she can help with more than entertaining Kenny, too. She can get the tea on. She can make biscuits with Mrs Buddle. She's playing tip with Gladdy on the way home. Reading her stack of library books by the fire. Without me. Yeah, that's what my sister is doing right now, while my sack of shit runneth over. I am fucking up a storm, I know I am. But what else am I supposed to do, Ag? Just stand there and have Welfare take you from me in the street? Farm you out to some stranger? How many ways do you want me shattered, Lord? No: you're better staying where you are, Ag. The Adamses are good people: the best there are. Everyone in Balmain will tell Welfare that if they've even got up to asking yet: my sister is safe with the Adamses. There's no chance Welfare wouldn't let Ag stop with them. And it's only while I'm working out where . . .

Where am I going, Aggie, my beautiful girl? I'm so sorry, I can't even see straight. But I'll come home. I will. I will get back to you when I've got . . . something. What?

There's a glass in my hand again and I can't keep hold of anything.

Ag, I'm so sorry. I've got nothing but shame to give you. Thought I was something special once, didn't you, Miss Greene? So did I, my beautiful Olivia, so did I.

Now I'm going down to Botany Bay in the morning, down to the tanker docks. Going to Mexico, rolling out barrels of Texaco Oil.

After I've had this beer, with Ced. Big Red Ced. I raise my glass to him. Ced is only a little fella, flyweight, jockey-sized.

The bar stops sliding around for a second as I look at him: 'Opening bowler of the Unemployed Workers.'

He raises his glass back at me but he's not laughing. 'Oath I am, mate,' he's saying. 'Oath I am. Stick with me and I'll show you how it's done.'

Six

Olivia

'I don't want to go to Mass,' Agnes says, her first complete sentence, not forgetting her manners: 'Thank you.'

I understand her silent protest: the tight little fists balled in her lap. It's been a week now. Mr Jabour has sent the word out to everyone he knows in every trade, to look out for a lad called O'Keenan, and he even sent Glor's Paul off to the police to press them to search for him. They said no – you need to get yourself an actual genie for that. If the police took to searching for every man who walked off from his responsibilities, that's all they'd ever have time for.

I also understand, too well, that there is nothing I might say to soothe Agnes's abandonment. Anger and fear must be in constant quarrel inside her, as they are in me, an argument that never settles but can only be packed away, so I can only tell her: 'I don't want to go to Mass, either. Let's make new bathers instead.'

She doesn't smile, but when I give her a pencil to sketch us up a design she bends to it diligently. She draws us into purple halterneck costumes, with orange belts and matching bathing caps, flowers all about our feet and the rays of the sun spreading down to the ground, all around us. It is a desperate need for beauty, for happiness, for losing sadness to a task, a need I recognise, and I shall indulge her however I can – forever if our kismet allows.

We can't stay malingering here forever, though. I've got to get back to the salon, assess what's left of my clientele – Coralie's taken three cancellations already, one of them from the Mosman set too, one of the Shadfords. Damn them all. And just as urgently I must sort out school for Agnes. It's about halfway through the final term and she's too clever at her books to miss out on any of it. She can't go back to Balmain, though: it's too out of the way, for me, and I truly don't want her wandering around the city on her own. It's too dangerous around the Quay, equidistant as it is between the Labour Exchange and Parliament House. There aren't enough policemen to keep the streets safe. Just this Friday afternoon past I listened to a whole conversation outside the wardrobe window between a group of those New Guardsmen on their way to the ferry, deciding on which workingmen's hotels they were going to 'raid', from the Rocks to Woolloomooloo, to stir up trouble and then blame the pursuant punch-ups on the trade unionists. 'God save the King,' they all shouted down the steps. Good God, what are we coming to?

Agnes looks up from her drawing, her blue eyes huge with searching. Lost in somewhere else. Wondering where he is, and if he's gone for good, if he might be dead, fallen down a ditch, hit his head, or if he's just somewhere round and being despicable. And as I wander those same threads myself, I wonder if we should both go to London, Agnes and I, so that we're not here waiting for him if or when he bothers to come back. But then my heart squeezes tight around some deeper knowledge: if he is alive, whatever has driven him to reject us, to reject his adored sister, it must be unbearable. What could it be? Shame at not paying the rent on time? Really?

Oh, but I want him here, I do. So that I might slap him – quite hard – for this pain he is driving into me. How dare he. How *dare* he do this, dead or alive. I want to scream it out into the wind.

*

The Blue Mile

It's odd how nature can occasionally throw up a perfect substitute object for one's anger and frustration precisely when one is in need of it. The shop bell dings and in walks Cassie Fortescue, this very Monday morning, and after all this time. I haven't seen her since that night at the Merrick, and this is the very first time she has ever set a white patent pump in the salon. Curious, most curious, and those shoes are an abomination – with those fawn stockings, *really*?

I wave, above the telephone. I'll finish my conversation first, with Gloria.

I say: 'I'm thinking of North Sydney Girls Grammar.' For Agnes's schooling. It's not ideal: a little too Pymble Ladies, a little too one hundred percent Church of England, but convenience might have to win, only four stops on the Cremorne tram, if I can afford it. Agnes is in the stockroom with Coralie right now, setting up a nook for her in there so that she might keep ahead with her school texts and her increasingly voracious reading in the meantime.

Glor says, entirely impractically: 'No, Ollie. Put her in at Sacred Heart. Then I can have her with me in the afternoons.'

'Dover Heights is not exactly easy to get t–'

'I'm only going to be bored with the baby.'

I hear her mother in the background yelling: 'You won't be bored, Gloria, I can promise you that.'

'Mum, shush, I'm on the phone,' I can hear Glor roll her eyes. 'I've got to go, Ol. She's giving me a hard time about everything at the moment. You do what you think is best; Dad will agree. You're such a good soul, Ol, you always do the right thing.'

Perhaps not always. 'Thanks, Glor. See you soon.'

I place the phone back on the cradle and wait another moment before looking up again to say: 'Hello there, Cassie.' I remain seated at the table. I'm not getting to my feet for whatever has finally brought her here. There can really only be one reason she is here, and it's certainly not for style. She's come to crow. The tide of Sydney Witches is turning, she wants to tell me, even the Hardys are going to abandon me now, or perhaps she's going to announce that the King has just recalled the Games. Whatever it is, she looks dreadful and I'm not being entirely unkind with this observation: she is greyish and gaunt and cigarette-scented. Losing all of her snub-nosed sweets. The ravages of cocaine and hobo-murdering, I suppose.

'Hello, Olivia.' Her smile is drawn on with a blunt pencil. She runs a finger along the top of my jewellery cabinet, as if she pops in here regularly for a browse. 'Amazing what they can do with fakes these days.'

'Isn't it?' I say, as if any costumière would carry real gems. Get to the point and get out.

She says, peering into the lower shelf of bangles and brooches: 'It can be so hard to tell what's what and who's who. So confusing . . .' Scrutinising the earrings now. I see what she's doing. The inspection: that was always one of her tactics of intimidation, particularly on house parade, looking for signs of mended stockings and homemade bloomers.

She turns to me: 'But you've never been confused, have you, Olivia?' There is a look in her eyes that can only be described as diabolical, and I am well and truly intimidated. She says: 'You've always been the real McCoy, haven't you? Always so far above the rest, haven't you?'

I'm not sure what she's referring to. Somehow I manage to raise my voice above the pounding of my heart to say: 'Not always above the rest, Cassie, no – certainly not when you had my head pressed into the lavatory bowl at school. What do you want?'

She doesn't reply. She just stares at me. She's mad. Quite mad, I'm sure of it. And she always has been. I want to ask her, scream at her: Why do you hate me? Why are you such a horrible bully? You have everything and you always have had: you're the daughter of a banker. Go away and enjoy your life. Lady Game's a banker's daughter too – go away and be impressive like her.

But she can't and pity swooshes through me, through that place where revenge used to be. Who would ever be Cassie's friend? Truly.

Cousin Min's finally ditched her for a public servant, for purgatory in Canberra. Even Denis has ditched her: five minutes after his father paid the fifty pounds worth of good behaviour bond to the Crown.

I say: 'Cassie, can I help you with something?'

She shrugs, but awkwardly: 'Help me? No. I want to ask you something, though. Is it true, what I've heard along the grape, that you've got a certain boyfriend? A labourer? Irishman. He has a child, hasn't he?'

My heart is pounding faster. How could she know? I might have been seen with him, yes, someone's seen us on the ferry with the picnic basket or whatever, but that detail? Wrong as it is. No one knows about us but the Jabours and the good people of St Gus's in Balmain. No one else would know he's Irish. My mind swoops around the Witches, to Mrs Bloxom, to Warwick at his Hunter Street chambers, and to the magistrate at the Children's Court: an old chum of Bart's. I can't at this present moment recall the man's name, nor the name of the clerk at the front desk, but they'd know mine from the vague exchange that day retrieving Agnes and this nasty snip has somehow swept from the court and along the grape like fire, growing horns and a tail as it goes. Who knows? Perhaps it's on its way to London now. And I won't deny it. I won't deny it ever.

I could not look more imperious as I tell Cassie Fortescue: 'That's right. His name is Eoghan O'Keenan. Go tell the grape he's Catholic and unemployed now too.' Wherever he damn well is.

Not the retort she was expecting, and it takes a moment for her to state the obvious: 'You're finished now, you know.'

'In your world, perhaps,' I scoff with disgust and I mean it sincerely. 'For whatever that might be worth.'

She snorts in return: 'That's right – you don't need us.' The blunt pencil line of her mouth twists downwards. 'I'd always wondered why you were so stuck-up. You're a viscount's bastard, aren't you? And your mother was always a slut. Never wondered how she danced till two?'

I did, once. Bit of magic Merrick fairy dust to see the long show through, might I suppose? But I am no *bastard*, no suppose about that. I look down at my hands on the table, at the blades of my pattern cutters too easily in reach, and I tell Cassie Fortescue: 'Get out.'

*

'My dear, we have ourselves a boy!' Mr Jabour waltzes me across the tiles of the ground floor as only a father of daughters might and I hug his precious joy to me. Finally, a boy for Mr Jabour.

'What are they going to call him?'

'Robert,' his chest puffs out over his belly. 'Robert Nicholas Gallagher. A fine name, don't you think, dear?'

'Yes,' I whisper. 'It's a beautiful name.' Nicholas is Mr Jabour's name. 'Is Gloria terribly bored?' I ask him.

'Lost her mind to it – Robbie, Robbie, my little Robbie, that's all she can say now.'

'Good.'

He squeezes me tight for a moment, in wordless consolation, for all that is not good. It's mid-December, eight-thirty on a Wednesday morning, and you wouldn't know that Christmas is nine days away. The arcade is a crypt and will stay that way most of the day, doubtless. I listen to his steady genie heart telling me that this isn't the first or last time the till has been empty. Things will work out. Maintain consistent quality, be confident of your stock and your expertise, always keep an attractive window display, give the impression of opulence and ease, treat every customer as if they were special. Simple; but for the last: largely impossible. I'm reduced to relying mostly on passing trade now, and that's a little difficult up in the gods, on the very top floor. Mr Jabour sends what custom he can my way, but it's not going to be enough; his clientele all sew: they don't need me. I'm going to have to make a move. Sometime in the New Year. London. Paris. Chatswood. Homebush. I'm a little paralysed in the face of it. The decisions that will need to be made.

Numb with worry at what might have happened to Eoghan.

Has he disappeared, a swagman hobo trudging out into the countryside, hanging his head in shame on a road gang somewhere, or is he . . . ? Say it for real, not a wonder. He is dead. He must be. How else can he keep away from Agnes like this? Almost seven weeks now, seven long, slow weeks without a word. It's not like he's some poor illiterate, not like he can't put a sentence together. Why not send a note? He has to be dead. Or he should be bloody well dead. In the New Year, if we still haven't heard from him, the Jabours will apply to adopt Agnes. Did you hear that, Eoghan? They're going to adopt her. You won't *have* a sister anymore. And then . . . and then . . . we're all going to disappear. We're going to leave you. Should you ever come back, we won't be here. The Jabours will help us. You'll see. I should . . . I should –

'I should go up and put the shingle out, I suppose,' I say with my last cellophane shreds of defiance.

Mr Jabour gives me one last squeeze: 'Sometimes that's all you can do.'

Whatever it takes, to keep going.

I go up and stare at the telephone. Should I call Government House? Beg for custom. Should I dare? The Games were booed at the opera on Saturday evening, quite overshadowing *The Mikado* at the Conservatorium Hall. Some would say suffering an Australian performance of any opera is torture enough. But publicly booed? In front of the students at the Conservatorium? What sort of barbaric society is this? If the King wanted to sack the Premier, he'd have asked the Governor to do it by now, and being insufferably rude and obnoxious isn't going to achieve anything but insult to one least deserving of it: poor Lady Game. I doubt she's much interested in how she might be attired for being ignored and booed at wherever she goes. But . . . damn it, I will dare. I pick up the phone.

'Yes, good morning,' I say to the butler at the other end. 'Miss Olivia Greene, couturier, for Lady Game, please.'

'One moment, please, madam,' and I get Miss Crowdy's impatient: 'Who is it?'

'It's Olivia Greene, from – '

'Yes, what is it?'

'Ah. Um. I'm only enquiring as to whether Lady Game is in any need of ward– '

'Not at present, thank you, Miss Greene. Good day.'

Well. There the dare came and went. Perhaps the nasty snip has reached vice-regal ears, despite no one speaking to Lady Game. Would Lady Game really not want to be served by a labourer's girlfriend? Perhaps. But *really*? Not too saintly of her, but it would depend upon how great the horns and tail have become on the story, wouldn't it. How could she trust me with a confidence now? Perhaps she's decided she can trust no one at all in this big, fat small-minded city anyway, and who on earth could blame her?

What's left of options here for me? An advertisement in the papers? Pathetic little black and white box under DRESS, FASHION, ETC. I've never done anything like that; never had to. Mother would be more and more appalled, and I doubt it would do anything for me now anyway. *Exclusif* can't compete on the same track with ready-to-wear . . .

'Morning, Ollie,' Coralie's bright face comes in with the bell.

How am I going to tell her I'll have to let her go? She'll find a place somewhere else – if Mr Jabour doesn't whisk her off somewhere, one of the department stores will snap her up as soon as look at her. I've heard that Hordern's might be expanding their fabric department to include a sewing school – Coralie would be perfect for something like that. I don't want to let her go, though. I don't want to let any of this go. My life. My world.

Mais non, chérie. Hold on. It's not over yet. Hold on, until the last fingernail breaks.

Hold on? What to? It seems that someone's let the water out of the harbour and we're all whirling towards the plughole.

You'll find something. And you will hold on.

*

I find Agnes up the top of the ferry steps, making her way round from the tram. Lugging her satchel on her shoulder, it's almost as big as she is. I call out: 'Poppet!' And when she turns, for a moment, in her smile, in the bounce of her thick beribboned plaits, everything is beautiful. It's beautiful that business is so slow I can be here at the top of the ferry steps at four o'clock on a Wednesday afternoon two ticks away from Christmas, be here to see Agnes smile. There's my branch out of the whirlpool.

She waits for me to catch up and I ask her: 'How was school today?' looking for signs every day, as I do, that some B is getting into her.

But she smiles again: 'Miss Rosewood picked me out for reading.'

That is the world to Agnes, all that she is holding on to. I have to find a way to keep her at North Sydney Grammar. I'll beg for the money. My next letter to Mother might need to be a most interesting one, mightn't it? Whether we remain in Sydney or not. Small matter of a child I have acquired . . . if she hasn't already been informed. I'm expecting that telegram any day now: *OLIVIA JANE! WHAT HAVE YOU DONE?*

Not today, though. Only our McIlraith's box waiting for us at the door. Annoyingly dumped on the step. I expressly asked them, as Mother has always done, to deliver it in the evening, in person, so that it doesn't get pinched. The miracle that it hasn't been makes me clap my hands: 'Here's Christmas!'

'Oh!' Agnes's deep blue eyes grow wide as the sky as I heft it inside and unfold the cardboard flaps of our bounty on the kitchen table.

'Behold the infamous Mexican chocolate cake.' I lift it out first, and hold it aloft in its red and gold striped tin.

'Ooh,' she says with giggling reverence, 'it looks like a little circus tent,' and so it does, becoming something new and lovely through her eyes. And so we go through her discovery of the tins of almonds and walnuts, the cherry shortbread tarts, the fruit mince for our pies, for which she will make the pastry, while I eat all the Paradise pineapple creams and caramel fudge bonbons.

'What's this?' Agnes holds up the bottle of French cognac that by some inexplicable force of habit I keep ordering.

I laugh, at myself. 'It's a brandy, for sauce my mother used to make. But we have custard with our pudding, don't we? Silly.' I don't know how to make Mother's brandy sauce. I take the bottle from Agnes's half-quizzical, half-repulsed frown and shove it in the cupboard with its fellows: last year's full one and three opened others, languishing at the back of the top shelf with the soap flakes and turpentine. A short, sharp scald of sadness at the back of my throat.

But when I turn back around, my little poppet is grinning, asking me, 'So, where does the Mexican infamous circus cake go?' Ever helpful, ever doing the job that needs to be done, there she is picking up the tin.

'In the sideboard,' I say and step back into the sitting room to open the doors of it for her.

She kneels and peers in, telling me: 'It's very dusty in here – you need new paper put down.' To line the bottom of the cupboard section. Was there ever a more perfect child?

I say: 'Well, we'd better do that, then, hadn't we?' For I certainly never have in my life, and I doubt Mother ever did either.

Agnes carefully removes the jumble of silver and vases and china oddments that live there and pulls out the paper that lay beneath them. I had never noticed that there *was* paper lining there – and with it comes a cloud of ancient filth, and something else... A certificate of some kind swishes across the floor, lodging under the toe of my right shoe.

I pick it up. The paper is equally ancient, yellowed, but thick: TICKET-OF-LEAVE it's entitled. From the *Principal Superintendent of Convicts' Office. Sydney, New South Wales, 12 August 1842. It is His Excellency, the Governor's, Pleasure to dispense with the Attendance at Government Work of Tobias Weathercroft, who was tried at* somewhere indecipherable in *London, 25 May 1831, Convict for 14 years . . .*

'Oh dear God.' I almost drop it, as if it's a spider.

'What is it?' Agnes is alarmed, as if it might have bitten me.

'Grandfather Weathercroft – my mother's grandfather – he was a convict.'

'Oh?' Poppet face relaxes; relieved: is that all? She asks me: 'What did he do?'

'I don't know. Doesn't say.' I read it again. 'This paper says he was allowed to work, in the District of the North Shore, for good behaviour.'

Agnes is not particularly interested in that. She sets about wiping the insides of the sideboard. While I laugh again – and darkly. Well, there's something else for the grape, isn't there. At least something to toss back to Mother when I get the dressing-down from her that's coming. A convict? I've always known this little stone house was made by convicts, the stone cut by them, but Grandfather Weathercroft a convict *himself*? I'm not merely half-cash-strapped Australian, then, am I. The Honourable Olivia Jane Ashton Greene is half-convict. Not the right sort, all right. I wonder, is that why Mother truly wasn't an acceptable bride for his Lordship – *really*? A dramatic discovery of convict stain. Atrocity of atrocities. I wonder if Barty Woo knows. I'd almost want to go all the way to London to ask him in person.

Oh God, but that catches me. London: no. I'm not going to London. I live here. And Eoghan should be here, laughing at this with me. My ultimate emancipation via this little certificate. My ticket to love whomever I choose. Too late. I could tear it up with my own outrage; stamp these convict-sawn floorboards with it.

But I don't. I hide my anger from Agnes. I must, for I know she has enough of her own to grapple with, and later, after dinner, as I cuddle her into bed, I ask her before she sleeps: 'Where shall we go to Mass on Christmas Day? You choose.'

She shakes her dear little curly head: 'I don't want to go to Mass at all.'

'No?' For all that religion has barely touched me, I must say: 'Agnes, it's not God's fault your brother isn't here. We must pray for him anyway.'

'Yes,' she says. 'I know that. I pray for him every day. All day. I don't need to go to a church to do it. God hears me. It's Yoey who isn't listening.'

'Hm. Yes.' I look up at the Bridge, crisscrossed black on indigo through the white slats of the venetians. The road is complete now, only waiting to be opened. You made that Bridge, Eoghan. I am begging you now. Please come home. A train rumbles out across the viaduct and into the tunnel below us. Hear me, if you can. *Me* – begging. Not something I enjoy. *Please*. Where are you?

Yo

'It is not in my power to say where the child is,' the fella at the Children's Court says.

'I just want to know if she's all right. That's all. I'm not going to bother anyone.' I'm not going anywhere near Balmain, the way I am, if that's what he's worried about. Shame enough running into Ellen Callaghan yesterday up near Taylor Square, *Oh, I hardly recognised you, Eoghan*, she could hardly wait to tell me she'd heard through Father Madigan that Ag had gone to a good Catholic family, looking down her nose at me as if her own brother doesn't manage a fucking brothel.

This court fella rubs his eyes; tired of arseholes bothering him every day, then he says, again: 'You must make application to the court to resume guardianship of your sister, otherwise I can't help you.'

I don't want guardianship of Ag. I'm not fit to polish her boots. I am an arsehole, as O'Keenan by definition must be, and I can't even look after myself, never mind a child. It's Christmas. I just want to know she's safe and happy, I just want to be sure. It's hard enough being this sober, to have come here; I'm sweating with it.

I don't deserve to be near her. I just want to know if she's all right.

He takes pity; he says: 'It is my understanding that the people who have her in foster care at present are considering adoption.'

'The Adamses? I know them — they wouldn't mind you saying.' Though I'm certain Mr Adams wouldn't mind ripping me apart slowly for what I've done.

'It is not in my power to say.'

'Yeah, right.' I wander back out. I don't deserve to know.

'How'd you go?' Ced asks me, leaning against one of the columns by the door.

I shake my head. 'Drink?'

'Yeah.'

We start walking back up to Flinders Street, up to Taylor Square, to the other Court House there on the edge of Darlo, where we're on the Communist Party tab. We're to be there at four o'clock anyway, expecting the King's own Girl Guides to arrive about then. I don't care where I'm going or what I'm doing. I can't stop thinking of Ag. It's Christmas. Jesus. It must be Mr and Mrs Adams that have Ag, mustn't it? It has to be. The only way I'll know is to go and front up to them. Sober up and front up to them. Front up to Mr Adams and tell him what exactly? Look, I'm not fucking pissed, yet, today. See — too fucking sober. I'm not on the dole yet, either. I've been getting piece work at the Texaco dock, a day here, a day there, rolling out them barrels, but mostly I'm getting paid to drink and run. Aren't I worth knowing.

Getting the Tooths into me at this pub; and three schooeys down, the Girl Guides are here to divert what's left of my attention. A bit early. It's only a quarter to.

They're into it quickly. Five of them, and one says to the barman: 'Two bottles of KB and dead Commie bastard, if you don't mind.'

And then he doesn't know what hit him. Ced is that fast and that small, they never know who or what has hit them. There's some power in him, for a little fella, he comes up from under:

crack. And then all they see is me.

A smile and a wink and I say: 'Come on. Take this outside.'

That's what they want, a public fight, to show everyone what a pack of arseholes we are and how it's all the Big Fella's doing, and how the only ones who can stop the fighting is the Girl Guides. This arsehole gives them something more than they're after. I start running. They follow. The five of them. Pack of spoons.

I run them round into Little Bourke Street, down the length of it, and into the lane behind the empty warehouse there, where the real arseholes are waiting. They step out of the line of terraces across the road: a dozen wharfies, going into bat for Australia.

I watch them beat the living shit out of all the King's men, and something in me enjoys it. Watching them covering their heads, scared for their lives. They're not going to get killed, just expertly hurt, but they think they're going to die. I know what that feels like: you think you just can't take another hit. But you do. I keep watching until they're finished and one of the wharfies says, 'Get scarce, kid.' Then I walk back up to Flinders, get on the tram, on the next one heading for La Perouse.

'Fancy meeting you here,' says Ced, got on the stop before me.

I say: 'How's about a drink, then?'

'Oath, mate.'

Olivia

'This is him, isn't it? That's the name?'

'You've found something?' I follow the Supreme Court clerk's finger down the ancient page. A register, of labour assignments, 1836, and here he is: *Weathercroft, Tobias – Aged 21 years – sent'd 14 years, theft of small pig – CCC 1831.* A small pig – made all the difference between hanging and transportation that *small*, I suppose. Good God, and this means he was only sixteen when put out to sea? But I ask the clerk what's not clear to me: 'What does CCC mean?'

He smiles at me in a bemused way that suggests such convict enquiries are not a part of his everyday; he says: 'CCC is the Central Criminal Court – the Old Bailey, in London.'

Where Bart prosecutes criminals nowadays. How funny. Round and round the wobbly wheel of fortune goes.

The clerk says: 'I must say I'm surprised there was anything to be found here at all – these records are destined for destruction. Library doesn't want them, nor the Attorney-General's Office. Seems a shame, in a way.'

In every other way it's shame that will see these leather-bound volumes burned to dust. Who in their right mind would ever want this sort of ancient filth lurking at the bottom of the Supreme Court's sideboard waiting to fall out and humiliate them? I look at the *Assigned to* column and see that Grandfather Weathercroft was sent to work for a man called Joseph Johns, a pie-maker, of George Street North, at the Rocks. Look at it hard, before it disappears. I look up at the clerk again and ask him: 'Might I have this register? Or just the page?'

'I'm afraid not,' he smiles again, and regretfully: 'It's property of the Crown.'

Aren't we all. I smile in return and thank him for his time. Something I have plenty of. Now that the discovery of fourteen small-pig-theft years is complete, I'll have to find some other lunchtime diversion. I pass the Thomas Cook travel agency on the way back to the arcade and resist making the booking, again. For passage to London. Stamped return to sender. But I can't – not yet. Not London. But where else might we go? There is no other logical place for us to go. So what am I waiting for? I spy the spine of the arch vaulting beyond the Quay and I'm waiting for the Bridge to officially open. That's the line in the sand at present. The nineteenth of March, the date has been set for the ceremony, thirteen days from today. If Eoghan doesn't show up then, I'm going to ask Mr Jabour to sign the adoption form and then Agnes and I will get on a ship. And Mother will get an awfully big surprise. I still haven't written to her about any of this, and the grape has evidently been just as remiss. I still haven't mentioned the idea of London to Agnes, either. If fate is a wheel, mine's got its gears stuck and left me dangling in midair.

With a riot of rayon in the window of the Emporium, the first thing I see rounding the entrance of the Strand. *Rayon.* Japanese rayon, one shilling, nine pence a yard. Uncrushable. Utterly fake: aren't we all. Mr Jabour waves to me across his cutting table – three customers in line. I smile back and mouth the word, 'Rayon' at him in mock contempt just as I turn to the stairs. How often did he make me promise I'd never stoop to synthetics? Now look at him! Busy again. And Coralie with him as Velma is busily in production of a new grandchild for him now, too. They're scheming to set up a sewing school of their own, the genie and Coralie. And I will be busy again one day too. Hold on.

Go to London, insists some whisper under the clop of my mary-janes. Take up the shop that Mother has picked out for me in Piccadilly. *Noooo*, the remnant child in me wails at the idea. At the defeat. Can't I set up again in Chatswood? Not likely: it's too close to Mosman, and I shall forever carry the stain of Lady Game, wherever I go in this city. The Witches are baying for blood, with Premier Lang daring to declare that he will open the Bridge himself instead of the Governor. The New Guard have declared on the King's behalf that this must not be allowed to happen. The newspapers read as a wild colonial opera of high dudgeon; the Games must feel besieged on all sides. I should try to telephone Lady Game again, or leave a card: *You can always run away with me and Agnes, somewhere . . .*

How long before these putrid streams of bile reach my little poppet at school? I would like to think that is far-fetched, that the Witches would not stoop to such pettiness. But I am too well acquainted with them. Their mystifying hatred. It is frightening. Look at my salon: not one order in my register. I would like to write to Governor Game myself and beg him: *Please, sack Mr Lang and be done with it. Sack him now.* If it really would make the difference.

I see myself in the window, under the backwards OLIVIA COUTURE. Lost. What happened to the girl who dreamed magic-carpet odalisque dreams of Paris?

She is here, says Madame. *Work. You have not broken one finger-nail yet – not one.*

Yes. Work. There is always work to do. I true up the edges of the Irish linen that's waiting for me, draped over the back of the chaise, spread it upon my table and start chalking up. A handkerchief shift, this will be. Gypsy-twirl from the hip. And if no one else will, I shall wear it myself. I shall wear it across the Bridge. Let the women of Sydney revert to type if they must: tasteless and inelegant in the fifty-three shades of beige that's just arrived, a freshly discarded season from Home: Bois de Rose Beige, Rose Beige, Ashes of Roses Beige, Beige Beige, Fawn Beige, Mushroom Beige, Biscuit Beige, Apricot Beige, Vanilla Beige, Coconut Beige, Peaches and Cream Beige. They won't miss me. My gypsy handkerchief is bright apple green.

*

'But I don't want to go,' Agnes whispers, as if in whispering it quietly enough the whole idea might go away. The whole Bridge might disappear. Her class is among those invited to parade across the span for the special children's day ahead of the opening. I understand her reluctance: the Bridge is Yoey, to us both. Can't look at it without this torment of wondering; can't not look at it, either. The damn thing fills the sky outside the front door, sneaks through the slats of the venetians. Where are you, Eoghan? Why have you left us? You nasty, sneaking, horrible coward.

I promise her: 'You don't have to go.'

'I won't get into trouble?' deep blue pleading.

'No, of course you won't.' I hold her to me, and hope.

She wakes with a bit of a sniffle on that Wednesday morning anyway, and it's raining. So we malinger together in our hideaway. We devour a box of Mr Hillier's best. We watch the raindrops ball on the petals of the geranium she planted in the window box I bought her for the back wall. We screwed it onto the sill together, facing north to catch the sun. She pinched the geraniums from the yard of the boarding house on the bend of Bay View Street, poking through the iron spokes of the fence. They'll plant themselves anywhere, those geraniums: Mrs Buddle told her so, in long-ago Balmain. Bright coral splash against this grey day today. Agnes spends the rest of it in a book and I don't mention London as ten thousand children trudge across the Bridge in this pouring rain.

And sometime in the night my little poppet moans: 'Olivia?' A great heaving sob – and a raging headache. 'It hurts . . .'

It really does. I hold her to me tight and terrified all through this night. If there is such a thing as God I'm telling him: don't you bloody dare let her get ill. Hasn't this child been harmed enough? You want to give her a good dose of the flu too? I rail at God until the dawn. Don't you let her be ill: this is not that kind of tragedy. No. I rail at Eoghan, for this is his fault too. His fault most of all. You hurt this child again and I'll – I'll –

Agnes wriggles around in my arm and says: 'You can let me go now. Please. I'm a bit hot.'

Fever?

No. I'm only squashing her with my fears.

*

It's the storm over Mr Lang's hat that almost pushes me across the line and into the travel agency, though. He didn't wear a top hat to the opening ceremony. No top hat. No frockcoat. *Quelle horreur!* the Beige Witches shriek across the front page of the paper. He wore a homburg! The indecency! What do you expect from one who doesn't even own a dinner suit and is wedded to a feminist frump? Well, you'd expect some fool from the New Guard to be so outraged he'd charge at the Bridge ribbon on horseback and make a complete laughing stock of the whole nation by attempting to cut it with a blunt ceremonial sword. That's how one properly declares a bridge open in the name of a king. The newsreel is playing at every theatre in town – at two-hour intervals. I haven't seen it. An Irishman, this rogue ribbon-slasher purportedly is – all troublemakers must be, mustn't they? They locked him up in the lunatic asylum for the weekend, last heard babbling incoherently about top hats. Apparently Mr Lang's speech on the day was quite stirring nevertheless. Jolly good. Sydney is a lunatic asylum.

And yet I stop on the footpath at the window of Thomas Cook, staring into one of the posters there: *TO ENGLAND VIA CANADA AND BEAUTIFUL LAKE LOUISE.* A couple of dancers cheek to cheek in the top right corner and suddenly I can't conscience going anywhere. I am dancing with Eoghan under the Christmas bell of St Augustine – *I will wait for you,* I told him that day. And how can I conscience taking Agnes away from *her* country? Take her from all she's ever known? Take her from Eoghan, and take me from him, too, so, so far away? What if he really does come looking for us at Lavender Bay and finds us gone? I can't bear that thought. My determination to hurt him back vanishes, nothing but a puff of smoke on the breeze. I shall continue to wait, a little longer. Perhaps I should wait until after my birthday, just a few weeks more. I'll be so much more certain of what I'm doing at twenty-one, too, won't I. At twenty-one Grandfather Weathercroft was a convict slave to a pie-maker at the Rocks: then went on to play for sheep stations, and lose them. Life is long. And life is too short. Act now. Before the rent on the salon bankrupts you. But still, I resist. London – nooooo.

The Jabours are offering no encouragement, no help at all with this decision to take myself sensibly Home to Mother. My genie says: 'Well, my dear, you know I will be sad to see you go.' His eyes are a pitiable deep umber glum and not for me alone. He holds no love for London or King George the German: they killed his brother, for thirty miserable million pieces of silver. Gloria gives me an outright: 'No – you *can't*,' and little Robbie cries: are you insane? While Coralie suggests, most sensibly: 'Come in on the sewing school with us, Ollie – it'll be buckets of fun.' It would too, and it is so obviously set to make a decent couple of buckets of money, but I don't want to teach. I want my salon back. I want my own dreams back.

I take my scattered self up to David Jones, for some chinchilla trim – can't get it anywhere but there and Foys at the moment. I'm so distracted by the time I get to the haberdashery department, though, I've forgotten what I want it for.

Kim Kelly

SYDNEY HARBOUR BRIDGE EXHIBITION
A miscellany of construction and design

The sign by the escalators directs me, through the shopping crowd. It's a steel-girder smash to the heart, this crowd, always is for me: how can the arcades be so quiet, so empty, and here, cash registers going *ding ding ding* everywhere. It's business, simple business – the buying power of bigger creatures – but it's not fair. Haute couture and crepe chaff bags all jumbled under the one convenient roof. I wander into the exhibition, all snaking pin-boards of draughtsmen's sketches and photographs and tables and tallies, and I'm still searching for why I'm here, when I'm drawn to a small glass-topped plinth at the end of one of the snakes. I wonder what's sleeping under the glass box: peer in and it's a pair of scissors. Mr Lang's ribbon-cutting scissors, when he got to have his go at it. I'm struck by how gaudy they are, a bright yellow gild, with flannel flowers and gum leaves twisting along the handles, around a likeness of the Bridge. Something from a pantomime. A prop. *Hand-wrought of Australian gold and containing six flame-coloured opals, quarried from Lightning Ridge, created in Angus & Coote's workrooms by Sydney's finest craftsmen,* says the card by them. I say they are just a pair of snippers: overwrought.

And suddenly I see in them that the argument is finished. It's time to cut my ties here. Eoghan has cut his: he is lost to us. Admit this most terrible of defeats. It's been five months now. And if he's not lost to us then it's him whose action, or inaction, is unconscionable. He can forget me all he likes – we were nothing but a blue mile of silly dreams. But how can he forget Agnes? How can he not fight for his sister? How can he not see all the wonderful things he had and might still have if he were damn well here? Mr Adams is still keeping his mail for him; keeping the light on for him. The Adamses loved him without question or complication. Why run from that? Why not see sense and damn well come back? Because he's dead, isn't he. Dead to me. He has to be. Took the ultimate coward's way out.

The Blue Mile

Despair: it's a leading cause of death among young men today.

For the life of me, I can't remember why I'm here. And I can't stand this city anymore. I have to get out of the DJs *ding ding ding*, and back down on Pitt, Ned the barrowman nods over his apples and oranges as if he knows what's happening here: I'm gone, I'm next, I'm packing up and moving on. Last week it was Monty – moving his photographic studio to a barrow at Manly, for the Sunday seaside trade, scrabbling for pennies from those who've got them. And now it's me, pulling the closed sign round early. Going home. To wait for Agnes to come in from school. I'm going to tell her today, this afternoon: we're going to start again. We're going to London. An adventure, together. Grab your hat and coat . . .

And hesitate once more at the top of the ferry steps, at the 1847 staring down at me from the lintel. How can I think of leaving my little stone fortress above the bay? Mother'll sell it for a carport for the flats next door as soon as I'm out of it, as soon as the price is right, won't she . . . and the price will be right. Bridge views around here are in bonanza, with the trains going across taking the traffic jams away, with plans now for a fun park to be built on the site of the old workshops.

I almost slip on the mail as I open the door. Pick it up. Jolly good, it's from his Lordship. How exciting – it'll be the birthday card, by the feel. Must do something extra special with this month's pitiful pittance remittance in celebration, apart from paying the shop rental: buy us fifteen pounds' worth of new shoes with it, all of it – in snakeskin – see if I don't, you horrible fool. Completely, utterly, mystifyingly lacking in embarrassment at being the worst excuse for a man I know. I almost don't read the card. He never has anything to say to me apart from *trust you are well*. Couldn't care less, et cetera. But this time, his few soulless sentences say something quite different.

I will arrive in Sydney in June and once established I shall make my search for a suitable property, for a vineyard, to make my retirement in kinder climes.

My heart stops.

I am very much looking forward to seeing you. It has been far too long.

It has been sixteen years, almost. I was five when he left for Flanders, left me for the last time. Honestly, all I remember of him is his nose and his stink; not one kiss, not one smile or tender word.

And he wants to see me now. He wants *kinder climes* now?

Happy 21st birthday, Olivia.

Ah. Finally, I see my path ahead.

Beginning with an ungainly sprint up to the post office and a reply telegram:

FATHER! HOW EXCITING! BUT ALAS I AM BROKE. IN TROUBLE. PLEASE CABLE £200. No, I am calculating madly how much it will cost me to set out my shingle at Piccadilly, under my own terms – not Mother's. Make that: £350. THRILLED TO SEE YOU IN JUNE.

And not before hell freezes over and I'm compelled to go ice-skating across it. He wants something from me – at long, long *last*. And he will give me whatever I want in return. Three hundred and fifty pounds is lunch money to him. Just as I know that tomorrow, I will be stepping through those travel agency doors. I will be booking our passage for sometime in May – that will give me time to tidy all squiggles here. Agnes and I shall arrive in England in July. Midsummer. Good. A flicker of raindrops balling on lolly pink snapdragons by a duck pond, somewhere in Hyde Park, that other Hyde Park, far far away. Soon to be dancing gaily with Olivia Couture pea-style gamboge, with my teals and my violets, all my lush lapis dreams. Done. And all fingernails intact, too.

But still, my fingers tremble with the key in the door as I return to my little haven of stone, and my shoe garden whispers from the wardrobe as get in: *No – wait.* You promised him under the bell. *I'll wait for you, Eoghan. I'll do whatever it takes.*

No: no more. I glare at the blackened tin vine leaves arabesquing up the sides of the shelves, lily trumpets spilling round the copper pipes. So beautiful: you, you and your fine tailor's hands, should be in business with me: my poet, my dancer, my lover, never to be.

You are gone.

Sit down to the letter I must write.

Dearest Mother, guess who's coming to London . . . and find us a decent flat, will you, dear, because we won't be living with you.

This is *my* adventure. *Just Aggie and me* . . . *and just Aggie and me* . . .

Yo

'They're planning to kidnap him,' Ced says at the bar of the Botany Bay, where we drink in the day, most days.

I laugh, on my second. 'The Girl Guides are going to kidnap the Bank Robber?' Because Lang is just not going to pay up. The United Australia Federal Spoons have tried to force him to kiss them British bondholder bollocks but Lang won't have it. Get fucked. I don't give a fuck, either. It's Olivia's birthday today. But then, I don't give a fuck any day. I tell Ced: 'Get me a front-row ticket, will you?'

'I'll get you more than that, you lousy bludger,' he says. 'Sometimes I do question your commitment to the cause.'

'Why? Because I don't have any?'

He laughs now. I'm a good Communist. Only ever wanted a simple life, and that's what I have now: do as you're told and you'll get a drink, comrade.

Ced has stopped laughing, though. 'The CMF have been put on alert by the Federals.'

'Who?'

'The Citizens' Militia Forces, mate – the army.'

'Oh. So?'

'They have guns.' He shakes his head at me: spoon.

'So do the cops.' I shake mine back. I never thought I'd ever sit on the same side as the cops, but here we are. This is an entertaining show.

Ced says: 'That's right, Paddy. And what happens when two sides in a conflict are armed?'

'Oh.' War. 'Right.'

I don't know that I like the sound of that. Unlikely to be a pipe band at this type of war.

Have another ale or seven, and another game of fucking billiards, and then Ced's boring my brain out my arsehole and up the road with another capitalist conspiracy: 'That's why Phar Lap had to die, you see. They had to kill him — he was upsetting the numbers. Too good. Hadn't lost a race since the Cup, had he, the bastard horse? So the Yanks had to poison him, didn't they?'

Did they? Amazing. It's a long walk back to La Perouse from here. Two miles of nothing, the trams don't come round this part of the bay, and I know I'm on the grog properly because of how I'm walking. I've been drinking all day, not quickly but solidly, and I'm not in the least bit shickered from it. I know where I'm going: into the gutter. Or into the sand. There's no gutters round here. I'll just have to fall through the sand, like piss.

As it's Saturday evening, Ced says, 'We'll get some goods of exchange, ay?' and we stop halfway to make a visit to the Chinese market gardens. Some beetroot, some carrots, we grab whatever there is down the ends of these rows along Bunnerong Road. One of the Chings sees us and starts up yelling, setting his dog after us, but we've already gone. Running. Ced's nearly as fast as me, too; amazing, for such a little fella. I've never been a thief, though, and this raiding doesn't sit too well in me. Ced reckons it's not technically thieving if you take stuff off the Chinese, but I don't know. I've got carrots spilling out of my pockets and I didn't make them. I miss making something. Anything. But I can't think about that. What would be the point?

The dog gives up and we stop running just past the kiosk at the Yarra Junction tram stop, where we follow the line down to the tin and board humpies of the camp, for something to eat, for Ced to keep our presence up round here, and for his weekend supply of Happy Valley Special Reserve. That's what the beetroot and carrots are for: Granny Smith lets him have two bottles for five bob if he brings something for the kids.

'What you got for me tonight then, love?' She's at her flyscreen. She's as fat as she is short, made just like an apple, with a face like a picture-book granny, but you wouldn't want to cross her. She'd have you razored. She runs the groggery and feeds the kids round here off the proceeds of her sly rum when the Governor's wife isn't having her photo taken with a soup ladle. There's plenty of kids and only dole rations to keep them. I don't come here in the daytime: kids running around everywhere, happy kids: they don't care they've got no shoes. Running round on the sand. I can't look at them. I see my sister in every one. I see my failure in every one. In everyone.

I am not on the dole, though, I tell myself, like it means anything. I'm not on the dole. Not on the capitalist shut-up, sit-down payroll. I'm on the payroll of the righteous. Righteous anger: it's the last of anything of any worth I have.

Some other dog is barking somewhere and I look across Granny's back fence, into the darkness. I look along the line of wire fences that go down to the beach, separating the Abos on the reserve further round, from the campers here in the gully on the point, and a cop looks back at me: 'Evening.' Making his rounds. There's usually a cop or two keeping an eye, especially of a Saturday night, keeping them no-hoper blacks from mixing too much with us good folk. I start laughing at I don't know the fuck what.

Granny Smith pulls me inside her tin and board palace: 'Get in here, young fella, and eat something, will you?'

She's got fish on. She's always got fish on, caught fresh off the rocks here, by the Abos next door. It smells good and probably tastes good too. I don't seem to taste anything anymore. Ced is jawing on to her about something, more conspiracy horseshit – that we'll likely come down here if it comes to a war. We'll likely sabotage the Bunnerong Power Station, put the streetlights and the trams out, and make La Perouse a stronghold. Yeah, that's what we'll do, won't we.

Granny Smith says: 'You'll give us fair warning to get the kids out.' Or she'll put our lights out.

We give her sixpence each for our tea and then we walk up the hill, to our own shit box back up past the Coast Hospital, where they put you if you've got a plague. The Communist Party of Australia has all the best squats. Interestingly, they all come with wireless phones, though, on loan from the socialistically minded of the sly betting industry. On the right side of the tram tracks, we are here, too. Lots of fresh air, it comes screaming up straight off the sea, over this high ground between Happy Valley and Long Bay Gaol. Ced is pulling the cork on his Special Reserve already as we walk up through the thick scrub here and I'm telling myself I've still got a way to fall yet. I can get up, I can get out. I can get back to Ag, one day. I'm not living in the humpies down in the gully. I'm not on the dole. I'm not on the rum.

I tell Ced: 'You'll kill yourself with that one day.'

He says: 'So?'

I don't know what his story is, I don't know who he is really, but I know what he means. We're dead men already. But I don't want to go that way, on the grog. Fuck no, I don't. I roll a smoke. Happy birthday, Olivia. How do the rich sleep in their beds at night? Better quality alcohol. I have none left tonight that I can drink and no business thinking about Olivia at all. I don't sleep for reckoning it'd be good if I just didn't wake up one day. Drag my arse along a wide-eyed dream up to the Bridge and take a dive.

*

'Well, well, well. Look who we have here.' This barmaid is looking at me across the taps of the Alexandria Hotel. Red lips on a mouth that's sucked too fair a share of lemons.

I'm thinking she's a whore on the side and that I don't want to go from the clap either. Jesus, but it takes me a minute to recognise her too.

It's Nettie Becker, looking about twenty years older than the last time I saw her, though it can't be two years.

'Yeah,' I say. 'Well, what do you know.'

And then I just stand there like a spoon, thinking: horseshit. We don't need a scene here. Ced and me have pulled up at the bar, waiting for Girl Guides. They've been making their presence known and their intentions spill around the produce railhead. Ced is leaning over at the barman now, asking him who's on cockatoo and where, to warn us of how many.

Nettie seems to know about that; she says: 'I always told you, didn't I? Lang is right.'

'Yeah.' I give Nettie a smile at remembering: she always did know everything and she did love her Jack Lang. I say: 'Good on him.' And I mean it today: he's just withdrawn the whole of the Treasury funds from the Commonwealth Bank – every last cent. Set up his own separate cash economy out of Trades Hall, at the Haymarket, under police and union guard, so that public employees, such as the railways fellas in this bar, can get paid. He's accused the United Arseholes in Canberra of enforcing an illegal state of slavery otherwise. He's a fucking hero, however monkey-nutted that might be. Political suicide.

Nettie's saying: 'Careful you don't get that pretty face bashed up.'

'They'd have to catch me first,' I laugh; I've never got caught at this game.

'That's right. You're not an easy catch, are you?' she says and presses those red lips together, little red lines running off round her mouth, look like they're painful.

I could tell her it was never her business to try me, but I keep my mind on the job, don't make a scene. I ask her instead: 'How's little Johnny going?'

She shakes her head; she just says: 'Measles.'

'Shit, no.' He's died from it, those lines say. A kick in the guts just to hear it. I say: 'That's rough.'

She doesn't say anything, giving me a long hard stare as she slides the ale across the bar at me. What? Blaming *me*? It's not my fault you're a loose bitch with a dirty mouth that got you turfed into the street. But something in me takes it anyway.

I say: 'I'm sorry to hear that.'

She turns away to serve someone else and I tell my glass: we're all to blame. For all this shit.

Some more than others.

'Seventeen of them – coming down Henderson Road!' the cockie screams in through the pub doors.

That was quick, I've hardly touched my beer, way too fucking sober yet, and that's too many to keep out of the bar this time, so we have to wait for them all to get in, count their khaki armbands. This National Guard. Who the fuck do they reckon they are? Masters of hypocrisy: King's men who would have the Governor-General sacked for being a Jew, if they could, and would cut all Welfare to women, let the daughters of Eve starve and all their snot-faced children with them. Hollow men. Tight-fisted greengrocers thieving fruit and veg wholesale. Ced bolts the doors behind the last; I bolt the doors round the Garden Street side. And then the bar turns to them as one representation of the Railway Workers Union, about thirty members strong.

The head of them here, an engine driver called Gil Gregory, makes himself known to the Girl Guides: 'This is as far south as you blokes go, right? You're not welcome here.'

The head of the Girl Guides steps up to him. 'We've only stopped in for a drink. This is a free country, is it not? This is a *public* bar?' He flicks his oiled hair off his face with a jerk of his head, the tosser he is. 'Or have the Communists decided to make it illegal for an honest man to enjoy a beer after work?'

He takes a baton out of the inside of his coat, one like the cops carry, turned handle with a leather strap, and the bad end about eighteen inches long.

Gil Gregory nods at it: 'I'm not a Communist. I'm an Aussie, and you're a fascist Pommy scab.'

The barman shoves Nettie out the dining room door and it's on.

I don't watch today.

'Oi.' I get smacked across the shoulder with a baton.

And then I get stuck in.

I don't know who this fella is that's just smacked me, but I've slammed his hand up against the wall behind him and he's dropped the baton. I hear it hit the boards, and I am pounding into him like he's got to take every punch I've never thrown but wanted to. He gets one in but I don't feel it. I can only feel my fist smacking into his head, his fat bastard roast-ham head. He falls down. He's got his hands around his head. He's had enough. I know he's had enough.

I scream at him: 'You had enough?'

'Yes,' he's crying for me to stop, on his knees.

But I keep going. I smack his head into the boards by the back of his collar and I tell him: 'This is your interest payment.' I get up and I have every intention of putting the boot into him too, but one of the railways fellas has the back of my collar now: 'You're not supposed to kill them, lad.'

No. I look around me. The Girl Guides are getting turfed out onto the street, red faces, ripped shirts. The cops are waiting out there to move them along quietly. It's over. One of the railways fellas picks up a baton and taps one of the Girl Guides on the arse with it: 'Naughty, naughty boy.' The bar falls around laughing.

But I don't laugh.

'Eoghan O'Keenan,' Nettie comes at me with her handkerchief. 'I see you got caught.'

'What?' I back off. I taste the blood on my lip. I say: 'That's nothing.' And it isn't.

But I find I've suddenly had enough. Had enough of what? I don't know. My own hollow.

'Toast to the King, mate?' Ced says. 'Jeez, you might have earned one today.'

I say: 'No. I haven't earned shit.'

I'm as surprised as Ced. I want to stay sober. I want to be sober, tomorrow and the next. I want to be ready for this war that's coming. I am an honest man: I want to pound another filthy fascist head.

Olivia

'The Governor has sent for him.' Glor's eyes are huge with the scandal and not a small amount of fear. One moment she's having afternoon tea with Paul at the Aristocrat downstairs, as they often do of a slow Friday afternoon, and the next she's raced up to the salon to tell me: 'He's going to sack the Premier this time – he must do. And Paul's been sent over to Trades Hall – to explain to the unions that it's not against the law. Mr Lang can't have the Governor arrested in response. Or he can, but that would be revolutionary. My God, but the Governor sacking the Premier – that's revolutionary anyway, isn't it? Oh, Ollie . . . what's going to happen?'

Little Robbie holds out his hands to me from his mother's hip. He is, in fact, the prettiest baby that ever there was. I'm so going to miss watching him grow, seeing who he's most like. I cuddle him up and pretend to eat his left cheek and tell Glor: 'It's Friday the thirteenth – anything could happen.'

'Don't be so flip,' she snips. 'Trades Hall is under barricade. What if –?'

'I'm sure he'll be all right.' I hope. Paul plays football – he's had a black eye before – and Agnes and I couldn't be leaving Sydney too soon. Tuesday week we'll be away. On the waves. I look over at my poppet now: sorting buttons and bits at my table, just as she did that day . . . so long ago. How she's grown. Straight-backed, picking buttons for a blouse we'll make for her. She's not entirely thrilled at the idea of London, changing schools again, missing so many weeks of it too, including these school holidays now, but it's as good an adventure as any. It is what I will make it for us. She'll brighten up once we're on the ship. So will I – we're stopping at Suva, Pago Pago, Honolulu, San Francisco, Vancouver . . . It will not be possible to be too miserable, will it? I say to Glor, dragging her towards the stockroom, our Aladdin's rainbow bomb of never-ending sorting: 'Come and see what bits you might want for yourself.'

'Ol,' she blinks away tears, 'I don't want anything. I don't want you to go.'

'Have to, don't I?' I smile, blinking my own away, holding each one deep in my heart: 'Must make way for the sewing school, mustn't we?' The genie is taking over the lease here and under Aunty Karma's supervision this will be Coralie's new world. I am happy about that: it warms that cold stone of regret that's sitting in the pit of my stomach. For London. Never been my number one choice of fabulous destinations, has it, but it's Piccadilly, it's a fresh start. In the stale Old Dart. But it's sensible. It's logical. It's Home, the land of my birth. I can make a fair fist of it and I shall. I have £350 of successful paternal extortion swelling my account and Mother is so thrilled I'm finally coming she is looking for a flat for me right now, said she quite understands a girl's need to bach these days. She'll do anything for me, to see me again. Can't wait to see her face go fifty-three shades of puce when she sees I shall be baching with a child. I smile: I'll get to meet my real little sister too. Two little girls in my world . . . .

'But you don't want that teal Shantung for yourself, do you?' Glor sniffs, recovered enough to see something here for herself after all.

I shake my head: I have seventeen trunks of essential can't-bear-to-leaves going with me. I say, 'There's almost eight yards there. I had something strapless with bolero planned for that – have Coralie magic it up for you.'

She sweeps her hand across the weave. 'Things change, Ol,' she says, wishful, wanting. 'Things change so quickly sometimes. If there's a revolution, you won't be able to get on the ship, will you?'

I frown and smile at the same time: 'That's desperate logic, Glor.' She's already tried to convince her father to refuse to sign the papers for Agnes to be allowed to travel abroad. The adoption papers. And they're still unsigned, but not so that we won't be able to go. Mr Jabour won't sign them until the very last moment. Just in case. What? Eoghan turns up to unabandon his sister? It's not going to happen, but still none of us can conscience the signing of the papers, not until the eleventh hour. The terrible no-turning-back of it.

Glor smiles back at me, right into my soul: 'I am desperate. But you never know, if the Governor does sack the Premier and *avoids* a revolution, perhaps Lady Game might even need you back to design her a special party dress?'

'Oh, Glor.' I cuddle up her and Robbie both and for Agnes's ears I say: 'You're just going to have to come and visit me in my London salon, aren't you? I'll be world famous most likely by then, too.'

'Yes,' Glor smiles, her canny crooked smile, 'you will be world famous, one day,' but the fear has returned to her eyes. She looks at her watch: 'After five.'

'God, is that the time already?'

'Hm,' she says. 'I told Paul I'd wait in town with Dad for him – till whenever he's back from Trades Hall. Wait with me, Ol?'

'Of course I will.'

A chill shoots through me, swooping, tingling. I'm not sure why I should be, but I'm a little unnerved now too.

Yo

The clock on the Town Hall is striking seven as I'm tearing up George Street, tearing up through the city from Trades Hall to the Treasury building. I haven't been into the city for a while and it is a strange place tonight. I look up as I pass the Strand Arcade: Friday night late shopping and all the lights are out there. Not a soul on the street round la-di-da town. Jesus, but this city will wake up in a minute. With Lang's next word, these streets will not be quiet.

I run faster. I run as if I might beat Lang there, to his office at the Treasury. He'd be there by now, back from Government House, with his pink slip. Dismissed. How can that be legal? The Governor – the King of England – can't sack a democratically elected leader of another country. But he can. He's just done it. If I was ever lacking in political motivation, I'm not now. I take that hill up Martin Place, past the fancy cars and cabs outside the Australia Hotel, and my chest is burning with it. I am giving away the smokes this day too; I've been three days off the grog completely and I'm still greasy in my guts from it like I've never known before: fucking arseholes, all of them: slave-driving, fascist, murdering arseholes.

Up into Macquarie Street and along the blackness of the Gardens, I am running through my life again, and every beating I've taken I will return with increasing interest. At the corner, this side of Bridge Street, the Department of Public Works looks at me with its blank stone face: my one good opportunity given to me and then taken away. Why? I am not a perfect man, but I am a decent man. Hardworking, honest man. Who has taken my life from me? The King of England: fuck you. This night, this black night, I will pay with whatever is left of me, I will do whatever needs to be done to fuck you as painfully as you have fucked me.

I look down Bridge Street, note the public telephone there – the one I will use to call on this war. There'd better not be a coin jammed in the box, for at my word hell will visit this city. The lights will go out from Bunnerong and White Bay; the wharves will shut down; the trains and trams will stop. The Governor will be arrested by the cops. It will be down to Lang: not some stiff-collared solicitor saying it's against the law. Whose law? The National Girl Guides will march out from the suburbs for us then, about twenty thousand of them, and only half that number again of Militia rifles. There are more than a hundred thousand of us: pistols and kerosene bombs enough to match, and ten times the heart. My blood is so hot for it, I want to call it on now.

Soon enough. There's cars lined up outside the Treasury: Lang's already inside. There's suits going everywhere up and down the steps on Macquarie Street, carrying boxes and files and all sorts of shit, in a hurry. Messengers darting off as I've just stopped.

At the bottom of the steps, I steady my breath and I'm unsure for a second: they look like they're clearing out, these busy fellas. What are they doing that for? Don't waste time wondering about it: I push in through the suits, and follow them round, to the Premier's office. He must be having to move somewhere. Safer. Where? La Perouse? Find out.

'Empty those cabinets too,' a woman is pointing into a room

full of them as I go down this hall; her voice is high and loud, directing bedlam. I'm supposing it's been called on already, the Governor's been caged and I'll be killing myself running back to the Haymarket in a second.

'Who are you?' some fella goes to stop me getting any further down the hall.

'Trades Hall messenger,' I say, pushing past him.

I see Lang now, half out a doorway built too small for him. He's putting on his coat. Putting on his hat. Going somewhere, briefcase in one hand and shaking some fella's hand with the other, saying: 'Good. Thank you. I beg your pardon?'

He's smiling, looking sad about it, though, tired, bending his head to hear the fella repeat: 'What happens now?'

'I go home.' He straightens up again. He is fucking enormous, telling the whole hallway, the whole world, with a wave: 'I am a free man tonight. I am sacked today and tomorrow we shall have an election campaign to be getting on with.'

'What do you think your chances are?' the fella asks him.

Lang laughs at the question, a short laugh – 'Ha' – is all he gives him, and he walks away, towards me.

He holds my stare for a second as he passes. He looks nothing like my father. He nods and smiles: 'Good evening, lad.'

I don't know what to do with myself, what to make of this, as I watch him walk towards the main doors, shaking hands and having a few words with each as he goes. He's taking it on the chin? That's a big chin he's got, but . . .

The fella beside me, the one who tried to stop me, says: 'Now *that* is a man.'

'What?' Something crashes in my head, falls through my guts, through the boards beneath my boots. 'He can't walk away.'

'But he is,' the fella beside me laughs, shaking his head, in a wonder of his own. 'The best of men always do. That's true nobility for you. Live to fight another day.'

I put my head in my hands, trying to make sense, understand:

'It's over?'

'No,' this fella says, and I look across at him. I've never seen him before. He doesn't look like anyone in particular; just another stiff-collared grey head, a public servant or a lawyer type. He says: 'It's never over. But there will be no blood spilt in his name – no pride is worth that price. You go and tell that to Trades Hall now, lad – tell those who need to know, the police have already been informed and instructed. Go now.'

I can't move for a second. Stuck stupid as if I've just met with the Lord incarnate. And I have, haven't I. Being told here something I've somehow always known but let go of in all my anger and shame. The Lord is here with us: in every good man. And nothing, nothing is ever over. Not one bashing; not one knock-back; not one prayer for something better.

I start to run again, with the power of this revelation. I start to pray again, for the first time in what seems like forever. Lord, hear me, please, for the wretched pile of horseshit I am. Forgive me. No. Fuck that. Take me to Aggie. Take me and throw me at her feet so that I can beg for the only forgiveness that matters: hers. Let me be a free man tonight, too.

After I tell the fella on the end of the phone in Bridge Street: 'Lang's called it off. It's definitely off. He's gone home. To Auburn. The cops –'

'Yeah,' I hear; a voice I don't know, taking the piss: 'The butler just phoned from Government House to tell us the same.'

He goes on about something, there's a feed on at the White Horse on Sussex, but I'm a lifetime past it already. I put the phone down and walk away. I'm heading to the Quay, to catch a ferry to Balmain.

Olivia

'I don't want to go to Hawaii, I don't think,' Agnes tells me as I tuck her into bed.

'Why ever not?' I ask her, surprised as much by the particularity of her doubt as by her mentioning our impending journey at all. I take it as a good sign, of facing up to it, and tell her: 'I'm looking forward to that bit. Don't you want to learn to hula-hula dance on Waikiki Beach with a flower necklace on? Grass skirt and all that?'

I wave my hands either side of her, hula-hula style, and she giggles.

And then she frowns, doubtful again: 'That's where the cannibals speared Captain Cook in the side like Jesus. Then they cooked him up in a big pot and ate him.'

'They did not!' I don't have to pretend to be shocked at the scandal of that. 'Agnes, wherever do you find such stories?'

'In the library... At school...' She looks into the lines of the venetians above her bed and I feel her real trepidation as she swallows hard against it: another new school, another new home, somewhere too far away to imagine.

I snuggle round and look into the blinds with her. Then I close my eyes and tell her, promise her: 'The library at your new school will be twice the size, you know. It'll be ten times the size of North Sydney public library too.'

'Really?'

'Yes.' If it's not I'll somehow make it so. I tell her: 'The libraries in London are so vast you have to have a great big long string tied round your finger before you go in, so that you can be found when you get lost.'

'That's not true, Ollie,' Agnes says, squeezing my hand close to her heart with wanting it to be.

I squeeze the whole of her perfect little girlness back. I adore it that she calls me Ollie now. We are real sisters too, in every way that it is important. I whisper into her wild sprawling curls on the pillow: 'It is so true.'

The ferry pushing off below us concurs: *toot tooooot*. All is quiet. It must be half-past eight at least; it was quarter to by the time Paul telephoned the Emporium with the news that civil war had been averted. Even weary revolutionaries must be tucked up in their beds now. All is right with the world. Our world. As right as it will ever be. Little ferries all, pushing out into the night, and a ukulele plucking out 'Blue Heaven' . . .

Yo

Get back to the Devil, you stinking sack of . . . some Ulster Gaelainn I don't quite catch. Mr Adams has the back of my neck in his iron grip. He has my face pressed into the bricks of the wall by his front door. I don't open my mouth for certainty that in doing so I will lose teeth.

He says, in English: 'You derelict, verminous son of a –'

That is what I am.

'You dare turn up here? You think I don't know where you've been? What you've been doing with them Commie mongrel sons of –'

'Wal, leave him,' Mrs Adams comes out the door: 'Leave the poor boy be.'

But he'll have his gobful out an inch from my ear: 'To leave your sister for that – for fighting. For what?'

I can't disagree with him but I can't yet reply either: the grains of the brick are one with the skin of my face now.

'Let him go, Wal,' Mrs Adams lowers her voice with some threat I've never heard from her before. 'Let him go, unless by some mistake you were made a saint yourself today.'

He lets me go; for Mrs Adams is actually a saint.

I turn around. His pit-bull head stares back at me not with hatred now. Worse: disappointment.

He says: 'You should have come to us.'

I know that. But I didn't. I couldn't. I had to work this out my own way. I don't know why. I can only say: 'I'm here now.'

'What do you want, then?' Mr Adams is not going to fatten the lamb for this prodigal. His iron-forged arms across his chest, still telling me to fuck off.

I say: 'My sister. Can I see her?'

'No, you cannot,' he says, 'She's with the girl, Miss Greene – they're off abroad.'

'What?' No. Jesus. Please. I never thought – *Olivia?* What are you doing to me now? Abroad? No, I don't believe what I just heard. That fella at the court said it was a family adopting her. The Adamses had to be adopting her. 'You're saying Ag's not here?'

'You don't deserve –'

'Wal Adams, you are a cruel man when you've a mind to be.' Mrs Adams steps down beside him and says to me: 'Aggie's only across the way, at Lavender Bay. They don't leave for another week.'

'Leave for where?'

'London.'

Horseshit she's leaving for London, I'm thinking, but Mrs Adams is saying it's true with all the kindness in her eyes. What I think is no longer applicable. I've lost Ag. I'm too late. From the first step I took running from her, too late.

But Mrs Adams is telling me now: 'Go on then – go and speak with Olivia, sort it all out.'

'Mum – Mummy!' Kenny is calling out inside. 'My button is loose!'

'In a moment, my love, we'll fix it,' she says to him over her shoulder and then she says to me: 'Wait a second, Eoghan.' She steps back into her hall and then back out again, handing me something. 'I kept your mail for you. I knew you'd be back. See?'

I look at the letters in my hand. Two of them. Won't be anything important; probably my eviction notice and termination of employ with Dorman Long, but Mrs Adams is telling me: 'You're a good lad. Go and make things good.'

I could kneel at her feet for a few hours first but instead I just stand here, like the emptiest spoon that ever was, shoving the letters into my coat pockets, one in each fist, crushing them with my shame.

'Good enough, lad,' Mr Adams gives me a shove. 'Go on. Off you go.'

Olivia

I'm in a dream. I've left the window open and the venetians are knocking in the breeze. Cross with myself even through this sleep: *You left the window open onto the street?* I've never done such a reckless thing. But I am rather preoccupied at present, aren't I. I've fallen asleep in my clothes, too, I realise: I can feel my belt buckle twisted and digging into my side. Hundred things on my mind: counting trunks, on and off a thousand ships. I feel Agnes still there under my arm, dreaming on, and all is well. All right. I rouse and blink into the dark, feeling across her for the cord to lift the blind and –

Tap tap tap . . . It's not the blind.

It's . . .

'Olivia – Olivia, are you there?' through the mail slot up the hall.

That can't be. I blink again.

'It's me – Eoghan.'

No. It's not. But it is. Before I've sat up, a bolt of anger has flashed and smashed through me.

I straighten my blouse and my skirt; smooth the tempest of my hair.

The Blue Mile

I open the door. I only want to check.

It's him. In silhouette, with the light from the ferry steps behind, collar of his duffel coat turned up against the night, black on black. Damn shoulderline. Damn him.

I say: 'Go away.' Cold as the air.

I shut the door; shut him away.

Slip back into bed beside Agnes: to check again. She is here, with me; there will be no upsetting our plans, our calm sea: *go away*. I breathe in the sweet scent of her hair... our camomile shampoo. Will they sell it in Piccadilly? It's the only one that doesn't crisp my –

'Was that someone at the door?' she whispers.

'No,' I whisper back. 'It was just the wind.'

I lift the bottom of the blinds and see the toes of his boots; his knees: he's sitting on the front step. Oh dear God, it is Eoghan. Not a dream. He's come back. My heart swings through several breakneck revolutions of joy and fear. And crashes back into rage.

Damn you.

DAMN YOU.

He has no right to come back. No right at all.

My heart is hammering as I plummet now into relief, into the want of folding him into me and never letting him go again. I want to run to him and hold him safe from whatever harm kept him from us all this time.

I close my eyes, shut them tight, see him dangling by a thread against the sky: *You can stay out there for a good while yet.*

Yo

I don't beg, though it's that cold now, a man less warmed by his own disgrace might die here. On this damp stone step, must be four or five hours now or more. But I will sit here, I'll stay here until . . . Until I'm told to clear off. I stare out over the harbour, into the black. The lamps along the Bridge road are floating in the night like a string of ghosts: sad. A train goes across the span, and with the stillness that follows its clattering comes the full power of my shame.

I can't blame Olivia if she never wants to see me again. Who would want to? I only want to see Ag, before they leave. That's all I will ask and then I'll leave them be. I should know where they're going, too, so that in time I'll make myself worthy enough to follow, so that I can know my sister. That's all I want, Lord. Please. Let me remain in my sister's heart, in some small way. If you grant me this, I'll join the seminary. I'll be a priest. I'll be a good one, too. One that doesn't drink; one that bans the form guide from consecrated ground. A bargain that brings the Lord to speak to me directly now, for the first time in my life and unhappily: *No, you will not become a priest, O'Keenan – I don't want you darkening my door either.* No,

I don't suppose you do. Apart from every other sin I've committed lately, I haven't been to Mass for more than six months.

Six months.

Six fucking months? What was I doing? How am I going to make it up? What penance? Any penance. Tell me. Whatever you want me to do, Lord, I will do.

He goes silent on me again and my hand goes to my pocket, to roll another smoke I don't want. Before I do I feel the letter there in that pocket and take it out; strike a match against it with the intention of burning it. I don't know why: mad. Cold. Fucking freezing. My hands are shaking and not only from the cold when I see in the light from the flame that this letter was addressed to Myrtle Street. Chippendale. It's been crossed out and found Fawcett Street via the presbytery at St Gus's. Now found me here, finally, on Olivia's doorstep. I don't ever remember getting a letter from anyone at all in Chippendale.

I'm just about to open it when the door opens behind me. Olivia.

'Get inside,' she says. 'You'll freeze to death.' The tone of her voice says there'd be a bother for her in having the body removed if I did.

I stand up and see her now, in the light coming through from the sitting room, though she won't look at me. She's tying a ribbon round her hair to take it from her face. Her hair has grown, the waves of it curling down to her shoulders, and it's more golden. She's more beautiful than ever and something else . . . her skirt is as crushed as the letter in my fist and her shoulders are hunched round, hunched away from me with worry. The worry of what I'm bringing her here. I resist saying anything at all.

She says: 'I'll put the kettle on.'

I follow her out to the kitchen, where she points to the table: 'Sit down.'

Then she turns to me, with the full power of Oonagh in a fury now: 'Well? Speak.'

'Olivia, I . . .' What else can I tell her but that: 'I made a mistake.'

'Indeed you did,' she says, slamming the tea caddy into the bench by the sink so I can feel how much that hurt her hand. She says: 'I got you a job, you know – friend of Gloria's brother-in-law. At Tycoon Clothing – shirt-making machine thing.'

'You did?' As if that's at the top of the list of reasons I shouldn't have gone off as I did.

'Embarrass me, hurt – you. Horrible. What was I to –? Hateful. Stup– not to mention.'

For all that she can't get the words out, I nod at every one.

As Ag comes in through the sitting room in her nightgown, rubbing her eyes to see that it's true: 'Yoey?'

She narrows her eyes when she sees that it is; then she turns her shoulder to me too: *You bastard.*

Olivia

He falls to his knees from the kitchen chair. 'Ag. I'm sorry,' he says, and in such a torment I see that however he's betrayed her, he's paying for it, and will continue to do so for a good while yet if Agnes's sustained glare of contempt is any indication. He's so pale, so thin; scooped out. He looks to me: 'If you think it's best, I'll come back, later, in the day. It's –'

'No! Don't go!' Agnes throws herself at him now, her arms clinched desperately around his neck, and the revolutions tumble round and round again in me, between alleluia and how bloody dare you. Look at you: filthy fingernails, trousers smeared with oily grime. And your coat stinks like some feral animal yet to be formally identified.

I rub my eyes and ask the back of my lids: 'What now?' Our passage is booked. My life is half-packed. I can't remain in Sydney. Not *now*. Not even –

'Now is whatever you want it be, Olivia,' Eoghan replies. 'I've not come here to make claims on anyone. I know you've made your own plans. The Adamses said you were off to . . .'

I look at him through my fingers, through my weary

delirium: his every breath is a claim on me, a claim on all my plans.

And now he smiles. I tumble into his left dimple. Good God, truly: what now?

Yo

'I don't have any bread,' she says and she goes to step round me and Ag, as if she's going up the road for some now.

It's not quite five o'clock in the morning; but I say: 'I'll go.'

'No.' Ag doesn't want that, she holds me tighter, but I take her hands and tell her: 'It's all right. I'll come back in a little while. You want some of that apple cake, if the baker's got some?'

My sister's eyes are telling me what I might best do with some apple cake if I walk out that door again. But I have to go. I have to let Olivia be for a bit. It's a shock. I shouldn't have turned up in the middle of the night like this. When is a good time to turn up like this? To make apology for the unforgivable.

I tell her too: 'I'll be back, don't worry.' And I will apologise for the fact of it a thousand times – daily, if that's how it's to be, until you believe me. I will cut a thousand petticoat skirts if I have to, and enjoy it. I will go anywhere, sewing beads along the edges of the path you take. I will do anything.

She nods, but she's gone back to not looking at me again. I go out the door to wander round the streets for a while, down to the old workshops and up under the northern approach, to the new station there, all silent; dead with silence and empty but for my praying, into the water, into the black sky: *Please. Please, take me back.* I have never been so alone and wanting as this. Sober and alone. And hungry, aching with it. I haven't eaten anything since I had a fist full of chips sometime yesterday morning, some strange other life ago, fist full of hours ago. I wander back around the bay, back across to Blues Point Road, down to the corner where Dean's is. It's still not open yet, though the baker's at work, banging around in there. I sit on the high gutter's edge by the doorway, to wait for the bread. There's a lamp directly above, glaring down on me, showing me where I belong, for what I've done.

I reach in my pocket, to roll that smoke I don't want, and my hand goes straight to that letter again. I pull it out and open it, not so much to read it as to keep my thoughts well away from the idea that it might be better for all concerned if I keep walking north all the way to China.

Dear Yo,

Two pages of handwriting, I don't know who from. I turn over to the end and see the name.
And shout myself to my feet again with seeing it: 'Saints alive!'
It's a letter from my brother Brendan. My little brother. Jesus. Sweet Jesus.
He says:

> *I hope my letter finds you well. I'm sorry now that I didn't say anything to you when I left but I didn't want to say anything then to anyone in the family. The circumstances were difficult. I hope you understand that.*

I do. Jesus, but I hardly even know the kid writing to me now. When? Almost a year ago. The twenty-second of July 1931, it's dated. How old is he now? Twenty. When's his birthday? I can't exactly remember at this minute. August – sixteenth?

He's saying:

For all that I could never find a job in the Neighbourhood, as soon as I stepped foot out of it, I got one almost straightaway, as a boy on the first ship I saw at Darling Harbour, which was an American mail steamer. I ended up in San Francisco next, working in various jobs around the shipyards where I was fortunate to get in at the office of an engineering firm, as a messenger, that got me on to another job as a trainee wireless technician for the railways. It's a bit of a long story, but from there I've ended up in New York. I am now in partnership with a friend I made along the way. His name is Edwin T Figmore, and we're in the wireless business now. We have a company that sells and repairs radiograms – those wireless-phonograph combination pieces that are becoming all the fashion – and although we are only a small concern, we are doing well, our shop is in Manhattan, in a good part of the city. I'm no good at selling anything – I'm still as quiet as I always was. I just do the repairs and Ed does all the selling.

Getting out of our own bad neighbourhood was what I needed to get myself going, getting well away from those difficulties, so that I could see what was out there for me in the world, what I was good at. I found it and I have not looked back. But I have never stopped thinking of you and our sister Agnes. If there is anything I can do for you – anything at all – please write to me. You only need ask. Things are really very good in New York for me. Things are starting to look up for business generally and for work of all types, too. If you want to come to America, I would be happy to help you get a start somewhere if I can. Ed can sponsor you if necessary. Just say the word.

I've never forgotten how you looked after me when I was small, making sure I was all right at school, making my breakfast and tea from whatever you could find, and standing in the way of that devil's hand for me when it came, or our brother Michael's. You said we'd run away and join up with the Connaught Rangers pipe band one day. You'd shove some schoolbook at me and say, 'Shut up and go and practise your reading or you'll get six from Sister Joe', while you took a dozen for me at home. Somewhere past that time, though, the bitterness got into me, the shamefulness at our poverty and our particular difficulties, and I shut up so well I didn't want to know even you – not any of my family. I am sorry for that now. I will never forget you, Yo. You were mother and father to me when we had neither.

Please give my love to our sister Agnes. She probably doesn't remember me. Maybe you don't either! But I wish you all the very best.

God bless you and keep you. You are in my prayers every day and will always be.

Your brother Brendan

And he gives the address, of his flat and his business. I forget about waiting for the bread. My feet are moving again before I've thought another thing, back round the corner, back to Olivia's. The dawn is cracking now, the sun coming up over the water, a golden road coming up under the Bridge for me, up through my feet, filling me with this golden light. My brother Brendan has written to me. Who? My brother has come back from the dead. He's a radiogram repairer. In New York. This is the word of the Lord.

And every good thing is possible again. No, not possible – it is mine to make happen, and it's happening this day.

Olivia opens the door to me. Olivia. This girl I will marry. She looks hardly less dismayed than she did when she first opened the door to me six or seven long hours ago. As well she should: I have no more to offer her than I did then either.

Apart from not wasting any more of her time; I ask her: 'You wouldn't consider changing your plans, would you?'

'Plans?' That tin whistle of hers singing high up to heaven.

The Blue Mile

Frowning at me through it, too; disbelieving of whatever I'm going to say next.

But life is all chance, isn't it, Lord? Every blessed heartbeat of it. So I have to ask her: 'Have you ever thought you might want to visit America?'

She straightens her back, stares down that fine, long nose, far too fine for me, and she says, disdaining: 'What America?'

Seven

Olivia

'New York, America,' he says. 'I'll take you there myself if you'll loan me the fare, yeah?'

Yeah?

Dimples, shoulderline, Irish eyes pleading at the doorstep. How does a girl say no?

This one says: 'You don't speak another word until you tell me precisely where on earth you have been.'

He hands me a letter that appears to have seen a good deal of weather, and he tells me precisely, plainly: 'Drinking.'

'Drinking?' I don't believe him. He's been gone for more than half a year – drinking what? 'Some poison that must have been.'

'Yes,' he says, unblinking. 'True. I was drinking, night and day, and otherwise getting into fights, living rough and being an idiot, running away. Disgrace that it is, it's all I can answer you with, Olivia, and I'm more sorry for what I've done than I can say. I was mad, with thinking I was worthless, that Ag would do better without me. I didn't know what else to do. But I do now. I will do anything you want me to. Tell me to go, I will go now. But if you'll have me back, please – read this letter. It's from my brother,

Brendan. Mrs Adams just gave it to me . . . I had it in my pocket and I . . . Please.'

It's trembling in his hand, trembling like a leaf between us.

I take it from him and I read it, and it is every heart-rending and mending thing I must know about the burdens my love has carried. True. Read it again: *You were mother and father to me when we had neither.* You are a good, kind man, and have always been. I blink out through the Bridge into the blinding rise of the sun, and I think I know we will go to New York. I can hear the gears of the wheel cranking, I'm sure. I don't quite yet believe it, though, so I can only manage to respond with: 'You didn't get the bread, then?'

'No. I'll go up now, will I?' He is ready to dash at my word.

'No,' I stop him. 'We'll all go now.' I don't want to let him out of my sight again, not ever again, or at least not for a good while. I turn around and shove the letter into the hall stand drawer – this flimsy slip of the truth, mine, *ours* – and as I do I call, 'Agnes?'

But she is already here. Her little face peering round the bedroom door by my hip, she sends him a scalding final notice: 'It's going to take me a long time to forgive you.'

He nods: 'I know it is, Ag.'

We start walking and she slips her hand into his, as he slips his hand into mine, and as the warmth of it swoops softly through me, he says: 'This is the best thing I will ever do, the best thing my hands will ever do – just to be holding yours.'

Oh God, I am not going to forgive you that easily, either, Eoghan O'Keenan. Trust is too precious a commodity. Why are you really here now? Trouble with the law? So eager to skip town? To *New York*? I ask him: 'What's this getting into fights business all about, then? Hm? What did you do?'

'Oh,' he tells the road with something of a shudder, 'you don't want to know too much about that.'

'Yes, I think I do. Actually.'

'Ah . . . er . . .' He kicks a stone and I eye the state of his sand-shoes – he's been working hard at a hole in the left toe, that is evident. 'It was just some scrapping with them fascist fellas, you know – that New Guard lot?'

'The New Guard? Oh really?' *What*? I look at him, all of him, shabby and unshaven. 'Political brawling?'

'Yeah,' he winces under a glance, shaking his head at himself, at the road. 'I sort of fell in with this Communist lot, dossing out at this place near La Perouse, and one thing led to another and . . .'

Something about Waterside Workers and Unemployed Unionists, and being too ashamed and angry to see what he was doing until he met the grace of Mr Lang last night, but I'm no longer listening. Whatever he did, it was heroically awful. And I know I will forgive him everything, filthy fingernails and all. I might even smile at him in a minute.

*

'New York?' Glor groans, as she's groaned a thousand times across this last week and now over her cheesecake, here at the Pav Cafe at the Quay, for our second-last goodbye. 'London was bad enough. But *New York*? I'm so racked with jealousy, Ol, I don't know what to do with it all. *Manhattan*? That's what you call *haute* romance, isn't it? I bet you go ice-skating in Central Park this Christmas just to make me crazy.'

'Well, yes, my darling, ghastly job but someone simply has to do it, don't they?' I pretend worldly ennui. 'Who else will educate these Americans against their fondness for frills? It's my duty to go, and you know it is. Must stamp out overflouncing wherever I go.' And I'm only half-joking at this: even Madame Chanel has given way to this present international festival of Chantilly blancmange. '*Sacré phlergh*,' I add, but Glor has glanced away out the window, towards the ship.

Our ship, a great black bow and red funnels, towering over the ferries below. So small they seem, my ferries. Little black and white blobs . . .

I pull my brim down against the midmorning sun, my eyes stinging with its brightness, and yet it is near impossible to look away. Today, this last day in Sydney. The water beyond the wharves is an unfurled bolt of wild bespangled magic and the thrill of untold adventure swoops and zooms through my own heart again. I reach for Glor's hand across the table: 'Oh but I want to take this harbour with me, in sequinned chiffon – plunging backline with diamante straps.'

'God, yes,' Glor whispers, reverently, seeing so exactly what I see.

God, I'm going to miss my wonderful friend.

I bite my bottom lip, stop the damn thing quivering.

'But what if he doesn't show up, Ol?' Glor clasps my hand in her mocha doe-skin vice grip. 'You won't go to New York then, will you? You couldn't go without him. What's the time?' she looks at her watch. 'It's ten-thirty, just after. He's late.'

'Nice try, Gloria Gallagher, but he's coming. Don't you worry about that.'

At seventy-eight pounds' worth of last-minute cabin class extortion, I'll have him hunted down and hanged if he's not here by eleven.

Yo

'And another thing, lad,' Mr Adams is not letting me go at his front gate, his fist round my elbow, and I'm listening as I'm counting the minutes down to the next ferry. But he's not saying anything. He's just stopped, here at the gate, Mrs Adams and Kenny behind him at the door, smiling me some sunshine to send me on my way, only I'm not going anywhere just yet.

'Yeah?' I ask Mr Adams. Come on, hurry up with it. Among all the advice he's bucketed on me throughout these past seven days, he's said at least a hundred times *Never make her wait for you again, lad – don't make her wait for you to tie your bootlaces, don't make her wait for anything at all.* Well . . . ? I really don't want to miss this 10.43 to the Quay. Please. But I'm not moving, for all that I owe him. Taking me into his home all this week, taking me back into his heart, and with not another word about arse-brained exploits undertaken on the way to learning my particular lessons. 'What is it, Mr Adams?'

He clears his throat, bastard pit-bull eye on me: 'You'll write, won't you?' Not a suggestion but an expectation with consequences for failure attached. 'Mrs Adams, she likes a letter. Right?'

'Right. Of course I'll write.' I had every intention anyway. There's a lot I want to write about: what I've seen, and all I will see. I might be writing down more than letters about it once I get going. I tell him. 'I won't ever disappoint you again.'

He nods: 'And you'll call me Wal.'

'I will.' Jesus, he's going to weld his hand to my arm if he doesn't let go.

But then he lets go and I'm wishing he didn't, and then he's crushing the breath out of me one last time, telling me: 'Good enough, son, good enough. Better than good.'

It might take me another minute to find my legs to leave at that: to be called son by him. To be someone's son, however borrowed.

'Best wishes, dear boy! Our hopes go along with you always,' Mrs Adams waves another kiss over with her handkerchief. 'Good luck!'

'Good luck, cheery cheerio lucky Yo,' Kenny waves too.

'Cheerio,' I tell him, and I wish I could bring him over to the dock with me to see the ship, but Kenny doesn't do well in a crowd. It has to be goodbye here at the gate, but I can't say it. I tell all of them: 'I'll write – every week. I won't miss a week, I promise.'

'Right.' Wal Adams turns away. 'Go on then, slán.' Get lost.

That's one thing I will never be again: lost. But I am running again. I am tearing down Darling Street, past Mrs Buddle's geraniums for the last time, hearing her call after me: 'God bless you, Eoghan O'Keenan!'

And I am the wealthiest man alive. Shillings jangling in my pocket, making me laugh as I go. Parting gift from Dorman, Long and Company, they are – for the underpayment of a total of £9/7/6. That's what that other letter waiting for me was, a request that I go into Public Works to pick it up and accept their apologies for the inconvenience of the miscalculation of my wages. *Most convenient,* Olivia said of it. *At least you can buy your own suit.*

I did. I am a man in a suit, starched collar and a blue silk tie, running for the ferry in new shoes.

Running for my life.

Olivia

Agnes skips along outside the windows of the cafe, a wisp of fairy dreams come true, skipping beside Mr Jabour, coming back from seeing our luggage onto the ship. Chattering on to our genie as she skips, she is so high with excitement, she might flutter up and away if he wasn't keeping hold of her hand.

'Ollie!' she shouts into the china-clinking interior of the Pav when she sees me, the sound of my name zinging round and round all the mahogany and glass. 'Guess what?'

'What?' Glor and I reply together, exchanging smirks at snooty stares.

'The man at the ship said we had too much luggage, and he was going to make us get a – get a, what was that thing, Mr Jabour?'

'An export certificate,' he chuckles beside her.

'Yes, an export certificate,' Agnes chirps, bouncing about from toe to toe with the fun of it. 'The man said he was going to send it all to Customs House – he wouldn't believe it was only your wardrobe. But Mr Jabour talked him around, didn't you?'

She beams up at him and genie laughter booms as he tells me over a job-done belly rub: 'Indeed I did, my dear. Fellow insisted on opening one of the trunks there and then – one full of hats – and he said, "What's all this, a sale on at Hordern's?"'

'Hordern's? How dare he!' I snort and grimace under my brim, for I might well have to sell off a few creations once we get to the other end. Only just over one hundred and eighty pounds of ill-gotten Lordship-avoiding patrimony left and New York is notoriously expensive. We don't even know where we will live, much less set out my shingle. *How* will we live? Will it all shrink and warp to rags? Fear catches at the edges of adventure. Am I really forgoing a window in Piccadilly prime position with ready-made Hyde Park Corner clients for . . . ? Insane. Mother will be waking up to the telegram sometime in the next few hours, I suppose, screaming: *WHAT? NEW YORK?* She'll storm across the Atlantic for me soon enough, soon as we do have an address. And she will be horrified rigid at my choice of husband. *An irresponsible, possibly alcoholic low-class nobody?* I imagine she will shriek. And I am already retorting, *Takes one to know one,* before I smother her in kisses, and my baby sister too. Squealing my happiness: Mother, look at me. I am everything you wanted me to be. Happy.

Happily terrified.

And then something else altogether when I see Eoghan dashing along the back of the wharves through the ferry throng, dashing through the door of the Pav Cafe. Our future, there in his long stride. And that beautiful suit – black on taupe pinstripe, midweight worsted, simply gorgeous. Eddie Nasser's cousin Danny Karam is a tailor of undoubtedly magical skill. But it's not just the suit. It's the man. If there is no man, there is no suit, is there?

Mais non, chérie. You were right. I must admit, he does scrub up quite well.

And there is no thrill like this: the tips of his perfectly manicured fingers touching my wrist as he bends to kiss me on the cheek: 'I'm so sorry I'm late, I –'

'Late? You're right on time. I make it two minutes to.'

My flame-caped dreams coming true: somewhere in

Manhattan . . . our salon is waiting for us. A real salon, where I will style and he will cut for me, filling up my sketches with his dancing words, and we will attract the most fabulous clientele to our famous circle toastie soirees. Artists, movie stars, fortune makers. He wants to meet them all; he wants to go back to school too, to learn about politics, to change the world. I want to clothe it. I can see our salon already. Bright daffodil Shantung drapes thrown open to the day. Our day. Whatever it might bring. Beginning this second. God, who's a little bit excited? What am I going to be like when I get him into that white tux? Outrageous, that's what I'll be, swathed in midnight velvet chiffon.

'I want to go *now*.' Agnes is dragging on his coat sleeve before he can sit down to join us.

'What? *Now?*' he teases her. 'Can't I have a cup of tea and a scone?'

'Noooo.' She's pointing out at the ship: 'Look – the engines have started going. See the steam coming up?' As if it might leave without us; not due out for another hour yet.

'What ship?' he says.

'Yoey, *don't*,' she continues to tug and he relents, letting her pull him back towards the door. 'Our ship, our RMS *Aorangi* – see? Over *there*. The RMS. Stands for Royal Mail Service, and *Aorangi* means cloud – in Maori. One of the sailors said so. We're going to float across the ocean like little clouds.' She twirls ahead of him, waving Hawaiian hands and flitting out into the sun, imploring us all: 'Come *on*.'

'Well, shall we?' Mr Jabour offers an arm each to Glor and me and we ramble after them around the Quay, as a brass band strikes up behind the far wharf to McMahons. What's that knee-stiffening tune they're playing? Good God, it's 'God Save the King'.

'Save us,' Mr Jabour says under his breath as we pass them and it is a bit much for an otherwise ordinary Saturday morning, their thrumming blasts not letting anyone forget this latest British victory in the colonies: the Bank of England will get their interest payments now that Mr Lang is gone. Hooray. The Games received a ten-minute standing ovation for it at their attendance of *Tosca* at His Majesty's on Thursday night, and the Federal Parliament has opened the national till to the new United Australia Premier – with a blank cheque, so that Mr Lang can't possibly be returned at the election. Mr Jabour dabs his brow with his handkerchief: quite furious, in his way. There is nothing to celebrate here in the King's name or anyone else's: unemployment has climbed over thirty percent, the shanties of Happy Valley creep almost three miles up towards the city now, and still the Bank of England maintains that it will continue to charge Australia its highest rates. That is truly and unfathomably outrageous.

Still, I clutch my handbag tighter to me as we walk, tighter round my own hypocrisy: round the letter in there, arrived Wednesday afternoon, hand-delivered. From Government House. An open letter of introduction from Lady Game herself, one which refers to me by my actual name, too: the Honourable Miss Olivia Ashton Greene. Curious eleventh-hour timing – to seal my silence at her esteem for the Langs, or to acknowledge my service to her? I'll never know and I don't much care. I won't betray her anyway. That's not my way. I'm far too well bred, aren't I. And I will use her introduction until the paper crumbles to dust.

I look over my shoulder, to the point beyond the Quay, where the Gardens meet the water. Where the teal meets the green, the horizon shimmering aquamarine, the colours of my city. Something catches at me again, at this leaving. How can I be leaving? But then, I imagine a conga line of Sydney Witches making their way along the seawall to Government House to have their names hastily reinstated in the visitors' book, and it can only be toodles and farewell from me. To this big bulging city, one of the biggest in the world, but one with a small mind.

As we can all too often be, and this catches like a claw at my hem, so that I'm suddenly exclaiming: 'Oh – I've forgotten to –'

Slip away back to the kiosk.

'To what?' Glor calls after me.

The Blue Mile

'Don't worry,' I wave. 'I'll catch you up.'

I have to tip the contents of my coin purse into the blind digger's cup.

'Ho, ho! Thank you, miss,' he says as they plink and spin. 'You're a lovely one!' he grins as if he might know me, as if he might see. 'Have yourself a good day, won't you.' He winks.

Winks? He *does* see? The rogue. He smells of stale wine and sun-crisped damp, and I tell him: 'I shall. I'll have an especially good day every day, just for you.'

'You do that, sweetheart!' he crows as I hurry off again, with once last glance up Pitt: goodbye, old friend, adieu.

By the time I've caught up with the others they are stepping into the shadow of the bow, Mr Jabour with his hand on Eoghan's shoulder now, something vaguely threatening in the gesture. Though he's probably only saying, 'You make sure you look after my girls,' for the thousandth time, there is a warning growl beneath his every word to Eoghan that tells him the international Lebanese drapers association will track him down and turn him into meatball soup if he so much as looks at a pub again. That makes me smile. Never mind that he'll have a hard time finding a pub in prohibitionist New York, he won't want one. I am more sure of this than anything. Besides, he'll be far too busy with . . . other activities I have planned. We'll be married tonight, at the captain's pleasure, somewhere between here and Auckland – surprise! All arranged by Mr Jabour, too, including the tux, and an entire masculine travel trousseau containing the most sublime Fuji pyjamas ever made – fine charcoal paisley on an ivory ground. Oh God, oh God, oh God, I can hardly wait. I can hardly breathe with thinking about it.

'Ah, there you are.' Mr Jabour turns to find me now, chuckling as if he might have heard my thoughts. I blush, lavishly. And then here I am; this is it. The keeper of my kismet is giving me away, at the steps up to our Aorangi Cloud.

'Photo!' Gloria is reaching into her handbag for the Kodak Petite Paul bought her for her birthday, so that she might document every move Robbie makes. Oh Robbie, little Robbie, who is distracting his grandmother and Aunty Karma this morning so that half of Beirut wouldn't turn up to say goodbye. My heart flies round the globe and back once more: when will I see you again, little one?

'Dad, you get in the picture too,' Gloria is bossing, squeezing us all together by the stair rail. I straighten the clasp of my cape, and Glor is reaching into her bag again, to throw handfuls of confetti at us. 'Say peas and cheesy beans, please!' We do – about seventeen times, until Gloria decides, 'Dad, come back here,' pushing us up the steps demanding: 'Up you go, up to the top, and I when I say kiss, I mean it. A proper kiss.'

We clatter up the steps after Agnes, laughing shoulder to shoulder, step for step, so together, Eoghan and I. In a few short hours, this shoulderline: mine forever. And I will be Olivia O'Keenan – initials OO'K. How fabulous will that look on a label? My black on white. I look up into the sky, sending my schemes straight through the zigzags of the Bridge, this great length of gun metal rickrack arcing up from the Rocks against this blue, blue –

TOOOOOT! The funnel blows and Agnes covers her ears on the step above us, shouting: 'Oh!' Then she grabs her brother round the neck in last-moment panic: 'Will there be trees in New York?'

'There will be trees, Ag,' he assures her, gathering her into our arms. 'Wherever we go, we'll find them. We'll always find them trees.'

Yes, we will. We will find everything we need.

'*Those* trees, Yoey,' she corrects him.

As Glor calls: 'Kiss!'

And we do. We kiss now for all the world to see, how rich we are in love and dreams.

We are streamers on this autumn breeze heading into summer. Wherever we go, there we shall be. New York, Paris, Madrid, Shanghai. Each other's safe harbour. Each other's way home. A solid steel rainbow across the sea.

The achievement of this bridge is symbolical of the things Australians strive for but have not yet achieved . . . that bridge of understanding among the Australian people will yet be built, and will carry her on to that glorious destination which every man who loves our native country feels is in store for her. I now officially declare the Sydney Harbour Bridge open for traffic . . .

Right Honourable JT Lang, 19 March 1932

Author Note

A *Blue Mile,* like its sister novels *Black Diamonds* and *This Red Earth,* is a fiction inspired by the history and squiggly contradictions of the land I love – this time Sydney, my old home town. With a pocket full of family lore from my grandparents' glory days, a long-held political crush on the Big Fella, Jack Lang, and a perennial wonder at our magnificent harbour and its Bridge, I set out to discover my city anew, finding all its beauty and its brashness glimmering as brightly then as now.

It's well known that the construction of the Sydney Harbour Bridge took eight years, six million or so rivets, £4.2 million, and sixteen lives to build, and at least eight hundred families lost their homes to make way for it. It was a lifeline in a dark time to the families of those several thousand men fortunate enough to obtain work on it, and brave enough to work on it at height. There were no pesky safety regulations in those days – men still 'rode the hook' at the end of crane cables on construction sites into the 1960s, until the Builders Labourers Federation began the fight to outlaw the deadly practice.

It's less well known that, as the Bridge was being built, the consequences of the Great Depression in New South Wales, especially in terms of unemployment and suspension of credit, seem to have been second in severity only to those in Germany, our enemy in the Great War and a nation subsequently crushed by war reparations. Why the British banks were so miserly towards their Australian cousins and allies over this period, when they reduced interest rates for others, is a question I have not been able to find an answer to. While I'm no perfect student of the past, neither is my country. We continue to struggle with our ever-shifting lines of bigotry, our fearfulness of difference, our terror at dips in the property market, and the sometimes vicious ideological divide between left and right. But there is an indefinable and indefatigable energy about Sydney, some loveliness humming underneath the frenetic pace and ruthlessness of the place, something that has perhaps always helped us resist letting radicalism or hatreds take hold for more than five minutes. Perhaps there's something in the water that makes us reluctant to spoil the barbie with any serious political engagement, or maybe it's just the way the sun shines on us here. Whatever it is, I hope the peace it brings continues.

My sun wouldn't shine at all without those who aid and abet my quests for tales tall and true. Selwa Anthony and Cate Paterson, without whom there is no book, thank you so much and forever for your belief and guidance. Julia Stiles and Emma Rafferty, thank you for sharp minds, kind hearts and all your editorial care. As always, I couldn't go anywhere much without the National Library of Australia's Trove newspaper and picture databases for the bulk of my research. And I wouldn't find the beauty, the terror or inspiration in any of it if it wasn't for my boys, Tom and Cal, the children who've raised me, and my own darling big fella, Dean, whose unwavering faith is my brain glue when nothing else seems to make sense.

A very presumptuous thank you, too, must go to the Langs and the Games and Miss Crowdy for the loan of your characters. Although obviously I have shamelessly invented words and actions for you here, I hope I have captured a little of the essence of the good people you really were, remaining so staunchly decent when all about you went bonkers

Last, but never least, this novel is my small but earnest tribute to all those who get up every day and simply go to work. Whatever it is you do, you make life better, safer, easier, cleaner, brighter or more beautiful. You make the world go round.